Roll the Credits

a Hector Lassiter novel

CRAIG McDONALD

BETIMES BOOKS

First published in the English language worldwide in 2014
by Betimes Books

www.betimesbooks.com

ISBN 978-0-9929674-1-3

Cover design by JT Lindroos

This novel is for Yeats and Madeleine, who willed it

PRAISE

"A writer of truly unique voice, approach, and ambition, Craig McDonald delivers again with ROLL THE CREDITS. Hector Lassiter is a compelling character but also a fascinating forum for McDonald's historical, social, and artistic observations. For all the wonderful action, slick dialogue, and plot twists McDonald throws at the reader, he's equally interested in saying something substantial about time and place. Not to be missed." —Michael Koryta

"With each of his Hector Lassiter novels, Craig McDonald has stretched his canvas wider and unfurled tales of increasingly greater resonance." —Megan Abbott

"Reading a Hector Lassiter novel is like having a great uncle pull you aside, pour you a tumbler of rye, and tell you a story about how the 20th century 'really' went down." —Duane Swierczynski

"I don't think there's anything quite like them. These are incredible novels... Not only is the series a one-of-a-kind, but Craig has done one better by trying to make each novel a different novel." —James Sallis

INTRODUCTION

If any label best describes the Hector Lassiter series, it's probably "Historical Thrillers." These books combine myth and history. The Lassiter novels spin around secret histories and unexplored or underexplored aspects of real events. They're set in real places, and use not just history to drive their plots, but also incorporate real people.

As a career journalist, I'm often frustrated by the impossibility to nail down people or events definitively. Read five biographies of the same man, say, of Ernest Hemingway, and you'll close each book feeling like you've read about five different people. So, I've concluded, defining fact as it relates to history is as elusive a goal as stroking smoke or tapping a bullet in flight.

History, it's been said, is a lie agreed to. But maybe in fiction we can find if not fact, something bordering on truth. With that possibility in mind, I explore what I can make of accepted history through the eyes of one man. The "hero" of this series, your guide through these books, is Hector Mason Lassiter, a shades-of-grey guy who is a charmer, a rogue, a bit of a rake, and, himself, a crime novelist.

Some others in the novels say he bears a passing resemblance to the actor William Holden. Hector smokes and drinks and eats red meat. He favors sports jackets, open collar shirts, and Chevrolets. He lives his life on a large canvas. He's wily, but often impulsive; he's honorable, but mercurial.

He often doesn't understand his own drives. That is to say, he's a man. He's a man's man and a lady's man. He's a romantic, but mostly very unlucky in love. Yet his life's largely shaped by the women passing through it.

Hec was born in Galveston, Texas on January 1, 1900. In other words, he came in with the 20th Century, and it's my objective his arc of novels span that century — essentially, through each successive novel, giving us a kind of under-history or secret-history of the 20th Century.

Tall and wise beyond his years, as a boy Hector lied about his age, enlisted in the military, and accompanied Black Jack Pershing in his hunt down into Mexico to chase the Mexican Revolutionary Pancho Villa who attacked and murdered many American civilians in the town of Columbus, New Mexico. Villa's was the first and only successful assault on the United States homeland prior to the events of September 11, 2001.

Much of that part of Hector's life figures into *Head Games*, the first published Hector Lassiter novel and a finalist for the Edgar and Anthony awards, along with a few similar honors. That novel is set mostly in 1957. Its sequel, *Toros & Torsos*, opens in 1935. Subsequent books about Hector similarly hopscotched back-and-forth through the decades upon original publication.

The Betimes Books release of the Hector Lassiter series will try for something different, presenting the books in roughly chronological order—at least in terms of where each story starts as the novel opens. The series now opens with *One True Sentence*, the fourth novel in original publication sequence, but the first novel chronologically.

Set in 1924 Paris, that novel is now followed by its intended sequel, *Forever's Just Pretend*, enjoying its first-ever publication and completing a larger story revealing how Hector became the guy we come to know across the rest of the series: "The man who lives what he writes and writes what he lives"; friend to Hemingway, Orson Welles and other 20th-Century luminaries.

The rest of the repackaged series unfolds in similar fashion, a mix of the old and new titles.

The Lassiter novels were written back-to-back, and the series mostly shaped and in place before the second novel was officially published. It's very unusual in that sense—a series of discrete novels that are tightly linked and which taken together stand as a single, larger story.

Welcome to the world of Hector Lassiter.

Craig McDonald

"Perhaps our eyes are merely a blank film which is taken from us after our deaths to be developed elsewhere and screened as our life story in some infernal cinema."
— Jean Baudrillard

FRANCE:

1940

In the old days, if a horse stumbled three times you shot it in the head.

As far as I was concerned, our driver had just made his second stumble.

Well, arguably it was his *third* if you counted a certain slip of the tongue earlier in the late-morning. I'd wondered at Billy's fluent German before, but *now?*

Following the twisting, mounting road toward the Alps, we were still thirty miles from our unstated destination. I was chewing my lip and weighing when best to kill our traitorous driver.

From the seat behind us, Gertrude Stein yelled over the Renault's engine's roar, "Hector, perhaps we will at last have the windows up. It looks like rain, does it not?" She was tugging the window crank on her side with no success.

More bellyaching. I twisted further around in my seat and said, "Sorry, darlin', but this heap's side and rear windows are all broken out. As a humble war correspondent moving in enemy territory, this Juvaquatre van was all I could wrangle under the gun."

That was true enough. I'd doffed my correspondent's duds for native street clothes, and then stolen our current ride. According to my hastily forged papers, I was Günther Hess of Lyon, one of the guys in charge of retooling Renault for German war production.

I had a smattering of rusty, Great War-era German and figured to get by just fine if chitchat didn't go far beyond basic weather, bathroom and sporting house directions or drink orders. I said, "Still, you're maybe right about the weather turning. I've got some rain slickers stowed behind you there. We'll stop and break those out, just in case."

Might as well get the bloody deed over with now, I told myself. I glanced at Billy, finding little stomach for the wicked task to come. I promised myself that for both our sakes, I'd try to make it quick. That was a sop to my sometimes not-elusive-enough conscience.

To distract myself, I smiled at Alice B. Toklas. Alice had never cared for me, not a lick, but the same was true of all the men that Gertrude doted over—all the male fiction writers and poets Gertrude had mentored or fed through the poorer times in older, better days in long-gone Paris.

Alice and I had exchanged perhaps a half-dozen frosty words since we'd hit the road seven hours ago. Now I said to the little bird-like woman with the dark, hairy upper lip, "Think we might even have an extra-petit raincoat that will fit you, Miss Toklas."

Turning back around, I tapped my driver on the arm and above the wind's sheer hollered, "You find a shoulder that looks firm enough, you pull over, okay, Billy? We're going to need to stretch our legs and get some provisions out of the back."

Blond, blue-eyed Billy, looking very Aryan to my own pale blue eyes now, shot me this suspicious look and said, "We're making good time, Hec. How much further do we have to go? Where are we going, exactly?"

Not subtle. But then subtle and Billy didn't seem to be acquainted. I shrugged and smiled. "Told you, kid, I'm only allowed to go where we're going so long as I keep my secrets until we get there. And it's far enough away yet to warrant a break from this kidney-busting heap of ours, son." The Renault's shocks were well past shot.

Yessir, I had decided now. Billy was going to be going further away than the rest of us, quite soon and for keeps.

I shook out a cigarette, offered one to Billy — his last, after all. I fired him up with my windproof Zippo. Alice coughed as our smoke blew back past her face. The little dame would just have to tough it out. Gertrude was diverting-enough company when she wasn't complaining, but Alice? I could feel her hateful stare at the back of my head, even now.

Billy nodded at a wide spot in the road ahead, a scenic pull-off at an ascending curve, and said, "It'll do?"

It was a picturesque place to die with that mountain valley view.

"If you think it'll bear the weight, why not, kiddo," I said thickly.

He pulled over and set the brake against the incline. Last moves.

I swung out and stalked around to the back of the van; dropped the tailgate. "Gonna need a hand with this, son."

Billy sighed and hauled himself out from behind the wheel. It was just starting to rain now, cold and stinging. Blinking back the rain and fumbling with the fasteners, I stepped aside as Billy said, "Here, Hec, let me." He got her open and I loaded his arms with stuff. Billy was now burdened with tarps and rain ponchos. Perfect. My stomach churned.

Gertrude had moved around in her seat to try and watch us. That was too bad for her. She was going to hate what she was about to see. Probably be haunted by it. She held her hand out the broken back window, palm up against the needle-spray rain and said, "Hector, hurry, the weather." She said it like it was news. Well, that was Gertrude in a nutshell, always discovering the world for the rest of us. Or at least presuming that she did that.

In the distance, I could hear truck engines. Those coming our way precluded me taking a gunshot at Billy. The sound of the approaching caravan also put the boot to my backside to take action, *now*.

I dipped my hand in my coat pocket and wrapped it around the bone handle of the SS knife I'd taken off a dead Kraut a few days ago. Sudden-like, I got around behind Billy, or maybe he secretly was a "Wilhelm," and wrapped my left hand around his forehead. I jerked his head back hard to expose his throat.

Gertrude gasped; Alice turned.

Billy, who evidently had some commando training, dropped his load and, snarling, elbowed me in the gut. He stamped on my foot with his heel, then he twisted in my arms. He forced his forearm against my neck, pushing at my windpipe. With his other hand, Billy went for my souvenir Nazi knife.

He was half my age and all my height. Billy was also trained in hand-to-hand combat—that was all-too-evident now. More wisdom come my way too late.

Billy snarled, said, "You Jew-lover! I'm going to kill you slow with that knife, Lassiter!" He smiled meanly and said, "Werner Höttl sends his regards."

Höttl: Would-be German film expressionist and auteur turned Hitler stooge.

So, it *was* Höttl behind this chase after the women. Hell, I'd suspected as much.

Billy's hand of a sudden clutched at his own throat. The curved handle of a walking stick was digging into *his* windpipe now. Gertrude and Alice were pulling on the other end of the cane, bless 'em.

I kicked Billy hard between the legs, three times though the second two kicks were admittedly meanly gratuitous. Clutching at his crotch, Billy fell gasping to his knees in what was quickly turning to mud. I got around behind Billy and slit his throat down to bone. I let his corpse fall face first into a blood-spritzed puddle.

Gertrude said, "What is this, Hector? Why did you kill that young man?"

"He's a spy," I said. "New Yorker from his accent, but Billy was German American Bund, or something, I'm guessing. One way or another, Billy-boy here somehow threw in with der Fatherland. Had my suspicions about him the past couple of days. I sorely owe someone in intelligence on our side for saddling me with this one. Close as we're getting, well, to keep you two safe in this new, good place, this *had* to happen, bloody as it was. Sorry, ladies. And thanks a million for the assist. Billy was a tough little traitor, sure enough."

I looked at the boy's body bleeding into the mud. Now he looked like just another luckless young one undone by our latest World War. Kid was going to stalk my dreams.

Gertrude said, "We do not care for these times."

"Ain't lately finding much to love myself," I said, standing over the dead boy in the stinging rain.

Those trucks were rumbling closer. Chewing my lip, I planted a boot against Billy's hip, pushed hard and sent his body tumbling down the muddy mountainside.

Shaking my head and wiping the kid's blood from the back of my hand, I said, "Yep, moments like this, I ain't remotely crazy about times myself, Ma'am. Now we best get moving, *vite*."

I helped the ladies out from the Juvaquatre and passed out the raincoats and some tarps to spread over their legs.

Alice reluctantly accepted my steadying hand as she climbed back into the rear of the Renault. Helping in short, stout Gertrude took a bit more effort. She finally opted to sit up front alongside me, wrapped up like a damp mummy. I handed Gertrude the cane she stumped around on and she stowed it between our seats. Gertrude said, "You know how to get us there, my Hector? I mean, without his help?" She nodded in the direction of the hillside I'd sent Billy tumbling down.

I released the brake, got us going again. "I was checking the maps," I called above the engine's roar. "Yeah, I can do it. Should be there before late afternoon. Hold on tight now, you two. We'll see if we maybe can't outrun this rain."

Gertrude and Alice were settling into their new home. Rich friends were sworn to protect the women from the Nazis here in the so-called Free Zone. The village mayor said, "Though we're not occupied, I am still under strict orders to provide the names of all those living here to the Germans. Regardless of the risk, I will of course omit Miss Stein's and Miss Toklas' names from that list, Monsieur Lassiter."

I slapped his arm and said, "You're a good man, brother. Maybe the only politician on God's crazy earth I admire." I grinned, added, "I mean, besides Churchill."

He said, "Not your own president?"

FDR? I had longstanding reservations about that one.

I looked around: Gertrude and Alice's new home was on the banks of the River Rhône, near the foothills of the Alps. It was a good and pretty place for a couple of famous female Jewish American lesbians to hide from Hitler's minions until we kicked Adolph's ass.

The mayor said, "You'll stay the night, yes? I'm a fan of your novels. And of the films. We'll have some good wine and you can tell me of your books, and how the battle truly goes. You can tell me when your countrymen will at last join the war. You can—"

I shook my head. "Glad you like the books. The movies are for money. Sorry, but I'm kind of AWOL from my *reporting* duties smuggling those ladies here, Sir. Have a lot of ground to cover, fast. Dreadfully late getting to Lyon." It wasn't quite a lie.

The mayor smiled. "Another time, then?"

"Count on it, buddy," I said. He saw to a refueling of my jalopy. They finished up that task as the rain returned. As I settled in for the long wet ride to Lyon, a middle-age woman handed me a wicker picnic basket.

"Provisions, for your trip back." I was surprised to see Gertrude and Alice behind her.

Leaning hard on her cane, Gertrude said, "Again, much gratitude for bringing us, my star."

I waved that away. "*De rien,*" I said. "Just keep a low-profile and stay well until we hand Hitler his head, right ladies?"

Alice surprised me by passing me a bottle of red wine. She said, "Please try not to get yourself killed in *this* war, Hector. It seems to again be a time for men like you."

When we first met in Paris after the Great War, when I was just a kid struggling to make a name as a writer, I still had a bum leg from the German-inflicted wound that nearly killed me.

I squeezed Alice's hand and hefted the bottle. "I'm going to save this, darlin'. We'll toast the death of Hitler and Germany's defeat with this very bottle of vino."

After stowing the wine in my picnic basket, I turned over the engine. The mayor said, "I'm more than surprised you weren't assigned a driver."

Gertrude and Alice exchanged uneasy looks. I said, "Men are in too-short supply to be hauling around American war correspondents. And I lived in France for several years after the Great War, so I know my way around your country well enough."

Smiling at Gertrude, I said, "Take care, Miss Stein," then tore off down the road. As I left, I shoved an arm out the window and held my hand up in the V for Victory sign; cheers at my back.

I'd lied to Gertrude. For me, these were very good times, heady and satisfying.

At the edge of the village I slammed on the brakes, sliding a bit in the mud. Standing there in the middle of the road, straddling water-filled tire tracks, was a half-starved black Labrador Retriever.

I swung out and walked slowly toward the dog, one hand out. Tail down, the stray smelled then licked my hand. Fella had no collar and looked as though he had gone many days without food. Still some puppy in him: he hadn't yet grown into his own big feet.

As I headed back to the Juvaquatre, the dog followed on unsteady legs. I rooted around the basket of food and stripped a sandwich of slices of ham and fed morsels to the dog. He weakly wagged his tail while he wolfed it down. When he was done, I swung up into the Renault. "You get clear now, old pal," I told him.

The Lab tried to jump into the car with me through the window, but his back legs were too weak to do the job. His front legs, now hooked over the Renault's open passenger-side window, began to fail him. He sat down and scratched weakly at the door with a clumsy front paw, whimpering.

Behind us, some trucks were headed our way. I thought about it, then reached over and opened the passenger-side door. I grabbed the dog by the scruff and hauled him up into the Juvaquatre with me. He collapsed onto the floorboards on the passenger's side and looked up at me with grateful dark eyes, panting tiredly.

I grabbed one of the tarps Gertrude had wrapped herself in and swaddled the dog in that to keep him warm and dry from the now harder rain. We tore off down the sodden road as the impatient truck drivers on our tail began to lay on their horns.

Close by Lyon, German troop trucks began to ride my bumper. The Kraut soldiers sounded drunk, boisterously singing "*Drei Lilien, Drei Lilien*" and cursing at me.

I scratched the black dog behind his ears and ground my teeth.

I thought to myself, *If I only had a machine gun and enough ammo, I'd fix all this world's sorry present troubles.*

BOOK ONE
The Girl in the Wall
November 1942

1

A drafty apartment in Lyon. We were seated around a table, now littered with empty bottles, well-worn maps and precious, damning notes bound for the stingy fire. Pancho, my adopted black Labrador, was curled up at my feet, the only part of me that was warm. From some adjacent apartment, I could just make out a scratchy recording of "I'll Be Seeing You."

Jean Moulin, resistance organizer supreme, a man I knew and trusted from a brief brush during the Spanish Civil War, said, "This new man the Nazis have put here, this Klaus Barbie, he is ruthless. A bloody fiend."

I ground out a Pall Mall's stub. "So we've heard. Hope to meet that hombre one day. Just once would do."

"Worse still might be his right hand," Moulin said. "His name is Werner Höttl."

That got my attention. Him again. This time, I'd been sent to spy on Höttl. But it was starting to turn into something more like a duel. "I know that sorry one by name," I said, telling half-truths. "Or at least I knew another who went by that name. I met him after the Great War. Höttl was around

Paris in the early 1920s, too. He was starting to do some stuff around the German cinema industry at the time."

"Sadists, both of them," Moulin said. "Butchers of the worst stripe."

Hefting my notepad, I nodded, said, "Anyway, I will carry your requests back to Wild Bill. We'll see what old Bill Donovan can do about meeting your needs here. Supplies really aren't the issue. It's the delivery here, you know?"

"Always the problem." Smiling ruefully, Moulin freshened our cups of wine and said, "For a crime novelist turned war correspondent, you're remarkably connected, Monsieur Lassiter."

I smiled and ran fingers through my dark hair, now graying at the temples. "At forty-two, they tell me I'm somehow too over-the-hill to be simple infantry. So I keep a hand in where I can." I grinned and said, "I look forward to dancing on these Nazi monsters' graves. Soon."

Moulin smiled and rose. "As do I. Now I must go." We shook hands and I watched him leave. He had to be the most hard-hunted man in France. Couldn't envy him that distinction. I poured myself another drink, again scratching Pancho between the ears with my free hand.

We were left alone with our host, a carpenter named André Babinot, and his wife, Babette, who was bustling around in the kitchen.

André and I chatted for a time, more on the war effort, the deprivations of his people. Fantasy stuff we'd like to do if we had a dull knife and Hitler to ourselves.

Pancho sat up suddenly, cocking his head on side. He began to scent the air.

Wetting his lips, André said, a bit anxiously, I thought, "Perhaps your dog needs to go out, Mr. Lassiter?" A low growl now.

Frowning, I said, "No, I know the signs and these aren't those."

Pancho suddenly bolted, sliding nose-first under a battered sideboard. He began to whelp and scratch furiously at the baseboards there.

I smiled and said, "Sorry, I'll stop him before he scars the walls."

My host shifted his feet, a tad nervously it seemed to me. He said quickly, "It is nothing. Probably just a mouse. Pay no attention, please."

Mice? Maybe. Or maybe not. Looking closer at the baseboards now, I saw seams. I tapped on the wall. Sucker gave off a hollow sound.

I said, "What, or who, have you got hidden behind this wall, *mon ami?*"

André had a Luger pointed at my chest now. He looked heartsick. "Leave, please Mr. Lassiter. This is nothing to concern yourself with, I swear to you. Let it be, my friend, please. I beg you do that."

The Jews in occupied France had recently been ordered to wear yellow stars to identify them. That was an ominous sign. Worse, some of them had begun disappearing a time back, or so I had heard tell. I played a hunch.

I said, "Easy there, André. We're fighting on the same side, remember? You've got someone hidden behind that wall. Someone Jewish? If that's so, maybe I can help."

He sighed and lowered his gun. "It's a lone child," he said. "A Jewish girl of nine my wife and I took in." He said softly, "I think my neighbors begin to suspect. And they're collaborators, spies for the Germans."

Not good news, that. Not for André, and not for the little girl hiding behind the wall.

I pointed at the false wall and said, "I'll help you move this furniture. I want you to introduce me to this child, brother."

2

The dark-haired, dark-eyed girl's name was Myriam Dreyfus. Dressed in a careworn tweed skirt and handmade sweater, she was skittish around me, choosing instead to focus her attention on Pancho, who sat with his paws across her lap, frequently licking her cheek as she petted him.

We had crawled through the small hole in the wall to visit the girl in her cramped hiding place. Mrs. Babinot passed some coffee cups and a flask through the hole, then crawled in to join us.

André said softly in English, "Myriam was in the orphanage until a few weeks ago. Her parents were said to have been murdered by drunken Nazis in 1940. Killed for their race. This man, this monster Barbie, raided the orphanage where Myriam was kept. I was there making new slats for the children's beds. Myriam stayed behind, watching me. The other children were playing out in the yard when Barbie and his man, this creature called Höttl, came and rounded up the children. Although I was terrified, afraid for myself, I'll confess, I hid Myriam under a bed and then smuggled her out of the orphanage after the others had been taken away."

He pressed his hand to his forehead. "You can't imagine how terrible it was, the crying. The screams. Nazis everywhere, questioning me as to whether I had seen this child. I was sitting on the bed, trying to brazen it out, knowing the child was hiding underneath the bed, hiding there because I had told her to. All the time I was thinking, If they find her, and she tells them I helped her hide? God forgive me for thinking that."

"It was a very dangerous thing you did," I said. "But you're a brave man. Don't beat yourself up over things that never happened. How'd you get her out of that place?"

"I had brought some tarps to spread on the floors, to protect the tiles," André said. "I hid a couple of the tarps in a storage closet, then rolled the child in the two remaining tarps. I carried the bundle out, slung over my shoulder."

He shook his head, squeezing the bridge of his nose. "One of the Nazis stopped me, making small talk. He insisted I smoke with him. I nearly suffocated the girl loitering with that soldier. All the time I was smoking I thought, 'If she moves, just a little? If she should sneeze, or cough?'"

I squeezed his arm and nodded, whispered, "You're a brave man, like I said. These other children, they were taken where?"

His wife shot André a warning look. He said, "I can't say in front of the girl. But I've heard terrible rumors. I believe they're beyond help. Barbie, he has an evil bloodlust. And Höttl? He is even worse."

"I get the drift," I said through gritted teeth. I wanted to kill Klaus Barbie, wanted to renew my acquaintance with Werner Höttl and give him a little of his own, regardless of my current orders to the contrary.

All bloody things in their time, I promised myself. For now, I was at least in a position to maybe save this child, and I surely meant to do that.

"These neighbors of yours," I said, "you think they're a real threat to little Myriam?"

"Very much," Babette Babinot said. "They'd turn us over, and the girl, to curry favor with the Nazis. I know it's coming, and any moment now."

"Well, then, I should take the girl away from here, *vite*. Tonight. I'll get this child to safe territory. Try and get her to England and sent on from there to… hell, somewhere better. Some place safe at least. Maybe back to the States if I have to go that far to protect her from the Nazis' reach."

Mrs. Babinot squeezed my hands hard, her eyes shining and wet. Her chin was trembling. "You can really do this? *Really*? Please don't lie about this."

"I can surely try." That didn't seem enough for the woman. I added, "I mean to do this, and when I set my mind to something, nothing stops me." I squeezed her hand and said, "Does Myriam have surviving family anywhere? I mean somewhere outside German occupation?"

The woman said, "None she knows of. How will you do this? The Germans are hunting for her, even now. They counted beds after André spirited her away. They checked registries at the orphanage. They know one child escaped them. Höttl seems committed to finding her. There have been stories in the papers about his search."

This was just getting hairier and hairier. Any second it seemed to me, the girl could be handed over. And these turncoat neighbors? There had to be a reckoning.

And why the obsession with this particular child? Could it be that famous surname of hers? It was a theory, anyway. And either way, Höttl must truly be one nasty piece of work, worse even than I knew.

"There's a new organization my side has formed," I said carefully.

That was the Office of Strategic Services—but I couldn't tell them that. Instead I said, "Some of its members are filtering here into France. Good and smart people."

I was a kind of adjunct OSS operative, though I couldn't risk telling my hosts that, either. Not them, nor all the other war correspondents who'd lately begun to give me the eye, actually making trouble for me with the brass with a whispering campaign that I was playing soldier and should be stripped of my reporting credentials and booted back home. Maybe even put in jail for violating the Geneva Convention.

I said, "I'll have some travel documents prepared. Some false identification made for Myriam. The two of us will travel as father and daughter. I'm going to run get you some hair dye, Mademoiselle. I want you to dye the girl's hair blond. You know—to help the cause."

It hung unsaid between us: Make the little girl look less Jewish. Do it *muy pronto*.

Babette said, "Of course. I can do this with no real effort."

"I should leave now. There's suddenly much to do." I scooted over closer to Myriam, said softly to the girl in French, "Honey, if you had to have another name for a time, to pretend at being someone else, what name would you pick for yourself?"

Avoiding my eyes, focusing instead on Pancho, she said in a little girl's contemplative voice, "Maybe… Sara."

Something closer to her own name would be better, something easier for her to remember. I said quietly, "How about *another* name?"

"Marie."

"Perfect. Can you watch Pancho for me for a time, *Marie*?"

She giggled as I called her by this new name. "*Oui.*"

I shook her foot. "Thanks, darlin'."

"Prepare her, best you can," I said softly to André and his wife. "Assure her the dog will be coming along for the trip, because he is. That alone might be enough to make her willing to leave here with me."

"It's very dangerous," André's wife said to me. "A terrible risk you run for yourself. I don't think you begin to grasp what a devil this man Barbie is. If you succeed, and he ever finds out you thwarted his will, then *you* will—"

"I know something of his minion, Werner Höttl, so I can make a wild guess what the boss man might try and do," I said. "Simple fact is, I'm not having that child fall into those butchers' hands. That's decided, and so the rest is of no consequence, just rearview-mirror stuff. We simply drive on."

I waved a hand and grinned like it was all nothing.

Sure.

I said, "I whipped Werner Höttl's ass in one war. Expect I can do that thing again."

Of course, I had nothing to make me think any of that was true, but I sounded convincing enough for the scared couple, I reckoned.

André smiled uncertainly and shook his head. "You crazy Americans…"

"Huh-uh," I said. "The Germans are the crazy ones. Hitler is quite and completely mad. Arrogant and twisted. That's why, in the end, our side will crush this Nazi scourge. Say what you will, but we Americans know how to kick German tail. This time we mean to do it for keeps."

From my lips to our dead God's ear, I thought.

3

We were in the back room of a bar run by the brother of a resistance chief. The room was swept regularly for bugs, and admission to the private space was strictly controlled. It was as close to an unofficial HQ with a liquor stock as could be found in occupied France.

I shook out my match. "Werner Höttl again," I said. "Swear, I can't seem to swing a dead cat without hitting up against something tied back to that son of a bitch."

"It isn't his real name, you know," Jimmy said. James Hanrahan was about my age, about my size. Jim was also forty-ish; wide at the shoulders and stood six-two. Jimmy had a few pounds on me. He had blue eyes, iron gray hair and a nose that had been broken more often than some men change socks—the bulbous remnant of a youthful and soon enough discarded boxing career. Jimmy had come stateside after what had sadly proven to be our *first* World War. He still retained his Irish tenor.

Long-in-the-tooth as we were for frontline service, Jimmy, a veteran Cleveland cop, had finagled an intelligence role for himself, just as I had done.

Through a haze of smoke, I said, "Höttl's not a real handle?"

Jimmy nodded. "Try this one on for size: Rudolph Van Ostrand, born in Bad Wildbad... Baden-Württemberg. His father was a butcher. Mother was an Austrian musician. Sounds an uneasy match to me. Boy helped out around the family business through his early teens. Might explain a few things about his blood-lust, I suppose."

"Not sure which name I like least," I said. "How'd you dig up this nugget on Höttl/Van Ostrand?"

"Wasn't particularly easy, that's for sure," Jimmy said. "These career military intelligence dolts treat information like it's private wealth. They hoard and protect it and fret over it. So in other words, I stole this gen."

Jimmy pulled two shot glasses and a virgin bottle of Glenmorangie from the pocket of his overcoat. "The stuff these Frogs call whiskey is swill," he said. "So I brought a wee dab of civilization. Proper single malt whisky, with no 'e', that is to say." He passed me the bottle and said, "You'll do the honors, won't you, Hector?"

I broke the seal on the single malt and poured as Jimmy lit his own cigarette. I said, "How many of these soldiers did you bring over with you?"

Jimmy held his glass up to the overhead light. "Probably the cleanest glasses in this God forsaken land," he said. He set his down for filling and said, "Smuggled in a case. So go easy, we're not beating back the heathen Hun with anywhere near the alacrity I anticipated. I'd like to have at least one bottle left to toast *der Fürhrer's* demise."

"May yet come sooner rather than later," I said. "Rommel got his ass kicked on the way to Tunis, I hear from my buddy Henry J. Jr. And Ike's 'Operation Torch' came off pretty well.

And the Russians are gathering force again in Stalingrad, they say, siphoning off more of Hitler's assets to shore up there in Russia. There are hopeful signs."

"Tell that to Vichy, France," Jimmy said.

I shrugged. "We'll get Southern France back too, in due time."

We tapped glasses. He said, "*Slainte.*"

I added, "To the death of the Reich," and we winced together at the burn. I said, "That is good stuff."

"Ah, yes, it is. But I feel a bit the traitor. I actually prefer this Scottish brew to Jameson." Jimmy hesitated, then said, "This child you're trying to save, to smuggle home, it's a salutary notion, Hector. But why personally make that run with her? I'm sure you could pull strings to get some sturdy lads to do the job for you."

"Maybe. But they wouldn't be committed like I am. The girl's also very withdrawn. She's been living behind that false wall for some time, Jimmy. She's, well, mildly troubled, I fear. I'm the only person she's willing to make the dash with, and that's mostly because of my dog."

Jimmy smiled. "Ah, grand! Yes, the canine. How you've managed to keep a pet in this bedlam's another thing I can't get my brain 'round, Hector, not one bit."

I trailed a fingertip around the rim of my glass. "Pet? Nah, *partner*. And Patton is toying with getting a bull terrier, I hear. If that cretin can have a dog in theatre, I certainly can. And then I'll be able to say Patton's copying me."

Jimmy roared. "Ah yes, the estimable George S. You two go back to Mexico, to the Pershing Expedition, if memory serves – and it always does. You Yanks do hold a grudge."

"Look who's talking," I said. "Besides, the older I get, I come to see we just become more the men we are. Patton started out bottom rung, and he avowedly ain't improving with age."

"Well, a child, a dog, and Höttl hard at your heels. It'd make a fine screwball comedy for back home. *Andy Hardy v. the Nazis… Abbott and Costello Meet Hitler*, maybe. It's a daft notion, Hector. The deck is already calamitously stacked against you."

"Maybe, Jimmy. Thing is, Höttl wants this child, badly. Or his boss does. It's the same thing in the end, really. They want this little girl, the only one to evade their grasp in this purge they ran on an orphanage a time back. So for all kinds of reasons, they're going to be denied their desires. I wanna shove this stick in Höttl's eye, and I want him to know exactly who gouged him."

"Hokey-dokey, then," Jimmy said. "So. Where are you taking her?"

"First objective is to get her on a plane or boat back to the States somehow. Of course that means getting her out of occupied France. If I can successfully cross that frontier, then I'll figure out where to send her and my dog. One miracle at a time."

Jimmy shook his head. "That last sounds like an afterthought, Hec. Getting her settled I mean. And that's no way to repay that child's trust. Hell, there are plenty of anti-Semites back home, even in the midst of this damned war against the greatest Jew-haters of all-time. Just getting her to the States isn't enough. She needs a good and loving home, Hector. You going go back with her? Are you prepared to be a father to this child?"

"I'm not remotely equipped for that," I said. "And I have work here. I—"

"You don't know a single family back home to place her with," Jimmy said. "You don't move in those circles, ever the committed bachelor and skirt-chaser." He drummed his fingers on the tabletop. "I've a kid sister in Euclid. She and her husband have been trying to adopt for a couple of years, without success. Lately, they've been looking to older war orphans. Also without success, so far."

"They're good people?"

This look. "She's my sister, Hector."

"You can make this happen, for sure?"

Jimmy nodded. "If you can get her out of this Hades, yes. I'll see that it happens."

"Well, bless you James Hanrahan and family." Then I hesitated. "A good Irish-Catholic family? This little girl being Jewish…?"

Jimmy shrugged. "I can't swear she'll not be changing her religion, Hector. Fionnula might contrive to undertake that conversion. Or maybe not. But fact is, that little Colleen staying here, under Nazi rule? Have you heard about these death camps, Hector? We hear they may be gassing the Jews."

I nodded. "Heard whispers of the same. Fact is, if the kid stays here, she's doomed."

"That's the way I see it," Jimmy said. He raised his glass; winced over the rim. "I truly don't envy you the chase. This Nazi, he seems pitiless. It's a fearsome tough run ahead of you, I think. I'd frankly hate to be you."

"Really, Jim?" I freshened our drinks. "Knowing you think that way makes it much tougher."

Jimmy bit his lip. "Sorry, Hec, I didn't mean to be a pessimist. Not out loud, at any rate."

"I didn't mean it like that," I said.

The big Irishman narrowed his blue eyes. "You're no dancer, Hector, so just say it."

"It *is* a tough sprint for one man, even the right man," I said. "But for two of the right men?" I smiled. "We could have ourselves a time, Jimmy. Could have us a grand lark."

Jimmy slapped his hand on the table. "Ah, Hector, you're a pistol!"

"I'm serious."

His smile went away. "I see that you *are*. You don't ask much, do you, Hector?"

I glossed it, or tried to. "Figure a silver-tongued operator like you can contrive some intelligence nonsense to inveigle a few days for a romp across France," I said.

Jimmy stared at the end of his cigarette. "A romp? Suicide run is more the term for it. Of course the intelligence gambit is easy, Hector. It's the prospect of drawing air even an hour into this run that strikes me as the long reach. Still, this poor little darlin'…" Jimmy looked as sick and gut-knotted as I felt inside.

I said, "Together, we can—"

"Hector."

"I know, Jimmy. You said it up front, insane."

"But a necessary madness, if there can be such a thing," he said. "Jaysus." Jimmy picked up the Glenmorangie bottle and weighed it in his hand. "Damn it!" He shook his head. "So be it. You bring the next bottle of whisky and I'm in, Hector."

I shook his big hard hand. Our pact stood a fair chance of getting him killed alongside me. We both knew that. Jimmy said, "And when do we commence this lunatic foray?"

"Six hours. I'm going to get our new identity documents. She and I will be traveling as father and daughter, at least in the countryside. In the cities, I'll be playing Nazi and I guess she'll be my prisoner. I'll fetch her and Pancho, then I'll pick you up at HQ at seven."

Jimmy shook his head. "No, Höttl's file has got me spooked. I'm not sure he hasn't penetrated the official infrastructure to some extent. There are at least two guys in my side of things I could figure for Bund or actual double agents. Pick me up here." He smiled. "Do I get a new identity in this crazy operation, too?"

I squeezed his thick wrist. "Just need you to be you, Jimmy."

"I can do no other." He re-corked the Glenmorangie and slipped the bottle in his pocket. "I've much to do. And ammo to gather, I suspect. Don't you forget the single malt, Hector. And I'll need a uniform. That's the tallest order, and I mean literally. Despite all these Teutonic delusions of Aryan grandeur, these Krauts seem to run to the short side."

Jimmy slipped on his hat. "And now, I'll see you in five hours and forty five minutes." He crossed himself and added, "I'll see if I can't wrangle some treat for the dog and lollipops, too."

4

It wasn't my neighborhood, but I didn't have to be a local to see something sinister was afoot. The streets were empty of civilians a tad too early in advance of curfew. Military presence however, was quite heavy, and it was steadily increasing.

Those damned nosy neighbors.

The Nazis weren't fully in position yet—they were still massing. I was driving a freshly stolen Opel Olympia that had been converted into a Nazi officer's personal car. The car had all the right insignia to carry me through the post-curfew darkened streets of Lyon. I was also wearing a German SS uniform. I just had to remember to keep my palm pressed to the belly if I had to talk to any real Germans—had to obscure the bullet hole there in the stomach of the jacket.

I pulled around to the back of the apartment building, positioning the Olympia under a balcony I figured to be roughly across the hall from the Babinots' place. I caught a break—someone had discarded a mattress. Scrounging up some empty cardboard boxes, I placed them on the roof of the Olympia, then balanced the mattress atop them.

From under the passenger side seat I pulled a bag and took out two hand grenades and a length of rope.

I aimed to misbehave.

André Babinot eyed my uniform and said, "You must wear that terrible uniform?"

"Only way to get around at this hour like I need to," I said curtly. "Now you and your wife need to go. Take what you can carry that matters most, but I doubt you have five minutes. Go out the back—the Nazi's are massing out front. I think your neighbors' poking their noses in has come home to roost." Remembering, I snapped my fingers. "The bottle of hair dye, I don't want to give the Krauts any hints to the girl's changed appearance in their search if they choose to make one."

André looked ashen. He nodded at the trash, then called to his wife. Seems they had long prepared for flight: Babette began pitching papers in the fire. Then she snatched up a box filled with what I guessed would be money, jewelry, maybe some photos.

The empty hair dye bottle was on top of the trash. I shoved it in my pocket.

I said to André, "Do me a favor, please. When you go, put the dog in the front seat of the Olympia parked out back. Just lash the leash to the steering column. You'll know the vehicle—it's the one with a mattress balanced across the top." I passed him a card. "The address of a safe house. Tell 'em Lassiter sent you. You need to memorize that address and then destroy it before going outside."

"Of course." André nodded. "And the girl?"

"She's still going with me," I said, helping his wife pitch paper in the fire. "But first she and I are going to pay a visit to your neighbors."

He gave me this wary look. "Why?"

"Candidly? I'm a vengeful man."

"It certainly smacks of pique, Monsieur Lassiter. And the girl should not see—"

"She's not going to see anything bad. It's not going to be like that. Actually, it's a tactical thing I'm doing, too. Yet she won't see anything, I swear to you."

He chewed on his lip. "When the Nazis find that hole in my wall?"

"You'll both be safely under my people's protection," I said, wrenching loose the panel. I held my hand out to the little girl. She was a blonde now, and she looked terrified. My damned Nazi uniform wasn't helping with any of that. I said, in French, "The dog will be waiting for us downstairs, *mon coeur.*"

Nodding, chin trembling, she took my hand.

"Chances are the Nazis know about that fake wall now," I said to André. "But when I'm done, at least the evidence of the hiding place will likely be obliterated."

Now André looked even more worried.

I said, "Two minutes, then you'd better be gone like your lives depend upon it."

"Marie" was frighteningly quiet and very focused on the gun in my other hand. I positioned myself next to the nosy neighbors' front door. In belligerent German I said, "Gestapo! Open the door now!" I looked briefly back over my shoulder and saw the Babinots hustling down the hallway to a back stairwell. They had Pancho in tow—dragging him, really. The dog's head remained cocked in my direction, straining against the leash. I nodded at the old couple. "Marie" weakly waved goodbye to them.

Then I pounded on the door again. "Open the door now or we'll break it in," I yelled.

René and Gabrielle Lambert sat in their chairs, fidgeting and wide-eyed. They exchanged frightened glares at one another. René had a nice sheen of sweat going. That made me think the missus was the one who had the informer's zealous streak. She just seemed tougher, meaner… like she had more to lose. So far, I wasn't relishing this confrontation with anywhere near the level of enthusiasm I'd anticipated.

We were just getting to the meat of the thing. The Lamberts exchanged confused looks but obeyed when I asked them to slide their chairs up against the wall that abutted Marie's hiding place.

They were sitting in those chairs, now. I'd made them sit down, one at a time—I made them sit in those chairs at gunpoint.

Marie was fidgeting with a doll by the front door. I gestured over my shoulder with a thumb, my Mauser trained between the informers. "How could you rat out a little girl to that murdering, goose-stepping fools gathering forces out front?"

Gabrielle said, "Times are hard. Food is getting scarcer." She shrugged. "If it had not been us, it would have been another, you must understand that." She just couldn't shut up and end it there. She said, "And anyway, she's a Jew if it even needs saying."

I nodded, staring at her. René looked even more scared of me now, must have seen something in my face. Time was getting short. Any second those storm troopers might come bounding up the stairs.

Time to get down to cases.

Glancing back at the girl by the door, I said softly, so she wouldn't overhear, "Here's the thing. When I made you each sit down one at a time, I slipped a hand grenade under each of your seat cushions. The pin has been pulled on each grenade. Only your body weight is preventing detonation. If you run or you stand, the things will explode in less than fives seconds. In this confined space, just one grenade could be lethal. Do you understand what I'm saying?"

Tentative, grave head nods. I smiled. "Good. Splendid, really. The little girl and I are going to go out your front door, now. You two count out loud together. Count to one hundred. When you reach a hundred, you run as fast as you can for the front door. If you make it into the hallway, you'll probably survive. But you'll certainly be losing all your precious valuables." I shrugged. "*C'est la vie*, eh?"

I aimed the gun from one to another. "Now, important thing is if either of you leaves those chairs before you reach one hundred, if you put your head out this front door, I'll shoot you dead. So just stay calm, count to a hundred, and then run together. Then you can have the rest of your lives to mull over the monstrous thing you did tonight."

Vigorous nods.

"Well, then I leave you now. I'm not joking. If you come out ahead of time, you'll be just as dead as you'll be standing close by those chairs when they blow."

There was a third way out of their predicament, of course. They could reach under their cushions, get a grip on those grenades, then make a run for the windows. They could break the glass with their elbows and pitch the things into the street.

Of course, then they'd be blowing up German soldiers. The Nazis who weren't killed by the grenades would likely see the Lamberts paid with their lives in an even more agonizing way than being blown to ribbons in their apartment.

I said to Marie, "Into the hallway with you. I'm right behind you."

I closed the door behind, me, then looped the slip knot I'd made in one end of the rope around the knob of the Lamberts' front door and cinched it tight. I looped the other end of the rope around the knob of an apartment across the hall and tied it off tightly with a bowline knot. Neither door of either apartment could be opened from the inside with that rope in place.

Booted feet pounded up the stairs now. I opened the door of another unit on the side opposite the Babinots and Lamberts' apartments. I'd cased the place earlier: confirmed it was vacant and left the door unlocked.

We hustled to the rear window.

One thing was going to plan. I'd parked my Opel under the right window. I lifted Marie in my arms and smiled. "We're going to jump onto that mattress there," I said. "It's going to be fun. And Pancho is waiting down there for us." He was—I could see his tail whipping out the cracked passenger side window.

With luck, the boxes and mattresses would keep the car's roof from caving in.

I took a deep breath, then made the leap. We hit the mattress and the cardboard boxes collapsed under us. Startled,

Pancho began barking. I rolled off the mattress, down the boot and onto the street, still holding tightly to the girl.

"Fun, like I said, yes?"

Wide-eyed, Marie shook her head *no*.

There was an explosion then. It was quickly followed by a second blast. I twisted around, getting myself between Marie and all the falling glass from the overhead windows.

Adieu to the Lamberts and more than a few Germans, with any luck.

I cast the mattress off the roof of the Opel and knocked off the cardboard boxes. I got Marie in the front seat of the Olympia. There were shouts throughout the building now, screams. People were yelling "Fire," and "It must be a gas explosion!"

More shouts in German, very angry Nazis.

Smiling at Marie, I got the car in gear. I ripped off down the alley with the headlights off, on my way to meet up with Jimmy Hanrahan: Marie whimpered softly to herself, until she fell asleep.

5

Jimmy had scrounged up his own German uniform. He loaded in his bags, then swung into the passenger seat. He looked me over and said, "Ah, you're on the right side of the flivver."

"What do you mean?" I got the car in gear and slid off the curb.

"I outrank you, Hector." He tugged at his coat's sleeves. He said, "If only the boyo I took this from had been half-an-inch taller. Maybe I should be in back. To further the ruse you're my chauffeur, I mean."

"Not much room back there between the child and the dog," I said. "Besides, with those two in the back, you looking the convincing Nazi is the least of our problems."

"No travel papers, then?"

"None that would explain this motley quartet."

Jimmy nodded and looked over his shoulder. He smiled at the child and said softly to me, "Does she have any English?"

"Of course not."

"Then here's a thought or two in our lingo. The dog is well-trained? Won't growl if he smells Nazi scum?"

"He's excellently trained," I said.

The Irishman squeezed my shoulder with a big hard hand. "She's already nodded off. No problem getting her out of that void in the wall, then?"

Jimmy had worries enough; couldn't see heaping on more by confiding what I'd blown up extricating the child. "It went well enough," I said. "We got away without any tagalongs, that is to say."

"Ah, you may fool some, but to me, you're such a cruddy liar, Hector." Jimmy ran a hand back through his graying hair. He rolled his window up tight. "There was something on the radio before I headed out. How much, exactly, did you blow up?"

I shifted in my seat. "Not so sure about that. I wasn't that close to the detonation site." I clicked the car heater up a notch. "It wasn't at all gratuitous on my part, Jimbo. The Germans were all over that place. I needed a distraction. And far fewer Nazis."

"The girl didn't see—?"

"We were outside, like I said."

Jimmy grunted and reached into a knapsack at his feet. He pulled out a long silver thermos and a couple of cups. "Did some more digging on your friend Höttl," he said, pouring us each some steaming brew. "Our boys seem to think he might actually have had some hand in shaping *Mein Kampf*."

"They're likely right about that," I said cagily. "There were some indications in old days of that."

Jimmy handed me my cup. I sipped and said, "You Irished it up."

"A dash of Jameson, yes," Jimmy said, replacing the thermos and sipping from his own cup. "Single malt and coffee seems an uneasy mix. So it's Jameson for this duty."

"This stuff with Höttl makes little sense to me," I said. "Höttl's not a career soldier. Not even much of an idealist, in my experience. He's an artist. Well, at least he's the creative type. Cinema. What in hell is he doing here?"

"Who knows?" Jimmy said. "Frankly, a lot of stuff that the Germans do flummoxes me. And look at the boyos Hitler surrounds himself with: Goebbels, Goring, Himmler, Bormann, Hess, Speer and von Ribbentrop? Can you believe some of his crew?" Jimmy shook his head and sipped more spiked coffee. "And Hess and that crazy flight to Scotland? You know, I heard a rumor that you were tied up in that whole—"

Spooked, I cut him off, said, "We got into this fight at least a year too late, Jimmy. Should have gotten in back in 1939, I think."

"Spilt milk now, Hector." He drank more java, whistling through the burn. He said, "You knew Höttl in Paris, in the 1920s."

"We weren't friends by any stretch, Jimmy, if that's what you're implying." I checked the rearview mirror. Maybe I was wrong about having no tagalongs. I said, "Someone is back there, Jimmy."

"Christ, and we've hardly even begun." He drained his coffee and cast the cup out his window. He reached for his gun.

"Whoa there, buddy. He's flashing lights."

The Irishman checked over his shoulder again. "Funny pattern to those headlight flashes. Code?"

I palmed the wheel, pulling curbside. "Just in case," I said, "go ahead and have that gun out, but hidden."

Two men exited the light transport parked behind us. The men were carrying German rifles. They approached along either side of the Olympia. The one on my side of the car rapped on the window with his knuckles. He let the rifle drop at his side, hanging there from a strap. "Jean sent us. I'm Bertrand. Please, Monsieur Lassiter, there isn't much time."

I rolled down the window. "There's a problem?"

"*Oui*. We picked up radio chatter. You were recognized. The Germans are looking for you, a blond girl child and an Olympia with Nazi insignia."

"Wonderful," Jimmy said. "Truly grand."

Motion in the rearview mirror: a third person was exiting the light transport. From the gait, and the silhouette, it looked like a woman in pants.

Bertrand said, "I'll take your car. We'll lead the Nazis away from the old city. My partner will drive you in our truck to your next rendezvous point. Please, we have to hurry, Monsieur Lassiter."

Cursing, I slipped out of the car. Jimmy started handing bags to the second man who hustled them back to our future ride.

Pancho leapt out of the back seat. Marie was still asleep. I lifted her in my arms. I said, "Where are we going to be while these vehicles are being moved around?"

"We'll be escaping, moving through the city clandestinely," a husky female voice said.

"You're American," I said, turning to face her.

"So are you. Small world." She was tall, nearly six feet and all of that topped by strawberry-blond hair, blue eyes. She looked like she was dressed for a fox hunt: jodhpurs, riding boots and a tweed jacket. All she needed was a riding helmet and crop. Fetching though... *very* attractive. She looked down at Pancho sitting there and wagging his tail. She said, "Really? A dog, too? You sure don't make it easy."

"When you're starting out at impossible…" I shrugged and smiled and put out a hand, balancing the child on my forearms. "Hector Lassiter."

"I know who you are," she said. "Don't wake the child. Now, we need to hustle." She leaned into the Olympia and snatched up the doll on the backseat—the girl's only toy. She thrust it into the pocket of her jacket, one arm and its head hanging out. "Let's shake a leg, boys, the Krauts are hard on our heels."

She trotted across the street. Jimmy and I exchanged glances, then followed. Trying not to jostle the girl awake with my running, I followed at some distance, but stepped it up a little as I heard the rumble of heavy trucks echoing off those sleeping storefronts.

I ran up a short flight of stairs toward a very old building. The woman was holding the door for me. Pancho was again sitting at her feet, looking up at her and wagging his tail. Sucker seemed strongly drawn to her. Well, he wasn't alone in that. I said, "I didn't catch your name, sweetheart."

She nodded and toed Pancho through the door behind me. "Duff Sexton," she said. "Now more walking, *sweetheart*, and less talking."

6

We were moving through a tall arched passageway, following Duff. Jimmy said, "What is this thing? Where are we going?"

"It's called a traboule," Duff said. "Lyon, particularly in the 1st, 4th and 5th arondissements, is honeycombed with them. These tunnels were built by textile merchants long ago, to move silk and other fragile fabrics in the rain."

Jimmy said, "And now?"

"Mostly used by the resistance, to move around the city at something like will," Duff said. "Very few Germans know about them, and the few they've found they haven't really explored fully enough to realize they form a secret means of navigating the city. Hell, plenty of Lyon residents don't really know about them, or how extensively they spread."

"But you do," I said. I was a little short of breath from lugging around sixty pounds of child down the long, echoing corridors. "Seems strange a Yank would know this route. Seems the devlish maze."

"I've lived here since 1938," she said. "My late husband was an architect. The traboules fascinated him."

I said softly, "How were you widowed?"

"The Germans," said she flatly. "He was a Jew."

"We're in the Croix-Rousse quarter, now," Duff said. "This is the *Traboule de la cour des Voraces*, or the Traboule of the Voracious Court."

Jimmy said, "By the way, my name is—"

"James Butler Hanrahan," Duff said. "Born March 17, 1902 to Stephen and Molly Hanrahan in Rathgar, Ireland. Your father was an English professor who moved the family to the States when he accepted a teaching position at Western Reserve University in Ohio in—"

Jimmy cut her off. "Your scaring me now, lass."

She shrugged and said, "It's just that you're in your brash friend's KA file."

I said, "*KA*?"

"Known associates," Jimmy said.

"Just so," Duff said. To me she said, "Although in your case it could as easily be called a Rogue's Gallery." She gave Jimmy a faint smile. "Compared to some others in Lassiter's file, you seem pretty okay, James."

Jimmy nodded. "Damning with faint praise?"

She smiled again. "Could be."

"All this information on Jimmy—you're not just an ex-pat resistance fighter," I said. "Not with all this information you have on us. And I don't care how good you are, or how strong your local ties are, the resistance would not be working hand-in-glove with you unless you're something more."

"Same as you, I'm OSS," Duff said. "Well, as much as they'll let me be a part of the team. It's still kind of a boys' club." She stopped us and said, "You're clearly beyond spent from carrying that child. You need to rest."

Her voice made it sound like that would be a very bad idea. Jimmy said, "I'll take her a while, Hec." I passed the child over into Jimmy's arms. I shook my burning arms and wiggled my fingers to get the circulation going again. I dipped a hand into my Nazi uniform for my cigarettes and lighter. Duff said, "Put those away. No wonder you're short of breath."

"Yes, ma'am," I said. Duff narrowed her eyes and then poked my belly through the bullet hole in my jacket.

"Took this the hard way, eh?"

"It's one less German in the world. You truly care?"

"Not at all," she said. "Let's get moving again."

After twenty minutes of brisk walking, we hit a fork. Duff led us to the right. Jimmy huffed, "How much farther?"

"Quite a ways, I'm afraid," she said.

I said, "Those men you were with. They said they'd heard on the radio I was identified by name."

"That's right," Duff said. "It seems Werner Höttl was there at the building, setting up cameras around the site. He was there at the direction of Leni Riefensthal."

Riefensthal: she was Hitler's designated filmmaker. Her name had come up before, in old days, when she was friendly with director Josef von Sternberg.

Duff said, "They seemed to be intent upon filming the raid for propaganda purposes – to try and dampen the mood of the resistance. Instead they accidentally filmed your rather flamboyant escape." That seemed to please her.

"They took the trouble to film the back of the building?" I scowled and said, "That makes no sense."

"Struck me as queer, too," Duff said. "Anyway, he recognized you from your old Paris days. Guess you haven't changed much, since then. Men are fortunate that way."

"I'm only not different on the outside," I said. I added, "Despite the cigarettes."

"You seem to know everything," Jimmy said to Duff, sounding very short of breath himself, now. "Any notion why Höttl is so driven to get this particular child in his clutches?"

Duff put out her arms. "I can take her a while. I'm stronger than I look." Jimmy didn't argue—he handed the child over to the woman. She smiled sadly at the little girl in her arms who had now fully awakened, eyeing this new stranger. Duff reassured her in French and the child nodded and then put her arms around Duff's neck, her head on the woman's shoulder. "I do have a notion," Duff said in English. "But it falls into the realm of rumor, really. Still, if it's true, it explains everything."

Jimmy rubbed his biceps and said, "What do the wagging tongues claim?"

Duff set off again. "They say this child's true father is the Butcher of Lyon's right-hand man, Werner Höttl."

7

Jimmy said, "You believe the rumors?"

Over her shoulder, Duff said, "It would explain a lot."

"But to kill a whole orphanage to slay one little girl?" Jimmy rubbed his shoulders. "That is goddamn cold."

"Wouldn't be the first time someone committed a slaughter to murder one child," she said.

"Sunday school stuff aside, it's coldly calculating," I said. "What better way to make it look less than personal? Kill two-dozen children to ensure the death of one girl."

The tunnel system was looking gloomy up ahead. Duff slowed and said, "Can you take her again, Hector?"

"Sure." We traded-off the girl and Duff pulled a flashlight from her coat pocket. Her pale skin glowed eerily in the torch's light. She aimed down the center of the traboule and Pancho wandered out a few paces ahead of us. I said, "How'd you draw tour guide duties for us?"

"Goes a good bit further than me playing tour guide to you fellas," Duff said. "I'm with you into England."

"Really?"

"Yes, I'm closing out my life here. And a female child making this trip exclusively in the hands of a couple of childless Neanderthals like you mugs? That won't do."

I said, "So you're coming along to play nanny?"

Duff shot me a look. "And they call you a gifted writer. You're not impressing me as the silver-tongued devil I was warned to expect."

Ouch. "It's already been a long night," I said. "You're catching me at ebb-tide."

"Well, pull it together, Ally Oop. Night's far from over." Despite herself, she smiled at me. "It was some fine mayhem you caused getting that little darling out of that place. I hear those neighbors were vaporized by the blast."

"Enough," I said. "Please. I'm already feeling some guilt for that. I wanted to trash the two apartments. Knock down both walls and erase any trace of the hidden room in case this child's protectors got caught. I probably could have done it without locking those snitches in there with the grenades."

"I wouldn't have had you do it any other way," Duff said. "Not after what they did."

There was a flash of light at the end of the traboule. Duff flicked off her light. She whispered urgently, "I hope that dog can be quiet."

"The dog can," I said. "He can also take down the person holding that other light, if need be."

I passed Marie back to Duff. Jimmy and I drew our Mausers from our holsters. "Wait here, dear Duff," Jimmy said. "We'll be back in a jiff."

I pointed and Pancho sat down next to Duff. I said, "Just whisper the word A-T-T-A-C-K to him if we go down. Pancho will do the rest or he'll die trying. The word S-T-O-P will break off his attack." I paused, then said, "Do you have a gun with enough ammo in case?" I looked from her to the child sleeping in her arms.

"I do," she said earnestly. Duff's eyes searched mine. "And I will if I have to. Now go handle this so I am not faced with that awful choice."

Jimmy and I were slowed by having to run on tiptoes to suppress the click of those Nazi boot heels on tile in the long, vaulted, high-ceilinged tunnels.

The flashlight's glow from the intersecting tunnel was getting stronger.

I could hear German being spoken, now. Two men. There were no alcoves or doorways to duck into for an ambush. The two tunnels, ours and theirs, met at right angles. We might surprise one of the Germans as they turned the corner, but not both. Both sides would likely take casualties.

And the sound of gunfire in the long echo chambers of the tunnels might draw down a platoon of Nazis.

I whispered, "Your uniform come with a knife, Jimmy?" I held up my own blade. "This one did."

Jimmy smiled thinly. "Yes, mine has a silver death's head and crossbones on the pommel. Delightful SS toys for something close quarters. You've a plan, Hector?"

"More or less. We put our trust in these damned uniforms and my German. Get in close as can be, then use these blades."

The Irishman frowned. "He looked at his own uniform. "Good thing we have vintage SS togs." There weren't many of these black S.S. uniforms like the ones we were wearing in circulation anymore. Himmler had recalled most of them in recent months.

I arched an inquiring eyebrow.

Jimmy said, "Black doesn't show blood. *Close in* is hard on clothes."

8

According to Duff, we'd reached the rendezvous point a full hour early. It was safer, she said, to stay in the tunnel system than to loiter on the streets. That was hard to argue given the motley crew we were.

We sat on the floor of the traboule. The child was curled up on Duff's lap, asleep again, but with troubled dreams. I said, "That little angel could sleep through the end of the world, I think."

"I'd settle for her sleeping through the end of this war," Duff said. "What this child has already seen in her short life? My God." She stroked Marie's hair. She made a face that made me think she didn't approve of the hasty dye job.

Jimmy shoved fingers down his boot and pulled out a silver flask. "Whisky," he said. "Hector? Duff? It's Glemorangie."

I pulled a flask from my left boot. "Got my own. Well, really it was meant for you, Jimmy. Your fee for riding shotgun. Talisker."

Jimmy swapped flasks with me. "This might even make it worth it," he said.

Duff took my flask from me and finished unscrewing the cap. She sampled the Glenmorangie. "Wow." Her voice sounded raw from the Highland single malt. She took another hit. "Okay, it gets smoother."

"It'll warm you at any rate," I said. "All this encyclopedic knowledge you have on us and others sets me thinking. What do you know about Klaus Barbie? I want the good, inside stuff."

"Golly, I wish I had it to give you," Duff said, handing me back the flask. "I know a lot less about him than I know about you, frankly. He's about twelve years your junior. Born in Bad Godesberg. He's zealous for torture and very ardent about Nazism. That's about all I know. He's still a bit of a cipher."

I finally allowed myself a cigarette, or rather, Duff allowed me one. Clicking shut my Zippo, I said, "So the girl's presumed parentage is what's driving all this support from the resistance?"

"It is a child's life, Hector."

I blew some smoke and rested my head against the wall. "You think that way, honey, and I cherish you for it, but the resistance leaders do not operate that way. That's not the way things are done in bad times like these. To risk all these so-called assets for a single child's life? That doesn't strike me as credible. It's not sound strategy."

Duff searched my face, then nodded. "You're right, of course. It's all about who she is. If she escapes, it will drive Höttl crazy. Also, the revelation he fathered a Jewish child can be held over Höttl. Maybe even used to control him. But this child has to make it out of Europe alive. America might be far enough away for her to be safe. Short of that?" She smiled and said, "If only we could kill every Nazi…"

"You're a woman after my own heart," I said.

That earned me a look. Duff said, "What about you and Werner Höttl? According to your file, you were in Paris together in the 1920s. We have some time before we can go out there. Tell me about all that, Hector."

PARIS,

JANUARY, 1925

They were sitting in a café on the Rue Vavin.

The whippet-thin German blew smoke and smiled, a death's head grin. He was so undernourished-looking, his eyes so sunken into their that sockets, one was made aware of the contours of the skull beneath the pale, nearly translucent skin.

"People will more easily fall victim to a big lie than a small one," Werner Höttl said. In addition to his unsettlingly scrawny frame, Höttl's face bore a wicked scar. The livid, fat red welt started on the right side of his forehead, just at the border of his black widow's peak, trailing down to disrupt a rather bushy eyebrow, then resuming at his too-prominent cheekbone. The scar ended at the edge of his upper lip. "The things fools will fall for at the mere promise of hope…" A wicked grin.

Hector said, "That wisdom sounds cribbed from Abe Lincoln. You know, 'You can fool all the people some of the time…'"

The German had just more or less latched onto Hector, probably because he was the only one sitting at a table alone in the crowded café. They'd met once before, years ago, but

Hector sensed the man didn't remember that, and so hadn't raised it in conversation yet.

There was some motion in a mirror beside their table. Hector turned and saw his date had arrived. Smiling, he rose and kissed her on both offered cheeks. The woman straightened his tie and kissed his mouth. "Who's your friend?" She ran her fingers back through her long, blue-black hair and whispered in Hector's ear, "He must be a *lousy* fencer. I know they pride themselves on such scars, but most of those look dashing or piratical. That wound is truly horrid."

Hector held her hand as she sat down and smiled at the bone-thin German. Hector took his own seat and said, "This is Werner Höttl. We just began talking a few minutes ago. Werner, this is my friend, Victoria Jensen. Victoria, meet Werner. Werner here has been going on about this prison writer."

Höttl shook his head. "*Prison* writer? *Nein*. That's not right at all. He is a thinker, a kind of philosopher-warrior, who is unjustly in prison and writing a book. My friend, Hess, has sent me some excerpts. They are powerful meditations and indictments on how the Jew is wrecking the world."

Victoria confiscated Hector's wine glass, took a sip and licked her full lower lip. "What prison? What thinker, this anti-Semite? And really, how smart can he be if he's in jail?"

Hector shifted uncomfortably. Less than the diplomat, was beautiful Vicky.

"He's in Landsberg Prison," Höttl said cooly. Höttl went on a bit from there, more anti-Semitic rants. He said, "I think this book could be very important. Soon the world will be discussing it. Mark my words here, and mark them well, you'll hear of it, and of its author. It's called *Mein Kampf*, and—"

"We're already late, Hec," Victoria said curtly. "I know it's my fault for being tardy meeting you here, but either way, now we're both late."

Hector stood and pulled her up to him. "Vic is right. We need to shove off, Werner. Maybe we'll see you around the Quarter again." He hesitated, then said, "This fella, this *writer*, what'd he do to get himself in prison?"

Höttl waved a hand. "He was convicted for his part in the rebellion the reporters called the Beer Hall Putsch."

"I remember reading something about that," Hector said.

"It's an injustice what has been done to him," Höttl said. "Herr Hitler is a visionary." A terrible smile and another death's head grin. "He greatly admires your countryman, Henry Ford."

Hector nodded. Ford: that racist son of a bitch. Hector said shortly, "Me? I'm a Chevrolet man, myself." He took Victoria's arm. "As you said, darlin', we have places to be."

Walking in the crunching snow, shivering and looking for a cab, Victoria said, "He's unattractive on the outside *and* the inside. Werner Whatever, I mean. How'd you meet that creep?"

"You were late," Hector said. "He found me."

"He's horrible."

"He is surely that." Hector wrapped his arm tighter around her waist. "To be completely honest, tonight wasn't the first time he and I crossed paths. I remember; I don't think he does."

"So you know him more than just tonight?"

"Sort of."

"You met here in Paris?"

"No, in Berlin," Hector said. "Just after the war. I was making my way here. I decided to see the country we'd beaten. See how it was rebuilding itself after all the carnage and our imposed penalties. There was a short story of mine that had been purloined and printed in translation in some German magazine. A director in Berlin read it, liked it, and asked me to spend a few days in the city on his nickel helping him adapt it for the screen. Höttl was a kind of understudy to the director. I guess he doesn't remember us meeting. It was very brief. And I had the impression Werner was under the influence of something at the time. Opium? Cocaine? Something like that."

"Did he have that wicked scar, even then?"

"Nah. Anyway, he was about as charming then as now. Only loopier back then."

Victoria shook loose his arm and waved her hands over her head, calling out, "Taxi!" She pulled Hector across the slick pavers of the boulevard. "Our cab, thank God. This wind is cutting through me."

Hector helped Victoria into her seat, then swung up into the carriage beside her. They snuggled close under a blanket. Hector called up, "27 rue de Fleurus, *vite!*"

He said to Victoria, "Better to get there sooner rather than later tonight. This frigid wind is killing me, too. I'm near finished with this weather." They were scheduled to leave for the States soon—Hector for the Florida Keys, Victoria elsewhere.

Victoria rested her head on his shoulder. She said, "I wonder how he got that scar. I've seen dueling scars, but that's about the nastiest, if that's indeed what it is."

Hector took her hand in his under the blanket. "Rapier? Epée? What difference does it make?"

"Quite a lot if it's your face on the receiving end," she said. "An épée would make a smaller scar than a rapier. And a saber? Though I have to say, that scar looks like it was made by a broadsword or an axe."

They'd nearly reached the door of 27 rue de Fleurus. Across the chilly courtyard, a voice called out, "What is this? You're friends of Miss Stein's, too?"

Werner Höttl trotted across the ice-glazed pavement, hands thrust into the pockets of his greatcoat.

Victoria whispered, "Friend? There is no way on earth this anti-Semite doesn't know *Gertrude Stein* is Jewish."

"I don't think he cares," Hector said. "Maybe he's here to solicit an endorsement from her for his prison-writer friend, for this *Mein Kampf.*"

"Not funny, Hec."

"I wasn't necessarily making a joke. Some authors will solicit an endorsement from an arch-enemy if it will sell them some books."

Hector thrust his hands into his own pockets to short-circuit Höttl's attempt at another handshake. He said, "You're an invited guest, Werner?"

"A guest of a guest to be strictly accurate," Höttl said.

Well that other guest must be no real friend to Gertrude, Hector thought. He said, "Really? Which guest?"

"The poet," Höttl said, smiling. "You know, Ezra Pound."

Quelle surprise.

It made sense. Ezra was another one of *them*—increasingly given to horrific anti-Semitic rants and grand conspiracy theories regarding Zionism.

Hector nodded at the door. "After you, Herr Höttl, I insist."

It was an unusually busy night at Miss Stein's salon. A haze of cigarette smoke obscured those famous walls lined with modernist paintings. The pungent scent of sweet cakes and candies and Alice and Gertrude's personally distilled fruit-derived liqueurs was cloying.

And then there was that *other* odor—the stench of sweat from all the nascent novelists, poets and playwrights granted audiences by the mercurial Miss Stein—exchanges that often ended in cutting, even career-stunting *bons mots* from the short, heavyset and tart-tongued Grande Dame.

Alice B. Toklas peeled Hector away from Victoria and steered him toward the Great Woman. "Gertrude Stein saw you come in and insisted I bring you right to her," Alice said. She cast a look back at Werner Höttl. "I must admit, your presence here tonight might be a kind of blessing."

Hector wet his lips. That was a surprise coming from usually testy Alice. He followed the little woman through a tangle of tipsy painters, intellectuals and slightly addled sycophants—Alice sometimes crept hashish into the baked goods she fashioned for these heady soirees; Hector had been steering clear of them since February.

Gertrude was holding court in her usual chair, ponderous and pitched forward, forearms resting on her knees. Above her chair hung a portrait of Stein as painted by Picasso. The pose in the painting mimicked or anticipated Miss Stein's present posture. When she saw Hector, she waved her hand, dismissing some heavily perspiring and foppish-looking young man.

Hector said, "That boy looked a bit too fey to be a novelist."

"Poet," Gertrude said. "At least in his mind he is so. My star, I saw you come in. But the man you came in with? You didn't bring him, did you?"

"Of course not. You know all my guests to your salon are of a type."

It hung there between them, unsaid: *Female and comely. Worldly.* Guests like Victoria, like the also raven-haired female crime writer Brinke Devlin who'd preceeded Vicky.

Hector accepted a glass of red wine from Alice. He nodded his thanks and said, "He happened to follow me and my date up. We're at best fleeting bar acquaintances. Fact is, I don't even like Werner. Hell, if I gave him any real thought, I'd probably hate him." He sipped his wine, then added, "He claimed to have been invited by Ezra."

"Pound?" Gertrude glowered. She gestured at an empty space up against the wall. "Pound hasn't been welcome here since he broke that chair." She again pointed at the emptiness. She shook her head. "Well, if Pound is the one I have to thank for that man being here again, it explains a few things. That horrid man, Mr. Höttl, he showed up three nights ago. He left me a packet of writings. One was some execrable, dreadful and ineptly composed kind of manifesto."

Hector shook out a match. Through a haze of smoke, he said, "And the rest?"

"His own works. Some kind of cinema treatments, I gather. They, too, were terrible. And… racist."

"Have you given him your appraisal of these works?"

"I suspect that is coming momentarily," she said. Gertrude watched the German talking to Victoria. The raven-haired, blue-eyed Victoria looked to be at wit's end while having to suffer his company. "I'd have you stay close, my star," Gertrude said. "Close by me, I mean. In case he reacts badly to my critiques."

Hector smiled thinly. "Much in his reaction might be determined by the way in which your criticism is couched."

"Of course," Gertrude said. "That hardly needs to be remarked upon. But I have a reputation." *That was true.*

"I have a reputation for honest, blunt criticism," she finished. *That was true with caveats.*

Hector smiled again, shaking his head. He doubted others who'd been on the receiving end of Miss Stein's criticisms would put it quite as diplomatically as she had.

He shrugged. "Why me?"

"Don't be daft," Gertrude said, waving a hand. "Don't play dense, Hector. Look at the men in this room. I can't look to them for defense. But you, my star? You can more than deal with that one."

Werner Höttl was drawing closer. Gertrude looked apprehensive, even frightened. Hector had never seen her quite like this. He said softly, quickly, "No worries, Miss Stein. I'll stay right here. Still, you can probably let him down more gently than you incline. He is a man who moves in unpleasant circles. There'll be other nights when I may not be so close to provide muscle."

"One cannot think like that," Gertrude said, wetting her lips and watching Werner draw closer. "If one did that, one would never do *anything*. Analysis breeds paralysis. Now, he's almost here. If it comes to fisticuffs, remember my furnishings, my paintings. I want you to finish him with a round-house or whatever you call them in those pulp magazine stories of yours. Lay him out flat. That's what I expect of you, Hector."

The lady didn't ask much, did she?

Hector rolled his eyes and sipped more wine. He said, "Right. No repeats of Ezra and the ill-fated chair. No worries. But if you put this to him in the right way, we don't even have to worry about—"

Gertrude cut him off, raising her voice over the din of all the chattering intellectuals crowding her salon. "Herr Höttl," she said loudly, saying it for the benefit of the room. This was, after all, a reputation-enhancing moment for Miss Stein. At least Hector wagered Gertrude figured that was so.

"No doubt you've come for the manuscripts and my opinion of them," she said.

"Just so," Höttl said, smiling and bowing exaggeratedly.

Gertrude glared at him. "Your racist diatribes provoked me to consign all of the papers you left me to the fire." She nodded at her fireplace. "From that reaction, even you can certainly infer my personal appraisal of those so-called writings."

Höttl's smile faltered. "You're joking, surely."

"The only amusing thing about any of this is your temerity to ask me to suffer to assess that racist drivel," Gertrude said. "No, Höttl, I'm quite serious. Believe I burned the writings. *All* of them."

Gertrude flicked her hand, as if she was shooing away a fly. "You, Herr Höttl, are dismissed and may not come back here, not ever."

Well, that had torn it. Hector dropped his cigarette into his empty wine glass and handed it to Victoria as she sidled up beside his chair. She whispered, "Go get 'em, champ!"

Werner Höttl's expression had quickly passed from incredulity to panic and now, all too swiftly, to rage and gathering wrath.

"Easy," Hector said, standing. "Let's take the air, eh, Werner."

Höttl took a step toward Gertrude. Hector slipped between them. At six-two, Hector had at least four inches on the German, and, he figured, at least forty pounds of muscle.

The salon had grown eerily quiet.

"Step aside, Lassiter," Höttl said. "This woman has my writings and those of my friend. Even this silly, poseur Jewess couldn't destroy the work of another writer. I mean to have my materials back. Some of my own were single copies… originals!"

Hector pressed his hand to Höttl's chest. "This lady is no practical joker," Hector said. "If she said she burned them, rightly or wrongly, that's what she did. I'm terribly sorry, Werner. Now come on, old pal—we'll find a café and I'll buy you a drink."

He swatted Hector's arm aside. "Don't! Don't involve yourself in this, Lassiter. It's between me and this treacherous Jew bitch."

Hector pressed his hand to Höttl's chest again. "That'll be enough. Out the door with you, Werner."

Höttl cocked his arm back. It was a ridiculously exaggerated attempt at a punch that went well beyond telegraphing intent.

Mindful of Gertrude's warnings about her furniture, Hector let Höttl swing at him. He caught the man's smallish, bony right fist in his own big left hand. Hector squeezed tightly, crushing the man's fingers in his grip. As he did that, Hector pivoted rightward, spinning around to gather momentum.

Turning almost 180-degrees, Hector drove his right elbow into the man's right temple.

Höttl crumpled to the floor, unconscious.

Hector said, "Someone open the door." He shouldered the rail-thin German across his back and rose, knees cracking.

Gertrude said, "What are you doing?"

"Putting this fella in a cab to the other side of Paris," Hector said.

Victoria smiled and shook her head. "You better make up a couch, Miss Stein. For safety's sake, I think Hector better camp out here tonight."

"Perhaps that is wise." Alice said it as though the prospect truly pained her.

Victoria said what Hector was thinking. "There goes our night."

Shifting the load across his back, Hector said to Gertrude, "Maybe you could get word to Hem. Maybe he can take tonight's shift. Perhaps Mal can cover tomorrow night's guard duty." Malcolm Cowley, like Hemingway, had some boxing skills.

Grimacing at the load, Hector said, "I'm not sure after what just happened here that this man's anger is going to pass in a single night."

9

Duff said, "Men get into fistfights all the time. To still carry a grudge from back then over some tipsy dust-up?"

I shrugged. "For some men I've crossed, that would be enough for a lifetime's resentment. Especially with so many witnesses, and, particularly, *those* kinds of witnesses. But, to be fair, we had other dealings, later. Until then, Höttl really carried his grudge for Gertrude most strongly. I suppose because she actually burned his and Hitler's writings. When France fell, through channels I got word Höttl was coming for Gertrude and Alice. I got them out of Paris just ahead of the storm troopers."

"Are the ladies still safe?"

"I believe so," I said. "It's been rather hectic these past two years. We can't exactly correspond as they're in hiding and I'm always on the move."

Duff nodded. "Fairly put." She looked at Marie. "My arms are full. What time is it now?"

"Five more minutes by my watch," Jimmy said. "I'm thinking I should take a peek at the street."

"Not a good idea," Duff said. "We stay here. That's the plan. If it goes badly, you two might at least hold them off long enough for me to try and lose them in these tunnels again."

"I think she's probably right about staying to plan," I said to Jimmy.

The Irishman considered, then said, "Yes. I do concur."

The child's eyelids were fluttering. Her hands and feet were twitching in her sleep, some fresh nightmare. Perhaps she was running in her dark dreams. I smoothed her hair. Its texture *was* very wrong because of that damned dye. I stroked her cheek. She turned in her sleep, quietening.

Duff, watching, said," Some dreamy childhood she's been handed."

"That is to say no childhood," I said.

"How'd we come to this?" Duff rocked Marie gently in her arms. "This war?"

I sighed. "How'd we come to the last war? And having done that bloody, crazy thing, how'd we let ourselves get to this sorry place again? Hell, I can't fathom it."

"Mass suicide pact, maybe," Jimmy said.

"Almost feels that, way, doesn't it?" Duff tried to stand with the child in her arms.

"Here," I said, "I'll take her again."

"We may need your hands free for other things," Duff said.

Jimmy and I each took one of Duff's arms and helped her to her feet. She said, "Five minutes must have passed by now."

"One minute ago," Jimmy said.

"Well, watches can vary a few seconds here or there," Duff said. "But this might be trouble."

I said, "Explain."

"Our driver, he's supposed to send a man down here to get us. Plan never really was to go directly to the street. We're supposed to be fetched."

"Do you know these two men? You'd recognize them?" I checked my own watch.

"You met them too, on the street," Duff said. "Do you remember their faces?"

"Probably on sight," I said. "Either way, like you say, it's a deviation in plan, isn't it? His not coming down, I mean."

"Could be good reasons," Jimmy said. "Unexpected Hun presence on the streets, say. Or maybe the Nazis overtook them shortly after we left them up top."

I chewed my lip, then unholstered my gun. "I'm going up to take a look around. If I'm not back in five minutes, flee. I hope these tunnels run a good bit further, far enough for you rest to get lost in again." Pancho started to follow me. I said, "Stay."

Duff said, "Don't exaggerate about this. How is your German?"

"Better over the past two years," I said.

"Give me a little something in the tongue," she said.

From memory, I rattled off the opening paragraph of one my novels, but in the German. I finished and said, "It'll do?"

"You might really pull it off," she said. There was a new tension in her voice. "Of course it may all be fine. Maybe they're just running late. Maybe it took them a bit longer than they anticipated if those Nazis did give chase."

"Sure," I said. "It's probably all dandy. How do I get out of this labyrinth?"

Duff was rocking Marie again, soothing her troubled dreams. "Up those stairs, veer right, up another flight, then a short distance to the left. You'll find yourself at the foot of a stairs that will take you into the lobby of a hotel. The truck, our transport, should be waiting out front."

"Right. If things are okay, how many men should be waiting up there for us?"

"Only the two you already met," Duff said.

I patted her shoulder. "Back in a jiffy." I slapped Jimmy's arm, trying to think of something worthy and clever to leave him with if I didn't return.

Jimmy raised a hand. "This is not a *moment*, Hector, so don't go all solemn and portentous on me. I sense much mayhem ahead for the two of us. I mean years going forward. So shake a leg, boyo."

"Five minutes," I said.

Before I reached the lobby, I paused to check the identification papers Jimmy and I had taken from the two Nazis we'd encountered in the tunnels. I committed the names of the dead men to memory. Then I ground out a cigarette on the sole of my boot, straightened my Nazi hat and pulled its brim lower to shadow my face.

The two men were loitering around the troop transport that had delivered Duff to us. The milling soldiers, based on my memory, were not the ones I was expecting to see.

Something had gone haywire on us.

I was toying with heading back down into the tunnels. I'd grab my friends and we'd push on through the underground. But then one of the German soldiers outside saw me and saluted.

There was the possibility Höttl hadn't adequately communicated my appearance to his stooges. If my German accent survived scrutiny?

Roll the dice? I decided I'd better do that.

Strutting outside, I said, "Have you seen them? *Der Amerikaners*? Any sign of them at all?"

The men exchanged a glance that made my stomach flutter. Both were probably in their late twenties and tough-looking young bucks. One had sandy hair, the other red.

Red said, "*Nein.* We weren't—"

"The child is very important to capture," I said. "I'm here to see Herr Höttl's will is done. I think something has gone wrong down below. Hans and Josef—" the Nazis Jimmy and I had killed in the traboules, "—never found them down there. They're pushing on, still looking for them in the tunnels."

Red said, "What would you have us do, sir?"

"The two you took this from," I pointed at the truck. "Did you get anything from them before you...?"

Sandy shook his head no. He drew his index finger across his throat. "Both took suicide pills disguised as buttons on their tunics. They got at them before we could stop them. We didn't get to question them."

"This whole operation is turning into a mess, and someone's going to pay for that," I said, trying to make it appear I might be looking to them as worthy candidates to play scapegoats. Giving them room for a dodge of sorts, I said, "You have a radio?"

Red nodded. "In the truck, in back. You want more men to come? More to explore those tunnels?"

"Fruitless," I said. "This Lassiter, I think, is far too clever to do anything obvious or expected. Maybe they were never even in those damned tunnels. I knew we should have followed them down, not tried to intercept them. I argued my case, but…"

Sandy and Red nodded, commiserating.

Time was getting on. Any second, Jimmy and Duff might decide to follow me up street side. Or they might become lost to me as they pressed deeper into the tangle of the traboules.

I pointed across the street. "Did you check the tunnel access in that building?" Hell, there *might* a traboule access point in the joint. It *seemed* a safe enough bluff. My question drew headshakes from the young Germans.

"Then go and do that right now," I said. "Stay at it. Some of these tunnel entrances are well hidden. If in a half-hour you've found nothing, return here. I'll stay with the vehicle just in case they should turn up."

I watched the two young German soldiers disappear into the building across the street. Then I ran back inside the hotel to find my friends.

Jimmy slid into the seat next to me. He said, "How many were there and how'd you take this truck away from them? Black doesn't show blood." He eyed my uniform. "But I don't smell blood, either."

I slammed the truck into gear. "We're leaving, fast," I said, "Because they may come back any second. I've got them looking for tunnels in the foundation of that building over there."

Jimmy smiled. "If they're good little tin soldiers they may spend weeks poking around in there. Congratulations, Hector. That shows rare restraint on your part."

I almost remarked on that, then decided to let it go. I said to Duff, "Now, as you're our guide, where do I point this heap?"

"Le Havre," she said from in back. "Although, frankly, I argued for Spain. Easier to move through, I think: the Nazis aren't so thick at the Spanish border. And Spain's arguably closer a safe place."

"But not so safe for me," I said. "You see, I have a standing death warrant against me in Spain. Somethin' tied to a visit there during the Civil War back in '37."

Duff raised her hands as if to say, *of course*. She said, "Well, if any man would have something like that hanging over his head, it would be you, wouldn't it?"

I saw the map of Europe in my head. Spain would have been a bit closer, the Nazi occupational forces sparser in between, just as Duff said. The run to Le Havre was a god-awful distance to traverse clandestinely. And it would take us dangerously close by Paris, where the occupying Nazis were thickest of all.

"Le Havre, was that always the plan?" I searched her face in the reflection of the rearview mirror. "If it was, and the plan has already begun to unravel on us as it has…"

"I know what you're thinking and I agree," she said. "We probably need to do something else. It's the only safe course."

"La Plaine-sur-Mer," I said. "Along the way, somehow, we'll try and make contact with the underground or the OSS. Get word back through channels to see if Wild Bill might not be able to get us some kind of boat from there to Britain. Maybe to Plymouth. Once we're in England, we can make our way easily enough to London, sans these SS duds." I fingered the lapel of my uniform.

"It does narrow the distance we have to travel by a good bit," Jimmy said. "It's not quite the sticks, but it's certainly less populous than that other route would be."

"Yes, let's try this," Duff said. "We're not exactly spoiled with options, after all."

I winked into the rearview mirror. "Right. If things do get too dicey, we'll veer south and I'll take my chances with the damn Spanish. Most of my problems there were centered around Madrid."

"Then let's put some miles between us and the city," Duff said. "We'll make as much time by night as we can. Come morning, we'll need to find some breakfast for the child. That couple did a decent job of caring for her under the circumstances, but I can feel her ribs through her coat."

I got us underway, giving her the gas. Jimmy said, "One thing's certain, we can't drive until dawn in this vehicle. When those Krauts get tired of searching that building for hidey holes and find this truck gone, the call will go out."

"They'll raise an alarm, of course," Duff said.

"Let's give it an hour or two," I said. "Then we'll steal some other transport."

10

Duff said, "The woman at the grocers must have seen me climb out of this thing with all these Nazi decals. She was quite cold. Even hateful. Probably thought me a collaborator. Can't blame her, but it certainly wasn't a pleasant feeling."

I stared at the dull black '35 Juvaquatre with the swastika plastered across the hood parked across the street. It was much smaller than our present truck, but it would do. Duff held up a movie camera. "Looks like the Germans planned to film our arrest."

I was focused on the car across the street. Of course the thing was Christ-awful old. God willing, it would be sufficiently reliable to carry us to the coast. I said to Duff, "So long as you were vigilant with that clerk. Hate to think she might have poisoned the food, or spat in it."

Duff said, "I was very vigilant. That car across the street, you can steal it?"

"Probably could, but stealing cars is more Jimmy's exotic forte," I said.

"It's sadly true," Jimmy said. "Some lads who were running a car theft ring in Parma Heights taught me a few tricks of the seedy trade, hoping for a lighter sentence." He opened the door. "I'll signal when I think it's time to go. Hector, you best start gathering bags and other sundries."

When he was gone, Duff said, "I quite adore Jim. He's a very good man. And some fast friend to do this with you."

"He is that—a great man, I mean. And he's a true friend, too. In a fix, you can't do much better than to have Jim Hanrahan in your corner."

"You inspire loyalty from your friends," she said. "That counts for something."

I rubbed my eyes. I could use some caffeine; unfortunately Jimmy and I had exhausted our spiked coffee. I said, "Did my file fill you with that much concern about me?"

"'The man who lives what he writes and writes what he lives,'" Duff said. "A reputation like yours makes a woman like me wonder a little about your motives for any given undertaking. Take now. Are you acting from conviction, or because you might get a book out of all this?"

"That's just an unfortunate publicity tag," I said. "I don't even like it. I'm a writer, yes. But my life is something else, particularly this phase of it. I'm fighting the fight, not gathering source material, Duff. I may use some of it in fiction, someday, of course. But this thing we're doing now? Never."

Jimmy waved his arm out the window.

Smiling, the little girl waved back.

I said, "You see to our little friend. Pancho will follow you. I'll get the bags."

Two trips—that's what it took to shift everything to the Juvaquatre. Jimmy said, "You look beat to the wide, Hector. I'll take first shift at the wheel."

"Great. But I want to do something first." I reached into the knapsack and pulled out a grenade and some string.

Jimmy smiled and shook his head. "Ah, Hector. Can't say I disapprove, but do be quick about it."

I ran back to the transport truck and rigged the grenade, weaving the string around the steering wheel to the driver's side door handle. Then I let myself out—gingerly—through the passenger side door. I told myself it was revenge for the two resistance fighters they'd killed.

It was four in the morning. Jimmy was sacked out in the back, wedged across the back seat with Marie sprawled asleep across his chest. Both were lightly snoring.

As we bumped along a rutted rural road, Duff turned around in the passenger seat, putting her back to the door. "Did you get any sleep when it was your turn back there?"

"Fitful," I said. "But I'm fine." It was a lie. I'd been awake back there the whole time, eyes closed, trying to sleep, but finding myself eavesdropping on Jimmy and Duff. I'd hung on all her questions about me and my past. About sordid stuff from my "unofficial biography."

Some of that scuttlebutt was one-third distortion, some one-third hype and a third all-too-true. I said, "You get any sleep?"

"Not tired enough yet," Duff said. "Maybe dayside I'll sleep a bit. At some point, we may need to switch to civilian clothes and steal a civilian car."

"Yeah, I'm keeping all options open," I said. I smiled at her. "You've got me at quite a disadvantage, you know. This dossier of mine, I mean. My life on paper as written by others than myself for once. You having access to all that is not good and certainly not fair, because I know hardly anything about you."

"We've got time now," she said. "Ask."

I faltered.

Duff said, "How about my middle name?"

I smiled. "Sure. How about that?"

"Mildred," she said. "Named in honor of a grandmother I never met. Horrid name. I don't ever use it. I'm just Duff Sexton."

"That surname? Sexton's not your married name?"

"Maiden name. I kept it." She shook her head, looking out the window. "I had a small career going in entertainment. Singing in clubs. I thought I was going to be doing it professionally and didn't want to lose the little marquee value I thought I'd earned for myself. My husband hated me not taking his name. But he let me do it anyway."

I grasped his position. She was that kind of female—the kind of woman for whom a man would swallow his pride. The kind of woman to make a man cede principles, relax otherwise rigorous standards of personal conduct. If you were married to Duff Sexton, did you really need her to carry your last name?

I said, "My first wife kept her last name, too. Just didn't care for the name Lassiter, I guess." I hesitated, then said, carefully, "Your husband—his passing?"

Ah, Duff, so blunt: "How'd it happen? That's what you're wondering, isn't it?"

"If you don't mind," I said.

"Without getting too specific, it was in the early days of the resistance," she said. "Things were still, oh, *rough*. Unorganized. There were early days kinds of problems, you know? They cost him his life." Duff tipped her head back against the seat. "I hated him for getting involved in all of it. From the first, I wanted him to run. I was desperate to hightail it back to the States and to hide from history. Bolt to California, maybe Washington State. Anywhere, really, but Europe."

Squirming a bit, I reached down, fumbling around my boot with my left hand. I handed her the flask of Glenmorangie. "Your present involvement in the OSS and the resistance—what's that about? Penitence? Revenge?"

Was that a little flare of anger in those pretty blue eyes? I accepted the flask back, took a swig, then handed it to her again. She ran her fingers back through her hair once more. It somehow looked redder in the dark. She sipped more whisky. "Both, I guess. But there's more, too. Friends, family of my husband's, they were made to wear these yellow stars. Some Jews began disappearing. Even children, like that little girl back there."

"I know. Like I said, I'm not over here looking for book material. I tried to sit this one out a while, too, at first. Just like our motherland did. It got under the skin of some folks in Spain because I wouldn't engage the Fascists there directly at the time."

"Why?"

"Even in early 1937, when I was in Madrid, it was clearly a lost cause," I said. "By '39, or so, I knew this was the fight, and one we'd have to win."

"This little girl—think we'll make it? Will we really save her, Hector?"

"Sure, we'll do it."

Duff laughed softly. "Is that cocky you, blarney you, or is it *sincere* you venturing that baseless guess?"

"Jimmy would probably tell you it's all three."

"But what would you say?"

"I mean to save her. And I mean to deny Werner Höttl his desires."

"Revenge? Penitence?"

I sighed. "Maybe both."

Duff surprised me by taking my hand in hers. "You said you met Höttl another time after the 1920s."

"Yes," I squeezed her hand.

"Was that in Paris, too?"

"Nah. We crossed paths again in Berlin, in 1929. I went there on some film business, again."

"Another of your works?"

"No, a screenwriting thing. I was brought in to punch up some dialogue and inject some character business."

"Another of your pirated works?"

"No, someone else's screenplay that wasn't quite up to snuff," I said. "It's where I got my start in that business, really."

"Might I have heard of this film?"

"Perhaps. It was called *The Blue Angel.* Josef von Sternberg was the director. Marlene Dietrich was the star. Well, eventually she was. It was the movie that really launched the Kraut."

"Marlene, 'the Kraut.' Another of your famous friends and a KA entry," Duff said. "That where you met her?"

"No. We just missed each other, that time. She hadn't yet been cast in the role. I met Marlene in Hollywood, in 1932, on the set of *Blonde Venus*. That was another von Sternberg picture. He and several other German filmmakers had fled for the States by then, already eager to escape Nazi Germany, even if it meant trying to start over in Depression era America. But there in Berlin, in 1929? Höttl was there."

BERLIN,

SEPTEMBER 1929

Hector had tried to stay on his best behavior during the previous evening's dizzying, noisy, liquor-soaked crawl through the bars and nightclubs of decadent Berlin.

He had nursed drinks or let comely women commandeer them. He'd stayed dangerously sober as director Josef von Sternberg led Hector and a few others attached to von Sternberg's new film, *The Blue Angel*, through a procession of smoky cabarets and jazz clubs.

Von Sternberg had eventually taken them to a lesbian bar called Maly where the femininely dressed women wore violets pinned to their dresses. After that, the director had hauled them to transvestite bars in which some of the people wearing slinky dresses might even have been actual women.

"It's vital that you absorb the atmosphere, the milieu for our nightclub setting when we start filming," von Sternberg said. He'd argued this position when Hector and a few others had balked at being ordered to the lesbian and, especially, the transvestite joints.

Standing sweating and a little drunk in the first of the cross-dressing joints—some place called Eldorado—brushing his unruly hair back off his forehead, the director said, "*This* is Berlin!" He was flanked by a pair of six-foot, two-inch blondes, both of them a bit broad at the shoulder, a bit too-possessed of too-prominent Adams apples. They were wrapped in snazzy, spangled cocktail gowns.

Hector had begged off at that point, choosing to make it an early evening much to the annoyance—perhaps even the disgust—of von Sternberg. But Hector didn't care about any of that. He was tired of the director's insistence upon steeping his crew in Berlin's decadent nightlife. Hector was no Pollyanna, and von Sternberg's campaign to that end had started almost from the moment Hector had stepped off the train at the Am Zoo railroad station a week before.

For his part, Hector was much more enamored with wandering through the city dayside, exploring the copious gardens, the parks and the forests that abutted the cityscape in several locations.

As to feminine companionship, Hector was drawn to the civilian female population of the city, not the bawdy and often coarse working girls selling themselves on the streets and in the bizarre nightclubs of decadent Berlin.

Decadent, yes, that was certainly the word for the city. And it was a city headed down a dark path, Hector sensed.

In one of the parks, the bucolic surroundings were undercut by a group of men, all members of the National Socialist German Workers' Party. Wearing matching crimson armbands emblazoned with black swastikas, they were singing an off-key but enthusiastic rendition of "Germany Awake":

> *Wir wollen kämpfen für dein Auferstehn*
> *Arisches Blut soll nicht untergehn!*

We want to fight for your resurgence!
Aryan blood should not perish!

It was half-past-eight in the morning and raining hard in Berlin. Hector sat in an artist's café on Rankestrasse, sipping bitter black coffee, watching the scurrying, sodden pedestrians and exchanging occasional inquiring looks with a pretty blonde at an adjacent table when Josef von Sternberg plopped down across from Hector.

The director shrugged off his soaking coat and tossed it across the back of an adjacent chair. The mustachioed Austrian was broad-shouldered and rather thick across the chest, but not very tall—actually several inches shorter than Hector. Von Sternberg wore a blue blazer, white pants and a black beret. He whipped off the hat, slung it on the table, then ran his fingers back through his unruly, graying hair. He rubbed his temples, wincing. "Such a headache, I have!"

Hangover, more likely, Hector thought.

The director said, "Where did you go after you abandoned me last night?"

"I spent a quiet evening with my typewriter," Hector said. He signaled the waiter he was ready for another coffee. "So, in your seedy wanderings through the underbelly of Berlin, did you find your leading lady?"

Von Sternberg was desperately looking for an actress to portray "Lola-Lola," a dancer and femme fatale in the "Blue Angel Cabaret."

"No, not yet," von Sternberg said. "I think that my friend, her name is Leni Rifensthal, desperately wants the part, though she hasn't come right out and asked me for the role.

She's wrong for it, at any rate. Every woman so far is wrong for it. This woman at *Der Blau Engel*, she must be a sublime temptress. A consummate Circe."

"The kind of woman a man would burn his life down for," Hector said, "I know." Hector specialized in writing such women.

"That's it, exactly," von Sternberg said. He appropriated Hector's second coffee as the waiter sat it on the table. He said to the waiter, "I'll need cream and sugar for this, too."

"And a second black coffee," Hector said, eyeing his stolen java.

"It would be easier, marginally easier, I think, if we weren't filming in German and in English," von Sternberg said.

The director was essentially making the same film twice, one version for the domestic market and one for the English-speaking world. *The Blue Angel* bore the added weight of being Germany's first major talkie.

"I'm having a meal at Horsch's," he said. "I'm taking another look at this actress, Marlene Dietrich. Why don't you come, Hector?"

The waiter handed Hector his coffee. "A meal? That's all?" He sipped his coffee, then said, "The event won't devolve into another freak show sortie through strange cabarets and bottom-feeder nightclubs?"

"Not this time, Hector, no. I'm taking this woman's measure, that's all. I'm asking Werner to come, too."

"Werner?"

"A kind of protégé, studio ordered, if it matters. I met him through Leni. They both have directing ambitions. I think Leni is probably the more promising of the two, but that may change after Werner has worked with me a for a time. He'll learn. What about you, my friend? Do you perhaps want to direct, too?"

Hector smiled and shook his head. "I write—that's all. This cinema business, I don't know how hard I mean to pursue this stuff down the road."

"You don't see the medium's power?" Von Sternberg struck Hector as incredulous *and* angered by Hector's admission. "Film will kill books, you'll see."

"It's not like that at all," Hector said. "Film is a collaborative medium, Josef. I'm more of a solitary artist, I think. And this notion of actors and actresses trying to *fix* my dialogue on the fly grates, frankly. Anyway, tell me more about this Werner, fella. What's the guy's last name?"

It didn't come as a particular surprise:

"Höttl. Werner Höttl." Von Sternberg sipped his sweetened, diluted coffee and shrugged. "That name will have to be changed, of course. If he ever wants to direct in your homeland, that is."

Several years before, when von Sternberg had come to America to direct films in Los Angeles, he had also been made to tinker with his name. That "von," for one thing—it was an addition insisted upon by some studio-type who thought it made the director's name "more regal sounding."

Watching Hector's reaction, von Sternberg narrowed his eyes. "You know Werner, don't you? And you don't like him. I can tell."

"I might even loathe him if I gave him any serious thought," Hector said. "We had... a scuffle. It was in Paris a few years ago. He insulted and even tried to physically attack Gertrude Stein."

Von Sternberg looked skeptical. "Are you serious? *Why?* What was the problem? Her pretension, perhaps?"

Josef von Sternberg was born Jonas Sternberg to Viennese Orthodox Jewish parents. Knowing that, Hector went ahead and said it. "Huh-uh. It was Gertrude's Jewishness. Also a little something over some things she said about the head of the Nazi party."

The director waved that last away. "The thing to do with the Nazis is to ignore them," he said. "A passing fad, at best. Political winds will shift, as they always do, and the Socialists will soon be swept from power. Just politics. As to Werner's behavior, well, I've always maintained the only way to succeed is to make people hate you. That way they remember you."

Hector couldn't quite buy into that philosophy. He said, "I'll think about your dinner invitation, Josef. I have no trouble seeing him again, but if Werner is to be there, too, well, I somehow doubt he'll be as sanguine about a reunion."

"I'll lecture him," von Sternberg said. He stroked his thick moustache. "I would have your opinion of this woman, Hector. Your opinion as a writer, an artist, an audience member, *and* not the least, as a noted lady's man. I know Marlene will be acceptable to German audiences, this film will make her a star here. But you have a better sense of American tastes. I need Yankee men to want to bed her."

Hector rubbed the back of his neck. "And so why would Werner be there?"

"I told you, he's a protégé," von Sternberg said. He put back on his beret. "You didn't actually strike Werner, did you, Hector?"

"Hell I didn't. And just as hard as I could, Josef."

Von Sternberg just shook his head. "So juvenile. So American."

Killing time before dinner, Hector decided to wander the seedier corners of Berlin, *solo lobo*. First, he had fortified himself with some theatre—Kurt Weill.

Humming "Surabaya Johnny," the tune presently stuck in his head, Hector warily made his way down the sin-soaked streets. Prostitutes, underdressed for the weather, tried to catch his eye. Having walked the district for half-an-hour, he figured he'd gotten—and on his own terms—more than enough of the flavor for Lola-Lola's tawdry world.

So he veered back to the better parts of the city, looking for another park he might wander in the rain.

It was then he got his first sense of being followed. Two German soldiers were shadowing his steps at some distance. Hector didn't think they were following him with any particular intent, not yet, anyway.

Cursing under his breath, Hector headed back to his hotel. He'd loaf there for a time, let the bastards lose interest in him.

More pounding rain. Hector's cab rolled up curbside in front of Horsch's, splashing rainwater from the swollen gutters several feet onto the sidewalk.

Hector settled up with the cabbie, then slid out and trotted under the offered umbrella of a doorman to the shelter of the restaurant.

Across the street, a couple of Nazi party members were standing in the rain, trying to force leaflets on the soggy passers-by. They were boisterously singing:

Wir werden weiter marschieren
Wenn alles in Scherben fällt,

Denn heute da hört uns Deutschland
Und morgen die ganze Welt....

We shall march onwards,
even if everything crashes down in pieces;
for today Germany hears us,
and tomorrow, the whole world...

The men watched Hector closely as he trotted into the restaurant.

Hector shrugged off his long black overcoat. He slid the coat check ticket in his suit-jacket pocket and shook out a cigarette. Flicking closed his Zippo, he blew some smoke and said to the hostess, "Von Sternberg, party of four."

The hostess was honey blond. She smiled with not particularly good teeth and said, "Herr Sternberg hasn't arrived yet, but another member of your party was seated a few minutes ago. This way, please."

"*Danke.*" Hector figured it was fifty-fifty: the first arriving party was this actress, Marlene Dietrich, or it was Werner Höttl. Given his luck in such matters, Hector figured it would almost certainly be the latter.

The German glanced up at Hector, forced a smile.

Höttl hadn't changed much. He hadn't put on any weight. He'd lost more hair. His scar was just a little less livid than it had been in Paris. Or maybe he was using makeup of some kind to try and reduce its ghastly prominence.

"I'm not standing up, and I'm not shaking your hand," Höttl said.

"Hell, that suits me." Hector took up a chair on the opposite side of the table. He ordered a glass of wine. When the waiter left, he said, "When did you leave Paris to return to Germany?"

Höttl scowled. "Why do you care?"

"Truly? I actually don't care. I was just making polite conversation. I figure as soon as the Nazis got their foothold here, you dashed back, looking to become some kind of wheel in the Socialist party."

"For von Sternberg's sake, I will be civil to you, Lassiter. I will do that until we complete filming."

"And then?" Hector sampled his wine. It was a shade too sweet for his tastes.

"Then I'll take my revenge. Consider yourself fairly warned."

Hector shrugged. "You may want to revise your timetable. I'm only here for another day or two. Von Sternberg and I have completed script work. I'm more or less hanging around to help him cast his female star. We could settle this now, really. Afraid I don't fence, but then judging by your ugly mug, neither do you, at least not competently. Suppose we could find some seconds and pick a location. You know, pistols at dawn and all that European nonsense."

"It is very tempting. Excuse me for a few moments." Höttl rose and walked to the front of the restaurant. Because of the position of their table, Hector lost sight of the man as Höttl approached the front of the restaurant. He returned a couple of moments later, dabbing at his face with a handkerchief. His suit coat glistened with beads of rain.

So, he'd stepped outside for a minute... *Hm.*

When Höttl resumed his seat, Hector said, "That scar—it is a fencing wound, isn't it?"

"Ah! My good friends, I'm delighted to see you are speaking!" Von Sternberg spread his arms. He embraced Hector, kissing him on both cheeks, then repeated the action with Werner Höttl.

"Sure, it's been just like old home week," Hector said. He pulled out a chair for von Sternberg. "Truth is, it hasn't been much of a conversation, Josef."

The director rolled his eyes. "More sparring, you mean? You're both good with words, so I expect I'm to be treated to more verbal jousting. Well, stop it, you two. We have a film to make. And anyway, life is too short for petty squabbles."

"For petty squabbles, yes, I would agree with that," Höttl said, looking at Hector with blatant contempt.

Hector shook his head, and inspected some other diners. "Christ's sake," he muttered under his breath. He scooted his chair around to face von Sternberg, essentially showing Werner Höttl his back. "Juvenile" behavior? Sure, but Hector was never too far above a bit of that.

Hector said, "Where's your potential leading lady, Josef, this Miss Dietrich?"

"She called to cancel. Something about her daughter being sick." Von Sternberg helped himself to what was left of Hector's Riseling. He smacked his lips and said, "I begin to think she's playing hard to get, as you Americans say. I think Marlene knows I'm leaning her way, and her evasiveness, it's a negotiating tactic."

If that was so, it seemed to Hector to be working just fine. He said, "Well, as the lady isn't coming, I'll leave you two fellas to your film talk."

Von Sternberg frowned. "Again you try to leave me, Hector? It's miserable outside, a hard cold rain. Stay and eat, and I'll see if I can't lead you both to one another's more winning qualities. I'd not have you two leaving it like this."

Hector pushed back his chair. "Thanks, Josef, but I like the rain, and I don't like this son of a bitch."

"Well, then let's still plan on breakfast tomorrow, Hector, just the two of us. Our usual café?"

"Sure, Josef. I'll be there."

Hector took his leave without so much as a head nod to Werner Höttl.

As he stood waiting for his overcoat's return, Hector peered through the rain-streaked window. Those same two Nazi party members who'd been singing out front were now across the street, watching the diners leaving Horsch's. Hector had the sense they were waiting on him.

Hector retreated back into the dining area enough to spy on Werner Höttl. Von Sternberg was going on about something, gesticulating dramatically to drive home points. Werner wasn't even watching the director, staring instead out the dining room window at about the place Hector figured those singing Nazis were positioned.

A soft voice, "Sir? Your coat..."

Hector smiled and walked back to the coatroom desk. He generously tipped the check girl. He said, "This is important, darlin'. Is there a way out of here other than that front door?"

She handed him his coat and he shrugged it on. He said, "Really, is there another way I can get out of here, and quickly?"

The young woman bit her lower lip, deciding. He said, "What's your name, sweetheart?"

As he asked that, Hector glanced out the window again. One of the Nazis was checking the toggle lock on a Luger. The other had his hand in his overcoat pocket, as if he was gripping a gun hidden in there.

This wasn't going to be a simple tailing as it had been with the German soldiers. This might well be an assassination on the street. Werner Höttl's brief excusing of himself, and his return with rain-stained shoulders, told their own story now.

The coat check girl's gaze had followed Hector's. She had also seen the gun being prepped. "I'm Liesl. Are those men waiting for you?"

"I'm guessing so," Hector said. "I haven't done anything wrong, honey, I promise you that. Those kind don't need much in the way of excuses. Now, about that back door…" He said it with some urgency—it didn't take any acting.

Guns drawn, the Germans were waiting for a break in traffic to cross the street.

"Liesl, I really don't have much time here, darlin', *please*."

She pointed. "Through the kitchen doors, at the back of the room."

"*Danke*, sweetheart." He lifted and kissed her hand.

Hector couldn't help himself. He risked detouring to von Sternberg's table. Josef smiled up at him, and said, "Hector! The foul weather has changed your mind! I'm so pleased."

"Sorry, Josef, no. This is where you're apt to fire me, friend." Hector reached over, grabbed Höttl by the scruff of the neck, then slammed his face into the table's top, twice.

Hector dashed toward the kitchen. Cooks frowned as Hector weaved between their stations and crashed through the back door and into the alley.

Running in the cold, stinging rain, Hector made his way to Kurfürstendamm, where he finally caught a cab back to his hotel.

11

Duff said, "Between your file's biography and these stories of Paris and Berlin, I wonder when you ever go home. You're very well-traveled."

I gave her a taken-aback glance, acting a bit hurt. "You mean I look haggard?"

Duff shook her head. "No, I mean you've traveled, a lot."

"I do seem to get around."

"You lived many years in Key West," she said. "That sounds like a place I'd perhaps like. Sounds a fine place to live—sunny, tropical weather. Good seafood. Always a tan. For those who tan anyway. With my complexion, I'd be a goner there. But it sounds perfect for a man like you. Why'd you leave Florida?"

"Lost too bloody much there," I said. "That smallish island got to be positively crowded with loss."

"For instance?"

"I lost a wife there. A lover or two. And a best friend. And a whole way of life vanished there, right before my eyes. For that last, I blame FDR and his damned New Deal schemes. Those federal boondoggles all but ruined the Keys. FDR turned the island into a tourist trap. I'm no Roosevelt fan, quite the contrary."

Duff changed the subject. "And Puget Sound? You lived there, too."

"Souring, also, in some ways of late. I'm looking for some-place new."

Duff smiled. "I've been finding myself drawn to New Mexico. Something really foreign-looking and new. Not too many people to stir up trouble. Quiet and solitude. You chased Pancho Villa with Jack Pershing and Patton. You know the desert. Does it appeal to you?"

"In measures. And more so since they invented air-conditioning."

"Exactly." Duff sipped more whisky. "Downside of that is I've heard the military is looking at New Mexico as the place for some kind of bomb test site."

The sun rose bloodily over the quiet, dew-kissed country-side. While there was still a little darkness, I pulled over under some trees.

"Here in the boonies, I think we're at some risk with those swastikas on the doors," I said. "These uniforms Jimmy and I are wearing are a real risk, too. We're vulnerable to scrappy farmers. Independent or self-styled resistance types. Maybe to Maquis."

Duff climbed out of the car and stretched. Pancho fol-lowed her out, then promptly raised a leg at a tree.

She said, "You being ex-cavalry, I'm going to presume you can make a campfire, Hector."

"I can do that," I said, looking around. "Don't see any chimney smoke, so it's probably safe enough to light one. I'll get a fire started, then change."

"And then I'll make breakfast." Duff reached in and gently shook Marie awake. "Come on, honey, your kidneys must be in danger of bursting by now," she said in French.

Marie said she was hungry. Blinking, she rubbed her eyes, then slid out of the car and hugged Pancho. After that, she walked through the shimmering grass, almost knee-high to her. Her fingertips trailed across the tops of the blades of dew-kissed grass.

Of course it had been a while since she's been outdoors. But watching her, I began to wonder if Marie had ever been outside a city. She paused and touched a tree as if to confirm it was real.

It was good to doff those Nazi duds. Now I was wearing my ancient leather jacket over a fisherman's sweater; gray flannel pants and work boots. Duff said, "That's a much better look for you." She eyed an ancient lipstick stain on the woolen collar of my leather jacket, then raised an eyebrow. That stain: Brinke, February 1924. I shrugged at Duff.

Jimmy slipped from behind a tree. He now wore a leather coat that belted at the waist and brown corduroy pants. He carried a brown fedora in one hand. With the other hand, he scratched Pancho between the ears as the dog loped along beside him.

We looked like native civilians now. My French was good enough to pass, Duff's too. If Jimmy kept his Irish inflected French to a minimum, we'd get along just fine.

Duff said, "If only we didn't have swastikas all over that car."

"I'm going to tackle that now," I said. As Duff worked over the skillet and fire I'd set under the high canopy of the old-growth trees, I poked around in my knapsack and pulled out the four cans of paint I'd brought along. I'd chosen four shades: gloss black, matte black, olive drab and battleship gray—basic car colors.

I selected the can of flat black paint, then started painting over those wicked Nazi symbols.

Jimmy wandered over. Head on side, he surveyed my work. "When it dries, it should pass. Where do you think we are, Hector?"

"I'm thinking about twenty miles west of Limoges," I said, finishing up. Duff waved us over for breakfast.

I hesitated. Somewhere at the edge of my hearing, I could make out the hum of an engine, not a car, but of a *plane*. Jimmy gave me this look. I said, "Get the girls under the trees and close to the ground! I'm going to move our car under the trees."

Jimmy nodded. "Should I put out the fire?"

I shook my head, swinging into the Juvaquatre. "No. The smoke that'd result from dousing the fire would draw more attention than what it's putting off now."

The aircraft was still at some distance. Now I could tell it wasn't just one plane, but two. I pulled the car under a big old pin oak, up close to the trunk and well under the bronzed canopy. Most of the others trees had shed their leaves, the bare limbs like crooked fingers grasping at the clouds.

I shut off the engine, then ran over to the campfire.

As I sprawled out on the ground next to her, Duff said, "Could just be planes going here-to-there."

"Maybe," I said in English. I was very aware the little girl was eavesdropping, now—not understanding, clearly, she was listening to our tones. She was holding close to Jimmy, who was on the other side of the tree trunk, keeping his weight off her, but covering most of her body with his. Now that we were in street clothes, Marie seemed to be more strongly drawn to Jimmy. Well, that was good, wasn't it? If we succeeded in smuggling her home, he would, after all, be her uncle, and probably the doting kind.

I grabbed Pancho by the scruff and pulled him close to me. Planes were still a novelty for him. I wanted to be able to silence my dog fast if need be. Duff was stretched out next to me. In English, she said, "If they're looking for us, and should use paratroopers?" She drew a finger across her throat. She was clearly terrified.

"They're too low to the ground to drop anyone—not enough time or distance to deploy the chutes," I said. I was getting a better earshot at the engines now. I said, "And they aren't that big. They're single-seater crates from the sounds of those engines."

Now I could see them up there, gray and yellow: twin Messerschmitts.

Shaking my head, I placed my free hand over Duff's and squeezed. "If they've come for us, it's going to be a bombing or strafing run."

That was another bad sign. German pilots flying so low put themselves at risk from rifle fire, especially with those fabric-covered rudders. These *were* search planes, then. It was the only way they'd take that risk buzzing the treetops.

Now it was all down to the density of the foliage; all these pin oaks that held their leaves while the rest of the trees were already well into their fall shed.

Duff scooted closer. "You're trying to make me feel better, I can tell. They are looking for us, aren't they?"

"Pretty sure that's so."

"How'd they know where to look?"

I squeezed her hand again. "Höttl has the resources of the German military machine at his disposal. For all we know, these are two of dozens of planes dispatched in every conceivable direction from Lyon."

"Of course," Duff said, her voice thin and tense. "I wish now that I hadn't cooked. That smoke may give us away."

"It's nothing," I said. "With the trees and the morning light on the dew, there's already a fog coming off the low-lying fields around us. The smoke will just be construed as more of the same. The important thing is that they don't see us or the car."

"I knew this was going to be a dangerous undertaking, but it seems more hopeless now," Duff said.

"We've come a long way already," I said. "My bigger immediate concern is making contact with our people to have a boat ready when we reach the coast. I don't want to loiter in any place too long with this much attention being paid to finding us."

Duff said. "I'll get us in contact when we're in range, so no worries there. I've got something to do that. Unless, of course, they blow up the car now."

The planes were coming in close to our position. Pancho began to whimper. I wrapped my hand around his muzzle, said, "Hush," and then stroked his back.

The two aircraft passed swiftly over our hiding place, their shadows sinisterly sliding across the dew-beaded grass. After a few seconds, the sound of their engines changed.

They were banking back for a second pass.

Question was, were they doing that because they saw something, or were they just being damnably thorough?

They flew overhead again, a bit higher than the last time and a fair piece west of our position. The planes were moving more in the direction we were headed.

"I'm taking that as a good sign," Duff said, as if reading my thoughts.

"Yes, but if they mean to push on, they have to make one more pass to return to their original heading."

As I said that, there was again the change in sound as the planes' motors strained in their turns.

This third time, the planes passed by much faster and much higher. Another good sign.

"We'll give them twenty minutes to get further away, then we'll eat and move on," I said.

12

Marie abruptly said, "Monsieur Hector, I really need to go to the bathroom!"

Of course.

Hell, Pancho was showing signs, too.

We'd covered perhaps thirty miles since those planes had flown over us in the early morning. I found another dense cluster of tall old oaks that were still holding their leaves and pulled us under their canopy.

Duff took the little girl by the hand and led her off behind some trees. Jimmy and I parked our butts on the hood of the car and got a couple of coffin nails going.

From somewhere, just at the edge of my hearing, I thought there was somebody playing an accordion. I searched the horizon, what I could see of it around the trees and hills, for chimney smoke, any rooftops, but saw nothing to indicate civilization.

Jimmy said, "How are we going to call for that boat?" He was tinkering with his own small shortwave radio, trying to pick up a BBC broadcast.

"Duff's promised she has something to handle that. If whatever she has doesn't get the job done, I have my own gizmo, but it relies on Morse code, and so you never know who is on the other end."

Jimmy *tsked-tsked.* "Yes, it's a crapshoot, isn't it?" He blew three smoke rings, then said, "Hector, do you hear an accordion?"

"Funny, for a moment I thought I had," I said. But now I was focused on another sound. Something mechanical. Jimmy heard it, too.

He said, "Motorcycle?"

"At least one," I said. "We'll get some grenades, then send the girls deeper into the woods."

Jimmy shook his head, then called for Duff. He leaned in, gripping my shoulder in one big hand. "You're going to hide, Hector. Duff and I are wild cards. You and the little girl are known to these Huns. If this is trouble, we two will talk or fight our way out of it. You take the girl and go deeper into that tree line. Wait this out."

Though I was reluctant to leave them, Jimmy's logic was sound. I took Marie's tiny hand and said, "C'mon, honey—we need to play Hide 'n' Seek."

Marie said, "Are Duff and Jimmy going to play, too?"

"Sort of."

"And Pancho?"

"He's going to help Duff and Jimmy find us," I said.

Once I had the child farther into the woods, I lifted her up into the branches of an old oak tree. "See if you can climb up there and hide," I said, pointing at a recessed crook about ten feet from the ground.

Giggling, Marie settled into her hiding place. The branches were thick where she was hiding, more than enough to stop a bullet. I said, "Get down in there as low as you can, okay, honey? Only come down for, or answer to me, Jimmy or Duff. Right?"

"Or Pancho," I heard her voice say.

"Or Pancho," I said reluctantly. If the three of us ended up dead or captured, the dog might be her only slim hope for protection, if not for survival. That tiny voice:

"Where are you going, Monsieur Hector?"

"To trick our friends," I said. "Now, stay there and be quiet. Promise?"

She said, "*Promis, craché, juré,*"—"Promised, spat, sworn," and then spit on the ground.

I said, "Here's something better, a pinky promise." I held up my hand, little finger extended. She reached down her tiny hand. I wrapped her littlest finger around mine and said, "There, pinky promise. Now, hush please, honey."

Moving tree to tree, I worked my way back to the Juva-quatre.

Duff and Jimmy had spread a blanket out on the grass. Duff had broken out sandwiches she'd made for a late lunch. She's also conjured up a bottle of white wine. Pancho lay next to the blanket, eyeing the grub, salivating and beating his tail against the grass.

Overall, they looked like a couple and their dog out for an autumn picnic. But from my vantage point, I could see the gun hidden under Jimmy's napkin; the hand grenades that bulged the pocket of his leather jacket. I assumed Duff had a gun hidden close by, too.

Three brown-uniformed Nazis were crossing the field on motorcycles. One of those bikes had an attached sidecar, and a fourth Nazi squatted inside it, clutching a machine gun.

I drew my Mauser.

God willing, these Nazis would just pass on by.

But it wasn't to be. The motorcycles slowed, then rolled to a stop near the picnic site. The soldier in the sidecar leveled his weapon at Duff and Jimmy.

One of the Nazis turned off his engine and knocked down the kickstand with his boot heel. "Don't waste time lying to me," the solider said in German, stalking toward them. "I know you know who I'm looking for."

Silence… then birds, a cricket.

Jimmy shrugged, saying nothing in English, German or French. The soldier repeated his words, this time in faltering, ungrammatical French. Duff said in French, "What are you talking about? Who are you looking for?"

Under the edge of the blanket, I saw Jimmy pull the pin on a grenade.

Well, well. Reckless Jim. Now we were *fully* committed:

Five seconds, tops, until detonation.

The solider said in his schoolboy French, "It's no use to lie. You are with the ones we seek. Where is your friend, Hector Lassiter? Where is the girl?"

Good Christ, they were convinced that Jimmy and Duff were with me. Well, that had torn it.

By my count, there were three seconds left before that grenade hidden in Jimmy's big mitt detonated.

If I was Jimmy, I'd sling the thing into that sidecar. I'd lob it in there between the German's legs and blow it and the attached motorcycle to hell.

Just the shockwave of that explosion would knock the other soldiers off their bikes. Hell, they might even be incinerated in the resulting fireball when the gas tanks ruptured.

The flaw in that plan was the standing Nazi. He had his gun pointed at Jimmy's head. Jim would never get the chance to pitch that grenade before the Nazi put a bullet in his head. Jimmy's dropped grenade would then blow his corpse and Duff to rags and jam.

Two seconds.

Jimmy was going to have to do something rash and damned quickly.

I put my fingers to my lips and gave a whistle no bird known to nature ever made.

Jimmy's posture changed. He grabbed Pancho's collar; aimed to keep the dog from fetching, I guessed.

The standing Nazi looked quizzical, searching the trees.

I shot the man between the eyes.

Jimmy pitched his grenade. The man in the sidecar began frantically swatting at the grenade as it flew toward him. Unfortunately for the man, Jimmy had pulled the pin so many seconds before there was no time to bat the grenade back.

It exploded about a foot from the man's face, shredding him and his partner sitting on the attached motorcycle. Then the gas tank of the motorcycle triggered a second fireball.

The other Nazi was blasted off his bike and slammed to the ground, bleeding from his ears. I drew down on him, just as Jimmy was also taking aim.

Both guns barked. Hard to say which shot did the job, but both were fired to the face.

Jimmy, still holding tight to Pancho's collar, rolled over, sprawling half atop Duff as a second motorcycle's gas tank exploded.

The fireballs touched off the dried overhead foliage of the old oaks.

I shouted, "Duff, move our car away from this fire. Jimmy, forage what you can that might be useful from these corpses. I'm going to fetch Marie. Then we best get moving again. If this fire should spread tree to tree, we could still end up dead."

13

We reached the town of Bellac in the late afternoon. Storm clouds were rolling in and we'd been hearing thunder for at least ten miles.

Duff said to me, "Just in case they've put out leaflets with your picture by now—with all those books of yours in print your image isn't particularly hard to come by, after all—I'd better secure our rooms."

From the back seat, Jimmy said, "I'll see what I can do to scrounge up some more gasoline. I'll almost certainly end up siphoning it off from some other Kraut heap."

I saw the church then in the gathering gloom. It was gray and tall and imposing. "You leave Marie and I there," I said. "Once you're settled, you can come back for us."

I palmed the wheel, steering curbside. Duff smiled. "Seeking sanctuary? Somehow that doesn't tally with my image of you."

"I've always loved European churches," I said. "I find them comforting. Even inspiring." I smiled. "I fear you've spent way too much time with my clearly distorted files."

Duff looked at the church. "Funny, you don't strike me as the religious type, not at all."

"You're partly right. I mostly like to write when I'm in a church."

"Well, as you'll be entertaining a child this time, we'll try to be quick," she said.

It started to drizzle. I sensed this deteriorating weather was only the start of something. I grabbed Marie's hand and we ran up the steps together.

As we reached the door, the harder stuff started pounding down.

It always seemed to be raining now.

We were sitting in a front row pew. Marie was wide-eyed, surveying the statuary and the vaulted roof so far overhead. It seemed more than she could take in.

I said, "Been a while since you've been to church, hasn't it, honey?"

"Ours wasn't this big," she said. She pointed. "I like the windows."

"Me too. Each one of them tells a story."

"I miss my Mommy and my Daddy," she said suddenly.

I hugged her close. "I know, honey. Let's go up there. We'll light two candles for your mom and dad. It's something you do in churches like this one to remember or to honor people."

As we finished lighting the second candle, I saw she was misting up. I hugged Marie again. "I lost my parents when I was just about your age," I said softly. "You'll always remember them, but it won't always hurt like it does now, I promise you that's true."

She looked up at me, very solemnly. "What happened to your mommy and daddy, Monsieur Hector?"

Hell, I couldn't tell her *that* story. I said, "It was like what happened to you in the most important way. I was very suddenly left all alone. My grandfather, Beau, took care of me. He raised me."

She spread her arms and I knelt. She wrapped her arms around my neck and buried her face in my cheek. I could feel her tears, warm against my skin. She said, "Who's going to take care of me?"

"It's like we've told you. Jimmy's sister, Fionnula, is going to be your new mommy. Jimmy's going to be your uncle. I expect you'll be seeing a lot of Jimmy, especially after Jimmy and I beat Hitler."

Her voice choked, Marie said, "You and Jimmy are going to do it yourselves?"

"With some help."

Marie said, "Daddy thought this war might never end."

I shook my head. "It will end, honey. Soon. I think the end has already started. When it's over, you'll be safe. You'll never again have to worry about people hunting you."

I held out my pinky. "Promise." She smiled and wrapped her pinky around mine again. Then she threw her arms around my neck again. Still hugging me, she said, "Was it lonely for you? I mean when your mommy and daddy went away?"

"Sometimes. You lonely now, Marie?"

"Not as much since we left Mr. and Mrs. Babinot. At nighttime, in my room there, it got very lonely before I fell asleep. It was bad at night. And so dark."

I stroked her hair. I said, "And now, honey?"

"I hug Pancho. It's not so bad if he's beside me."

"Then you'll never have to worry about being lonely like that again. Pancho's going home with you. He's your dog, now."

"But he's yours. You'll be lonely."

"No, I'll be very pleased knowing he's safe and happy with you," I said. "Fighting Hitler, it's too dangerous for a dog to come along while I do that. I want Pancho to have a yard and a little girl to love him and play with him. If you'll take care of him, it will make me very happy. You will take care of Pancho for me, won't you?"

"I'll take very good care of him, Monsieur Hector."

I hugged her back. "Thanks, darlin'. I'm delighted to hear that."

"You will visit, too, won't you?"

"Every chance I get."

I picked her up and carried her back to a pew. She watched the two candles we lit flickering in the warm darkness. She said, "We forgot to light two candles for your mommy and daddy."

"It's okay, I've lit a lot of candles for them," I lied.

"When will I get to my new home?"

"Soon. It'll go faster once we cross the water to merry old England."

She repeated the phrase, *Merry old England*, and smiled. She said, "That's where Jimmy and his sister lives?"

"No, but it's a stop along the way," I said. "Then you go across a lot of water. You and Jimmy and Pancho. You go the safest place on earth. Then you'll be home."

Getting that dog back with them without some kind of quarantine was going to require some string-pulling I figured, but between Duff's connections, Jimmy's and my own, I was wagering we could get them on a military boat or plane that would let them travel as a trio. "Soon you'll be home," I said, "I promise. There, you'll never have to worry again."

This voice, old and warm: "My *son*…"

An elderly priest rested a slender, shaking hand on my shoulder. He had rheumy green eyes, thinning white hair and gin blossoms at his cheeks. His hassock was stained with something that might be spaghetti sauce. "You aren't in some trouble, are you, my son?"

Stomach tightening, I said, "Why do you ask, Father?"

"Some *men* are gathering out front. Sister Bernadette is talking with them now."

"Men. You mean Nazis?"

"Yes," the priest said. He looked very worried. "They are asking about a man whose description matches yours. A man named Lassiter." Softer, in my ear, he said, "They're looking for you and this little girl. This is a large old church, with many corners and crevices. Perhaps if we hide you really well? Maybe in a confessional or the bell tower?"

I shook my head. "I suspect they won't hesitate to look in those places, or anywhere else that strikes their fancy." I stood and pulled Marie to her feet. "Father, does your church have any interesting architecture of other kinds? Some tunnels, maybe? Hidden rooms or exits? I'd prefer tunnels leading to other structures. Even a sewer system access could do."

"You don't have to deal with anything that sordid," the priest said. "Follow me, my son. I can get you to the other side of the street, but after that..." He shrugged.

"I'll take it from there, Father. And thank you for warning us."

He squeezed my arm. "Let's go now, and fast, my son. Sister Bernadette is indomitable, but these are Germans after all."

Two blocks from the church we turned the corner into two German soldiers who leveled their guns at us. Marie squealed and leapt into my arms, wrapping her arms tightly around my neck.

One of the Germans looked to be about twenty, the other was maybe just a shade on either side of thirty.

They both looked at Marie, now trembling in my arms. I muttered, "*Goddamn it*." I bit my lip, said in German, "She's just a child, brothers. Let us go, please. I don't have much money on me, but I'll give you what I have if you'll just let us go. She's done nothing."

The young one sneered. The slightly older German looked heartsick. He drifted back behind his young cohort. I figured then he was just going to let his bloodthirsty young friend work us over, shoot us or turn us over to superiors. Maybe the young one meant to do all three of those things.

The elder German reached for the pommel of a knife.

Goddamn it!

I turned Marie's face to the hollow between my neck and shoulder so she wouldn't see what was coming.

Then, eyes wide, I stepped aside to avoid the blood-spray as the German soldier sliced open the throat of the younger Nazi. The German who had just murdered his fellow soldier said to me in his own language, "You did that. Do you understand me?"

"Sure," I said carefully in German. "I cut his throat." As I said it, I watched the boy on the ground bleeding out, twitching and damning me with his eyes and he clawed at his neck.

The other German knelt and wiped down the blade of his knife on the dying soldier's tunic with two practiced swipes. All the while, he watched me—as though I might actually somehow do something with my arms full of whimpering child.

"I have a daughter about her age," he said, rising and slipping his knife back into its sheath. "I hope to survive all this desolation and see my little girl again." He nodded at Marie. "I couldn't see her…" His voice trailed off without saying "killed."

"Right," I said. "I couldn't either, positions reversed."

"You better go, fast," he said. "Go that way. We were the last coming from that direction. But know this—if you get caught, I'll shoot you before you can betray me."

"No need to even think about that, brother. I wouldn't do that after the chance you've given us here," I said. "I'm going, but first, what's your name?"

He narrowed his brown eyes. "Why?"

"Because as you say, someday, a day soon, I hope, this goddamn pointless war is going to be over. When that happens, I mean to look you up one day. Buy you a drink and meet your little girl."

We shook hands. He said, "I'm Frederick Schmidt of Düsseldorf."

"I'm Hector Lassiter of coastal Texas. Stay alive, Frederick, and thank you."

"My legs are getting tired," Marie said.

"I know, honey. Come here." I lifted Marie and held her so she could bury her face between my shoulder and neck again. We'd been walking in a needle-spray rain for nearly twenty minutes. We were both soaked through and shivering. Marie's teeth chattered against my neck. She said, "Your skin is scratchy." It had been a couple of days since I'd shaved.

Marie asked me for a story. As a writer, my stuff usually walks darker, bloodier ground than even the unexpurgated Brothers' Grimm and Mother Goose tales tend to traipse.

Soaked to the bone, I told her some cockeyed fairytale about a pretty little orphan girl menaced by an ogre with a scar down his face. The little girl was saved by a wandering warrior bard who distracted the ogre with fanciful tall tales until the bard could ice the son of a bitch ogre with the big bastard's own writing quill.

Werner Höttl meets *The Thousand and One Nights*? I couldn't deny it. Like the old scribe said, "Bad writers imitate; good writers steal."

Marie said, "Where did that story come from?"

"I made it up."

Her forehead wrinkled. "Made it up just like that?"

"Sure," I said. "That's my job. I am a storyteller. I am a writer."

"I used to tell my stories in my room in the dark, the room without windows." Marie bit her lip then shook her head firmly. "I think I'm going to be a writer, too." I sensed she truly decided it to be so, right there.

A black sedan, a Renault, was slowing. It began to pull over toward us. As it reached the curb, I reached for my gun. My left arm was curled under Marie's bottom, supporting her weight. So I slipped my right hand into my coat pocket and wrapped my damp palm around the butt of the Mauser.

The driver cracked the window of the Renault.

Jimmy said, "Don't shoot, Hector. Seemed time for some new wheels. Now you two get in here before you catch your deaths."

I finished dressing in dry clothes, then sat down at a window-side table to eat the meal Jimmy had scrounged for us from a neighboring market while I took a hot shower. The room was gloomy, just a stark light over the table, spotlighting it. A knock at the connecting door. It opened a crack and Duff said, "Are you decent?"

"Just."

"I finished giving Marie a hot bath," Duff said, sliding in. "I think she'll be okay. She was sopping wet, but I don't think she's going to catch cold. It was a very lucky thing you and Jimmy crossed paths out there in the rain when you did. Jimmy agreed to sit with her so you and I can have dinner together. I mean, if you don't mind the company. No pressure for you to agree, but I am famished."

"I'd love the company," I said. Duff was wearing a dress. It was tasteful, nothing showy. I could see for the first time she had very nice legs. I pulled out a chair for her. She sat down, and I scooted her chair in. I said, "Jimmy said he'd ordered for two."

"Certainly looks that way," she said. "I love Jim more with each passing hour. I was just teaching him how to fix Marie's hair. After all, he's got to see to such things between England and Ohio. He was a good sport, but said he hopes all this domestic stuff doesn't pull his teeth. His words, not mine."

I laughed. "Impossible. Jimmy's solid iron. But he has a big soft heart when it comes to some. You were right, of course. In terms of my rogues' gallery of friends, to use your term, he's the real standout. Probably the best man I've ever known. I mean, at least since Hem kind of went to pieces in the late thirties."

Duff filled our wine glasses. I raised mine and said, "Let's drink to putting them safely on whatever craft carries them to America."

We tapped goblets. I looked out the window, sipping my wine and watching the hard rain streaming down the glass. There was lightning in the distance and the deep thrum of rolling thunder occasionally rattled the panes.

Duff licked her lips and nodded approvingly. "Who picked the vino, you or Jim?"

"The wine was Jimmy's discovery and it's lucky for us it is good as he's not a wine kind of guy. I've got a pretty formidable palate and so usually have to see to my own needs." I smiled ruefully. "What that palate boasts, my liver lacks."

Duff nodded spread her napkin across her lap. "So, another close call. But you again carried the day. You seem to have what they call the Nelson touch."

"Thanks. I just hope I come to a better end than the Admiral did."

"How close, exactly, did this one come?"

"Thanks to the priest, it wasn't much of a scene. I didn't kill anyone, for instance. But that would have been rough duty anyway with a child in my arms. I stole a German's motorcycle to get some distance from the church, then ditched it quickly and continued on foot."

"May be a good thing Marie was there to stay your hand, to push you toward flight. You strike me as the committed kind that would have stuck it out at the Alamo."

"No way," I said. "I'm much too fond of myself for that flavor of sacrifice. I got those death-for-country urges out of my system early on, during the last war. Any romantic notions I had about dying for Uncle Sam were ground out of me pronto in that majestic cluster fuck."

Duff sipped more wine, still savoring the taste. She said, "That crude admission aside, nearly as I can tell, if you ever had nine lives, you have to have exhausted eight of them before the 1930s wound down."

"Possibly." I started in on a bowl of soup, some too-thin, chicken broth affair. I sifted in some salt and pepper and said, "This evening's close call at the church brought home for me what I said to you before about Höttl having the resources of the Third Reich to pitch at us. If there had been any fewer of his minions swarming the church grounds, we might not have slipped safely out in the ensuing confusion."

Duff paused, a knife and fork poised over her meat. She put them down and reached across the table, placing her right hand over my left. She hesitated, frowning, then said, "While I bathed her, Marie told me her version of what happened after Jimmy and I left you at that church. The child's account was pretty harrowing, Hector."

I topped off my wine. "The state of fear is the sorry place that little girl has lived, and for a very long time. This wasn't that bad, Duff. Really." Well, thanks to Frederick Schmidt it had worked out okay.

Duff picked back up her utensils. I was very sorry she quit touching me. Her hand was warm, strong and silky. The memory of its touch lingered. She said, "Marie also said you told her a story, A story about your parents' deaths. Exhaustive as your file seems in some ways, it doesn't include the fact you're an orphan."

"It's not exactly something I trumpet," I said. "How's your food?"

"Adequate. Soup's quite disappointing. I deduce you think so, too, given the damage you've done to the saltshaker. What happened to your parents, Hector?"

Staring at my plate, I stirred my food around. I'd only ever told the story once in full. That had been done in France, to

Brinke Devlin, my eventual first wife. I gave Duff a drastically truncated account. Still, she was the second on earth to hear it. Maybe that should have told me something.

"My father murdered my mother," I said, staring at my food. "The state of Texas saw to my old man's demise. I was raised by my mother's father, a gallant old gent and infamous confidence artist."

Duff nodded slowly. After I was silent a while, she just said, "Did you see this happen with your mother?"

"The immediate aftermath? Yeah." I stared at my plate. "I've seen too many people I love bloody."

She took my hand again. She didn't say anything, just searched my eyes, smiling sadly and shaking her head.

I suggested walking off dinner. Duff was initially skeptical. "You're a hunted man, Lassiter."

It was still raining steadily, but not the bucketing rain that was falling during dinner together. I said, "The streets are all but empty. Even the goddamn Nazis are staying warm and dry inside somewhere. It's dark, too. With a fedora and an umbrella, I reckon I'll be safe enough company."

Duff took a look out the window and bit her lip. "Dinner was a bit heavy and could use walking off. So okay, it sounds nice. Like something one did before the world went to hell and gone. Just let me tell Jimmy we're going out for a soggy stroll."

We shared a big umbrella, Duff clutching to my left arm. The streets were very quiet, just us and the rain. "This *is* nice,"

Duff said. "Simple pleasures like this have been denied so long that it feels sadly alien to have them back."

"The good old days will come again," I said, smiling. "All these simple pleasures will become familiar again," I said. "The tide is already turning in some important ways. I can see it. We're winning this war."

"But there will still be battles lost. So many more lives taken…or squandered."

I said, "Have you thought about what you might do when this war is finally over? Will you go back to singing, maybe?"

"I was never that good," she said. "I've learned to let that dream go. And my imagination isn't strong enough to imagine all of this ending anytime soon. It seems too much tumult for things ever to return to what we'd call normal. Something has ended."

"Nah, it'll shake out, and the speed of the course-correction will leave you dizzied, honey. I thought the same thing during the Great War: 'We can *never* go back. It'll *never* be the same again.' People living in times like these always have such thoughts. But it does swing back. Things return to just the way they were, for the most part. We have a talent for forgetting. And then, somewhere down the road, goddamn us, we will do this bloody thing again."

"What will you do, Hector? What will your life consist of after this war?"

"At base, I'm a one-trick pony," I said. "I'll do what I always do. I'll write. Novels, screenplays. Maybe some journalism recording the aftermath of this war."

The wind was picking up, tugging at the umbrella with insistent gusts that blew a cold spray under the umbrella and into our faces.

We ducked into a recessed storefront—some jeweler's closed for the night. Looking around, I saw many vacant retail spaces.

War and occupation were not friends to local businesses.

I shook out a cigarette and fished out my Zippo. "Guess we best wait for a break in the weather before heading back. Sorry to have dragged you out in this, Duff. I thought the hard rain was behind us." From some upstairs window a phonograph was playing Edith Piaf.

She smiled. "There are worse places to be. I kind of like this, actually."

"Maybe you haven't worked out your career options yet," I said, "but when this war does end, will you stay here in Europe, or will you go home?"

"It's back to America, I think," she said. "I'd have left before now if I hadn't somehow gotten caught up in this OSS stuff. I thought I had an obligation to avenge my husband and the others we knew who've been taken or abused. I still feel I need to do what I can to that end. But once it's over, I won't be coming back to France, not to live. Once we get to England, I may make up my mind to stay there. Or, perhaps, to press on home. Either way, I left Lyon with you three knowing I'd never go back there. I guess, for me, that city is what you say Key West became for you."

I heard laughter from up the street. Some drinkers were half-carrying one another, passing by our little sheltered space from the storm. They seemed oblivious to the weather, but were not yet that wet from the rain.

"Must be a café or bar very close by," I said. "May I buy you a drink, Duff?"

She seemingly didn't have to give it much thought. "Sounds wonderful if it truly isn't far."

"I'm wagering it's just around the corner. Those boozers looked like they were just starting their night's soggy, liquor-soaked odyssey home."

Business was predictably light. We grabbed a table by a piano at the front of the café. Duff sampled her whiskey sour, then nodded at my glass. "So sorry you had to settle for your third choice." She raised her ginger eyebrows. "What *is* a mojito, anyway?"

"Cuban drink, made mostly of rum," I said. It had been such a long while…

"And a daiquiri?" That was longer still in the past.

"More of a south Florida, Keys or Cuba kind of thing," I said. "It was silly and sentimental to think a French bartender had ever heard of either, let alone could mix 'em."

I smiled and sipped my single malt. "I still own a little house in Key West. I rent it out now for walking-around money. If you do return to the States, I could shoo the tourists out for a couple of weeks. You could come down and take the guest room, and I could introduce you to any number of exotic, tropical libations."

This knowing smile. Duff said, "Those among other things you'd like to introduce me to, I'll bet."

Yes, she had me there.

Couples were taking turns at a piano in the corner, playing tunes; some singing along.

The latest duo of impromptu entertainers moved back to the bar. I looked at the suddenly silent piano. I said, "Come over here, won't you? Bring your drink with you." I moved to the piano bench. Duff smiled. "You're joking—you play?"

"Mostly by ear, but yeah, I can bang out a tune or two."
I played a few bars of Hoagy Carmichael's "Skylark." When
the bartender didn't order me away from the piano, I shifted
tunes.

Duff smiled, delighted. "You really can play!"

"And you can sing," I said. "Let's entertain the local elbow-
benders. Don't you dare say no."

I began to play "I'll Be Seeing You." Duff smiled uncertainly, but then began to sing, smoky-voiced, silky and sublime.

When it was done, the spare and scattered patrons
applauded.

Duff took my hand. "Let's get out of here, Hector."

"It's still raining."

"I don't care. Let's go, I mean right now." She wasn't to be
denied, whatever her reason for getting out of there in a jiffy.
Nobody was spying on us; we weren't drawing funny looks.
Hell, quite the contrary…

I followed her out into the rain, huddled close together
under our umbrella.

"Where are we going, Duff?"

"I have no idea. I'll just know when I see it."

She led me to a park. There was a gazebo there. "Perfect,"
she said.

Duff pulled me under the canopy of the darkened gazebo.
She led me to a bench out of the rain. Duff sat down on the
bench, shrugged off her coat, and then lay back on the bench.
She urgently pulled me down into her arms. I started to say,
"Here? Like this? This is a crazy place for it."

"Hush, Hector."

She kissed me hard.

14

We sat in the gazebo, waiting for some let-up in the intensity of the rain. The thunder and lightning, at least, had abated.

Duff was still trying to correct her wardrobe, to adjust her under-things, reattach her garters and to do something with her hair. She said, "Next time we behave improperly we must find a proper bed to do it in."

I kissed her another time and said, "Absolutely." It was bucketing rain again.

"My God, how you wrecked my hair," she said. "Do you think Jimmy will know?"

I swept an arm at the weather. "Time we get back in this monsoon, we'll both look like drowned rats. So, no, I doubt that he'll notice anything. All evidence of impropriety washed clean."

"It was a crazy time for this, but entirely my fault, of course," Duff said. "Selfish of me."

"I was there," I said, smiling, "and so much more than willing. So it's selfish of me, too."

"We have bigger things to do," Duff insisted. "Passing wonderful as this was, we should already be back with Jimmy, figuring out our next moves."

She was right of course. I said, "Very sorry to see this moment pass so soon. But, you're right of course. Duty still calls. You said you can get us in contact with the OSS when we get closer to the coast. How exactly will you do that?"

"I can even do it now," she said, adjusting her bra strap under her dress. "But I think it's best to wait until we're closer to our destination. In order to narrow the window for interception or any countermeasures by moles, or spies, I mean. As to how, I have a radio hidden in one of my bags. You hook jumper cables up to a car battery to boost the transmitter's signal. It's a very nifty gizmo. Of course, if it was found in a search by the Germans, it would be grounds for summary execution."

"Following torture," I said. "Yeah. Good. I'm glad you have something dependable." I pressed my hand to her heart. "I saw the necklace there when we…"

It was a silver pellet container on a chain. The container itself looked a little like a small bullet. I'd seen them before. They contained what the Brits called an "L" pill…"L" for "lethal."

I said, "What is it in there, cyanide?"

"I really don't know," Duff said softly. "But they say it only takes five seconds. They were evasive when I asked about whether it's painful. Yours?"

"I threw my suicide pill away within five minutes of being handed the goddamn thing," I said. "Slow-motion self destruction I might warm to, but dying like that? Not my style at all."

"Why doesn't that surprise me?" Smiling, she pressed her hand to my cheek. "We've really created some complications for ourselves with this sweet night, haven't we?"

"Not from where I sit." I laughed. "Hell, I had the sense you despised me before we even met. Now I'm giddy."

"Despised? No. More like I was intrigued by what I was learning about you in your file." Her fingers traced my mouth. "I'd definitely formed some harsh opinions, though. I even sampled a couple of your novels in preparation for encountering you. I quite enjoyed them. When I met you, I found you compelling. Vexing, but compelling. I expect you provoke that reaction in many women."

"You fascinate me," I said. "But I don't know nearly enough about you yet."

"We still have some time together." Duff checked her watch. "But for now, time has really gotten away from us. We better go." She looked behind me and frowned.

I said, "What's back there, darlin'?"

"Two Nazis. They're watching us, trying to decide if they're going to approach us, I think. Maybe they intend to tell us to move along. We're probably violating some damned curfew."

I picked up our umbrella. "Let's keep looking like tipsy lovers, but shake a leg doing it. Save 'em the trouble of that warning."

The rain had finally subsided when we reached the hotel. We seemed to have lost our two Nazi soldiers on the brisk walk back. But there was a new crop waiting outside our hotel, hard-case German troops massing around our hotel and the one across the street.

"Oh, God, this isn't good at all," Duff said. "How are they finding us?" She cursed softly. "And what fools we are! Passing time with one another like that while Jimmy and Marie sat in there with these Nazis creeping in around them."

I felt the same way about the two of us, but said, "We'll persecute ourselves later, honey. Now let's get in there and get them out."

Jimmy looked simultaneously cross and relieved to see us. "We need to *go*," he said emphatically, "and I mean goddamn now."

"We saw 'em getting in position outside," I said. "How're they finding us?"

"They haven't found us yet," he said. "I've got everything packed and moved it downstairs into the car with the dog." He handed the keys to Duff. "You drive. They may search for people, but I don't think they'll be going through bags and the like. Pick us up by the townhall at the end of this street."

Duff nodded at Jimmy. "You seem to have it all planned. How will you all get out of here to meet me?"

"I have an idea about that, too," Jimmy said. "Now get moving, Duff, darling. Time is in calamitously short supply."

Duff left and I scooped up Marie and her doll. I said, "How are you up on all this, Jimmy?"

"Having some more time to myself than I expected,"— Jimmy put just a little edge in his voice, I thought—"I was toying with this radio gadget the spymasters gave me. I was trying to coax a BBC signal from the thing when I tapped into the Nazi radio band. I've been eavesdropping and sweating ever since. Now let's move our asses, Hector. The Krauts are searching every hotel in town and they seem to be starting with this street."

Jimmy led the way across the treacherous, rain-slicked mansard roof of our hotel.

I've never been good about heights, and a vivid imagination was more the liability. Lugging a frightened, fidgeting child across that slippery, sloped roof, I was assailed by visions of loosing my footing and plunging us both to our deaths.

We finally reached the end of the hotel's roof. Jimmy slid over the side to the roof of the adjacent building. That one was blessedly flat and covered in tar. I lowered Marie over the edge to Jimmy, then vaulted the low wall to join them on the adjacent roof.

We moved across two similar rooftops after that one—it was very easy going. When we hit the edge of the last roof, we were confronted with a four-foot gap between rooftops.

The roof on the other side of the narrow abyss was about two feet lower than the one we were standing on.

Jimmy made the jump with no trouble and turned around to face me. I could tell he was trying to decide between urging me to make the jump with her in my arms, or perhaps tossing Marie across the distance. I was afraid if I did the latter, she might scream—it was a long way down.

Making the leap alone wasn't any problem I knew I could make the jump, even if I would hate doing it. But weighted down with sixty pounds of squirming child and a slick surface to launch from?

Cursing inside, I took a few steps back, started running, and kicked off.

I hit the other side, lost footing, then began tumbling backward. Jimmy said, "Whoa there, boyo!"

He grabbed my belt and waistband of my pants in his big hand and pulled me away from the edge.

I thanked him with my eyes, not wanting Marie to know how close we'd come to falling over the edge.

Short of breath, we made our way across the roof and saw we were now confronted with a ten- to twelve-foot gap between our building and the next.

"So much for this Spring-Heeled Jack nonsense," Jimmy said.

He began to scrounge around the rooftop for a tool.

"Hello! Here we go," he said. Smiling, Jimmy hefted a rusted lug wrench.

Jimmy crept over to the roof access door and broke off the outside door handle with a single swing. He turned the wrench around, then used the tapered handle to punch out the interior door knob through the hole left by the handle he'd sheared off. Through the weather-ravaged door panel, I heard the interior doorknob bounce off the floor.

Jimmy opened the door, smiling. The hinges were rusty and the door's opening sounded like some small animal being tortured. "We're in," he said redundantly, very proud of himself.

"And everybody in the building may know it," I said. "Way our luck's running, this will probably end up being the rooftop of some flea bag hotel being tossed by more Nazis."

I was nearly right: we made our way down three flights of warped, creaking, shadowed stairwells. Then we began to hear all the groaning and moaning.

Not moaning from pain. No, it was the *other* kind of moaning.

No hotel, this. We were in a bawdy house.

Marie said, "Monsieur Hector, is everybody sick in here?"

"That's it exactly, honey," I said. "Cover your ears and keep your face pressed to my neck. Can't have you catching anything. Keep those eyes tightly closed too, darlin'."

We made our way down two more flights of stairs and then tiptoed down a long, lowly lit corridor past more noisy rooms.

We ran into the boss whore at the front door. She was big, overly made-up. Confused, but glowering.

I shrugged. Jimmy said to her, "*Au revoir, Madame.*"

It was drizzling rain again when we reached the street. We ran another two blocks in the rain.

The Renault was idling at the corner.

I slid into the back seat with Marie and Pancho. I crouched down below the window level and pulled blankets over the three of us. Pancho licked my hand, then started licking Marie's face, setting her to giggling.

Jimmy slid in next to Duff and began checking his weapons as she slid off the curb. She flicked on the wipers and said over her shoulder, "Any trouble?"

In English, I said, "I nearly fell off a roof, but apart from that, *nada.*" I paused, added, "We found a sporting house."

"Useful knowledge for the future for you fellows, perhaps," Duff said. "Important thing now is that they don't have any roadblocks set up."

"We might catch a break there," Jimmy said. "They seem focused on the city's interior for the present."

I said, "Jimmy, you said you heard on your radio they were searching every hotel in town."

"Right." Jimmy got out his pocket radio and began to fiddle with it again.

Marie clutched a bit tighter to me at the sound of the German voices coming from the tinny little radio's speaker.

Half-listening to the radio, Jimmy said, "They knew you were in town, Hector, but not *where*. Seems you were spotted and recognized at that church. That's why they're turning the town upside down presently. They know you're here somewhere. They're starting with hotels, inns."

I pulled the rather itchy blanket from over my face. "How'd they find me at the church?"

"One of the nuns ratted you out," Jimmy said sourly.

Well, damn. I said, "Not Sister Bernadette, I hope."

"No, another of the penguins," Jimmy said. Under his breath I heard him mutter, "The bitch."

"When we get clear of the city," I said, "I think we maybe best head southwest, Duff. Forget the run to Niort. Hard as they're hunting us, they're going to figure us to go straight for the coast, hell-bent-for-leather. And it *is* my strong impulse to do just that. But if we mender a bit, trail down away from England a ways, well, it might confuse the bastards. Might at least thin them out in that direction as they try to block us on the straight run."

"Problem now is we're violating curfew and doing it in a civilian car," Duff said. "And driving with lights on at night this close to the city, we're also an easy target for airplanes. With these storm clouds, there's not even moonlight to navigate by with headlights out."

"We play the hand we've been dealt," I said. "We drive on, Duff."

On the outskirts of town, a single young dark-haired Nazi stopped us. He was polite, officious. He struck me as a conscriptee.

Yet for all that, he was a tad too nosey. Call it the misguided diligence of youth.

As he began to press, and then to grow suspicious, I saw where we were inevitably and bloodily headed.

From the gloom of the backseat, I said softly so only Jimmy and Duff would hear, "Marie is asleep."

That simple declaration was a death sentence for the young German. It was trading youth for youth, really.

In civilian life, I'd maybe have gotten on with the young guy.

I pressed my palms to Marie's ears.

Jimmy said, "*Right.*" He crooked a finger. "Here lad, I'll show you my papers."

As the young man leaned in with a flashlight, Jimmy grabbed him by the scruff of the neck.

The soldier opened his mouth to scream for help. Jimmy shoved his Luger inside there and shot the kid through his palate.

He let the young man's corpse slide down the side of the Renault.

Our car was black. As Jimmy said, at night, particularly, it wouldn't show the blood. The rain would wash the offal off, eventually.

"Get rolling now, Duff," Jimmy said thickly, wiping at his bloodied hand and gun's barrel. Duff watched the big Irishman. She looked pale in the low light. Her hands were tightly gripping the steering wheel. I said, "You okay, Duff?"

"I have to be," she said. She swallowed hard and got us moving.

15

In a glade, in a lull between rainstorms, we popped the hood on our car and connected the cables of Duff's suitcase radio to the car battery.

Duff said, "Who'll it be? The resistance? British intelligence? Our boys?"

"OSS," I said.

I put my back to a tree's trunk, smoking a cigarette and watching Marie play fetch with Pancho.

It wasn't really much of a game of "fetch" per se. When Marie could pry it away from him, Marie would hurl the stick, and then Pancho would lope after it. Head down, he'd carry it back to her, then, as she reached for it, he'd bolt, sending her chasing after him, laughing.

Duff put a shoulder to the opposite side of the tree, smiling and watching Marie and the dog. She said, "So, what's the plan, mister?"

"We'll be splitting up soon. They wanted to try and arrange some commando drop behind us. Thought they'd drop someone to protect our caboose. I nixed that. Sounds daft, and if they could really get a plane near here, I'd want to get on the sucker and fly the bastard straight out of here and back to England."

Duff nodded. "Okay, so you rejected sending in the cavalry. So from that nixed option, how do we arrive at splitting up?"

"Notion is it's better to divide the German's search efforts and give them something extra to chase," I said. "Can't say I'm fully sold on this scheme, either."

"What, exactly, is the scheme, Hector?"

"Jimmy, Marie and the dog will go north of Bordeaux. There'll be a small fishing boat waiting there for them. Some Greek salt of a sea captain the Germans think they have in their pocket. Old man is actually semi-retired British Secret Service. He'll run them into England."

"And us?"

"We go to a farm house where the split occurs. There, we're to be given a loaner black Labrador and a female midget."

Duff checked my face to be sure she'd heard right. "A female *midget*? You're joking."

"That's just what Jimmy said."

"Where is Mr. Hanrahan?"

"Back at the car, using your radio to try and get word back to Cleveland. Letting his sister know what's coming her way."

"What's the story with the midget?"

"Circus performer," I said. "At a distance of ten feet, she looks like a midget. But in a car, in the right dress and from a distance?" I gestured with my cigarette hand at Marie.

Duff scowled. "That's truly insane, Hector."

"No, that's military intelligence's finest planners at work," I said.

Marie was now rolling in the grass with Pancho. Duff smiled, watching me watch Marie. She veered: "You mentioned a wife. You two ever talk about children of your own?"

I stared at the end of my cigarette. "Sure. But that wasn't to be. How about you and your husband?"

"He wanted children," she said. "I didn't, then."

"And now?"

"Not for me, I think. It's nice being around her, even under these circumstances. But that responsibility forever? I can't fathom that. It scares me in some primal way. A way I don't think I could ever overcome. And unconditional love? That's some cross to bear."

"It's funny how things you thought impossible sometimes just become your life," I said, dropping my cigarette and twisting my toe over it. "But I understand how it's not for everyone."

Duff offered me her hand. "I can't tell which side of this issue you fall on."

I bumped my forehead head against hers. "It matters?"

She was candid. "I can see how it could come to count for something."

Hm.

I squeezed her hand, then lifted it to my lips. "Let's just say that under the right circumstances I wouldn't run from the prospect. On the other hand, I'm not hungering for it, either."

Duff smiled and shook her head. "You always manage to have it both ways?"

I shrugged.

"Our splitting up, does that mean the two of us aren't going to England?"

"Oh, we go. Got to give the Germans something to chase, like I said. And our side wouldn't mind netting a few Krauts at least connected to Höttl."

Duff said, "On that note, Jimmy said you're under strict orders not to capture or kill Höttl. Why is that?"

"I wish I knew," I said. It wasn't a lie. I hated those unexplained orders that tied my hands when it came to really laying into the German filmmaker.

"We'll be about two days behind Jimmy if all goes to plan," I said. "I'm to draw fire, like I said. But I do want to change the plan a bit. I want you to go with Jimmy and Marie."

"Huh-uh," Duff said. "You're under orders and you can't disobey those. And I was doing this kind of thing long before you and I joined forces."

She stared at her feet. "And I don't trust you alone, darling. You'll take bigger risks by yourself, I know it. I can take care of myself and you. I make my own decisions, too, Hector. So we're going to do this together."

I shook out a fresh cigarette. "I know you can handle yourself. But now, having talked to people, well, I have a sense of the real magnitude of what's been chasing us since we fled Lyon. The scale of it. And, honey, it terrifies me. I've been a nervous wreck since breaking that radio connection. Honest to God, it's a miracle we've come this far, Duff. We've been damned lucky to get here. It's going to be even harder to press on as we get nearer Bordeaux."

"I'm staying with you, Hector, it's a closed discussion."

I could see she meant it. "Okay, darlin', I hear you."

"Good," she said. "We'll waste no more time on such talk, then." Duff ran her slender fingers back through her strawberry blond hair and sighed. "If everything against us is of the scale they're telling you, it does settle one question."

"What do you mean?"

"All this being thrown against us, to justify that, Marie must be Höttl's daughter."

"That makes terrible sense," I said. "And if it's so, that's a story I mean to learn more about. Somehow, someday, I'll get that tale."

Some bars of light were breaking through the heavy clouds, stray shafts of light in sharp contrast to the slate-gray sky.

"Maybe the weather is finally clearing," Duff said.

"Let's hope not," I said. "So long as it stays like this, the search planes have to stay down. 'Tween here and the coast, stormy weather is our best friend."

Jimmy cleared this throat to signal his approach. That spoke volumes. He clearly sensed something had happened between Duff and I.

I said, "We were just talking about the weather and search planes."

"Yes," Jimmy said, eyeing the sky like it might try something. "Prayers for more rain are in order." He got out his own cigarette and I fired him up with my Zippo.

"It's all arranged," he said. "Even passage for that canine. Now we just have to reach the coast and make the boat. No mean feat that, of course." He watched Marie and Pancho gamboling through the damp grass. "God willing, in a few weeks, she'll be able to do that every day. Won't that be something?" His voice cracked as he said it. That pierced me.

Duff smiled and hugged Jimmy tightly to her. "Tonight, we'll practice pigtails."

Jimmy sighed and jerked his head in my direction. "You had to say it in front of *him*?"

We were bunked in the barn of an OSS-vetted farming family named Dupuis.

We weren't off to the most auspicious of starts with the Dupuis clan.

After introductions, we sat down together for a rather lackluster meal. When we came outside to fetch some things from our car, we found the rear tire was flat.

Neither we nor any Dupuis had a patch kit or spare tires. Christophe Dupuis said, "Don't worry. We'll loan you our truck when you leave in the morning. Somehow, we'll just have to see the OSS gets it back to us."

Then Mrs. Dupuis apologized for not putting us up in their main house.

"We do what we can for the cause," Gabrielle Dupuis said, "but we're not spies nor are we soldiers. I'm sorry we cannot offer you more."

Duff assured her the barn would do us nicely.

We'd pushed the car into the barn and Marie and Duff were already bedded down in the front and back seats. I inspected the tire. It looked to me like some kind of puncture.

Jimmy and I were wandering alongside a small stream, hands in pockets, breath trailing frosty in the crisp air. The skies had cleared a bit and the moon winked between the clouds.

Jimmy said, "Don't strain yourself with disingenuous denials, Hector. You know I'm no fool and I certainly know your urges. Let me just say this much about Duff and you. This one seems a keeper. Duff's a special one, and she clearly has your number, yet she's still drawn to you. Thus you'd be a goddamned fool to let her slip away."

"I agree," I said. "That's why I want you to convince her you need her along on the trip home to care for Marie. Orders be damned. I want Duff to go with you tomorrow, Jim. I'll hook up with all of you in London once I make it through. I really want you to convince Duff she's critically needed with you."

Jimmy chuckled. It sounded humorless. He slapped my back then squeezed the back of my neck. "Ah, Hector. As I said, that woman utterly has your number. Right here you've gone and proven that's so."

"I don't understand."

"Duff said you'd ask this of me, Hector. She saw it coming. She said you're badly shaken by what you heard from your spymasters about the scope of the search for us. Parenthetically, I'll ask you not to tell me about any of that, Hector. I have a comforting, false optimism carrying me forward and I'd not have it fecking compromised. Anyway, Duff thinks you think we've no chance. As to me taking her, it's no use, boyo, so you better be clever and best Höttl this one last time. Stay safe of that Kraut bastard's clutches and I'll do the same. Then, when we get to London, you and I will get properly plastered. God knows, as a proper Irishman, it's the only way I can enjoy myself in that damned country."

16

I was suddenly awake. I was *wide* awake.
But *why?*

Eyes open, I lay there in the semi-darkness, listening.

I heard whispers. The murmurs were not Marie's, and not Jimmy's, either.

Pancho was alert, head cocked. He was listening, too. His muzzle twitched.

Duff's lips brushed my cheek. "You sleeping?"

"Not anymore," I said.

"Good. I was thinking we might take a little walk." Her intent was really something else, of course.

I smiled. "This is *truly* a crazy time for it."

"Then say no," Duff said. "You're right of course. It's completely crazy." A little smile. "And yet…?"

I checked to make sure Jimmy and Marie were still asleep. I said, "As I'm awake now…"

We moved on tiptoe. There was a slight breeze across our faces as the brisk night air whisked through the widening crack in the barn door that had softly squeaking hinges. I closed the door softly behind us. Pancho had insisted on following us out; he promptly went off in search of some tree.

The lights were on in the Dupuis' house. I checked my watch: Three in the morning. "Guess we're not the only night owls," I said. It didn't seem right they'd be up at this hour.

Duff nodded. "Probably best we first take a moment and be the spies we're supposed to be, wouldn't you say?"

"You read my mind," I said.

Through a window, we saw the woman and two younger men gathered around the kitchen table, loading guns; slipping knives into pockets and boot cuffs.

Our host, the farmer Christophe Dupuis, crept into the kitchen with an oil lamp. His wife, Gabrielle, and his two "sons" smiled.

One of them feigned drawing a knife across his throat and raised an eyebrow. Christophe smiled meanly, nodding. He aimed a gun in the direction of the barn and feigned a shot and the recoil. I ground my teeth, deciding on the spot.

I'd already had my doubts about a familial connection between the boys and the Dupuis elders. The young fellas didn't look much like brothers, and they didn't look like either of their supposed parents, either. Christophe and Gabrielle didn't seem a real couple. I had this vision of the real farm family that was supposed to be helping us dumped in some silo or at the bottom of some nearby stream.

All four of the "Dupuis" were armed to the teeth now.

The woman was gathering a length of clothesline. It wasn't nearly enough rope to tie up all four of us, but it was just about right to hogtie a little girl.

Son of a motherless dog.

Duff whispered, "So it's like that. We're outnumbered and outgunned."

"But we're not surprised," I said softly back. "There's value in that."

"So what do we do?" Tension in her voice.

I smiled grimly. "We retaliate first." I pulled a grenade from my pocket.

Duff was horrified. "You're carrying those in your pockets?"

"Just this last one I have left."

"You think it will get them all?"

"Probably not," I said. "There's a front door on this place, and a back door. I'm going to break the glass here, shoot as many of them as I can, then shoot the lamp on the table—get that flammable oil out of the bottle, so to speak. I'll count five—enough time so they don't have time to throw this sucker back at us," I hefted the grenade, "then pitch it in. If any are still left alive after the explosion, eventually they're going to run out the front or back doors because I figure soon enough the house will be on fire. We'll shoot them as they come outside. Agreed?"

She looked sickened by the notion but nodded. "There's no other choice," she said. Duff chose the back door to guard.

I managed to get Christophe and one of the boys with my first two shots; my third took out the lamp. The woman and the surviving younger man made it to another room. I pitched the grenade in after them.

The ground shook.

Screams.

The back door opened and a lone figure ran out. Duff hesitated shooting—just couldn't bring herself to shoot another in the back, I figured.

Faced with the same choice, I wasn't so certain I'd have done better…or, to be fair, perhaps bloodier was the more precise word for the act Duff had failed to bring off.

A low growl at my side: Pancho, snarling.

I pointed at the distant figure. We just couldn't risk leaving one for seed or to tell the story. I was about to give the word when Duff beat me to the punch. She said, "Pancho—*attack!*"

The dog sprung from his sitting position, stretching out and tearing across the dew-kissed field.

Pancho seized the running figure by a hamstring, shaking his head side-to-side and dropping the person to the ground.

The dog moved up the torso next, grabbing the person by the upper arm, again violently shaking his head side-to-side.

Duff and I ran after the dog. As we got closer, we saw: It was the woman.

Gabrielle was already in shock.

I said, "Pancho, *stop*. For God's sake, stop." I got him by the scruff and pulled him back. He'd torn some kind of artery under her arm. Gabrielle was bleeding out. I wasn't compelled to help her, but I also didn't want to seen any more damage done to the dying woman. "For God's sake," I said softly to the dog, "please *stop*."

17

Marie was running across the field as I walked back from the stream, Pancho trotting at my heels in the high grass.

She said, "What's wrong? Is Pancho sick?"

That dog was very nearly Marie's exclusive focus. I said, "He's fine. Just had to wash out his mouth. He ate something that might be bad for him."

Duff was trailing behind Marie. "We're ready to go," she said. "Jimmy's almost finished moving everything into the Dupuis' truck." Their bodies were under a rat-infested hay mound in the barn.

"Good, 'cause I want to make tracks pronto," I said. "God only knows when those Germans are supposed to get here to take us off the Dupuis' hands."

Jimmy raised and locked the tailgate of the truck. "Guess we'll steal yet another vehicle, something a little less rural in character, when we get closer to Bordeaux. And we'll need an extra vehicle anyway when we split up."

"I've re-thought all that," I said. "To hell with that notion. There's been too many leaks, at too many levels. There seems to be deep German penetration of the resistance, of the OSS. I say we go straight to the coast, all of us, together. We'll arrange our own transportation to England. Whether or not it's a government boat or plane, between the U-boats and the fighter planes, it's a crapshoot anyway. Might as well be our show."

Duff said, "We go together to Bordeaux?"

"Nah," I said. "Not going there. Somewhere more obscure."

It was six in the morning. I was a wreck from filling my body with gallons of black coffee and streams of nicotine.

Duff stretched and turned around in her seat to face me as we bumped along the road. She said softly, "Sorry. I really meant to keep you better company. I have this sense you're going to be a mess any moment from all this pushing of yourself past all limits of endurance. I don't know how you're sustaining even now, Hector."

"Thing to do now is to sprint," I said. "I'm counting on you and Jimmy carrying the last leg of this thing when we run out of road.

Duff sighed and tipped her head back against her seat, eyes closed. "Now that you've scuttled all the official plans, what really happens now?"

"I've delved into my little black book. Going to reach out to another old friend."

"Another Hanrahan?"

"There's no such thing," I said. "But the man I'm thinking of is another friend. He's clever and scrappy. And, so, maybe just what we need now."

A dockside tavern in Gujan-Mestras: we were watching the wind make whitecaps on the Bassin d'Arcachon. Duff had shamed the keep into sending someone to fetch some milk and a sandwich for Marie. I'd also slipped him a few extra francs to allow Pancho to sit at my feet.

As Marie ate, sneaking morsels of meat to the dog, Duff stroked the little girl's hair. She eyed me and said, "Where is this clever friend?"

Jimmy sipped his ale and said, "Hec may have been glossing that last a bit, dear Duff. This boyo is a bit of a pirate, literally. He's a merchant marine who used to hang around the Keys when Hec lived there. When our current war started to heat up, our friend Trev thought he might take all his rum and refugee running skills and turn a buck this side while still helping the cause. He does all that when that help doesn't get in the way of his wallet, that is to say."

Duff said, "Trev?"

"Trevor Lord," I said.

She said, "A pirate, huh?"

"That's Jimmy's word for the fella, not mine," I said.

Duff nodded. "And what would your word for him be?"

"An adventurer, I guess."

"Ah, the Keys in the twenties! It was like a wide-open border town, and while the rest of the country was dry, we were positively bathing in booze." Trevor smiled and shook his head at the memory, or at what he remembered of the memory.

Lord knows I drank my share during prohibition, but Trev drank many people's share. "It was a hell of a great time." He smiled and winked at Duff. "The stories I have to tell you, pretty lady…"

"Another time, Trevor," I said. "How quickly can we shove off?"

Trev said, "When does Hanrahan get back? And where'd he go, anyhow?"

"Jimmy said he'd be back around three or four this afternoon." I yawned. My stimulants and lack of sleep were starting to hammer hard at me. I said, "As to where he went? He said he had some special things he needed to pick up from some people he's connected with. Ones he swears he can trust, at least in terms of supplies. When he gets back, we're all ready to go."

"Let's plan on heading out at 4:30, then," Trev said. "We'll keep on until it gets dark, then drop anchor. I don't like to run at night because of the submarines and overhead patrols. If you're not dark and still, you're begging to be a target."

"Makes sense," I said. "I don't care if it takes two weeks to reach England, just so long as we get there intact."

"Two weeks would be a very expensive charter," Trev said. "Think of my losses on other jobs."

I watched Duff watching Trevor, imagining him as she was seeing him—a lanky guy most women would probably call good-looking. He stood six-four, one of the rare men who eclipsed me. He was broad-shouldered and had an easy smile under green eyes. A full head of auburn hair. Yeah, she probably thought him handsome. Trev always did well enough with the ladies in the old days. And he was cocky. Like I said, a hell of a scrapper, too. What was there not to like?

He said, "Who's paying for this voyage, Hector?"

"Duff's hating you for a money-grubbing mercenary by now," I said.

Trevor shrugged. "I was trying to make a joke. Anyway, it's not like Duff's on the market, right, so why should I try too hard to be liked? I mean you two are a couple, yes?"

"Now I'm hating you," I said. I nodded at Marie. "It's all about her. If it's money you want—"

"I'm just joking, Hec," he said. "Someone else is underwriting this run back to England. My costs are covered with some special things in the hold I'm transporting. No, I'm doing this for the same reasons you all are, to get this little girl to safety. All I need from you is that you bring your own provisions for this sweetie, here." He chucked Marie under the chin. She squirmed, evidently ticklish there. Trev said, "I'm not exactly stocked or equipped to see to the needs of children."

I sipped some beer. "Right. So let's split up now, then we'll reconvene at your boat at 4:30 p.m. What's your current craft's name, by the way?"

"I bought the boat, and changing the name is bad luck," Trev said, skittish-like.

I smiled. "Sure, I've heard that. So what's it called? 'Daffodil' or something?"

Trev rolled his eyes. "No, not *that* bad. It's *Victoire*. Grandiose, I know."

"It is a tad much," I admitted.

Trev checked his watch. "Where are you all staying?"

"Doesn't matter," I said. "In a couple of hours, it'll be a moot point. And if you don't know and unfriendly types somehow how trailed us here?"

Trevor scowled. "Right. Now, joking aside, you're scaring me. This Höttl, he's really that bad?"

I said, "Every wicked and warty inch."

He looked at his watch again, then pointed at my glass. "How about another drink, Hec? It's been a long time. We have a lot of catching up to do."

"Thanks, pal," I said, "but we've got the trip from here to England for that stuff. I also haven't slept much in at least thirty-six hours. I still have things to do while I have half a brain left and before I simply fall over dead from exhaustion."

Trev bit his lip. "Sure. See you in a bit then."

I helped Duff on with her coat and whistled for Pancho. We slid out into the weather. There was a brisk, cold wind off the water.

Voices, carried on the breeze. I heard conversation, urgent, guttural and officious. *German.*

Holy Jesus!

I grabbed the girls by the arms, looking left to right and back again.

There was a run of stairs down to a small jetty.

I said, "This way, fast," and urged Duff and Marie down the stairs. There was a small dinghy tied-down there. The oars were still in the boat. I helped the girls in, toed Pancho into the boat, then untied it and slid in myself.

Using a single oar like a canoe paddle, I punted us along best I could directly under the overhead pier, heading back the way the German soldiers were coming directly overhead. From the sound of all the boots and glimpses stolen between gaps in the salt-sprayed planks, I figured there to be at least a dozen of them passing above.

We reached another small jetty, and I pulled to and roped off the boat again.

I crept back up to the pier, then signaled the girls and dog to join me.

We slid back into our truck and headed to our scheduled rendezvous with Jimmy.

"Another close one," I said, furious.

Duff toed around it a while and finally came out and said it in her way, "Those Germans, the questions Trevor asked you about where we're staying? His trying to get you to stay for another drink, while all the while checking his watch? I know he's your friend, but…"

"I'm thinking it, too," I said, seething. "Reason why I lied to him about Jimmy's schedule. Trevor's already sold us out, goddamn it. Swear to God, apart from you and Jimmy, I'm not trusting anyone anymore."

Duff placed her hand on my thigh. "What are we going to do now?"

"I used to have my own boat in the Keys," I said. "The Devil May Care. I can pilot at sea. I ran all over the Gulf Stream back in the day. So best figure I can find an island as big as England. We're going to steal Trevor's crate. We'll risk the run to Great Britain on our own."

18

Standing on the shore, steadying his elbows on the truck's roof, Jimmy scanned Trev's boat with a pair of binoculars. He must have heard my approach; his back stiffened. "Don't shoot, Jimmy, it's just me," I said, padding up behind him.

Jimmy handed me the binoculars. "I'm relieved to have you back, Hec. Where have you been?"

"Making sure Trevor isn't on that boat," I said. "After the Germans rushed the tavern I picked for our first meeting with Lord, I found a phone and called back there for Trevor. I directed him to our hotel, telling him there'd been an urgent change in plans. Bastard sprinted out of there right along with the Nazis. He drove off with them in one of their troop transports." I lit a cigarette and said, "Swear to God, I'm losing all faith in my own judgment. And if I ever cross paths with Trevor again, I'm puttin' him down."

"I trusted him enough to support you in this gambit, too," Jimmy said. "And you'll race me for the privilege of killing that bastard. We're just lousy with turncoats in our midst, it seems. Well, we best shake a leg before he comes back here."

He bit his lip and said, "The Keys are a few years behind you, Hec. You *can* really pilot this rust bucket, can't you?"

"I really can," I said. "No worries there. It's like falling off a horse."

"But you haven't had a night's sleep since I can't remember when."

I flung my yet-to-be-tasted cigarette into the water. It suddenly felt like one too many. "Trevor's basic plan for a crossing as he described it to me was the right one, I think. We should shut down engines and go dark at night. But first we'll get some distance from this place. Then, tonight, I'll sleep. Come morning, I'll get us underway, put us on our heading, then show you and Duff how to keep us on that beam. While you two take turns making that run tomorrow, I'll get some more sleep. But first, let's steal that Judas' damned boat." I hesitated, then added, "Ideally, we should kill him doing that."

Trevor dodged a bullet. When we stole his boat, he wasn't conveniently present to be put down.

It was a hellish first few hours. I felt nauseous and unfocused from all the tension, nicotine, caffeine and no sleep. The water was choppy and seasickness chased Marie and Duff below. Pancho had followed them down there, looking a bit punk, himself.

Jimmy scanned our wake with binoculars. "All's clear, so far. Of course they need only to radio ahead for a sub to intercept us and to sling a torpedo into our side. Perhaps a fighter squadron to find and strafe us."

"Yes, so I'm going to shut down in about thirty minutes," I said. "We'll hook up Duff's radio to the boat's battery. I want you and Duff to use that coded gizmo to see about getting one of our subs or frigates to intercept us and carry us the rest of the way to England. Wild Bill ought to be able to swing *that* much for us. I mean, the boys who'll be coming to lend us aid will have been to sea for a time, well outside Höttl's reach or the influence of his Nazi gold or whatever else he's using to pay off these traitorous bastards."

"Right," Jimmy said. "Sometime you're going to have to tell me why dear Bill Donovan would support—or at least appear to support—your bid to deprive Höttl his birth daughter, yet deny you the right to kill Höttl. With your wily ways and the right couple of snipers, putting old Werner on the south side of the sod should be a relatively simple task for you. Done-before-breakfast stuff."

"I wish I knew the story behind that, too," I said, raw-voiced. "Every time I make a pitch to end Höttl, I get a terrific tongue-lashing. They want Werner watched, and they seem to want him contained as it can be arranged, but they don't want him harmed. I'd dearly love to know why that is."

Yawning, I shut down the engines. We'd nearly lost the light. "Let's get her sea anchor down, then we'll get below and pull the shades. Biggest danger to us then should come from the stray pod of whales or some other damn ship running into us in the dark."

Jimmy sighed and clapped my back. "Ah, that's my Hector, every uttered syllable a comfort."

He began to sing then. The tune was one I knew as "The Minstrel Boy," but the lyrics weren't the ones I was familiar with:

A glorious band, the chosen few
On whom the Spirit came;
Twelve valiant saints, their hope they knew,
And mocked the cross and flame.

They met the tyrant's brandished steel,
The lion's gory mane;
They bowed their heads the death to feel:
Who follows in their train?

19

This shaking: "Hector? It's first light, Hector. You said to wake you as the sun rose."

Exhausted as I still felt, all dry-mouthed and cotton-headed, I groaned and said, "Yeah, right." I was grateful for Duff having woken me. I was having a bad dream that I was tied naked to a table and being "interrogated" by Werner Höttl and Klaus Barbie.

Duff said, "Some nightmare you were having, huh? You nearly cuffed me." She brushed the hair back from my damp forehead and then kissed each of my eyes. "I can't wait to get you to London and in a room away from the world. You make me a wanton."

"I desperately want that, too," I said, brushing her cheek with an unsteady hand. "Any luck last night with the radio?"

"We have some coordinates," Duff said. "A British submarine will meet us there. Based on our present location, or at least what you determined it to be last night, because Jimmy thinks we've dragged anchor some distance from that point, at top speed they estimate we should reach the rendezvous spot by six tonight."

"Splendid. Then all we need to do is stay alive and free about twelve more hours."

No mean feat with the German Army, Navy and her Luftwaffe potentially looking for us. Duff, I knew, knew it. But she smiled and snapped her fingers. "Easy enough."

Kidding myself a moving target is at least marginally harder to hit, I swung my legs off the bunk and stretched. My head was spinning. I said, "I feel like I've got one of the world's greatest but completely unearned hangovers."

"That's because you've hardly slept in days," Duff said. "I suppose more coffee is out of the question?"

"I can still taste the last couple of gallons in my mouth. But no, a bit more would be quite nice. I take mine black, but this morning, anything you can do to soften it would be appreciated, honey. My guts are a mess."

I stood up, very unsteady, pressing the palm of my hand to the low ceiling until I caught my balance. I figured it shouldn't take terribly long to reacquaint Jimmy with ship's steering. In the 1920s, in the Keys, Jim had shown some natural facility for piloting my pleasure boat.

Teaching a novice like Duff might take a good bit longer.

After an hour spent at the wheel with Jimmy and Duff, I'd staggered back downstairs to catch some more sleep. Marie was still asleep on an adjacent bunk. Pancho looked up at me from the floor where he was sleeping, then dropped his head again, looking sullen and sick. He clearly hated being at sea.

Poor Pancho—all the crazy things he'd seen with me these past couple of years. He must still question his own insistence to climb into my car that long-ago rainy day in the shadow of the Alps.

I collapsed on the cot, plumped my pillow, and closed my eyes. What seemed like a few seconds later, Duff was shaking me awake again, this time more roughly. "Dammit, wake up, Hector!"

"I just fell asleep," I grumbled.

"It's nearly four. We're two hours from the rendezvous site. But we have company, Hector! Two boats closing fast on us. German boats! Jimmy needs you up top, now."

Holy Christ!

Half-running, half-crawling, I rolled off the bunk and scampered up the steps to the deck.

Squinting in the light, I called up to Jimmy, "How far away?"

"Five minutes at most," he yelled down.

I hadn't often heard fear in Jimmy's voice, but I did now, and it unsettled me.

But he was out of his depth, so to speak. If we'd been on shore and armed, even pinned down, he'd have been in his element. Out here?

Jimmy said, "I've opened her all the way up, but they're sleeker and faster. Built for speed. I might have something that can help us, but I need you up here to steer, Hec."

I took the wheel at the flying bridge where I could see better. It also made me an easier target for a rifle shot, but if Jimmy didn't pull a rabbit out of the hat in the next four minutes, it would hardly matter how I died.

Jimmy scrambled to a tool compartment under a passenger deck in the pilot's cabin.

He tugged out what looked like some kind of ordnance box and something long and thick wrapped in oilcloth.

Whatever was bound up in the bundle was just slightly longer than a rifle.

"You've been keeping secrets," I said, smiling at Jimmy. "That what I think it is?"

"Probably," Jimmy said.

Duff poked her head up top, said, "Anything I can do?"

I said, "Make sure Maria and Pancho are safe below, then I need you to come up and take over at the wheel. I think I may need to give Jimmy some tactical support with this weapon of his."

The two pursuing crafts had halved their distance from us in less than two minutes. Duff called down, "Can we run this fast, this long, without burning out the engine or bearings?"

"Probably not," I called back, "but we just need a couple more minutes at this speed."

I lifted the binoculars back to my eyes. Trevor Lord was on the lead boat, waving his arms and yelling at the German sailors, probably besieging them not to shoot his stolen boat full of holes.

Jimmy had finished prepping his weapon. It looked more than lethal, but I figured it would take at least six or seven shots for Jimmy to get the range right on the Springfield rifle with its attached M1 grenade launcher. There would likely be several misses required to really get a feel for the targeting and the trick of compensating for the pitch of the ocean and the relative speeds of our respective boats.

Hell, Jimmy might have to let them come nearly alongside and then try and take them out at something like pointblank range.

The recoil from the grenade cartridge affixed to the M1 was notorious for its wicked-ass recoil, enough to seriously damage a shoulder or even the stock of the weapon. Jimmy put the butt of the rifle to the seat of one of the boat's exterior, bolted down chairs, and set the stock on side—that angle was textbook recommended firing strategy. He guessed at the distance between us and the first boat, then set the range ring.

To my astonishment and delight—Jimmy's too, I could tell—he deposited the first grenade squarely on the deck of the lead boat.

Wide-eyed, Trevor pointed at the grenade as it plunged toward the deck. None of the Nazis had the presence of mind, or the selflessness, anyway, to throw themselves on top of the grenade to muffle the imminent explosion and maybe save the boat catastrophic damage.

Evidently the grenade had also landed close by some fuel or ordnance containers; the primary grenade explosion was swiftly followed by several larger secondary blasts that vaporized the boat down to the water line.

Adios, Trevor Lord. That first explosion ripped him cleanly in half.

I figured Jimmy had the bead and could make short work of the second boat.

But his first two shots went wide.

I saw now there were men running movie cameras on the second boat.

Goddamn Werner Höttl!

Jimmy's third shot just missed the deck, but blew a hole through the hull of the second craft somewhere under water where I couldn't see. The boat rolled sharply on its side, then began to sink, nose down.

Most of the Germans scrambled to the back of the boat, just delaying their inevitable sinking into those cold, rough waters.

Jimmy loaded another grenade and started to take aim at the sinking boat.

Scowling at my raised eyebrows, Jimmy shrugged and said, "*Nazis*, Hector. Never leave 'em for seed. Anyway, it would be cruel to let even them drown, wouldn't it?"

Argue with any of that?

I couldn't. Not with the blood up. Not in that time and place, and not so fully in the moment.

20

W e'd been in London for several days. Duff had been growing increasingly morose as the time for our parting had drawn closer. Now, well into our last day together as a quartet, *quintet* if you counted our four-footed member, she'd taken Marie out on the town. She was committed to get Marie's hair "fixed," as Duff put it, as well as to finding the girl some new dresses and another doll.

I was a couple of minds about all that. It was nice they could wander the streets at something like will, but as I also pointed out to Duff, "Despite all the Nazis swarming around, Lyon was relatively intact. London's been being bombed for years. Seeing all that rubble may unhinge the child."

"Trust me to be judicious about where we go," Duff had said. "I don't want to unsettle her, you know that."

After they'd left, Jimmy and I had moseyed down to the hotel bar, where we remained. Marlene Dietrich on a radio: "See What the Boys in the Backroom Will Have."

We'd been in London nearly a week. I finally felt like I was truly catching up on all my lost sleep.

"It's finally all official," Jimmy said. "All the maddening i's are dotted and the irksome t's are feckin' crossed. We'll leave tomorrow at seven. We'll be taken home on a transport plane." He paused. "I've pulled some strings in the other direction, too. I mean for me, personally. I'm going back to my old post in Cleveland, Hector. This past week has been enough mayhem for me in-theatre. I'm no kid anymore. There's also an old pet case back home that may be heating up again. You know, Kingsbury. The Mad Butcher. I'm resuming the hunt. Afraid you'll just have to beat Hitler without me, boyo."

"I'll do my best," I said. "And I'm glad you're going home, Jim. Glad you'll be *in situ* to watch over Marie. Just in case Höttl should have any lingering connections to Buckeye Bund members or the like." I hesitated. "I can't thank you enough for making this run with me, Jimmy. It was well past above and beyond, my brother."

He waved a big hand. "None of that, Hector. Given what this will do for my sister, we're more than even."

Jimmy tapped the bar twice with his knuckles and said to the bartender, "Two double-deep shots of your finest single malt, can do?"

Watching the bartender pour our drinks, Jimmy said, "And you, Hector? Are you hell-bent on going back to France to further nettle Werner Höttl?"

"I need to play lip-service to my status as war correspondent for at least a few weeks," I said. "Besides, these past few days haven't left me with too-warm feelings about the condition of the newly-formed OSS, or about the internal security of the resistance. Often as we were sold out from somewhere while running this hellish gauntlet, I'm going to be a good while regaining my trust in the spymasters."

I accepted my whiskey and tapped glasses with Jimmy. "Besides," I said, "I'm still resenting having my hands tied where Höttl's concerned. So, I'm going to follow your example for at least a while and go back to what I do best. I'm going to write. Dispatches. Some stories and maybe another novel. I'm getting the itch for the latter."

"And you'll spend some quality time with Duff Sexton," Jimmy said.

"And I'll spend some time with Duff," I confirmed.

Jimmy smacked his lips and said, "Ah, to be in England now that war is here." He smiled and shook his head. "You just remember to obey the cautions you were urging on Duff before she ventured out onto the streets with Marie. This isn't safe territory by any stretch of the imagination. You never stray far from the cover of a bunker or a tube tunnel, right? The Blitz may be over, but those damned Germans, they're said to be experimenting with rockets."

I'd heard those rumblings, too, but in recent months, the Germans had shifted their air–attack focus. The Nazis were now bent on making so-called "Baedeker Blitzes" on tourist towns: Bath, York, Exeter and Norwich. Those were also much softer targets.

Jimmy shook his head and squeezed my arm. "When you do finally make it back to the States, I expect you to make Cleveland a first stop."

"Hell, it'll be the very first," I said.

We said our goodbyes to Jimmy and Marie at the airfield.

I scratched Pancho between the ears, surprised to find myself rather shaken to see him go. We'd traveled a lot of treacherous European ground together, that dog and I.

Marie hugged me hard. Then she wrapped her arms around the dog.

Jimmy said, "Remember, Hector—don't screw things up with this one." He pointed at Duff, then kissed her goodbye. He said, "Keep Hec north of the dirt, luv."

Jimmy thought about it, then hugged me so hard my ribs hurt. He said, "I dearly hope the world turns in such a way you get to kill Werner Höttl, up close and personal. And soon."

Two nights after we were left alone in London, three-sheets to the wind and huddled in a subway tube during a false alarm that had us all thinking the Blitzkrieg had resumed, I proposed to Duff.

She kissed me passionately, then said, "Give me a day or two to think about this, you lunatic." Her eyes searched mine. "Agreed?"

Then she went back to kissing me.

Three nights after that, during still *another* bombing run that turned out to be a another false-alarm, we decided to file for a marriage license:

"Just in case," as Duff put it.

A week later, following a romantic interlude in Leicester Square, with no threat of bombs falling, Duff and I were married.

BOOK TWO
The Death of Paris
August 1944

21

Paris, August 15. Technically, the city was still squarely in German hands. But the Nazis' grip was slipping. I had been in Paris more than a week. I was taking the battle directly to the Germans with my own ragtag recruits.

My crew included resistance fighters, fellow "foreign correspondents"—mostly Scots and scrappy Irish who'd ditched their reporters' duds and gone to war. Some soldiers and pilots cut off from their units... a handful of World War I vets and local Parisians at last emboldened to take up arms.

And we had a few very proficient, recently left leaderless, Maquis I'd dragged along with me from various previous forays into the hinterlands through late 1943 and the spring of the present year.

These motley "French Forces of the Interior" were equipped with grenades and cartridge belts. Also liberated weapons of English, German and American manufacture. They were adept at living rough. Capable hunters and fishermen. And consummate killers.

In all the heady to-and-fro, I couldn't quite decide whether they'd all chosen me to be their leader or if I'd more or less stepped into the void.

Either way, I was leading the charge.

And we were making real headway in Paris.

Still, we had our failures, too.

Today we'd just missed in our efforts to stop a convoy of several thousand prisoners being shipped to Buchenwald.

On the other hand, the Paris Métro, Gendarmerie and police had simultaneously called a strike. The postal workers were said to be planning to follow suit in the morning.

It felt like the momentum to free Paris was *mostly* on our side.

All the while, as I directed my irregulars and fought in skirmishes and hand-to-hand tussles in the streets, I was also hunting one particular man, and trying very hard to avoid another. The first was a sworn enemy; the latter, a former friend.

My ex-pal, a frighteningly capable man when he set his mind to such things, was said to be closing in on Paris with his own guerilla unit, actually running a good distance ahead of Leclerc and his forces. Through channels, I heard that after taking and holding Rambouillet until our boys could take over, he was now boasting he was going to liberate the Ritz. I had no reason to doubt he could do just that, and pull it off with grand panache.

Soon, it seemed, we'd all be here in the City of Light once more.

Hector Lassiter.

Werner Höttl.

Ernest Hemingway.

Paris was far too small for three such as us.

Bernard Reboul was one of my Paris resistance boys.

In an alley not far from the Rue Vavin where I lived in 1924, he said, "The Germans still holding out have been given orders to plant explosives in key locations all over the city. Hitler wants to decimate Paris, to burn it as his forces leave it. It seems if he can't have it—"

"Then he means to annihilate Paris," I finished for him. "Word of that ambition has come our way from many directions. How are you doing in the counter-efforts on that front?"

Bernard scratched his unshaven cheek. He was pretty ripe all on his own, but his clothes also stank of stale cigarette smoke. He reeked of cordite, and, yes, of dried blood. Bernard was a teacher before the fall of Paris, an instructor in military history. From an apartment somewhere above I heard music, *Le bar de l'escadrille.*

"Some more circumspect of his followers, already anticipating the war crimes trial to come, are stalling and some fewer of those even refusing," Bernard said. "Others are at least tipping us in time to disarm the explosives they've placed."

"Excellent," I said. "Stay at it, brother."

Bernard dragged a hand across his sweating forehead. "There is, however, one man, a German named Werner Höttl. He seems quite committed to fighting to the bitter end. He's also some kind of filmmaker for Hitler. He's been dispatched to help orchestrate, then to record the destruction of Paris. He's to capture it all on film for posterity. I know it sounds utterly mad, but I believe it to be true."

I could believe that well enough. Höttl was well capable of all that.

"Höttl and I have crossed paths over many years," I said. "He's a fanatic of the first water, believe that. Burning Paris and filming it would be right up his alley. Keep me informed on anything you pick up on him. Nothing is too small to interest me about that son of a bitch. I'll let you know what I hear from my sources. My side doesn't want him dead for some reason. But I have different aims. We just can't leave any fingerprints if we get a killing shot at him, do you understand me? Are we clear?"

"Fully," Bernard said. "Between us, perhaps, we can do it." More music from somewhere above, *Reviens mon amour.* Bernard hesitated, then said, "But if I may speak frankly, I fear for your duration in the final onslaught, Hector. I may be speaking out of school here, but you need to know that you are in some jeopardy of a very different kind. Rumblings are even reaching me and I am really nobody."

That got my stomach going. "What kind of rumblings?"

"Rumors that you may be in trouble with your own government. Your fellow reporters are raising issues about you and how you're helping us. They say you're callously breaking the rules of conduct for war correspondents. I tell you this because you are a valuable ally to me. I warn you because you need to take steps to look, well, to look somehow less *engaged* on our behalf. You need, at least cosmetically, to appear that way to your journalistic peers."

"Message received," I said. "Thank you for the warning, Bernard."

Journalistic peers? Screw them ten ways from yesterday. Yellow voyeurs. *Cowards.* In times like these, journalism was too often a hack's and a coward's sanctuary.

I'd heard many similar rumors about me over the past few years, of course. But it did seem these past couple of months I heard them more often and from more directions. If they'd reached into the ranks of the resistance I figured I might be in real trouble.

For nearly four days, I'd been bunking at 27 rue de Fleurus, Gertrude Stein's long-languishing salon. Enterprising Nazis were trying to steal art for themselves as their cause failed around them, looking after their post-Third Reich retirement needs, I reckoned.

In the rush to get Gertrude and Alice out of Paris in 1940, their apartment had been left more or less intact and in the care of friends. The arrangement worked well enough until the European war's tide decisively turned.

And, as she'd noted so many years before, Gertrude's other friends just weren't the scrappy types.

As the Germans' grip on Paris faltered, word had come my way some Nazis were eying Miss Stein's collection of modernist paintings as easy and vindictive pickings.

So I'd moved in to play watchdog. Me, and a dislocated Maquis named Robert Lécussan. Robert was small, smart and chillingly feral.

As I slept in a bed, Robert was most often to be found bunked on the floor of the salon, clutching a carbine and surrounded by grenade boxes, liberated firearms and all those modernist works of art he frequently disparaged.

I rapped lightly on the door three times and said, "Robert, don't you damned shoot me—it's Lassiter."

He opened the door a crack, confirmed I was me, then stepped aside so I could slide in. "Any problems while I was away, Robert?"

"Just a woman who came by. I sent her away."

"Christ, Robert, women we aren't worried about. What did this one look like?"

"Too tall. Pale skin and reddish-blond hair. Blue eyes. Some might call her beautiful."

"And her name is Duff," I said. "Right?"

"That's right!"

"You turned away my wife."

He shrugged. "Well, she will probably come back then, yes?"

What a chucklehead. Lethally effective, but decidedly not a thinker.

I shrugged off my coat. "You've been a while cooped up in this joint without a break, Robert. I'm going to be housebound a day or two, I think. Come back tomorrow evening, about seven. Between now and then, indulge yourself, old pal. Maybe think about finding a bath or a shower. Frankly, you'd be hard-pressed to sneak up on an unfriendly smelling like you do now."

He pulled his shirt collar up to his nose, sniffed, frowned, then shrugged. "You're certain you can spare me?"

"No worries," I said. "See you tomorrow night, *mon ami*."

Say this much for Duff: never the expected entrance with my darling.

There was this determined rap against the door, then, when she heard the floorboards squeak on the other side of the panel, she said, "I'm pointing a gun at the door and any shot can more than go through it and you, little man. So open the door so I can wait on my husband."

"Don't shoot, honey," I said. "It's me, Hector. I'm opening the door, and I'm doing it slowly now."

She wasn't bluffing: Duff was holding twin forty-fives. Given the flimsiness of Gertrude's front door, blowing holes through the thing with those automatics would have been easy enough.

I said, "You can put those away, love. We have the place to ourselves for the moment. I utterly surrender."

Duff kissed me and then slid past. "My bags are outside," she said.

As I bent to pick them up, she said, "That guy who sent me packing earlier, who is that psycho? He definitely qualifies for the Rogues Gallery spectrum of your burgeoning KA file."

"Maquis, named Robert. He's a great watchdog, and that's about all I can say for him on the good side," I said. "He is lacking in the social graces. Hell, any graces."

"He's lacking in any human qualities so far as I can tell," she said. "And hygiene, too. I could smell him through the crack under the door."

I put her suitcases down inside the door and locked up. We kissed again, then Duff began exploring the painting-filled main room. "So, this is the famous salon of Miss Stein," she said. "I'm not a writer or painter and even I've heard the legends of this place. How many times did you have to face Stein, here?"

"*Je ne suis pas certain.* Dozens, maybe." I followed Duff around as she surveyed the paintings. "Only my first couple of times here produced those kinds of exchanges with Miss Stein. You know—the storied, challenging recitations and the like. The insults. Only one of those, the first, I think, would even rise to the level of her more legendary confrontations. I stood about there, a callow kid from Texas with no high school diploma and dreams of writing prose. I was leaning hard on a cane with a bum leg. Yet I made the cut with Gertrude pretty swiftly, relative to most others. Alice, on the other hand? She's never quite come around to my charms."

"She's a lesbian," Duff said. She kissed me again, then continued exploring the salon. Hands on hips, Duff considered the famous portrait of Gertrude as painted by Picasso, hanging over Gertrude's favorite chair-cum-throne. The Miss Stein in the portrait looked engaged, intense... argumentative.

Duff said, "It captures her?"

"For all I know, it may have shaped her," I said. "That portrait predates my knowing Miss Stein by many years. Think that thing was painted about Ought-five or six. I was just a little boy back in Galveston, then. I came in with this bloody century."

In the portrait, Gertude still had long, dark hair, piled high—a far cry from the salt-and-pepper, Romanesque bowl-cut she was sporting the last time I saw her in 1940.

"All these paintings," Duff said, "it's amazing. And it's remarkable they've so far survived occupation."

"Friends have watched over the apartment. I moved in a few days ago when I heard fortune-hunting Nazis were mulling making a run at this place."

"So you and the psychopath 'Robert' are the new guardians of Modernist art. The world is now truly crazy. What would Gertrude think?"

"Figure we'll find out soon enough when the Germans are gone in a few weeks, and Miss Stein and her fearsome little friend can return. Good news is, I've gotten Robert out of here until tomorrow night."

Duff stroked my cheek. "Dreamy. You doing any real writing, Hec?"

"I've started to write again, yes. A novel about some of this. Mostly looking to damage some people's reputations under thinly veiled fictional guises. I've decided that as an author it's my sacred obligation to serve as caretaker of my enemies' memories."

Duff smiled fondly and shook her head. "So what else is new? I'm going to be hungry, soon. I suppose your sending your little crazy man away means we're hostage to this place until tomorrow night?"

"Hostage isn't the word I'd choose. And I'm making dinner for us. I've stocked the place, and very well. Good food, tasty baked goods. Some excellent liquor. That's no mean feat with all the rationing and siphoning-off of goods by the occupation."

She smiled. "I like this idea very much. Let's stay right here and pamper ourselves."

I broke the seal on a bottle of single malt and poured a couple of glasses. I poured a little water on top of the scotch to open up the taste. I said, "So, where have you been since Easter?"

"Probably easier to tell you where I haven't been," Duff said. She stirred the ice around with an alabaster finger. "And I really shouldn't tell you either of those things, even as pillow talk. It's all classified. Please don't get offended that I can't confide in you."

"I understand. What have you been doing generally then?"

"Can't say that, either," she said. "But for me, this is all winding down. I've already started to arrange travel papers. I've been kicked loose. I'm ready to go home."

"To the States, you mean?"

"Yes, to New Mexico or Arizona, I think—to scout properties for our house." She wrapped her arm around my waist and rested her head on my shoulder. "I'd ask you what you've been up to, but I'm afraid I know already. Frankly, I'm scared for you, Hec."

Something there in her voice. I said, "Höttl, you mean? I've weathered his storms before, no worries there."

"Not the kind of problem I'm talking about," she said. "You've got other worries. Maybe bigger worries than that crazy German."

"What do you mean, darlin'?"

"Three days ago, I was ordered in by SHAEF." She bit her lip. "I was ordered in to be questioned about you."

SHAEF: the Supreme Headquarters Allied Expeditionary Force.

I swallowed hard, then took another shot of what the Scots call the water of life. "The goddamn other reporters," I said, "they've raised some kind of ruckus?"

Duff sighed. "Exactly. They say you're compromising their protected status as war correspondents by taking up arms and playing soldier as a few have put it. Some people on Patton's staff are listening, darling. They're listening hard."

It would be goddamn Patton's staff, wouldn't it?

"Jesus Christ." For the first time, I sat down in Gertrude's favorite chair—always had wondered how the sucker felt. It was not worth the waiting for. But I couldn't really focus on that, just now. I reached up and took Duff's hand and pulled her onto my lap.

"I'm between a rock and a hard place," I said. "Can't let the damned correspondents know I'm really OSS, and the OSS can't admit they're using a journalist as an operative."

This knowing look. She wasn't buying it, not a lick. Duff ran her fingers through her strawberry blond hair, then traced my lips with her fingertips. "True so far as it goes, darling. But rumbles through the OSS also have it you're playing soldier, Hec. Going rogue and far outside the sphere of orders you might have, explicit or implicit, from Wild Bill to spy. They say you're a kind of *de facto* guerilla leader."

"That's... overstating it."

Duff cupped my chin in her palm. "Make me believe that, Hector."

"Höttl's here in Paris, Duff. He's one of Hitler's point men. That twisted cocksucker is charged not just with helping to incinerate this city when the Nazis inevitably have to abandon it, but also to film the place being destroyed. He means to turn the destruction of Paris into some kind of damn movie."

"That's some cinema Hitler will never see," Duff said. "He's already beaten. There's just nobody honest left in his bunker to whisper that truth in his ear." She brushed a comma of hair from over my right eyebrow. "Höttl aside, word is you're still more than pushing the line, Hec. They're going to haul you in and interrogate you. At least I've been led to believe that's so."

"To what end would they do that to me?"

"For a hearing," Duff said. "A hearing to determine if there are grounds for a court martial."

Well, *damn*.

I squeezed the bridge of my nose. "How long until they order me to appear?"

"Things are too busy right now to make you a priority," she said, wrapping her arms around my neck. "The thought is we'll take Paris back in a week, two at most."

"Sounds about right." I ground my teeth.

"Yes. And then they will have time to deal with you. Probably sometime in late September or early October."

"Goddamn it to hell," I said. "I'm just trying to help win and end this war."

"But you're doing that masquerading as a reporter," Duff said. "Look at it from the professional journalists' perspective. You carrying firearms and using your credentials to function as a spy and soldier undermines their protected status. You can't really blame them. Your actions threaten their lives if they're caught and presumed to be spies or secret soldiers like you."

"Sure I can blame them," I said. "I blame them every time I see these so-called journalists out on the street or in the fields, writing and taking pictures or rolling cameras instead of reaching down to pull one of our wounded boys to safety. Instead of picking up a dropped machine gun and strafing those German bastards back after they've shot to death a few of our boys as these *correspondents* look on. But let a journalist take a stray to the heart or the head? Holy Christ, then these reporters came all over outraged. Then not all corpses are created equal. I say we're Americans first and writers second."

"Well, for what it's worth, Hec, you're not the only one in this jam. Your former friend, Hemingway, he's in the same fix. Almost identical circumstances. He'll be pulled in, too. Same timetable. Maybe you two should patch things up, finally. You might end up in some room together, after all."

"Room? You mean jail cell." I closed my eyes and tipped my head back. "Hem and I are finished, and I mean forever. Stuff happened in 1937 between us that can't easily be taken back. Neither of us is what you call the forgiving or forgetting type. And what a Christ-awful mess I'm in."

Duff hauled herself off my lap. She walked around behind Gertrude's throne and began to massage my shoulders. "I've made some inquiries. Inside the OSS and inside the Inspector General's office. Even among a few friendly staffers I know of Patton's. Shared opinion is you should deny everything, Hec. Don't try to explain it or to rationalize it. Just deny everything and brass it out. You should disclaim everything they claim. That, and keep your nose clean between now and then, since people are actively looking for evidence now. Don't feed the fire."

"Fat chance of me laying low," I said. "Look around, this is practically the end-game so far as the European theatre is concerned."

"Exactly, and damn it, Hector, you've had more than your share of adventures. Sit out these last couple of weeks. We'll murder the days together in bed. The brass does not want Americans getting any glory, not an iota, in the liberation of Paris. Leclerc was handpicked for this honor five months ago. Quasi-celebrities like you and Hemingway undermine the public relations boys' plans to let the French liberate the French. Or at least to have it look as if they did that."

"But I need to kill Werner Höttl," I said.

"Hector, I know he's your longstanding *bête noire*. One of several I can count. But the OSS still wants Höttl alive."

"Any better sense of why that is?"

"Still a mystery," Duff said. "But the big boys want him left alone, so there it is."

"Can't happen," I said. "I need to kill this man, and I'm going to do it, regardless of the cost to myself."

Duff stopped massaging my shoulders. "Why? Why do you so want Höttl dead?"

"Because he sent me a message a few days ago. A letter, actually. Sucker put it in writing."

"A letter?"

"It's there on the mantle," I said. "He sent it to me via one of my friends, from the old days. I went by Shakespeare and Company, the American bookstore that was kind of a second home to all of us back in the great old days in Paris. The store space itself is empty now. The books are all in hiding from the Nazis. But Sylvia Beech still lives above the shop. She's Jewish, and therefore vulnerable. Höttl rightly guessed I'd check on her. That I'd watch over Syl during these treacherous last few days as the Nazis retreat."

Duff nodded. "Höttl threatened this Sylvia?"

"No, she was just the delivery mechanism, so to speak. Read the letter there, you'll see."

Duff squeezed my shoulder a last time, then headed over to the fireplace. She scooped up the letter, unfolded it. I watched her read. I watched as her jaw tightened, as her cheeks flushed. She looked up from the letter, blue eyes filled with hate.

"Threatening my life is a big so what," I said. I poured myself a fresh drink. "Offering to spare it in return for turning Marie over to him, or at least divulging her whereabouts?" I shook my head. "To hell with Höttl. I'll kill him first, whatever its costs me."

"He *is* blunt. Your life or Marie's." Duff couldn't conceal the hate in her voice.

"As if that's really a choice," I said. "Only question I have is if he's truly that obsessive, or just that delusional."

Duff arched an eyebrow. "What? Deluded enough to think that you'd actually disclose Marie's location so he won't kill you?"

"Nah. That he's so delusional as to still be chasing this child to save face when he has so many other things of moment on his plate."

I drained my drink and poured another. I said, "Hitler's all but through, yet Höttl seems to think he still needs to cover up his fathering a Jewish child. Hell, Höttl should be worried about his forthcoming trial for war crimes, yet he's acting like he still needs to maintain appearances with goddamn Hitler. Where's the logic in any of that?"

"I don't know." Duff put the letter back on the mantle. She sounded soul sick. "If you do kill Höttl, it could really cost you, Hector. You'd be directly disobeying orders."

"I know."

"Do you know where to find Werner Höttl, Hector?"

"Not yet, but I've got my people working on it. For sons of bitches like Höttl, Paris is shrinking by the hour. He can't stay hidden much longer."

"Your people." Duff poured herself a whisky. "I'm going to pretend I didn't just hear you confess you are running your own crew here. I'm going to do that just in case I'm hauled into your eventual hearing."

I stood up and stretched. "They can't make spouses testify against one another, Duff."

"Not back home in a proper court of law, sure," she said. "But consider where we are. And it's going to be a military procedure. I have this terrible suspicion they can do anything they decide they want to do once they've got you in that room and in that chair."

She handed me her shot glass. "You finish it off. I thought I'd cultivated a taste for single malt back there fleeing Lyon. Seems if I did, I've lost it again."

I drained her glass and placed it on the mantle. "You simply have to stay practiced."

She said, "This dinner you're preparing? It can keep for a bit?"

"Sure. Why?"

"It's been a very long time, Hec. Much too long. I need you."

We kissed. I said, "Likewise. Let's go upstairs."

Duff wrinkled her nose. "In Gertrude Stein's bed? Really?"

"No worries," I said. "I bought new sheets."

22

Duff stretched and sat up. I ran my fingers down her bare back and squeezed her hip. She slipped on a silky and slinky diaphanous gown that left nothing to the imagination.

She ran her fingers through her tangled hair and said, "You're sure your little psychopath isn't coming back?"

"Like I said, I've given him tonight and tomorrow off. He was getting stir crazy."

"That twerp had no distance to travel to crazy, Hector."

"Well, he was itchy to get out of here."

"Yes, to draw blood, no doubt." Duff raked her fingers through my chest hair. "I've thought hard about this," she said. "I'm now making it my mission to keep you in this apartment, in this bed if necessary, until Paris is liberated. I'm going to keep you out of harm's way, and well away from other kinds of mischief, until this stuff with the brass blows over or goes away. I'm gonna keep you here 'til Miss Stein sets us out."

I took her hand and kissed its back. "With you as company, the other stuff I can probably sit out or safely watch from a window. But if I get a line on Höttl, I'm striking."

"His death cannot be traced to you, Hector." She pressed her hand to her belly and her stomach growled. "I can't argue effectively on an empty stomach."

I scooped up my pants and shirt. "Then we must eat."

I freshened our wine. Duff said, "It's been two very long years. Any word from Jimmy about how Marie is doing?"

"No." I jammed the cork back in the bottle. "Jimmy and I agreed upon last parting that until this war is over and Höttl's dead or on the final run in some backwater this side of the ocean, we'd not contact one another. Neither of us wanted to risk even a tenuous link that might somehow lead Höttl to Jimmy and then to Marie. When I get back to the States, I'll beeline to Cleveland. But always checking my trail along the way."

She smiled. "We will beeline to Cleveland, you mean. I miss them both, terribly."

"That's what I meant of course," I said. "We will make that trip together."

"I'm serious about keeping you here these next days, Hector. I'll do it at gunpoint, if necessary. Handcuff you to a stout pipe, if I have to."

"I know you mean it, and I'll try to obey," I said. "You have properly spooked me with this court martial stuff. Hell, someone else mentioned to me ahead of you I might be in trouble on that front. If that much chatter is in the air, figure I better help myself by staying within those damned correspondents' lines going forward."

I sipped some wine and bit my lip. "But I can't lose any shot I might get at Höttl. If he shows himself, I'm going to strike at him, one way or another."

Duff shook her head. "This so-called crew of yours, Robert for instance, let them do it. You don't have to personally deliver the *coup de grace*, do you?"

"One of mine doing the deed works plenty fine for me, too," I said. "Hell, if I thought I could pay some of Höttl's own flunkies to turn on him, I'd happily pay real money for it to end that way, too."

"I feel better for you saying it," Duff said. "And I think I even believe you." She raised her glass and looked out the window. "You know, I don't really know this city that well. Many other cities in France I feel fairly at home in, but this one I've never gotten to explore. Soon as we can travel the streets safely, you must show me your Paris."

"We'll do it," I said. "Provided the goddamn Nazis don't blow it up first."

Duff gestured at Picasso's portrait of Gertrude Stein. "Picasso, where's he as all this bloody madness rolls along? Did he retreat back to Spain?"

I smiled. "Picasso just visits our world from time to time, I think. The city's fall, the occupation and the pending liberation? It's immaterial to him. By all accounts, Pablo just keeps his head down and continues to work in his studio, painting, sculpting,... Eating and drinking and making love to his wives and models. History is just another thing that happens around Picasso. Hell, the very business of living is the same way for Pablo, I think—a distraction between masterpieces. He's an artist in the purest, most terrible sense."

"As opposed to novelists who write books between revolutions, wars and chasing killer surrealists?" Duff smiled over the rim of her glass. "You know, men who blur the lines between their blood-and-thunder lives and literary productions?"

Not subtle. I said, "Picasso has to fill a single canvas at a time, and I've watched the son of a bitch do it in twenty, thirty-minutes and then sell each of the things for as much as I might net for an advance against a novel. But that novel? I've got three-hundred, maybe four-hundred pages of blank paper to fill. To do that, I have to feed the muse."

"Ah-hah."

"You sound less than convinced, Duff."

"I'm still trying to get a handle on you in some ways, Hector. Even if we have been married for a couple of years, because of this damned war we haven't spent that much time together." She smoothed the tablecloth with her hand. "I'm trying to decide how to put this."

I reached over and shook her foot under the table. "Just say it, Duff, that'd be best. I'm durable. I love you and can take it."

"Okay. The man who lives what he writes and writes what he lives. That's what they call you. Which half of that is true?"

"Right." I tried to shrug it off. "I have to choose?"

Duff was solemn. "Someday, I'm afraid you might have to do just that."

There was machine gun fire nearby; the sound of an explosion and screaming.

"Keep your butt in that chair," Duff said. "That's someone else's worry now." She looked around. "Stein have a phonograph or a radio? I'll find us some music and turn it up extra loud. Let's try really hard to forget we're in a goddamn war-zone."

23

I gave Robert a longer leash, let him have five days away from Gertrude's salon. At the end of that time, he seemed less edgy, but it hadn't helped his hygiene a lick.

Me? After five days cooped up, even five deliciously carnal days with Duff, it was harder and harder to keep from venturing out.

Sunday, the twentieth of August: the fight to liberate Paris was truly underway.

I sat out Saturday, but by Sunday afternoon, I was crawling walls to see the Germans lose the city. Hell, to *pitch in* toward that end.

Duff cursed and said I was making her edgy with my "goddamn infernal pacing." She said, "If you go out there, even for an hour, I know you won't go out as a correspondent. You'll pull your irregulars together and go after Nazis. I know it. You'll just dig your hole deeper with SHAEF."

"In this mayhem? Not bloody likely. This might be the one time in this war when I can truly act with impunity."

Duff looked at me, clearly exasperated. "If you go out there, you have to come back here for dinner and sleep here every night. And you have to bathe before bed. And that psycho, Robert—he's professional?"

"Surprisingly, one of the best."

"Then get him back here to protect me. Him and two more just as good. And you be circumspect. You must be very extra careful."

"I can do all that. I will do all that. Anything else?"

"Find a way to do it without leaving anything that can be traced back to you, but kill Werner Höttl. For Marie and Jimmy's sake, I've also decided I want that man dead."

In the courtyard of Gertrude Stein's building, Charles Delattre said, "Bernard is very busy now. As to Robert, I couldn't get him to bathe. But in deterrence to your lady friend, I liberated a bottle of the Prince Machiavelli cologne."

I offered him a cigarette and fired him up with my Zippo. I said, "Charles, you can speak French with me, and you can speak it with Duff, particularly as your English is still a little, let's call it faltering."

He looked genuinely hurt. "Where did I—your word—falter?"

"Deference, not deterrence. But you could also have said, 'Out of respect to your lady friend.'"

He nodded, glum. "Any other?"

"Prince Matchabelli cologne, not Machiavelli." Although I could imagine colorful ad campaign for the latter scent: "*Dominate* your woman!"

Charles stared at his feet. "I can only masterise the language by speaking it."

"Master the language," I said. "Mastery is indeed the goal. Stick with it, old pal. Just let Duff know, up front, if you want her to correct you if you step wrong again. Hell, she may even be able to coach you a bit."

"I appreciate... that, Mr. Lassiter."

"Right." I slapped his arm. "Just keep my lady safe, and we're even. And don't let Robert scare her, *oui?*"

He winked. "No fears. I will retain him."

"Restrain him. Great. I'll be back in time for dinner."

Bernard said, "You've been sorely missed. We're in a different game, now. I'll confess, I feel out of my depth. Fighting in the streets like this? My God."

"We're all out of our depth, now," I said. "There's never been a time like this one." I read his expression, added, "I know, I know. Every generation thinks they're the first to discover the world, but this is far from my first war and I'm here to say, it's a *très* different beast."

"It is a different kind of enemy," he said. "Evil personified."

"On that note, do you have any word on Höttl?"

"It's very confused, Hector. Chaotic."

"They call it the fog of war for a reason, Bernard. Just please stay at it. Höttl is a must for me."

Bernard squeezed my shoulder. "For me as well. Consider what this man is trying to do to my city. He means to plunder and then to decimate it. And to film all that as it happens. It's vile and insane."

"Your men know to look for cameras?"

"They do, but with so many real journalists polluting the town, it's vexing."

Real journalists: that dug at me in an irksome way.

I followed Bernard up several flights of stairs and onto the roof of a building overlooking Rue de Regard. I accepted the binoculars from Bernard. He'd done some work on them himself, touching up what he could with flat-black paint to reduce surfaces that might catch light and so draw fire.

After a blurry look through the binoculars, I adjusted the focus pin on the field glasses. "How hard are the Germans fighting?"

Bernard struck a match; I smelled cigarette smoke. "It varies, wildly," he said. "There are a few die-hards, as one would expect. But the others? We have some who can't surrender fast enough. Some others are fighting just enough to be protected if the battle should by some miracle go the Germans' way. But it's token resistance."

I didn't want to appear weak or too worried, but I said, "I've heard from some others a bit of the same you warned me about, the brass snooping around after me."

Bernard exhaled and said, "Yes, I've heard some more since we last talked. It's a serious thing, I think."

"The prisoners, how are they being held? Where?"

"Hector, we have no facilities for prisoners. I know you cannot be tied to any of this, now, my brother. From this point forward, I think you know me as a guerilla leader who gives you leads for your dispatches. I think these men are all *my* men, operating under my sole orders. And so the prisoners they take and what happens to those prisoners are my responsibility. Do you agree with all this?"

I thought about all of it. After a time, I said, "Yes, that's how it is. Thank you, Bernard."

He nodded. "I will of course alert you to any new developments regarding Höttl."

"Again, I thank you."

Bernard took back the binoculars. "It is less than a nothing. Forget it now and play—no, *be* the good reporter. We can handle this ourselves, Hector. It's nearly over, whether the Germans think so or not."

I pointed down at the street, "That man there, the German at the back of the crowd of six. Is that a movie camera he's holding?"

Swiveling, Bernard adjusted the focus pin on the field glasses. "Yes, that is a camera. Looks rather elaborate to me. I mean, not just some German with a personal camera making little movies for the folks back home. It looks a professional piece of film equipment to me."

He picked up his radio and rattled off some instructions in French and in English. To me Bernard said, "It may be some time, but we will try and take that one prisoner, Hector. We'll see if we can draw more from him in the event he is tied to Höttl's film project here in the city."

"I would very much like to be present for that talk," I said. "Somewhere private, if you can arrange it."

Bernard chuckled. "Hector, for these kinds of talks, we always seek private places. Soundproof, too, if at all possible." He went back to watching the man with the camera. He said, "Pitched floors and a center drain are also a boon for such," he smiled meanly and said, "...*discussions*."

24

It took every bit of forty-five minutes to make what should have been a ten-minute walk back to Gertrude's salon. There were sandbag barricades to leap, checkpoints to pass through after flashing my correspondent's ID, street skirmishes to skirt. And there were other war correspondents to try and placate or to dodge.

Some stray machine gun fire took out the window of a grocery behind me. A young woman was exiting the store. I grabbed her around the waist and pulled her to the ground, rolling half-atop her as the machine gun fire strafed overhead, peppering us with more glass and woodchips.

Someone from a floor above us returned fire on the German machine gunner. Screams followed and then the shooting stopped. Someone yelled in French, "All clear! The goddamn Bosch is dead!"

People began rising from the pavement. A few cheered. I hauled myself up and offered a hand to the girl, pulling her to her feet. I scooped up her grocery bag and handed it back to her. "Where are you headed, darlin'?"

Straightening her clothes, in a state of mild shock, the girl muttered an address. "You're on my way," I said. "I'll see you safely there."

She eyed my correspondent's insignia. "You're a reporter; you're not even armed. I don't think you can be much protection. But thank you for saving me from the gunfire."

I took her arm. "I am a reporter, but under these conditions, I've decided to bend the rules, just a bit. I do carry a gun. Now let's get you home. I hope you have enough in that bag to last you a few days. It may be another week before it's safe to venture out for such shopping trips."

Two blocks away from the scene of the machine-gunning, it was a much different story. I'd reached a neighborhood taken and held by resistance fighters. There was much drinking, partying… even a couple fornicating on a balcony in full view to drunken cheers.

Some of the Parisian collaborators had been dragged out into the street. The men were being beaten; one got himself shot.

The female collaborators were roundly spit upon, then their heads shaved.

Three men had a man in a German uniform on the ground. They were kicking and beating on him. I got a look at the bloodied man's face and was startled to recognize him. It was Frederick Schmidt, the German who had saved me and Marie when we were caught outside that church two years before— the one who had slit his fellow soldier's throat to give Marie and I a chance for escape. His was a face burned into my brain.

He looked at me for a moment, then I saw him make the connection, too.

I drew my gun and got out the right credentials for this dicey moment. I hauled one of Schmidt's attackers off him and said, "Allied intelligence. This man is my prisoner. Stop before you hurt his head. He knows things I need to know."

One of the bastard's got in a last kick, despite my orders to the contrary. I zeroed in on that one. "Help him to his feet," I said nodding at the prone German. "You can help me take him to headquarters," I said to the Frenchman. I sized him up with my eyes: he'd do.

None too gently, the Frenchman helped Frederick to his feet. I motioned with my pistol. "This way." I led the two down an alley, then pistol-whipped the Frenchman.

To Frederick I said, "One good turn…" I pocketed my gun and then bent to task and pulled off the Frenchman's shoes. "He's about your size, so the clothes should fit," I said.

Wincing and gripping his ribs, Frederick helped me strip the man, then wadded his German uniform into a trashcan. As he dressed, I sorted through my various documents. I found the ones I was looking for. I passed the sheaf of papers to Frederick. "My government made these and they are excellent. They'll get you through at the border. Between here and there, you're Günther Hess."

Frederick nodded and I helped him on with the man's coats. "Those ribs broken or just bruised, you think?"

"Not broken," he said. "I don't think so anyway." We shook hands. He said, "You've saved yourself a trip to Germany for that drink. We're more than even… *Lassiter*, wasn't it? I've thought about that day outside the church, often."

"That's right Frederick. I've thought a lot about that day, too. Stay alive, old pal."

Duff padded into Gertrude's bathroom, wearing a silk robe. I was in the midst of my second Duff-ordered bath. She handed me a glass of whisky over ice, then shrugged off her robe. Nude, she pinned up her strawberry blond hair. All curves and milky skin, she slid into the hot water with me.

She said, "So, how is it out there, heady? Intoxicating?"

I shook my head, savoring the whisky's first burn. "Few days from now, it may be all that. But just now? Now it's very messy and chaotic. A very bloody Sunday."

"Could I get out to see a little? I have the urge."

"I'd resist it," I said. "Hell, it's crazy enough, I'm loathe to go back out there just now. Barring something new on the Höttl front, I think I'm staying in for a few days. On one street you have Parisians partying like the war is all but over. A street over from that, you might find diehard Nazis still rounding up Jews. Most of the Germans are just sort of exercising due diligence, laying down random fire but not with much zeal or intent. Those know it's the endgame. Despite all that, it still makes for a hell of a lot of bullets zinging around out there. What do the British call it? Death by misadventure? In Paris, as things stand now, that's an all too real possibility."

I savored some more whisky and tipped my head back against the tub's rim "On the trip back here, I had three Germans try to surrender to me, despite my vaunted correspondent's insignia."

"What'd you do with them?"

"Directed them to some loitering resistance types, who probably promptly shot them."

Duff's hand was suddenly there, under all the suds. "Like you said, Hector, some Sabbath." She stood up and handed me a towel. "We have a while before dinner is ready," she said. "I have sinful notions about how to pass that time."

25

On Wednesday, the 23rd, I was again drawn out of Gertrude's salon, lured away from Duff.

One of "my" Maquis, Jules Poincaré, excitedly pounded on Gertrude's door, shouting, "*Grand Capitaine! Grand Capitaine,* I come with news!"

Through the door I yelled back, "It's Hector, remember? I have no commission and no title. I need you to remember that if asked by anyone."

Duff rolled her eyes at me.

I opened the door a crack, confirmed it was just Jules and his battered Sten gun. I let him in.

"Bernard sent me," he said, smiling and awkwardly bowing a bit at Duff. "The man with the camera, he tells me to say, we have him!"

I could suddenly feel my pulse in my ears. "Höttl? You captured Werner Höttl?"

Now Jules looked dejected. "*Non,* the man with the camera you spied from the roof a few days ago."

"Well… that's good news, too," I said. Reaching for my correspondent's coat, I said, "He's talking?"

"Not yet, but probably soon," Jules said.

I swallowed hard. I'd have not had Duff hear that last. And heard it she had.

Coldly, she said, "Give me a moment before you leave, Hector. I may be able to scare-up some needle-nosed pliers in case you want to personally pull out this prisoner's remaining fingernails for persuasion."

"I'm not gonna do that," I said. "Jesus, I'm no torturer. And neither are the boys. These Germans need to be focused on war crimes' trials and the like. It doesn't profit them to be closed-mouth now. I'm counting on this one cheerfully cooperating."

"Perhaps I should come along," Duff said. "I think I should tag along to provide counterbalance in case your boys haven't been so well-behaved." She nodded at Jules' feet. The tops of his brown boots were bloodstained, actually crisscrossed with patterns of blood spray.

"Traveling the streets is even more unsafe by night," I said to her. "Technically, we're still under German curfew, you know."

"Then you could wait until morning to go, Hector." Duff reached for my lapels, as if to strip me of my coat.

Jules looked agitated. He said, "The camera man, he is not in good health. It's true. And he says he will only talk to you, boss." He fidgeted, then added, "Bernard said you should hurry." He looked at his own feet. "He said you should really hurry."

He smiled uncertainly at me, then nodded again at Duff. "I didn't know you had a friend here, *Grand Capitaine*. I mean, Monsieur Hector. I mean, Hector."

I opened the door for him, urged him through it. He backed out, bowing again at Duff, clutching tightly to his

Sten gun. Through the closing crack, I said, "Give us a minute, Jules. I'll meet you in the courtyard. I need to talk to my wife, first."

Duff said, "Better you just follow him out there, Hector. You told him you'd meet him, so you've made up your mind to go along. Time spent talking to me is time wasted. It seems to me your prisoner—or rather, your boys' prisoner—is bleeding to death from whatever bloody things they've done to him."

Jules was choking down a cigarette, sweating in the moonlight. He saw me coming, said, "Monsieur Lassiter, I truly am sorry for causing trouble with your wife."

"I just need to not drag this out, Jules. Where are we going, and how far?" I pulled out my own cigarette and a lighter. "Please say it's close."

"It's very close. Rue de Vaugirard."

"I blew a stream of smoke and slipped off my jacket, hooking it over the crook of my index finger. It was far too muggy to be running around in the thing tonight. I said, "Lead on, MacDuff."

"What?"

"Show me the way, Jules," I said. "And let's do make it brisk."

Two Maquis dressed in ragtag bits of foraged uniforms stood sentry outside a shuttered café at the corner of Rue Saint-Placide. Jules said to them, "We are still in time, *n'est-ce pas?*"

One of the Maquis said, "It would seem so. They've hauled no corpses out, recently." They waved us inside with their carbines.

Moans of pain from behind a door I presumed led to the kitchen. I found I had no appetite to see the state of the man they'd been working over. I called out, "Bernard? Come out here, pal."

Bernard backed through the swinging kitchen door, wiping his hands on a blood-stained towel. His uniform and boots, however, weren't splattered with blood as Jules' were. Bernard tossed the town in a wastebasket and shoved his hands in his pants pockets. "I'm glad you made it before he expired."

I said, "How badly have you worked him over?" Frowning, I pointed at Jules' boots. "Figure based on those, it must be pretty nasty."

"*Non*, Hector," Bernard said, lighting a cigarette. "He resisted my men's attempts to subdue him. As a result of that stupid resistance, he was inadvertently gut-shot in the street with his own gun. Jules helped carry him back, hence the blood on his boots. Believe me, we couldn't add meaningfully to this man's pain at this point."

"It's a bad wound?"

"Fatal anytime now," Bernard said. "He asked for you specifically. There isn't much time left. We've done what we can, but none of us are doctors."

"If he asked for me, he must be tied to Höttl," I said.

"Of that there can be no doubt," Bernard said. "That connection he doesn't even try to deny." Bernard took my arm, guiding me toward the kitchen door. "Truly, he has little time left. We must hurry, Hector."

"Right."

They had the German sprawled out on a kitchen counter. They'd spread some towels under him, but more blood was already pooling at his back. I said softly to Bernard, "You did check to see that there's no spare cutlery in this place, right?"

"*Absolument.* And he's not moving with that hole in his torso, Hector."

The German was a bit older than I'd expected him to be, maybe pushing forty. Leaning over him, still a bit wary, I said, "You're a bit long-in-the-tooth, pal. I know you Nazis are down now to fielding old men and little boys against us lately, but you don't strike me as a fresh conscript. So you're what, an idealist?"

The German was husky and blond. He had gray eyes. His skin was very pale, possibly because of all his blood-loss. I'd wager his complexion otherwise usually ran-to-ruddy. Somehow, he found a voice, surprisingly firm: "Lassiter? Is that you, Lassiter?"

"That's right," I said. "What's your name?"

"Doesn't matter, now that you're here, Lassiter."

Again, the voice was surprisingly loud, even strident. As he said it, he turned his head away from me. I realized he was directing his words into the discarded movie camera by his head.

Bernard was frowning too. I nodded at the camera and said, "Hand me that, won't you?"

The French resistance fighter passed me the movie camera. I was no expert on such things, but I'd already spent some significant time around film sets. The weight and balance of the rig seemed all wrong. Not caring if I spoiled any film inside, I popped the latch and opened the camera. There was no film inside, just a radio with the transmission button taped down.

"This is a radio now, broadcasting to Höttl, I'm guessing," I said, as much to myself as to Bernard. "The objective was to get me here," I said. "This bastard's a decoy duck! He's nothing but damned bait!"

As I said that, there was gunfire outside. I was reaching for my gun when an explosion behind the restaurant blew off the rear door. The concussion from the explosion nearly knocked me from my feet. Two uniformed Germans ran through the black, billowing smoke. They strafed Bernard and Jules with machine guns, nearly cutting them in half.

They swiveled their guns at my heart. I stopped reaching for my Mauser. Cursing, ears ringing so I couldn't hear my own profanities, I raised my hands.

Through swirling smoke and dust, a slender man in an SS uniform stepped into the kitchen, pointing a Luger at my head.

That nasty, livid scar. That wicked grin.

Werner Höttl said, "Keep your hands raised, Lassiter. Then you'll be escorted outside by my men. We're going to take you someplace more private even than this."

Still unable to clearly hear even my own voice, I said, "Why not shoot me here?"

Höttl smiled. "We will take you someplace where your screams can't be heard, but where they can be recorded without any ambient distractions. You're going to suffer terribly, and I'm going to film your ordeal." He smiled and winked. He said, "I hope you're ready for your close up."

He looked down at the German laying on the counter with his fatal belly wound. He stroked the man's hair and said, "You did well, Hans. Now, your earned release." Höttl raised his Luger and shot the man in the head.

26

I was led at gunpoint by nearly a dozen German uniforms with Höttl at the tail, running a handheld camera.

The interior of the abandoned café now looked like a Chicago killing floor: Bernard, Jules… all my irregulars lay strewn around the floor in bloody pools.

I squinted into the late-afternoon sunlight. The two resistance fighters who had been guarding the door were also dead on the street, both shot through the head.

Höttl said to his men, "Turn him around, quickly." I was jerked around by both arms.

As Höttl turned his camera on me, he said, "See that setting sun, Lassiter? Observe the quality and warmth of its light. This is what we filmmakers call, 'the golden hour.' The shadows stand in greater contrast. The light at this hour, just as dusk is coming on, can flatter even the coarsest subject. Savor this sunlight, Lassiter. This is the last sunset you'll ever see. I'm afraid for many reasons, your screams not being the least of them, the rest of our film will be made under artificial lights."

"Why film me at all, Höttl?" Something wet was trailing down my cheek. Not tears. When it reached my lips, I realized from the coppery taste it was blood. But not my own blood; perhaps bloody spray from Jules or Bernard.

I said, "Hitler will be dead before he can ever screen your damned movie. And you? I figure another forty-eight hours, seventy-two at the outside, and your side will be routed. It'd be a better use of your time to try and get out of this city before it's locked down for your sorry types."

Höttl smiled from behind his camera. "Heh! All of this you speak of is hypothetical. Here is the one certain thing, Lassiter. You will be dead soon. That is coming, without question. The only mystery attached to any of this is how much pain you will suffer, how much of your body you will vaingloriously sacrifice to ruin, before you inevitably break down and tell me what I want to know. The faster you answer the question between us, the more swiftly you'll earn the gift of death, like that aide of mine back there."

He fiddled with his camera a bit, still filming me struggling against the quartet of Nazis gripping my arms. Höttl said, "As to me recording your agonies, well, that is a film for my private collection. At least at first. You see, I have built quite an array of such, we shall call them, *short subjects*. I don't have it readily handy, or I could actually screen for you the film I made of Jean Moulin's last hours. It would give a taste of what's in store for you."

Höttl smiled again. "Moulin endured longer than nearly any of the others. His fortitude almost pushed the duration of my film from what my peers would regard as a short subject into the approximate length of a feature film. My good friend, Herr Barbie, was most scientific in his handling of Moulin's torture. It was quite prolonged."

The notion of Jean Moulin's torture and death being preserved on film made me nauseous. I said, "Don't remember you being so sadistic in the old days, Werner."

"Sadism? *Pah*. I'm practicing my craft, Lassiter. The cinema is truth at twenty-four frames a second. When I film the agonies of Germany's enemies, I'm capturing another facet of life, that's all. One day, I mean to put some of these private films together for a public showing. Perhaps you'll make the final cut, Lassiter. I think I shall call the film *The Garden of Suffering*. Perhaps I will set the images against the music of Prokofiev. I fancy the *Dance of the Knights*. Say what you will about the filthy Soviets, but they certainly can write stirring music."

Höttl lowered his camera, frowning at the sky. "The light is failing. The magic hour is gone." He jerked his head at this men. "Load him up now."

I was hustled into the back of a truck. A black hood was pulled over my head and my hands cuffed behind my back.

Under the circumstances, I was hoping for a longer, more leisurely drive. Anything to postpone Höttl's bloody attentions.

What I got was a flurry of neck-snapping stops and jackrabbit starts. We made turns that threatened to take the truck up on two wheels and that twice threw me from my seat.

Yet I had the sense we traveled less than four blocks.

I was tossed into what seemed to be an abandoned meat locker. It was cold and dark and stinking of the ghost aromas of stale blood and old meat.

The walls looked thick, probably good as soundproof. As torture chambers went, Bernard would likely have approved.

There was a single, overhead bulb. For perhaps the thousandth time, I checked my watch by its light. I'd been in the room for perhaps four hours. The place was stifling. I doffed my coat and later, my shirt. The room's furnishings consisted of a stained mattress and a bucket for a slop-jar. Peeling paint and lots of cobwebs. Next to the mattress, there was a canteen of water that might not be tainted.

I'd expected immediate torture. Maybe Höttl was being the consummate *auteur*, ulcerating to get his "film set" and lighting just so before he set to work on me.

At midnight, overwhelmed by rising and falling blood-pressure, low blood sugar and an inability to soldier on awake in the face of mutilation and murder, I pulled back on my shirt and sacked out on that soiled mattress, tucking my boots and coat under my head for a pillow. I could hear the drip-drip of water from somewhere behind a rear wall; the soft scuttling of mice or rats.

I was nauseous, scared and cut off from any prospect of rescue.

It was hard to sleep with that light bulb burning overhead. It was just far enough from reach to make it impossible to unscrew the thing. It was also protected by a metal cage, so I couldn't break it with a thrown boot, either.

As I thought about my boots, I found myself focusing on their laces.

The bastards had taken my belt, but left me my bootlaces.

Unfortunately, there was nothing to fasten the other end to, if I did opt for self-strangulation to escape torture. Even the interior doorknob of my cell had been removed.

A little after five in the morning, stomach in knots and mind turned-in on itself in a dark and ugly way, I finally drifted off.

What seemed like minutes later, I was awakened by the slamming shut of my cell's metal door.

I sat up, startled and blinking.

A tray now sat inside my door.

Groggy, I want over to fetch it. Hard bread, cheese of dubious vintage and a cup of lukewarm coffee.

I didn't care. I wolfed down the bread and cheese and guzzled the sorry joe.

At seven a.m., the door opened and four German soldiers filed in.

Their leader said, "I need you to take off all of your clothes. Do that now and then you will follow me for interrogation."

27

They'd tied me naked to a stout wooden chair with my own belt and a few other sundry, bloodstained belts perhaps taken from the bodies of my irregulars.

The chair's legs were bolted to the floor.

In the semidarkness, I saw light stands, a couple of cameras on tripods.

Two Germans were equipping a battered table with the tools of their trade: brass knuckles, needle-nose pliers, matches, a bucket of ice and various cutting utensils.

For the moment, I was glad I was tied tightly to the chair. If I pressed my thighs to the chair's bottom they couldn't see now badly my legs were trembling. But there was not much I could do about the flutter in my belly.

I'd already been two hours in the chair, watching them slowly, deliberately laying out and arranging all those things they were going to use to destroy my body. I took it as a bid to try and break me down to betray that little girl back home in Cleveland, Ohio without having to take the trouble to actually cut into me.

The door to the street opened and a skinny man in an SS uniform slid in. He motioned over my two guards. Low murmurs ensued, those and frequent looks back at me where I still sat strapped naked to the chair.

My guards strode back over and began to unfasten my legs. "There has been a delay."

I said hopefully, "Höttl's been captured?"

"Delayed by events, that's all. You get to think more about what's coming. Early tomorrow, we will start this again."

"I could use some food," I said.

"You've had your last meal," the other said. He was about six-feet, well-built and dark-haired. In school-boy French, he said, "Herr Höttl has made it clear you will die tomorrow. He wants your bowels and kidneys empty so we don't have any extra mess to deal with when you inevitably lose control of yourself during interrogation."

That set my legs to trembling again. This time they noticed.

The other guard, very Aryan, said, "Let's not get him dressed. It will save time tomorrow preparing him."

And being held naked in a cell would meanly play with my head in the hours between now and then, demean me and maybe break me down that extra bit.

Of course, I'd played the game from the other side. I knew the drill.

They led me back deeper into the building and shut me away naked in that stinking meat locker.

Several hours later, one of the German guards who'd led me to my cell returned. It was the one with the black hair. He was maybe twenty-five or twenty-six. I said to him, "What time is it?"

"Eight o'clock at night," he said softly. "The city has almost fallen. Tomorrow, I think, the Germans will be in full retreat."

The Germans? Odd way for a Nazi to put a pending rout. I forced a smile, trying for some bravado. I said, "For a fella on the losing side, you seem to be taking it in something like stride."

The German licked and then bit his lip. Kid looked like he was trying to make his mind up about something. I said, "What's your name, son?"

"Doesn't matter. Look, Lassiter, I don't want what I'm going to do or say in the next minute or two to give you any hope of an outcome other than the bloody one you face tomorrow. I know the endgame is almost here, and it's cruel it has to come so tantalizingly close to your own fate being decided. You're... well, you're going to have to be a kind of a necessary casualty, Lassiter. I'll try and see you're awarded for your sacrifice."

What the hell? A necessary casualty? I'd always hated that term. I said, "You talking about a medal or something? If so, screw that! What the hell are you going on about?"

He said, "I'm working with your military. Sent to watch over Werner Höttl."

"*Watch over?*"

"Yes, to see he escapes harm or capture when the city falls."

"Are you goddamn joking?"

"Lower your voice, Lassiter! I'm supposed to be here to check your mental state, to soften you up for tomorrow."

I ground my teeth and said, "Right. You're American?"

"Yes, I am. And, no, I can't help you escape here. I just can't do that. I'm ordered to stay right at Höttl's side. From now, until we leave Paris, I'm tied to that man. So I can't slip away to get word to our side about you or where you're being held." He took a deep breath and shook his head. "I'm sorry, Lassiter. I am so truly sorry for what is to come, for what you have to endure tomorrow."

Watching him, trying to decide if he was on the level, I said, "If you're telling me the truth, and if they should break me, why tell me your secret? In desperation, I could think I might barter myself some advantage with the information."

He half-smiled. "I've read your file and made an assessment of your character. You'd gain nothing by doing that, and it would be same as you murdering me. You're not that kind. That's all on the one hand. On the other is the compassion I show you now." He checked the door again, then handed me a single tablet.

I said dully, "An L pill?"

"A very powerful suicide pill, yes," he said. "I only ask you let me be out of this room for an hour or so before you take it. They'll believe you snuck it from your uniform before you were undressed. That you were weighing your options and finally decided to go out easy. Well, comparatively easy. There'll be stomach pain, convulsions. But nothing like the pain you'll experience tomorrow if you let them set to work on you."

I looked at the tablet in my palm. "A suicide pill is your idea of a compassionate gesture?"

"Honestly, if our positions were reversed, I'd see it that way," he said. "You saw those devices we were ordered to lay out today. Höttl is going to dissect you alive, Lassiter."

"And you're going to stand by and watch?"

"I'm guarding you tonight so I can try and sack out through the worst of it tomorrow. Depending on how long you hold out, I might not have to see it at all." He hesitated, for effect, I reckoned, because he then added, "Doesn't mean I won't be likely to hear your screams, however." He lowered his head and said. "Again, I'm *so* sorry. And I urge you to act tonight, or as they lead you out of here tomorrow. Once you're in that chair, I don't think you'll get another chance to get your hand up near your mouth."

Jesus H. Christ! This son of a bitch really wasn't going to try and help me. Hell, he was going to invest all his energy to try and preserve Höttl's wretched life. And he was evidently doing so on orders from our side. It was worse than insane.

I said, "Do you know what that bastard wants from me?"

He shook his head. "I don't want to know. My knowing can't change my orders or your fate. I will follow my orders. It's just a shame you didn't show similar discipline. If you hadn't started playing soldier, you likely wouldn't be here now, frankly."

That again.

He said, "I'm sorry, Lassiter. This truly makes me sick inside. For God's sake, before dawn you please use that pill. Once things get started, you might not be able to change your mind. Hell, you might not even have fingers or hands left. Höttl's had us prepare materials for swift cauterization of amputation sites."

He got in a bit closer, whispering now. "I'm going to have to hurt you now, Hector. I have to do that to give myself cover. Maybe… maybe it will give you the push you need to spare yourself far worse suffering tomorrow. To help me do this, I'm going to make myself believe that's so."

I smiled, trying to project more of that false bravado. I said, "If that salves your conscience in some way, then by all means, you cling to that line of reasoning, you sorry son of a bitch."

He swung on me then. It was a hard shot to the gut that nearly set me to retching bile. In flawless German he snarled, "Fool! You could have ended this now and saved yourself much misery!"

It was an act of will to keep from pitching that damned pill through the cracked door after the bastard.

I held onto the suicide pill for one reason. The prospect that somehow, come morning, before I was tied down, I might find a way to shove the damned thing in Werner Höttl's mouth and make him swallow hard.

28

Cotton-mouthed, I said, "What time is it now?" I dug knuckles into my eyes. I could feel that suicide pill, still clutched in my right hand.

"Noon," a smallish, very young German soldier said. "Get up and go through that door. It's time to start."

It was maybe thirty paces back to that chair.

Each step along the way, I thought hard about that suicide pill in my hand.

As they grabbed my left hand and set to work on tying it to the chair, that pill weighed heavy in my still-free right hand.

I had about a minute to struggle with the notion of swallowing the damned thing.

Then they grabbed my right wrist and started binding it to the chair.

I'd lost my last option.

Twenty minutes after being strapped in the chair, Werner Höttl arrived, looking very crisp and straight-backed in his SS uniform. He nodded at my three German guards. The dark-haired boy from last night was still staying scarce, the craven son of a bitch.

Höttl put down the swagger stick he was carrying and slipped off his uniform jacket. One of his men helped him on with a long, bloodstained leather smock. My legs began to tremble again. As he pulled on surgical gloves, Höttl said, "Leave us alone now. I'll call you in when I'm ready to be relieved."

We both watched his men file out. When they'd gone, Höttl pulled a chair up about three-feet from mine and he lit a cigarette.

"Some of what you've said has proven prophetic," he said. "We are in full retreat. Paris has fallen, and, as you presciently pointed out, I am, for the moment, trapped. Consequently, we have a great deal of time to spend together."

"Why don't you just shoot me now, Werner? I can't help you. Not because I don't want to, but because I don't know where she is."

That earned me a sneer. "I don't believe you. You're going to have to tell me what became of my daughter, Lassiter. Don't waste time lying to me or trying to convince me she's dead. You killed that farm family, and we found their bodies. We found every one of the bodies of the soldiers you killed between Lyon and the coast. But no nine-year-old girls' corpses."

"Then just think of her as dead," I said. "You've lost the war, Werner. Hitler will be captured or killed soon. The Reich has fallen. You fathering a Jewish girl is irrelevant so far as your *career* is concerned. You Germans' efforts at genocide are at an end."

Höttl narrowed his eyes. "Not at all. Hitler is finished, yes, that is clear. But the party and its aims will endure, and the cause will renew itself. When I escape here, and I will escape, I'll be one of those uniquely positioned to rekindle the dream. Next time we will not fail. And the extinction of the Jewish race is still a worthy objective."

I said, "With your anti-Semitic feelings, how'd you end up impregnating a Jewish woman, anyway?"

"I took the child's mother by force," Höttl said, very nonchalant. "It was a party, the liquor was flowing." He closed his eyes, remembering. "Her name was Suzanne. She didn't look Jewish that night."

If I could manage the spit, I would have unloaded in his face. I said, "How'd you learn otherwise?"

He tipped his head back and blew a stream of smoke. "She tried to press charges for rape. Her family was…" He waved a hand. "She was a nothing. But there was enough information in the police complaint to determine she was a Jew. And to learn where to find her."

"You killed her parents? You tried to kill her?"

"Her parents sent her away before I could strike," he said. "They sent her away before she could begin to show and their family could be scandalized by a bastard grandchild. I was content to leave it at that. Years passed. Then, quite by accident, I found Suzanne. I went to Lyon, attached to SS-*Hauptsturmführer* Barbie. I saw Suzanne on the street. I confronted her there. That was stupid of me. It gave her time to hide the child from me. I should have followed her home instead of confronting her. Then I'd have taken them all. I killed Suzanne and her husband. Despite my *urgings*, neither would tell me where to find the wretched child. But I persisted in my search."

"And that search led to the orphanage," I said. "You and Barbie, you killed all those children?"

"Of course." He stared at me a long time. "That was the first of my films you ruined, Lassiter. For that alone you deserve all you're going to suffer today."

"I'd heard you had cameras at the apartment building the night I fled there with the girl," I said, desperate to keep him busy talking. "Struck me as strange you were filming the back of the building."

"I wanted good coverage, for later, in the editing booth," he said. "I had seven cameras running that night. I was going to show that cow, Leni, how to really make a film honoring the Party. I was going to title my film, *The Girl in the Wall*. It was intended to satisfy two aims. The protection of my reputation within the party, of course, and to create a super-lative piece of art-cum-propaganda that would underscore the futility of sheltering Jews. But you snatched her away. I ended up with a recording of you killing German soldiers and saving the girl. It was a disaster that injured me with Klaus."

I met his gaze; I couldn't quite suppress a mocking half-smile.

Höttl said, "If you gloat, I'll just hurt you longer."

"You're right," I said. "Under the circumstances, why rile you?"

He smiled now. "Indeed. But your suffering will be exqui-site, all the same. Screams for the ages."

Angling to delay that suffering for as long as possible, I said, "*The Girl in the Wall*, that was the first of your films I ruined, you said."

Höttl spread his arms. "All this," he said. "This city and its demise was to be another film. *The Death of Paris*. I was going to record the destruction of the city, but you—and countless others, to be sure—have ruined this project, too."

He stood and walked around my chair, his eyes on me, inquiring. I felt that flutter in my belly return. I fought to keep my legs from shaking harder. Höttl said, "Those whip scars on your back look rather old."

February 1924. I'd gotten them here, in Paris, under the damnedest circumstances. My beloved Brinke. Molly. A cult of nihilistic artists and this particular sadist...

His gloved fingers traced the scars crisscrossing my back. I couldn't suppress another shiver. "So many wounds. That tells me you have a high tolerance for pain. So I will adjust my own plans accordingly."

He walked to the front door, muttered something in German I couldn't make out. Two men in civilian clothes entered the room. Höttl said, "My cameramen. They're Polish. They speak not a word of English, German or French. I, however, know enough of their language to give them orders. I will interrogate you in your own language. Neither of us, therefore, has to worry about you compromising me."

The lights were turned on, nearly blinding me. The heat from those movie lights, almost from the first second, was intense, and with the summer heat of the room, I was swiftly bathed in sweat. As the men fiddled with their cameras, I said, "You might be wrong about my tolerance for pain." There was something quavering in my voice that unsettled me. "It's been a hard few years," I said. "They might have broken down my reserves. Made me weak for much suffering. I know you wouldn't want to pass me out or prod me to a fatal heart attack or the like before you get what you want."

"Nonsense," Höttl said. "I'm a Nietzschean. That which does not kill us makes us stronger, yes?" He nodded at his men and I heard the cameras start up. "We're rolling, now." He punched me in the kidney. "To business!" I gasped for breath from the blow.

Höttl came back around in front of me and sat down again. He lit another cigarette. "We would have started with such beatings, confined to your torso, of course—must protect the head with its precious knowledge stored inside. But those whip scars show me the futility of such prosaic forms of motivation."

"It could still be well worth the effort," I said again, squirming a bit in the chair. The seat was slick with my sweat. My mouth was dry and my kidney burned.

"*Nein*, Lassiter. You would suffer a few broken ribs, likely. Perhaps some organ damage. But you'd not tell me what I want to know because of a simple beating."

Höttl eyed the end of his cigarette, turned it, examining its golden-orange ember. "After the beatings failed, we'd inevitably come to these. Cigarette burns administered to the bottoms of your feet and the backs of your knees. To your throat, and, of course, to your testicles and penis. Cigarettes and ice, administered in tandem, of course."

"Of course," I said softly. My voice didn't sound my own. It was now thin and trembling.

"We may still get to that. As I am trapped by the city's fall, perhaps I should stretch this out."

"You have had a long time to hate me," I said.

Höttl laughed. "Indeed, my friend. Indeed. I did toy with taking my time." He was looking at the end of his cigarette again. He did that with something like intent, it seemed to me. I felt my sweat running in cold rivulets down my spine.

"But now, Lassiter, I find I have little zeal for the slow build. Of course I could delegate the early phases of your torture, but then there is the possibility of my men learning my secret, the fathering of that little Jew bitch. I think we will subscribe to that old movie axiom of 'getting in late and getting out early.' 'Cut to the action,' so to speak."

I said thickly, "Good. I concur. Kill me now and be done with it. If I knew where she was, of course I would resist telling you as long as I could hold out. But the bad news for both of us is I honestly don't know where the girl is. I turned her over to American adoption authorities and never looked back. She could be anywhere between Wildwood, New Jersey and Seattle, Washington. Between El Paso, Texas and Detroit, Michigan. Hell, she may have been moved to Mexico or Canada. It's a big goddamn continent, Werner, and American adoption records are sealed so tight J. Edgar Hoover himself would be hard-pressed to access them."

Höttl smiled. "Your legs are shaking very hard. Your heart rate is so elevated I can see the pulsing in your chest. Your ears are red with your spiking blood pressure. You stink of fear, *Amerikaner.*"

He reached over and ground his cigarette out in my thigh. I tried to bite back my scream and failed. He swung a fist into my mouth. Through bloodied teeth I said, "Typical director, abusing the writers who give you the material you need to realize your precious visions."

"That's right, Lassiter. You *are* a writer. You have to have dexterity to type, yes?"

God. I imagined him breaking my fingers, one a time, and maybe in multiple places. My writing was keyed, so to speak, to my fingers' ability to pace my mind. At forty-four, would my hands ever heal correctly? Would all those fractures to bone invite in the arthritis I constantly feared might someday rob me of my ability to slings words onto paper at white-hot speed?

Höttl was watching me closely. He lit another cigarette, then leaned over to the table and picked up a long knife. "Now, even though I promise you you're going to die here, today, in that very chair, even though I swear to you that is the truth, you still haven't reconciled yourself to the fact, have you, Lassiter? You still imagine some future for yourself. As a writer, you must have your hands, your fingers."

He turned the knife so the movie lights glinted along its blade. "I'm going to cut your fingers off, one at a time. If you're still holding out after your fingers are all gone, then I will set fire to your hands to cauterize the stumps. Then I'm going to castrate you."

I believed him. Oh, I believed every bloody word.

"For the love of God, Höttl, I don't know where that child is. I swear to God, I don't know where to find her!"

Höttl wasn't having any of that. He said, "It's that holding out of hope that always makes these sessions so sadly tedious in the early going. Once hope is taken from the subject, things continue apace. But it's shattering that fruitless sense of hope that there is a future that is so critical to obtaining results." He ground his cigarette out again in the same burn wound he'd made with the first cigarette.

When I stopped screaming, he said, "I know you still harbor illusions of hope, of escape, because you're still clutching to that pill my officer gave you last evening. Somewhere in your mind, you're hoping you pricked his conscience, and he perhaps got word to the outside world of your predicament."

I looked back at him, knowing I looked stricken but unable to suppress it.

Höttl was beaming. "Dear fellow, that suicide pill you were given last night is nothing more than a laxative. Günther is not American and he's not OSS or a spy of any kind whatever. He was, how would you put it? He was a plot complication. For our film together, you see?"

He lit a third cigarette. "This one," he said as he fired it up, "I'm going to put out in your left eye." He shook out the match. "It's like this. I arranged for Günther's little drama with you last night because I wanted to give you that fraction of hope, and then tear it from under you now. To hasten your reconciliation to the hopelessness of your situation and your inevitable death. I wanted you to see how completely you are in my hands, here. And, of course, I filmed the whole exchange. Now, on the subject of hands, this is your last chance to tell me where the girl is before I take both of your thumbs."

I was gagging, already visualizing him slicing off my fingers. And I was reeling from the disclosure last night's scene with the guard was just that, a bit of cruel theater. A put-up job and a nasty con. I was losing all control now, felt myself slipping toward the impulse to beg for my life.

Höttl grinned and stroked my cheek. "You're very nearly broken. But not quite. Therefore, I'm going to cut off your left thumb now. Only after, I'm going to put the question to you about where I might find my child."

The cigarette hung between his lips as he rose and held the knife up to my face.

He said, "It was perhaps thoughtless of me not to let a writer compose a few last words, to set down his last thoughts on paper while he still had the tools—the fingers—to do so. I suppose you could give some dictation to Günther. Some last true sentences."

Höttl gripped my wrist. He was surprisingly strong for such a scarecrow of a man. "Now, don't fight this, Lassiter, or else you might lose two, even three more fingers."

Although I knew the chair was fastened firmly to the floor, I still struggled to tip it over. I was bathed in sweat, trying to twist my damp wrist free from his grip; aiming to slam my forehead into his face as he clutched at my fingers and pried my thumb away from my fist for a clean cut.

There was gunfire outside, screams.

Höttl snarled, pivoting around to face the door. Someone was pounding at the door now, demanding in English it be opened.

Something about the male voice was vaguely familiar.

Now whoever was on the other side of that door was shooting at the lock.

Werner Höttl turned on me, wild-eyed, then slashed the knife across my chest. He raised the blade to plunge it into my crotch when the first bullets actually penetrated the front door.

Höttl tossed aside the knife and ran up a flight of interior stairs, screaming something to his cameramen in Polish. The two men exchanged looks, then got down on their knees and raised their hands, apparently opting to surrender rather than doing their fleeing master's bidding. There were more shouts from outside, and then the door was kicked open.

29

The first three through the door were our boys, machine guns at the ready, all business.

Two more soldiers came in behind them. The five of them made sure I was alone in the room, then waved in Duff and a medic.

When I saw Duff, I said, "Höttl, he just ran up those stairs! Send these boys after him. If they hustle they can maybe still get him!"

Looking stricken, staring at my sliced open pectorals and the burns in my leg, Duff shrugged off her coat and covered my lap. I said, "Damn it, Höttl can still be caught if we hurry!"

Duff stroked my cheek. "No, Hector. We were only allowed to come and get you if we promised to let Höttl go."

What?

My mounting rage at the prospect of letting Höttl escape was swept aside by a voice. From outside, *his* voice called, gruff and urgent. "Duff, is Lasso okay?"

Hemingway.

Duff and the medic locked eyes. He nodded. Duff yelled back, "He's okay, Ernest. We got here just in time. Hector will be okay thanks to you. *You* saved him."

"That's good," I heard Hem say. "That's really good. I'm going now, gotta get my fat ass out of here. I've got my own hearing board to sweat after all. Can't be caught doing things like this."

This long pause, then Hem yelled back, "Tell Lasso I hope he kills that Kraut son of a bitch someday. Tell Lasso I said that, won't you?"

They got me untied and up on my feet.

I shrugged off their hands.

Still naked, still seething, I kicked over the movie lights and tore open the cameras. I pitched the film reels of my inter-rogation out into the punishing sun.

30

I woke up in Gertrude's bedroom. Duff was sitting in a bedside chair. She put down the book she was reading, a French translation of my novel *One True Sentence*, and smiled.

She said, "Six stitches in your chest, a cigarette burn that will probably leave a small scar, one that won't show much under your leg hair, and a bruised kidney. Could have been so much worse."

Duff rose, parked her shapely bottom on the bed, then leant forward and kissed my forehead. "All things considered, not much to signify, and thank God for that."

She kissed me on the mouth. "It's your head I'm worried about, Hector. The terrible time you spent in Hottl's hands. I saw the stuff he'd set out on that table. To come so close to that kind of torture has to have done things to your mind. I tried to put myself in your place. Tried to imagine having to endure that. I can't. I couldn't. I'd break for certain."

"Oh, he broke me," I said flatly. I could feel my chin trembling. "He had me terrified, you're right. I was close to falling to pieces."

"You didn't tell him anything though, right?" Duff gripped my hand hard. "The important thing is he didn't win. Isn't that so? You didn't given up Marie?"

I searched her blue eyes. "I might have talked. I told myself I'd die first. But he'd nearly broken me and maybe I would have betrayed Marie if you hadn't come."

"I don't believe that, Hector. Not at all. Neither do you, deep down."

I said thickly, "We'll never know that for certain." I ran my fingers through Duff's ginger hair. "Goddamn wonderful Hem... How?"

"I sought Ernest out," Duff said. "I won't apologize for doing that, Hec. I don't know what happened between you two. He's not talking, and I suppose you'll never tell me, either. Despite it all, Ernest saved your life, Hector. I was at an utter loss to help you. Hem could."

"The brass wouldn't throw in?"

"Not at all. They were apparently willing to sacrifice you. One said it was what you earned yourself by playing soldier— yes, that very phrase again. I didn't know where to look for you. All my OSS connections pleaded ignorance."

Wincing, I shifted the pillows and sat up straighter. "So you went to Hem?"

"Word of mouth was pinpointing Papa's progress into Paris," Duff said. "He's a phenomenon, and the news of his arrival preceded him. I went to the Ritz, which is where Hem went almost immediately upon reaching the city. He was very gracious to me. He listened to my story. Papa has his own connections, sources. Despite everything, he didn't hesitate to help you, Hector. You two really should talk. He was thrilled to help save you."

When I didn't respond to that, Duff said, "Ernest pulled strings, found his own OSS source that confirmed Höttl was under observation. Our boys had seen you snatched and knew where you were taken. Because of Hem and pressure from a general friend, we were allowed to attempt a rescue on promise we'd let Höttl go, unmolested."

"Son of a bitch."

"That's just what Ernest said when he heard the terms of your rescue. Would you rather I hadn't done anything?"

"Christ, no! You saved my life. You and Hem."

"Hemingway really did all that. I was just along." She smiled. "Hem's arrogant, headstrong and juvenile in perplexing ways. Suspiciously too-macho and a terrible narcissist, I can tell. He's probably slightly mad now. But you know, I think I adore Ernest anyway."

"Hem has some great qualities," I said. "If you can get word to him, thank him again for helping me."

"He's still at the Ritz," Duff said. "He's liberating it. We can go together."

I shook my head. "No way. I was naked in a chair, about to be cut into pieces, Duff. Hem saved me from that, yes. But if he wouldn't walk through a door to talk to me when he was in the role of *über* hero...?" I shrugged. "Clearly, our central issues stand."

"I am your wife. You could tell me what caused this rift."

"Ancient history," I said. I waved a hand. "You know, I just want a drink."

"I have pain medicine for that."

"No, I want a *drink*."

Duff slid off the bed. "Okay. You've certainly earned one."

I said, "I did learn one important thing from the past couple of days. Regardless of anything else in this mad, bad and burning-down world, Werner Höttl is still committed to murdering Marie. She'll never be safe until Höttl is dead."

31

M ost of that Friday, *Liberation Day*, I remained in bed.
We found a radio station playing American tunes: *I'm
Gonna Love That Guy*, Kitty Kallen's *They're Either Too Young
or Too Old*, and *You'd Be So Nice to Come Home to*. Saturday,
I couldn't resist the raucous sounds of celebration filtering up
from the streets.

Duff found me struggling to put on a shirt. The blow to
the kidney and the stitches across my chest had severely lim-
ited my mobility.

"Let's get out there and see it unfold," I said. "We're missing *good* history."

She smiled and helped me on with my shirt. "Sure. Let's
go do that."

As I'd promised, I tried to show Duff bits and pieces of
my Paris as we weaved through the jubilant crowds down the
narrow twisting streets I'd once walked with Brinke and Hem;
later and even more fleetingly, with poor luckless Victoria.

In many ways, our passage was reminiscent of that day I'd traversed the distance from Gertrude's salon to the rooftop where Bernard and I first spotted that camera-toting German.

Most of the activity was celebratory, but there were still some reprisals underway—beatings or even shootings of male collaborators and a few stray Germans who didn't make it out of town in time. Some more women who'd consorted with Germans were having their heads shaved.

I held Duff's hand, wending our way to the Café du Dôme. I said, "Any word on Höttl? Did you, I don't know, maybe ask Hem to work his network on the son of a bitch?"

Duff stopped walking and turned me around to face her. "No, I haven't done that. I took you at your word that the door between you two was to be closed again and locked. As to me looking, *no*. I'm keeping you on a short leash. Pulling you from Höttl's clutches came at a price. I'd hoped to delay talking about this until you were feeling better."

It was a struggle not to put it to her in a snarl. "What price?"

"It was tantamount to acknowledgment you're sufficiently more than just a correspondent to justify Höttl snatching you. I'm afraid saving you strengthened SHAEF's case that's being built against you."

"I can't think about that now," I said. I thought, *Those sons of bitches!*

I looked around, spotted a closer café. I pointed. "Looks like they have some liquor stock. C'mon, I'll buy you some refreshment there. God, but I need a drink right now."

The next two days we passed indoors, holed up in Gertrude's salon. I was working on a new novel and trying to savor my time with Duff... the good food and the wine.

Word came with little warning that Gertrude was on her way back to the city, quite close to arriving, in fact. Duff and I hurriedly changed the sheets, straightened up the salon and greeted Miss Stein and Alice in the courtyard.

Gertrude, looking very much her nearly seventy years, a little gaunter than I'd ever seen her, limped up the path, leaning on a cane. Alice actually smiled at me.

I introduced Duff and said, "We've been here for a few weeks, bunked on the salon floor, protecting your place and paintings from Werner Höttl. Everything's like you left it. Except for one thing."

I hugged Alice then. She looked up at me frowning. I said, "That bottle of wine you gave me in 1940 is up there on the table, Alice. What do you say we all go toast the Liberation with that vino? After, Duff and I will get out of your way."

The rest of August we spent in a hotel. I was still trying to focus on the writing and keeping my nose clean, but it was hard to forget the SHAEF sword hanging over my head.

That threat didn't stop me from keeping an ear to the ground, still trying to locate Werner Höttl if he was still hiding somewhere in the city.

The last day of the month, malaprop-prone Charles, propelled by the bloody forces of attrition to the status of my primary operative, dropped by for a lobby lounge consultation. He said, "It is a mystery, *Grand Capitaine*—"

"*Hector*."

"It is a mystery, *Hector*. I have destroyed all my men to make infestations about Höttl's whereabouts, but to no success. I think this German has somehow invaded capture and landscaped to some friendlier country. I can find no feetprints of the man."

"*Deploy* your men again, Charles," I said. "Have them stay at their *investigations*. I'm convinced that son of a bitch hasn't *evaded* capture or *escaped* yet. I think we can still have him."

32

Duff and I wiled away the first two weeks of September in the manner of the long overdue honeymoon that the war had denied us when we married in 1942.

During those two weeks, I didn't play solider; I didn't play reporter. I even gave up, for the most part, hunting for clues about where to lay my hands on Werner Höttl.

Sitting in a café with glasses of wine, Duff said, "I've been thinking hard about this. Let's go home now, darling. If you leave the European Theater, it might just be easier for the Inspector General to drop all this, to simply abandon any notion of a hearing that would require them to fly you back to France."

"It *is* a thought," I said.

The fact I seemed warm to the notion seemed to surprise Duff. She said, "You'd really consider this?"

I took her hand, stroking its pale back with my thumb. "I would. Crazy as things are now, it's not as if Höttl could track us on our way back to the States. We could safely get some time with Jimmy and Marie, then disappear into the desert and our air-conditioned hacienda. Just live as a couple of anonymous, oversexed gringos stalking the borderland cantinas and bullfighting rings."

She smiled and raised my hand to her mouth. "You silver-tongued devil. Will you really consider this?"

"I'll really consent to this," I said. "I don't even need the time to think about it."

If only she'd suggested it a week earlier.

When we returned to the hotel, slightly tipsy and eager to get to our room, the concierge waved me over. He passed me an envelope with an army seal. Duff looked at the envelope and leapt to the obvious conclusion:

"Damn it."

The Inspector General of the U.S. Third Army was ordering me to appear for a "judicial investigation" in Nancy, France on October 6.

George S. Patton's Inspector General, of course.

33

The young military attorney, a guy named William Evans, Jr., said to me, "I want to assure you up front, Mr. Lassiter, I'm here as your advocate, and I will do my level best to get you out from under all this. I also want you to know, Mr. Lassiter, on a personal level, that I'm a tremendous fan of yours. Of your writing, of course. But I also admire what you did in theater, even if officially I have to lament it."

I looked the young man over. He was crisply uniformed, fresh-faced and quick-eyed. Seemed like a bright kid. And I had to count on Billy, as I'd chosen to call him, to pull my ass out of this latest fire of my own reckless, feckless making. One of the few that really had me sweating.

"Nearly as I can tell, Mr. Lassiter—"

"Call me Hector, please."

A smile. "Okay, Hector. Nearly as I can tell, the general sense is you were more armed combatant and guerilla leader than war correspondent. Some of your fellow journalists, the ones who weren't so, well, let's say patriotic, or at least not so intrepid as you, blew the whistle. You're going to be accused of serving as a forward observer, of having functioned as a liaison between OSS and French Resistance. Of acquiring and storing arms for the Maquis. There are reports you held a key town in France for two days with a band of irregulars until our boys could get there and officially secure it. You also made it into Paris a very good bit ahead of our own forces. Reputedly, you arbitrated local disputes, established a field command and accepted countless German surrenders."

All true.

And not nearly close to touching on the scope of everything else I'd done in zealous disregard of rules of conduct for correspondents. I'd been in it up to my eyebrows, of course, just as deeply as I had been in smuggling Gertrude and Alice out of Paris, in smuggling Marie out of Lyon and to the States.

I'd had me my own private war and I'd relished much of it.

"It's not true," I said. "Some of it is stuff presented in false light, without context. Some of it is just vicious whispers and tongue wagging from jealous sons of bitches who I scooped. Journalists are a low and catty breed, Billy. Take it from one who knows."

"Good," he said. "We hew to that tack. I'm sorry for all this, Hector. You did good, brave and important work. I have that from several officers who wanted to come here and defend your actions. But since we can't acknowledge those actions, we can't use those men to help us here today. I know that's going to be the hard thing for you, Hector. But you're going to have to deny every great thing you did for the war effort when we go before that board. You're going to have to settle it in your mind now that you can never talk about this, and never write about any of it. Not *ever*. There's no clock to run out on this, do you understand?"

"Completely." I didn't care about the rest; I knew well enough what I'd done, what I had contributed. All I wanted was to walk away from this drumhead trial with no sanctions from the Inspector General and no censure from some George S. Patton stooge.

Billy said, "If it's any consolation, Hector, you're not the only one facing this threat of court martial today. Just on the other side of that wall is the great man himself. Almost identical allegations have been lodged against him."

I frowned. "The great man? Who is that?" I suspected, of course, but that 'great man' descriptor chafed.

"Hemingway. His hearing is just before yours." Billy smiled. "Now that I think on it, aren't you two friends? I could take you over for a brief chat. Might take both your minds off this other stuff to commiserate for a time."

I looked at the wall as though I could maybe see through it if I stared long enough. "No, thanks, Billy," I said softly. "Hem's probably using this time the same way I am, to run practice answers through his head. You know—deny, deny, deny."

My young counsel smiled. "My friend caught Hemingway's case. My understanding is Papa will be doing just what you're doing. He'll probably walk away from this as you will. Well, except for one allegation. Seems there's a claim, with a witness, that Mr. Hemingway personally killed a sniper at the request of a Miss Sylvia Beach."

Christ. I'd heard that story, too. From Sylvia. I thought about it, then said, "When did this crazy thing allegedly happen?" I already knew the answer: August 25th, about six hours after Hem saved my ass from Werner Höttl. Billy rattled off the date from a clipboard.

I said, "That's so much bullshit, Billy. Hem was with me that afternoon into evening. At that time, he was supposedly shooting that Kraut, he was knocking 'em back with me and my wife in Gertrude Stein's place. We were among those babysitting the joint against Nazi art plunderers pending Gertrude's return. Hem was at the spirits a good bit harder than me. Probably lost track of time. But my wife and I can vouch for it all. That was us—just some drunk reporters playing unarmed art cops."

Duff had wanted to come to Nancy but I'd argued her out of it. I pointed out it she was *in situ* to use a term I'd come to mock, it made it too convenient if some son of a bitch did want to use her against me. And hell, she'd been in the Marie affair up to her neck, herself. I figured, if needed, I'd have plenty of time to get word back to Paris to Duff to support any cover story that would help Hem.

Billy wet his lips and said, "You'd testify to that?"

"Sure," I said. "And, Christ, I'm obviously close to hand." Hell, I owed Hem.

"Excuse me a minute. Going to go give a heads up to my friend."

I sat there alone, staring at the wall between us. Hopefully, Hem wouldn't be so pissed off as to reveal me as a liar despite the rope I was throwing him.

After about five minutes, Billy returned. He smiled. "Papa said I should tell you he wasn't that drunk but thanks you for correcting his memory. He said something about you being even. Well, that's good news all around. I think with your testimony on his behalf, both of you will walk, now. Honestly? You're both too famous, too important as men and writers back home for command to risk dressing you down for fighting the damned Nazis. Nobody would be served by punishing you two. I expect there'd actually be a backlash from home for that. They need heroes back there. Been a hard few years."

I slapped his arm. "Well, at any rate, I get it, Billy, and the secrets die with me. Tell you what, son. Next war, I'm going to get the Geneva Convention tattooed on my ass in reverse so I can read it in the mirror."

The hearing board was mostly an annoyance. Me in a chair sitting across from a bunch of pinch-faced, constipated looking officers and conscripted judicial types. I denied every single thing, re-contextualized other things. I embroidered, distorted and twisted damning actions through convoluted prisms to make them look innocent or misunderstood.

As a fiction writer, and a fast one, I have certain advantages as a liar.

My worst moments came very early, when I was first planted in that stiff-backed wooden chair. I realized that unconsciously, I was pressing my legs hard against the seat and chair legs to keep them from shaking. I was gripping the vertical posts supporting the arms of the chair in the same way. My posture and position was almost identical to that I had been forced into when Höttl's men had tied me to that other chair in Paris.

When I realized what I was doing, I crossed one leg over the other. I got permission to smoke through the interrogation. My hands steadied after the first blessed hit of nicotine.

After an hour, I figured I'd pretty well deflected every charge against me. Then one of the old warhorses threw me a wicked and charged curveball.

"Mr. Lassiter, what is your obsession with Werner Höttl? You've been making inquiries after his whereabouts for the past several weeks now. Why?"

Through the first smoke of a freshly lit cigarette I said, "The one allegation in all of your charges I don't deny is attempting to protect the life of female Jewish child from that bloody bastard's attempts to murder her."

"There are recorded threats you made against Herr Höttl's life in our records."

I shrugged. "*Herr* Höttl is a Nazi who revels in murder and torture. We've killed so many Nazis these past several years, what's one more?"

One of the hearing judges, a particularly patrician-looking man with gin blossoms in both cheeks said, "Werner Höttl has been deemed to be of future intelligence-gathering value to the United States government. *If* you are released back into civilian life, we'll need some assurance you will desist from your search for Herr Höttl, but also from issuing any more threats, even if they might be no more than swaggering macho posturing or you mouthing off in your cups. Do you understand, Lassiter?"

If you are released back into civilian life? That bit nearly sent me out of my chair.

I said tersely, "I hear you."

"But do you agree to these terms?"

What else could I say? In Army prison, I certainly couldn't kill the scar-faced son of a bitch.

"Absolutely," I said. "Okay."

"Okay? Well, then." The Inspector General tapped a hammer and said, "You're excused, Mr. Lassiter. An M.P. will escort you outside now while we deliberate."

I planted my ass in another goddamn chair for the better part of an hour. Most of the time, I found myself staring at that same wall, wondering how things were going for Hem, wondering if I'd be called to repeat the lie I'd told Billy.

Other than some news photographs and dust jacket photos, the truth was I hadn't seen Hem since 1937. Some mutual friends had said he'd undergone some severe personality changes in recent years. His marriage to his third wife, I'd heard, had also soured but they'd not yet divorced. That bitch had been a wedge between us, too.

The door swung open and Billy slid out, smiling. "You're clear. Hemingway, too. Now you both just have to walk the straight and narrow, and don't put anything contradicting any of what you testified to in there in any letters, novels or short stories. Got it?"

I stubbed out a cigarette, rose and shook his hand. "Oh, I thoroughly get it, Billy."

Billy grinned and squeezed my arm. "Great. It's been pleasure doing this for you and a personal thrill meeting you and your friend over there. Now, for God's sake, Hector, stay the hell away from this Werner Höttl, whoever the hell he is."

34

Over the course of a lazy, hedonistic weekend, Duff and I made our last tour of Paris.

We briefly crossed paths with Marlene Dietrich outside the Ritz. Marlene tried to drag me inside in order to single-handedly foster a rapprochement between Hem and I.

I kissed her cheek and urged the Teutonic chanteuse to drop it. "I want to leave Paris tomorrow only with good memories," I said. "Please believe me, Kraut, neither Hem or I are ready or any reconciliation like you envision."

As we moved through the city, I kept to cafés and restaurants that weren't filled with memories of Brinke, Molly or Victoria, the key women I'd memorably shared the city with in the 1920s. Still, Brinke visited me more often in my troubled dreams, her memory stirred by *our* city.

We dropped by 27 rue de Fleurus one more time to share a last late-afternoon drink with Gertrude and Alice.

Our last stop before heading back to the hotel was at Shakespeare and Company to visit Sylvia Beach and Adrienne Monnier.

The women were mulling whether to make a go of the store again, whether to move back into the shop all of the books and records that now resided in an apartment above 12 rue de l'Odeon, the place where they'd been hidden from the book-burning Germans. The books had remained safe even when Sylvia was interred by the Nazis for half-a-year.

Sylvia hugged me hard and said, "With you and Hem in town, it's almost like old home week."

We shared some wine with the ladies and talked about old days. Sylvia, something of a champion of mine in my hungry years, was careful to avoid mentions of the women who'd passed through my life whom she had come to know back then.

As we were leaving, Sylvia said, "Oh, Hec, remember when I used to play postmistress for you and Hem? Well, a letter was mailed here a few days ago. A letter for you."

I didn't even need to see the envelope to guess at the identity of the sender. I slipped the envelope in my pocket and hugged Sylvia and Adrienne a last time.

Pulling her coat closer against the chilly October wind as we slipped from the empty bookshop, Duff said, "The letter, is it from Höttl?"

"Who else?"

"Aren't you going to open it?"

I shook my head. "Not without a deep drink in front of me."

The letter was posted from the one place on earth I couldn't chase Höttl, much as I was spoiling to make him extinct. He'd mailed the threat from Madrid, Spain.

Huddled close against me at our fireside table, sipping some good red wine, Duff read along with me:

Lassiter:
Your luck, for the moment, is better than mine. But you're not safe. Any time left you between Paris and our next encounter you should regard as "found time." Accept it as an intermission, so to speak, before you again sit in my chair, subject to my bloodiest whims.

We will finish our <u>discussion</u> at that time, under the hot lights, and if in the meantime I should find the child on my own, I will still make it my mission to strip you and tie you to that chair under my bright lights, anyway.

When that day comes that we resume our talk, I will begin by cutting off your thumb. That will be a mere tease for the main show to come. I've determined your deconstruction will be the centerpiece of my film, *The Garden of Suffering*.

Duff hugged me close. She said in my ear, speaking above the raucous din of the café, "I'm so sorry, darling. I erred calamitously. I should have violated orders. I should have gone up those stairs after Höttl myself, all consequences be damned."

She pressed her forehead to mine. She said, "Hell, as we're married, maybe they'd even have let us rut and rot in the same cell. That wouldn't have been so bad, would it?"

That night, I had a dream about being back in Höttl's chair. I had the same dream every night until we reached New York.

35

It was a crisp November afternoon in Euclid, Ohio. Jimmy had insisted upon barbecuing, despite the cold.

Jimmy and I stood in the backyard of his sister Fionnula's place, drinking bottled beer and watching Pancho lope along after Marie as she ran through crunching leaves. She was bundled up in a puffy winter coat and wearing corduroy pants. She was much taller than when I'd last seen her and reedier, too. At age eleven, you could see the intimations of the teenager she would become.

Marie didn't seem to remember me much. Duff, on the other hand, seemed to ring a bell for the girl. Maybe it was that striking, long red hair of Duff's that made memories of her cling.

Pancho, seeming older and a bit fatter, remembered me just fine. In terms of table-scrap finger-food, he also rightly regarded me as his likeliest mark after Marie. Not a bad judge of character at all, that dog.

Jimmy pulled the zipper up higher on his leather coat. His hair was a tad grayer; his midsection a bit thicker. He said,

"Duff filled me in on the Höttl stuff while you were playing fetch with Marie and the cur."

"I'm so sorry, Jimmy." I ground out my cigarette on the sole of my shoe. "Duff had to agree to let Höttl walk in exchange for saving my ass. And then Patton's Inspector General made me promise—"

Jimmy waved a hand; with the other, he used a spatula to flip a piece of meat. "Forget all that, Hector. It's past and done, and it's not like you two were drowning in options." He turned over another piece of meat. "He was really filming your torture?"

"Really."

He shrugged off a chill. But then it was getting nippy. "Soon as I get these grilled through, we'll take 'em inside and eat by the fire. Fionnula, she keeps a cozy house."

"They're all happy together?"

"Ecstatic," Jimmy said. "Deliriously happy."

"Then it's been worth every risk." I lit another cigarette. "Duff and I, we'll be scarce for a time after this, Jim. I don't want Höttl, or some private eye this side he might hire, maybe some nested Buckeye Bund member, if such types exist, tracing you through me and maybe tracing Marie through you. Until Höttl is dead, I think it's best you and I keep it rather distant."

"Let's not be that extreme, Hector."

"I think we have to," I said. "I mean to at least keep Höttl on the run until I can strike at him through others. I'm working some angles toward that end, even now. A lot of these Nazi cocksuckers, they're fleeting to South America. I figure maybe Höttl's headed that way from Spain. I'm seeing if some of my hired hunters can get his scent there. Maybe I can at least cost him many a peaceful night's sleep. Just maybe I can keep Höttl looking over his shoulder."

"A salutary notion," Jimmy said. He shook his head. "Imagine that bastard filming your torture and murder."

"I don't have to imagine it. I was in the chair, facing those cameras."

Jimmy smiled sadly at me. "You artist-types are the strangest, damnedest lot. On that note, Fionnula says Marie's best subject is English. Ironic, isn't it? I mean, given she came here with hardly any of our language at all."

"Children are like sponges," I said. "If we could only learn foreign tongues as easily as they do, we'd all be cosmopolitan as hell."

"Well, Fionnula said Marie is top in her class for story and journal writing," he said. "Fionnula thinks Marie might grow up to be a writer, like you."

Jimmy smiled, added, "And wouldn't that be something?"

BOOK THREE
The Judas Kiss
September 1957

36

"**G**oddamn Krauts! Damned Germans think they're the only one's who can frame a shot or light a set. Screw that!"

Sam pulled his eye patch down over his empty socket. "In the land of the blind, the one-eyed man is king," he shouted after the French journalist now on his way out the trailer door. Then Sam added, "And it's goddamn *Samuel* Amos Ford! *Sam* Ford, *not John* Ford—he's a *different* one-eyed director named Ford, you goddamned frog! If I'd directed *The Quiet Man*, I'd have eaten a goddamned Winchester in contrition! Print that!"

Sam spat and poured himself four more fingers of rye. Softer he said, "Swear to Christ, Hector, I'm done giving interviews, especially to these goddamn so called *cinéastes*, whatever that means. Goddamn snooty French intellectuals have to contend they discover *everything*, and if it's something truly American, like the Blues or crime films, they slap some Frenchified label on it. So-called 'film noir', say. And is that enough for 'em?"

I started to comment but Sam forged ahead. "Christ no, it's not enough! Some frog journalist has to go and say we stole all our imagery from the Fritz filmmakers. All that piss water from a goddamn egghead who goes and confuses me with that oater director *John* Ford. Hell, John's eye patch is on the *other* goddamn side."

We were waiting out a rainstorm in Sam's custom silver Airstream trailer on the Universal back-lot. I'd been two-stepping with Sam for most of '57, fitfully squeezing in script work on a pet project of Sam's about cockfighting called *Rooster of Heaven*, a film he envisioned to be shot south of the border. Filmed, "Well away from the lying studio heads and their crooked accountants," as Sam put it.

But there were funding shortfalls. To fill the chinks, Sam had agreed to take over direction of a film noir called *The Judas Kiss*. The film's original, dipsomaniacal director had recently perished when he missed a turn high up in the Hollywood Hills.

Sam said, "The paycheck on this gig will give me some walking around money for location scouting in Juárez, Tijuana. Seed money to get *our* film up and running."

I said, "And I'm here because…?" Through the trailer window, I watched the bustle on the studio lot. Gregory Peck and Chuck Heston walked together under big black umbrellas. The rain percolated against the trailer's aluminum skin.

"Because this damned 'noir' script is a dog, Hec. Plot's okay. Basic beats are in place. But the dialogue's awful and the pace is a mess. Now, if you're finished dicking around with interviewers, stolen skulls and the Feds, I want to get to work and make a movie. Fast as you are, I think a week of your work will make the script *spank*."

It had been a bitch of a year in most ways. And as Sam had said, there had been this mess earlier in the year involving the severed head of a long dead Mexican revolutionary—*craaazy* stuff. I felt I was just starting to touch ground again. A berserk and probably boozy week hanging with Sam wouldn't be the worst thing in the world. I said, "Sure. What the hell is one week, after all?"

Sam grinned, wringing his hands. "That's the spirit, kid! Everyone's already buzzing about how that Welles' film, *Touch of Evil*, marks the end of an era for iconic crime films. The last great *film noir* they're already crowing. Screw that! We'll make a film to shame that goddamn whale's ponderous potboiler."

He poured me a drink and raised his glass for a toast. "Here's to *The Judas Kiss*!"

"That title sounds like some robe-and-sandals Bible epic," I said. I nearly gagged on the rye. "This stuff is terrible."

"Hell, it's just an acquired taste, buddy."

"If that's so, the price of acquisition is too high, Sam." I put down my glass. "What's the gist of this picture's plot?"

Sam ran his fingers back through his unruly salt-and-pepper hair. "It's a torturous potboiler sorely lacking twists and reversals, but with your patented touch I think it might be confused for something that isn't not art."

I squeezed the bridge of my nose. "I'm still parsing that one," I said.

"Don't matter," Sam said. "Here's the premise. A G.I., still having readjustment-to-civilian-life grief, is struggling to pull it all together in 1957 Los Angeles. This grunt's cross to bear is heavier than most."

"How so?"

Sam drove home points with his index finger. "Our boy, Hank Lasher, was caught by the Nazis and fell into the hands of this sadistic kraut named Aldrich Bieber. Bieber's an SS-type of your worst fucking nightmares. This guy is one ass-nasty son of a bitch with a real zeal for blood. I mean one wicked-ass Kraut monster. I'm trying to get Vincent Price to play Bieber."

"Price sounds good for that."

"In spades," Sam said. "So Hank was caught by the Nazis and fell into the hands of Bieber. The Nazis want these invasion plan details they figure Hank is privy to. They stay at him and stay at him, slowly taking him apart. In the end, he breaks. Hank sells out his unit, and his fellows are killed to a man, including Hank's best buddy from back home, Ernie Johnson. Ernie's devoted, doting kid sister is the luscious Lizabeth Johnson, a blond, blue-eyed looker. Hank *loves* her. No, more than that, he *worships* her."

Sam poured himself some more rye. "Flashing back, our boys raid the place where Hank is being tortured and get him out before anything too permanent happens to him. I'll push the torture scenes as far as the censors will allow, but we won't be seeing too much, I figure. Anyway, that nasty-ass Nazi Bieber escapes. Hank is saved, and as there is nobody left alive except Bieber to contradict him, Hank lies and swears they never broke him. But they *had* broken Hank, made him a traitor, and that intelligence Hank spilled gets Ernie and the rest of his buddies annihilated by the Krauts."

Sam bummed a cigarette. "Now, *flash-forward*. Hank's recovered and is ready to be sent stateside. He demurs returning. He's overcome with guilt for selling out his mates, so he stays on in Europe for a long time, hunting Bieber. He's sworn to kill the son of a bitch, whatever the cost, figuring it's the only way to make up for betraying Ernie and his band of brothers.

"After ten years of fruitless searching through the hell-holes of South America, no success in his hunt, not even a faint trace of Bieber to show for all his efforts, Hank finally returns home. He works up the courage to pay a visit to Lizabeth. Turns out, she's married, and very happily, for like, eight or nine years. Then, on the fireplace mantel, Hank spots a wedding portrait of the happy couple. The groom is fuckin' Aldrich Bieber, the evil bastard who tortured Hank! How dramatic is that?"

"Seems a reach," I said.

Sam shot me a look. "Nah, it's in the script… such as it is. When he was on the rack, Hank tried to stall and buy time by rambling on about his best girl back in Los Angeles, luscious Lizabeth. Bieber falls in love with the *notion* of Lizabeth, and after establishing his new identity in the States, he went in search of her. Seduced her. This damned Nazi set himself up as a respectable Los Angeles businessman with a pretty wife and a nice little house on the outskirts of the city. Mr. Joe Citizen, of a sudden."

Sam blew a few smoke rings. "All of that plot stuff I've told you, *all* of it, I need you to cram into the first fifteen minutes of the film. The current version of Vargas' script burns about three-quarters of screen time to set all that up. I need you to shorthand it, so we can get into the meat of the story pronto, Hec."

I said, "And the meat of that story is…?"

"Hank wants to kill Bieber, slow and bloody," Sam said. "Yet it seems Bieber somehow makes Lizabeth genuinely happy. She's utterly devoted to him. The Nazi may really love her. And, of course, Bieber could conceivably tell Lizabeth how Hank got Ernie killed."

"Not without costing himself his wife, he couldn't," I said.

"Not an insoluble plot problem with a crafty and creative sucker like you pulling the strings, Hec. And anyway, it's your logic issue to solve, buddy. I just make your words sing with pictures, as always."

Sam tossed me a dog-eared script. "Just fix it, buddy, and fast. And now, vamoose. I've got a hooker due here within the hour."

37

The security guard said, "Anyone ever tell you how much you look like William Holden, only taller?"

I smiled ruefully and got my Chevy back in gear. "Few here and there." I palmed my turquoise '57 Bel Air out of the studio's lot. The rain was picking up. I nudged the wipers on and dialed around the car radio to a country station. A horn honk. I waved at a passing convertible. Clark Gable, Cadiz Ohio's favorite son, waved back.

World War II.

Nazi torturers.

It had been years since I gave any of that any thought. That last war, for me, seemed to stand away from the rest of my life in a funny way, almost an annex from the main event.

Duff and I had split in late forty-six. Peacetime and much time alone together in the desert found us less than compatible. The split was all very amicable and tinged with real regret from both sides. We still talked, still wrote each other long, loving, funny letters. Before my rather disastrous last marriage, when our paths crossed, Duff and I would often as not end up between the sheets for a weekend or two.

We were still good together as lovers, just not for very long.

And the others of that time…?

Gertrude Stein died of stomach cancer in 1946. Alice had been left alone to try and nurse Stein's memories, to handle her posthumous works and to dodge money-seeking Stein relatives who saw all those paintings and thought, "There be *mucho dinero*."

Jimmy was still in Cleveland, still a cop and still hunting the Cleveland Headhunter on his own time.

Werner Höttl…? I spent the rest of the 1940s underwriting searches for that one. No trail of a flight to South America or anywhere else ever emerged. No trace, even, of his ever having left Madrid. As Franco was proving durable, Spain was still off limits to me.

Little Marie? Last word I had on her was that she was in school, studying English lit and film at some Cleveland-area college. She wanted to be a screenwriter, Jimmy said. That prospect made me wince.

And Duff? She was here in L.A., somewhere. She was a studio publicist, by day. By night, she sang in various nightclubs and reputedly was building a pretty good following. She'd be forty in a few weeks. I toyed with calling her. I hadn't seen her face-to-face since late forty-nine.

Given my rocky last couple of years, I decided it was maybe better not to re-open that door just now. I sensed I'd be clingy.

And, anyway, I needed to get my ass in the chair and my fingers on the typewriter keys.

The material Sam wanted me to distill down to fifteen minutes of film now seemed to comprise about seventy-five percent of the existing script, just as Sam had said. I had a week to essentially rewrite the whole damned thing and build in now-absent second and third acts.

I headed back to my hotel room at the Biltmore and bent to the task.

An hour of work down. Then the phone rang:

I scooped it up, said, "Lassiter."

"Mr. Lassiter, it's Fenton Young."

Christ. Young was some tinhorn scholar/biographer who'd been hounding my ass the past few months, trying to secure my "official blessing" for a biography he planned about me. He was too steeped in this psychological mumbo-jumbo for my tastes. Too focused on my World War II experiences and, most alarmingly of all, on the recent death of my wife and child.

"Listen, you son of a bitch—"

He spoke over me. "Easy there, friend. I saw in Hedda Hopper's column you're here in Los Angeles working with Sam Ford. As a happy accident, I happen to be here, too. I'm actually calling from the lobby and I thought over drinks—"

Goddamn it. And goddamn Hedda Hopper. Few years back, the old bitch had spilled the beans on Spencer Tracy and Katharine Hepburn. Tracy actually kicked Hedda in her fat ass in Ciro's. I figured I might do much worse to the failed actress-turned-gossip maven.

But first I had this scholar to cope with. The fact the son of a bitch was from Yale made him more the menace in my eyes. Probably a Skull and Bones member, the weasel.

"Fenton, the answer is, emphatically, *no*," I said. "You write about me, let alone publish anything, and I get wind, then I'll feed you your own hands. Now you best get back East, 'cause if I spot you in the lobby, or anywhere, I'm going to lay you out cold."

I slammed down the phone and then called downstairs and asked my calls be screened. Only female callers and Sam Ford were to be put through.

I passed my week in that chair, fixing logic problems, punching up dialogue. Laying in some flirting from Lizabeth's end to further stoke Hank's reasons for trying to find a way to burn down Bieber and so not cost himself Lizabeth's love.

I burned up nights with a notebook and pen, nursing whisky and waters in the Formosa Café, watched over by framed portraits of Hollywood icons as I wrote. It was a scripting *sprint*.

Each time I returned to the Biltmore, the desk clerk handed me a sheaf of notes from Fenton Young, my would-be biographer. Each of those scraps of paper I dumped in the trash bin, unread.

Sam turned the last page of my version of *The Judas Kiss* and said, "It *does* spank, Hec! We'll be great to go, soon as the director of photography gets here."

I slid off the trailer's couch to make myself a drink. I'd brought along my own bottle of single malt. "I thought you had Steve Janning on board. He's a local. Hell, by birth or for business reasons, all these film-types are Angelinos, aren't they?" I took my first sip of whisky.

Sam waved a hand. He shook his head in disgust. "Janning? That bastard bailed three weeks ago," Sam said. "DP now is this cat named Armand Vargas. The script you fixed is his. He's the one who recommended me for director, though I've never met the guy. We've just exchanged a lot of memos. He knew you and I had worked together a few times and he put a bug in my ear to get you here to polish the script. Armand says your last book, *The Land of Dread and Fear*, might be your masterpiece."

That assessment put this Vargas in a very small club. I'd taken a critical drubbing for the novel. It was, the wags said, "too dark, too noir. Too literary to be pulp."

I said, "Sucker has good taste." I sipped more whisky. "But he's still a shitty screenwriter."

Sam helped himself to some of my top-shelf whisky. He said, "This next item could be good news, or bad news, depending on your mood." He took a sip of Scotch, let the burn pass, then said, "You are a freshly reborn bachelor, ain'tcha?"

My stomach was suddenly sour. "That's right. You read about it in Hopper?"

"Nah, some scholar was by couple days back. Said he's writing your biography and you'd given your blessing for me to talk on the record about you."

I nearly came out of my chair. "Fenton Young?"

"That's the longhair!"

I growled, "Don't ever talk to him again, Sam. He lied. I'm trying to bury this book of his."

"Anyway, he mentioned this stuff about you being on the market again. This last wife, what, number three, four? She stick you for much cock tax?"

"Wasn't a divorce," I said. "I'm a widower. Maria died." I got up and poured myself more whisky.

"Sorry, Hec. Didn't know the particulars."

"Why the hell do you ask?"

"The publicity person for this film—I got word today they hired this particular woman. Her name is Duff Sexton. Me not knowing many *Duffs* in my life, hell, not more than the one you married few years back, I figured maybe…"

"She'd be my Duff," I said. I shook my head. "I mean, my former Duff. I mean, yes, it's my ex-wife. That is to say, one of them."

"You two still talking?"

"Yeah, we left it very well. You don't have to sweat keeping us apart, Sam." I said, "Do you have her current address? Her phone number?" Now our reconnecting seemed foreordained.

He winked his one good eye. "Guess y'all didn't leave it *that* well."

"We don't always send Christmas cards," I said, "but we are…friendly."

Sam struggled up out of his chair. "Let me make a call. I'll try and get you the dope on where to reach her."

38

Duff had settled into a cozy place on Los Feliz; the Griffith Observatory loomed above and behind.

I slid out of the Bel Air, bottle of wine in one hand and flowers in the other, running head down through hard autumn rain. I dashed under the shelter of her front porch awning. I knocked on the door with the toe of my shoe.

That voice through the still-closed door, silky and husky all at once: "Hector Mason Lassiter?"

"Jesus, Duff, you turn psychic?"

"Sam Ford called ahead," she said through the door, fiddling with the lock. "Sam said you'd likely drop by. He said you said we're okay, but in case that was less than so, Sam thought I should have time to run or turn off the lights and pretend to be away."

Surprising sensitivity from Sam. I said, "What's the verdict, darlin'?'"

"I'm opening the door, or trying to. It swells and sticks in the rain."

Duff cracked the door and smiled. Silk blouse and tailored skirt; killer heels that did wonderful things for her calves. At thirty-nine, she was still a looker. I wanted to think she'd dressed for me. "It's raining hammers," she said.

"Tell me."

She smiled and opened the door. She kissed me, then took the flowers and wine. "You're looking good, Hec. I've heard worrying stories about your last couple of years." She knew just how to put it. "I'm *so* sorry to hear about Maria. Much, much sorrier about Dolores. I was worried what might walk through my door. But you look *so* fine." She put the wine on a table and stroked my cheek. "Want to talk about it?"

"If I did, you'd be the one I'd pour it out to, darlin'. But you've heard the stories, like you say, and there's not much to say beyond that. Frankly, I find it's best at this point just to put it all away."

"But you're holding it together?"

"Better every day," I said. "You know me—despite all my efforts to the contrary, I'm the consummate survivor." I took her left hand, checked for rings, then kissed her hand. "Looks like you're single again, too. I'd heard differently."

"Didn't work out." She smiled and pulled me to the kitchen. "Good news is, from your perspective, maybe that means so far as we went, *I* was the problem."

"No way," I said. "I blew it. Can't cut off the dark parts of myself that fire the writing." I went back and scooped up the bottle of wine. "Got a corkscrew?"

"In that last drawer," she said, "left of the sink." Duff rummaged around cupboards and found a vase and started doing something with the flowers. "I really think it *is* me. I'm in love with being in love. Building intimacy is heady. But maintaining it?" A head shake.

The cork popped and I said, "Little late to let it breathe."

Duff smiled and handed me two wine glasses. "No bottle of wine ever gets to breathe around you, Hec."

As I poured, I said, "Word is you just signed on for this gig, for *The Judas Kiss*. They didn't tell you I was on board, or did you maybe agree despite knowing I'm in the fold?"

"If I'd known you were on this one, I'd probably have signed on just to see how you're doing. I've been quite worried about you, darling."

I smiled. "Like I said, I'm doin' okay."

Duff smiled and stroked my face again. "Those dimples…" She sighed. "I've been getting calls about you. Some guy says he's your official biographer."

Fenton goddamn Young. I was going to have to send him to the dentist, that was becoming clear. "He isn't. Don't talk to the bastard. Besides, he's from Yale."

"And that's a problem?"

"This year, yeah, it surely seems to be." I passed her a glass of wine. We tapped goblets and I said, "To absent friends."

"And reunited ones." She sipped, said, "You still know the best wines."

"Not the most destructive of my talents."

"No, it isn't." Duff took my hand and led me to the couch. "Fact is, I've been backing away from the movie business. The nightclub performing isn't going to make me rich, but it keeps me pretty well, and I've got my own little following. So I've been thinking about going full-time as a torch singer."

"Sounds a fine plan. So why take this job with Sam? Why really?"

"I was partly flattered into it," she said. She sipped some more wine. "Some guy raved to Sam about my skills. Stroking my ego's always been a pathetically effective way of getting my attention and into my good graces. But I also took it to help my young friend get a foot in the door. But you, actually, can do that more effectively than me."

"What, some would-be screenwriter?"

"That's right. Flies in tomorrow."

"Got talent?"

Duff nodded. "I think so. In spades."

"What's his name?"

"Her name," Duff corrected me. "Marie O'Rourke."

I said, "Not *that* Marie? Little Marie? Jimmy's Marie?"

"Jimmy's Marie," she said, "but not so little anymore. She's twenty-four, Hector."

39

D uff said she was feeling cooped up; she'd spent several days at home, coming off a cold. I'd caught her on the rally. After a light meal at the Pacific Dining Car, we took a rainy ride up into the Hollywood Hills with the corked bottle of wine and a couple of paper cups.

We parked and stared down at the lights through the rain-streaked windshield. The radio on low. Patsy Cline was crooning "Walkin' After Midnight."

I said, "Jimmy must hate this, his niece in this wicked town, in this business. This city is a shark pool, you know that. Jimmy certainly thinks that way."

Duff took my hand. "The fact you and I are here to watch out for her mollified Jim. And anyway, it's Marie's dream. We'll see she gets the right start. And we'll see to it that everyone in the industry knows you're watching over her. That will keep the wolves and mashers at bay. My God, you should hear the way people in this town talk about you."

I shrugged and said, "City like this one, it's better to be feared than loved."

Duff scooted across the seat and rested her head on my shoulder.

She said, "It's a beautiful view in the rain. But coming up here in this weather is probably borrowing trouble, Hec: these very hills already lost the film its original director."

"Yeah. Who was this admirer who drafted you for this gig with Sam?"

"Armand something," Duff said.

"Ah-hah." *Armand Vargas.* Suddenly I had acid stomach.

She looked around the interior of my Chevrolet. "I like this very much. It's new?"

"Relatively. It's a fifty-seven, that is to say."

This wicked smile. "You christen it, yet?"

I raised an eyebrow. "Define christen."

"You know, fool around in it?"

"That's kid's stuff," I said, laughing and shaking my head.

"I'm still a kid. Got a little while yet before I hit forty and am over the hill like you. The rain, the lights down below. That backseat. C'mon, Hec, you're not *that* old."

Business was light in the Brown Derby. I'd picked the place. Duff said, "You're a pushover for anything even vaguely Latin looking." *Yeah.*

They seated us in number five. Story went Gable proposed to Lombard in that very booth.

It was a weeknight and the rain was something more than just weather tonight; it was downright vicious now. Smoking a cigarette and listening to the rain lash the windows, I studied all those crazy caricatures lining the walls. Duff had excused herself to the ladies room.

Duff slid back into the booth and said, "Doubt we'll get another chance to do that again once Marie gets here. She's due in after lunch." Duff reached across the table and took my hand. She said, "So maybe you should spend the night. I mean, if you want to."

I smiled, uncertain Duff truly wanted that with me. "You're sure?"

"Hector, I'm virtually insisting."

A rusty red DeSoto was hard on our tail. Couldn't be anything good about that. Chewing my lip, I eased off the gas; let a red light catch me. I shifted into park, said, to Duff, "If something goes bad, slide across the seat and drive on."

Before she could balk, I slid out of my Bel Air. I recognized the man behind the wheel. I whipped out my Colt and used the butt to break the DeSoto's driver's side window. The man inside raised his hands, cowering and sputtering. I reached in and shifted his car into park then tore the keys from the ignition. I pitched them far.

My self-declared Boswell, my would-be biographer Fenton Young, sprayed spittle as he sputtered, "What in God's name, Lassiter?"

"Jesus," I said. "I should just shoot you and be done with it." The light had gone green. The drivers behind Young's car began leaning on their horns. I waved my Colt in their direction, and that shut them up.

I gripped Young's chin in my hand. "My last warning, pal. Come after me again and I swear I'll make you wish you were dead. My life is mine, and mine alone to write about. Drop your damned book."

After breakfast, Duff and I said our good-byes. I needed to dash back to my place and get some fresh clothes for a meeting with Sam and his prospective lead actor. Duff was on her way to the airport to pick up Marie.

I'd driven perhaps four miles when I got the sense the gray, fifty-five Olds back there was almost certainly following me. There were two men in the car. In the still-drizzling rain, and far back as they were, I couldn't get a good look at them. At first, I thought maybe Fenton Young had hired some help. But *two* men? That didn't compute.

I'd been in L.A. earlier in the year because of the caper with the skulls, so I still had the roadmap pretty squarely in my head.

Stubbing out my cigarette in the ashtray, I gave the Bel Air the gas and made a hard right onto Ventura Boulevard, tires squealing on the slick pavement.

The ones following me were dumb enough to follow suit and lay the hammer down, leaving no doubt but that they were shadowing me.

But I had horsepower on my side. I made a few more stomach-tugging turns, then got the boys on a straight-away. I put three blocks between us, then peeled through an alley. When I reached the street at the other end, I hopped out and wheeled a dumpster into the middle of the alley, blocking my pursuers' escape. I sprinted back to the Bel Air and whipped around the corners to block the *other* end of the alley, my pursuers' only route of retreat.

The boys in the Olds were backing up at speed when they saw my Bel Air slide into their path. I scooted across the seat and slid out the passenger side door. From the far side of my Chevy, I put two shots through the back window of the Olds with my civilian piece, a vintage Colt .73 Peacemaker. The first shot was to break the glass and reduce the risk of deflection; the second shot was to take out the passenger with a bullet to the left shoulder.

The driver flattened out on the front seat, probably being bled all over by his wounded buddy.

I hollered, "Out of there now, fellas. First fling your guns far out through the window, then you come out slow and with your hands up. Once you do that, you spread eagle on the ground."

Silence.

One minute passed, then another.

I yelled again, "The gun through the window, and you follow, or I'm going to start shooting again."

Two shots rang out.

The interior of the surviving windows of the Olds were sprayed with blood now.

Frowning, I gave it a minute.

Two.

I crept over to the Olds, Colt at the ready.

The driver had shot his passenger, then turned his gun on himself.

Two head shots.

What the hell?

Professionals wouldn't tote around wallets with identification. These fellas *did*.

"Joseph Brown" of Alameda.

"John Green" of Oakland.

Right.

I dug deeper. Yes, these suckers were very much amateur hour. In hidden wallet compartments meant for storing "getaway cash," I found their real identification cards.

The driver was Max Veidt. His partner was Dieter Dönitz. Max had killed himself and Dieter with a Luger.

I checked the bloodstained glove compartment, then under the seats, careful to keep my sports jacket clear of all that dripping blood and brain matter.

Sirens in the distance: maybe they were headed my way, but maybe somebody else had their own little blood mystery unfolding a few blocks away.

I slipped the men's wallets into my pockets, then swiftly patted down the corpses. In Max's shirt pocket I found a single slip of paper:

A.V., Biltmore Hotel
506 S. Grand Avenue
Room 603

The Biltmore. And, apparently, a *neighbor* of mine. I slipped the paper into my shirt pocket and fled the scene.

The present desk clerk at the Biltmore, fortuitously new to me, seemed to think he should be paid some gelt for information. His approach rubbed me the wrong way.

I said, "You really want to shakedown a cop?" I flashed an honorary LAPD badge Jack Webb gave me after some under-the-gun script-doctoring I'd delivered for the staccato, laconic Joe Friday. I think old Jack has boxes of those damned badges, passing them out to Hollywood scribes like candy bars.

Either way, it was a good enough hunk of tin to fool the hotel wage-slave. I said, "Room 603, who's in there, hombre?"

The clerk, of a sudden come-all-over-obsequious, checked his registration book. "Checked out an hour ago."

"His name?"

He squinted, said, "Hector Lassiter."

"Come again?"

"His name was Hector Lassiter."

"Let me see that damned book." I spun the registration book around. Sure enough, it was my name, but nothing close to my handwriting. And it sure didn't gibe with those initials on that slip of paper I took off the dead driver of the Olds.

I pushed the book back across the desk to the clerk. "Has that room been cleaned yet?"

"Probably not."

I snapped my finger and held out my hand, palm up. "Pony up the key, ace."

The bed was turned down and the sheets rumpled. I scooped up the note pad to check later for any writing impressions.

I emptied the wastepaper basket on the floor and sorted. Some tissue paper, a spent matchbook from Chicote's. That was one of my old Madrid haunts back when I could still go to Spain. I found an empty cigarette pack—a European brand—HB, or Haus Bergmann smokes. *German* coffin nails. I slipped the empty HB pack into the pocket of my sports jacket.

After checking my watch, I decided to give the room five more minutes of my time. There was a newspaper on the writing table with an empty Coca-Cola bottle. I flipped through the *L.A. Times*, looking for anything underlined, circled or torn out I might be able to check against a pristine copy.

Nada, nada and *nada.*

Whoever had been here had taken a shot at the crossword puzzle, abandoning all hope of cracking that sucker about a third through after several screw-ups in unforgiving fountain pen.

I moseyed back downstairs and tossed the key to the clerk. "Any outgoing calls this guy placed?"

He frowned and turned his back on me, digging through paper. He handed me a single sheet with three numbers written on it.

The first two phone numbers were identical and placed to another hotel on Rodeo Drive.

The third call had been placed to Sam Ford at eight o'clock last night, just about the time Duff and I were "christening" my Bel Air.

I headed back up to my own room. Someone was crouching by my door. I slowed, reaching for my gun. A man was sprawled there on the ground. Wary, I kept a hand on the butt of my Colt and eased up next to the body on the floor. I squeezed the man's earlobe, bringing him back around.

Son of a bitch if it wasn't Fenton Young. He had a black eye now... *and* a fat lip. Dried blood at both nostrils. He groaned and cupped his swollen, bruised eye. "What now, you sorry son of a bitch? Who hit you? And what are you doing outside my room? I told you—"

"Government men," he snarled. Young whimpered and pressed his hand harder to his eye. "Some crazy men stopped me. They beat me! They were dressed in black suits and ties. They said they were on official business. Wanted me to tell them something about you and some German man."

Black suits and ties.

Hm. FBI? CIA? Six-of-one, a-half-dozen of the other.

I helped the bastard up, said, "So someone is trying to get to me through you, huh, Fent? Let this be a lesson to you. You're not the only mouth-breather bent on the notion of harassing me, dumbass. And what were you up to, anyway? Trying to break into my room maybe? Guess so, given you're at my doorstop. Well, learn a lesson here. It's not just *me* you have to sweat when you nose into my affairs. I've got enemies by the truckload." I shrugged. "Guess I just live that kind of life. You stay out of it, now, yeah?"

"I need a doctor," Young said.

"Sure you do," I said. "I'll ask the hotel detective to see you get some help just as soon as I call down to have him haul your ass away from here for trying to burgle my room. I mean to see you do some time for this one, sport."

40

I drove to Rodeo Drive, foot heavy on the gas. I was squeezing in the trip before my scheduled meeting with Sam and his potential star who'd play "Hank" in *The Judas Kiss*.

My Jack Webb badge got the names of those registered to the room "Hector Lassiter" had called from the Biltmore, the two men who had followed me from Duff's apartment.

"I'm going to need to search the room," I said, hand out for the key.

Nothing too revelatory emerged: anonymous clothes, spare ammo for that Luger.

The boys had bypassed the requisite hotel Bible in the bureau in favor of a copy of *Mein Kampf* that one had packed.

This chilly epiphany tardily ambushed me:

They followed me from Duff's apartment.
They've been watching Duff's!

The cops would probably find this place, eventually. They'd start checking in- and outbound calls. I couldn't risk a phone call to Duff from this room.

I hit a payphone in the lobby. I called the airport. I had Duff paged. She said, "Hector? What's wrong?"

"Marie's plane land yet?"

"It's due in half-an-hour. Why are you calling me?"

"Try not to be obvious about it," I said, "but look around you, sweetheart. Anyone seem to be spying on you?"

Her voice, going tense, "What is going on, Hec?"

"Bloody trouble, darlin'. I think it's all tied up with your visitor. When you get Marie, don't collect her bags right away. Just beeline for a security guard and stay glued to that fella, heart of my heart. I'll come there and fetch you two. I'm leaving now."

"What's happening?"

"Germans, *Nazi* types, followed me from your place this morning. They're dead now, and *not* by my hand. Tell you more when I see you."

Fifty-five white-knuckle minutes getting to the Los Angeles Airport. I burned twenty more minutes wandering the concourse, frantically looking for Duff and Marie.

I finally found them in an airport lounge, chatting up an elderly airport guard. The old dude wouldn't do much good in a brawl, I reckoned, but his uniform and sidearm might cow a displaced German thug still finding his way in the States. I checked the guard's badge and said, "Officer Lynch, my thanks for watching over my gals."

He winked—a very grandfatherly guy. He said, "What kind of problems are stalking these lovely ladies?"

"Unwanted suitors," I said. I hugged and kissed Duff.

This young woman seated beside her stood, smiled. The last time I saw Marie in person, she was fifteen and a little gawky, still wearing braces. I'd seen photos since, but they didn't do her justice. She was dark and attractive, now. Hell, coltish. She had this charisma.

I pressed a hand to my chest, then hugged her. "Marie, you're a heart-breaker."

"So great to see you, Hector." Smiling, she hugged me back, hard.

"You've gotten *tall*," I said. To the old guard I said, "Any suspicious types around?"

He shook his head, setting his wattle to wiggling. "Not that I've seen."

I took his offered hand. Old guy had a creditable grip. "Again, thanks." I turned to Duff. "We'll get Marie's luggage, then—"

"The officer saw to that," Duff said, smiling at him. She obviously had him in her hip pocket. "He radioed for Marie's bags to be brought up. We're all ready to go."

"Then let's do that." I took Duff's arm. "We'll pick up your car later."

The old security guard said, "I'll escort you to your car."

Hell, he did carry a gun. "That'd be swell," I said.

41

Marie was squeezed into the front seat between us. After our dalliance in the back seat, guess neither Duff nor I could cotton to the notion of having Marie sit back there just yet. I turned down the radio on Sam Cooke's "You Send Me." Marie said, "What is going on Hector?"

I kept checking the mirror. Duff said, "That crazy biographer again? Or someone else?"

Marie said, "What crazy biographer?"

"Some academic is trying to write a biography about Hector," Duff said. "It's got Hec going crazy. Guy's been following him, snooping around."

"Makin' my life a living hell," I said. "You can't imagine what it's like having some would-be author with an axe to grind trying to tell your story." I checked the mirror again. No tails for the moment.

"My meddlesome biographer aside, there is some real trouble, I'm sorry to tell you, Marie," I said. "If I wasn't afraid of you being followed back to Euclid, I'd put you on a return flight to Ohio this instant."

Marie said, "Again, Hector, what is going on?"

I hesitated, said, "Understand, please, you were *so* young then. I don't know how much your mother or uncle might have told you about this particular German—"

"Werner Höttl?" Marie put it out there, blunt like that. She looked from me to Duff and back again. "Hector, Höttl was kind of my personal version of the bogeyman. Uncle Jimmy used to show me pictures of Höttl he'd gotten from his spy connections made during the war. Jimmy would talk to me about the man's scar. Unc wanted me to be able to spot Höttl in a crowd *like that.*" She snapped her fingers. Her nails were long and varnished. I still couldn't adjust to her being grown up, a woman.

Marie veered into an Irish accent now, close enough to evoke something of Jimmy's tenor. "Lassie, you ever see that devil's face, you *run!* You run and get word to me. If that Kraut devil ever gets me, then you get word to Hector Lassiter. Hec will know how to handle the boyo and for certain. If Hec isn't available, then you go to Ernie Hemingway."

"That sort of answers my question," I said, half-smiling at her impression of Jimmy.

"Uncle Jimmy was always running spooky scenarios by me," Marie said. "He'd take me for long drives and get me lost and say, "Now, imagine I'm Werner Höttl, and you escape from this car somehow. What do you do in those first moments you're shed of him?"

God. I'd thought when we got Marie out of France we'd delivered the child from darkness. Apparently, Jimmy had kept the specter of that Nazi monster front-and-center for little Marie in all the years since.

A part of me could see Jimmy's side in doing that. Hanrahan was a terrific cop who'd spent his life chasing monsters, including decades pursuing his own personal demon, the

Cleveland Torso-Slayer. So far as Höttl was concerned—my own personal demon, and Marie's too—I'd not delivered on my end back there in Europe. I'd failed to *kill* Höttl. Consequently, Jimmy wanted to keep Marie safe, whatever the cost. He meant to prepare her for any eventuality.

But *Christ*, I wanted the kid's life in Ohio to be sunshine and honey.

Duff said, "Hec, Marie and I have had some time to talk. She knows about all of it."

Marie said, "I also know about what Höttl almost did to you."

One thing still wasn't clear to me. Had anyone told Marie that Werner was her real father? I surely didn't want to be the one to accidentally drop *that* bombshell on her.

Duff said, "Now, what has happened, Hector?"

I sighed and said, "Two men followed me this morning from your place, Duff. There was a chase. The one shot his partner, then turned the gun on himself. The gun was a Luger. The two men had false identifications. They were stupid enough to carry their real papers on them. They were German. They were also packing a copy of *Mein Kampf*. That and the gun makes 'em throwbacks, to my mind. Die-hards, I guess you could say."

"And from that you make the leap to Werner Höttl?" Duff leaned around Marie, searching my face. "Question their reading tastes, sure, but—"

"It's my strongest instinct." I cracked the wing window to let in the smell of the resuming rain. "The man they were working for was registered in the Biltmore Hotel under my name."

I felt Marie shiver against me. Duff probably felt it, too. She said, "You confronted this man?"

"Just his empty room," I said. "But he made a phone call from that room I sorely need to follow up on."

I checked the rearview mirror again. "The good news is, for the moment, we're free of tails. Probably because our friend, the *other* Hector Lassiter, has had his ranks unexpectedly thinned this morning."

Smiling at Marie, I said, "Does your uncle let you drink?"

She shook her head. "He probably wouldn't approve, but I am twenty-four. I make my own wicked choices now." This pause as she read my expression. "Don't worry, it wouldn't be my first drink."

"We'll find a good place, then. Plot our next moves."

We headed over to Wilshire and Trader Vic's for some Mai Tais. When you're paranoid, there's nothing for distraction like crazy Tiki décor and island ambience.

Recent rum shortages had forced a change in the classic recipe: Duff and Marie seemed fine with that. Always the purist, disappointed, I switched to something with tequila.

I left them with their drinks and hit a payphone, patting some nastily sneering, hand-carved Tiki god on his potbelly for luck. I called the studio and found Sam Ford in his office, waiting for me so we could go to lunch. He was miffed when I told him I couldn't make that date with him and Rock Hudson.

Sam swore he hadn't received a call at eight p.m. last evening, the time indicated on the Biltmore's phone records. Sam said, "I had a woman here, Hec. So I had that cocksucking phone off the hook." Then Sam veered. "Rock and me will probably be migrating to some bars after lunch. Maybe the

Frolic Room. Check back here if you get free and I'll leave word with the front office what our libational itinerary looks like. Rock's really looking forward to meeting you. He's a fan, goddamn it."

Christ. I shook out a cigarette and fired up with my Zippo. I said, "You sure Rock is right for the part of Hank?"

Sam, cagey now: "What could be wrong?"

"He's tall, good-looking, most women claim," I said. "But word is, he's more than a tad light in the loafers."

Now Sam was being extra careful with word choices. "So what?" It sounded like Sam was lighting a cigar on his end, probably to buy himself time to think about his phrasing. He said, "Hector, there's what we are, and there's the image we project. In life, only the last really matters, and that's particularly true in the movie business. Perception is reality."

"Until *Confidential* and *Hush-Hush* knocks down that projected or perceived image," I said. "Hell, Hedda Hopper might go after Rock, like she did with Cary Grant and Randy Scott."

"*Ain't* gonna happen here," Sam said.

I said, "Yeah, *well.* Quick change of subject: Have you ever met Armand Vargas? In the *flesh*, that is to say?"

"Nah, just corresponded, like I said the other day."

"Not even a phone call?"

"*Nada*," Sam said.

"Know anybody who *has* met this cat?"

"Some front office-types who've employed him as a director of photography claim to," Sam said. I could hear the frown in his voice. "Why do ya ask?"

"Armand seems a mystery man," I said. "Have a feeling that handle's an alias."

"What's *that* matter? Goddamn movie business is full of folks who've changed their names. Rock—hey Rock, what's your birth name?" I could hear another voice mumble something. Sam again: "There, you *see*, Roy Harold Scherer, Jr. of Winnetka. So in this town, it's *gotta* be Rock Hudson, right? Anyway, I want to get you two together, so you can take his measure and tweak the dialogue to Rock's cadences and the like."

"Fine, we'll arrange it," I said. "Next time you talk, have the names of two or three guys who've met this Armand Vargas. I want the description of this fella."

"Anything in particular you're looking for?"

"A very nasty scar down the right side of his face would be a dandy start."

I slid into the booth and sipped my cocktail. Watching her over the salted rim of my glass, I said, "Marie, honey, how'd you choose this film as the one to wet your feet in the business? Earlier this year, I was in Venice, California, with Orson Welles on the set of a film that would have been a real experience for you—Marlene Dietrich, Chuck Heston and Janet Leigh."

"It was a contest," Marie said. "I got this letter sent to me at school. The movie was to be one chosen at studio discretion. It was just a wonderful stroke of luck it turned out to be a film you two were attached to."

"Very lucky," my ex said softly. "Almost an embarrassment of riches in terms of luck." Her gaze drifted to me. Duff gave me this, *You say it, Hector* look.

"Yeah," I said, toeing out there. "In my experience, luck simply doesn't run that rich, honey." Toying with my glass, I said, "Was there a particular name associated with this contest, Marie? Is there a contact name you can call to mind?"

"It was all handled by mail," she said.

Jimmy must have loved that. It should have had all his warning signals buzzing. But it was the kid's dream and she was probably indomitable. And as Duff had said, the fact I was here with Duff on the receiving end would likely "mollify" Jimmy, just as it seemingly had.

Duff said, "What exactly do you suspect, Hector?" Although I sensed she now shared my own fears about all this, Duff was playing fence-sitter to some extent, keeping a foot in Marie's pond in case we had to go good-cop, bad-cop on the darlin'.

"It's this *Armand Vargas* angle," I said. "Armand, the man who recruited you for this film, Duff. The mystery man who recruited me. The man Sam Ford hasn't laid eye on yet. Nobody I can find has ever seen this Vargas character, and I'm not finding anything on him in terms of a filmography. It's like Vargas just materialized in the past few weeks."

Maria put it out there, cold again. "You think Vargas is really Höttl? That's what you think, isn't it?"

"Maybe," I said. "Höttl's been missing for thirteen years. It's possible he's established himself in Hollywood under some other identity. Los Angeles is lousy with German film directors who fled the Fatherland ahead of the war and Hitler's increasingly heavy hand. Höttl could blend in, in that sense. This Vargas alias, if it is one, might be an identity cooked up just for the three of us, to draw us all in for a killing stroke."

I stirred my straw around in my drink. "Regardless of who he really is, Vargas is trouble. These dead Germans who chased me this morning had a slip of paper for someone staying in the Biltmore Hotel. That someone's initials are A.V. This same A.V. placed a call to Sam Ford's place last evening."

"Well, that is damning," Duff said. "More than a bit chilling."

Marie was more resistant. "If this is some kind of plot, it doesn't make sense to me," she said. "First, how could he find me back home? And if he could, why not strike at me there?"

I picked up a souvenir matchbox, struck one and lit up another Pall Mall. "It makes sense for Höttl to let you reach here if he wants it *all*—all three of us here to take down at once, maybe. Some sweeter form of revenge in his mind. As to how he found you in Ohio? Well, that does baffle me. And it makes it harder to know what to do next. If he did find you there, you going back home now, which is my strong impulse, doesn't truly solve anything."

Marie crossed her arms on the table, chin out. "Then you don't want me on the set?"

"Hell, I'm not going back to that set under these circumstances," I said. "And I'd handcuff Duff to a post if she tried to go there. This is all hinky and also getting bloody."

"So what would you have me do?" Marie looked from me to Duff. "Do you agree with him?"

"I do," Duff said. "Darling, Hector and I can get you on a set anytime, and Hector can likely do more for you than that given his own screenwriting credentials and connections. But this, *now?* Two men are dead and this stuff about Armand Vargas is more than disquieting. I'm scared for myself now, let alone the threat to you and Hector. So, yes, I have to agree with Hector. This all feels orchestrated to some bad end."

"I'm so sorry, kid," I said. "Duff's right, I'll make it up for you, in spades. This is merely a dream's delay, not a denial. I'll get you back out here myself, and we'll make a *good* movie together, not some potboiler like this one. You'll help me with the script, and I'll get you a screenwriting credit, and *soon.*"

Marie hung her head. "But *now?*"

"*Now*, for this moment, I think we're safe if we stay away from the studio, away from Sam Ford and away from any direct phone contact with your folks or Jimmy," I said. "The next step is for me to tuck my Bel Air away in a parking garage somewhere. I'll rent a beater car with something under the hood, then telegram your uncle. We'll shack up in some hotel for a couple of days to wait."

"To wait for what?"

"For your uncle to use his cop tricks to get out here without a tail," I said. "Then I'm putting you and Duff on a plane with Jimmy to Mexico for a little southern R and R while I close out business here with Armand, or Werner... or *whomever*."

In the near dark of Trader Vic's parking lot, I tripped over something bunched up alongside my Bel Air. A groan: it was a person sprawled on the ground.

I knelt down and turned the man's face into the light. He'd been badly beaten this time. An arm was broken. Duff and Marie were looking over my shoulder. "Who is he?"

"My would-be Boswell, biographer Fenton Young," I said, disgusted. I drew my gun. Once again, it seemed Young had run afoul of someone looking for me. If so, they might still be lurking, watching. I said, "You girls get in the back seat, quickly."

I pinched Fenton's earlobes to bring him around again and then helped him to his feet. "Let's get you in the front seat," I said. I folded Young into my Bel Air, then slid in behind the wheel.

I got us on the road fast, the Colt resting on my lap in easy reach. So far, nobody seemed to be following. My biographer was whimpering and clutching his belly.

"Okay, Young," I said. "I'm taking you to the hospital. You've lost at least two teeth and I think your left arm is broken. Who did this to you?"

Groaning, really milking it, I thought, he choked out, "Nazis!"

I shot him a look. "Come again? Actual Germans?"

"No, Angelinos, I think," he said through bloody teeth. "But they dressed like Nazis. I mean, they wore armbands with swastikas. They ran away, stopped beating on me, when some men came out of the restaurant." I glanced back and saw Marie's wide, frightened eyes in the rearview.

"And they were looking for me?"

"And for a woman they said is with you." Young tried to turn around in his seat then, to look back at Duff and Marie.

"Huh-uh," I said, pressing a hand to his bruised cheek and turning his head forward. "Eyes forward, egghead. Otherwise I'll drop you on the street here, and I won't even brake first."

"I *do* need a doctor," he said. "I feel like my ribs are broken."

"Could well be. If one of those suckers finds a lung, could be lights out for all time for you, hombre." Just couldn't help twisting that knife a bit. "How'd you find me this time?" If Young could tail me, I figured I must be losing my touch.

He groaned a little and said, "A fluke. I was at Vic's for a drink. I happened to see your car and—"

"You tried to burgle that," I finished for him.

"I'm quitting," he said. His chin was quivering. "I swear it."

I said, "You're quitting what, exactly?"

"This project. This book about you. Not because it's not my right and the public doesn't have a right to know about you. Not because you've threatened me. But I am quitting."

Arching an eyebrow, I said, "Why toss in the towel now?"

"Because these people around you are so terrible! My God, how do you go on living this life of yours? These terrible people hounding and harassing you? Chasing you? How do you stand it?"

Yeah.

And he said it without a trace of irony. Typical academic.

42

I left Duff and Marie at a hotel where I'd secured adjoining rooms. I'd hidden out in the same place earlier in the year. It held ghosts, but I knew it was safe.

While the ladies settled in, I tooled over to the Grand Central Market. I stashed my Bel Air in the Clocktower parking garage. Place was largely deserted at this hour, mostly empty spaces. I heard footsteps; figured I was being tailed. Then I realized it was the echo of my own skittish footfalls. Every shadow seemed nasty with menace, now. I have a strong imagination from the jump. It didn't take much of that to imagine myself right back in Höttl's chair in Paris, waiting to be dissected alive.

I hit an Italian restaurant and picked up three entrees to go and a couple of bottles of wine. I cabbed it back to the hotel. I rapped the door and said, "Don't shoot, gals. It's your favorite Texan."

Duff saw the restaurant bags, said, "Perfect. I'm starved. We'll have to wait a few minutes, however. Marie's showering. Have to say, she's pretty dejected, Hec."

"That can be overcome," I said, opening a bottle of wine. "Loathe as I am to do much more with film, I will suffer through in order to get Marie's foot in the damned door. I'll see we share a screenwriting credit, just as I said, and shiftless sort I feel as this goddamn wicked year winds down, I will see the words are really mostly hers."

I kissed Duff and said, "But there's something I need to know, sweetheart. Does that girl know she's Höttl's flesh and blood?"

"Yes," Duff said, offering me a paper cup to fill with wine. "Since she was about twelve, I think."

Duff sipped her wine. "Not bad, despite the paper cup. Look, I'm all for getting Jimmy here and having him and Marie disappear into Mexico, but I'm staying here with you. I saved you from Höttl once, and I have my own sources and skills. I can help you, Hec."

I poured myself some wine. "I well know what you are capable of. And I agree up to a point. But I think we're up against more than just Höttl in this mess."

She gave me this incredulous smile. "Such as what? Neo-Nazis, or something? They're mostly a joke."

"Maybe those, too. But more even than that."

"Who, then? What, exactly?"

"I'm still groping my way through on that front," I said. "It's more of a gut instinct than something I can point to. Höttl finding Marie in Ohio portends something bigger at back of this, I think. Grief you don't need."

"Well, when you have something firm on that front, then you can frighten me, Hector. Until then, we're going to pursue this Armand Vargas or Werner Höttl together."

"This could get very bad," I said. "There's real risk here."

"That's why you need me, Hector." Duff smiled and kissed me. "I make you circumspect. I always have."

The shower water cut out. I said, "Guess we can start preparing dinner."

Duff said, "Don't try and distract me. You haven't agreed that I'm staying."

"You noticed."

She said, "I know all your tricks, Hec. Never forget that."

Forget? Hell, I loved her for it.

Marie fiddled with her food more than ate it. After a time, she said, "You really think Höttl still wants me dead?"

"Yeah," I said. "Don't ask me why that is still so after thirteen years. Originally, he claimed it was because he saw big things for himself in the post-War Nazi movement. I reckon he had visions of himself as a kind of neo-Führer, or the like. Hell, even Ezra Pound's protégé, that nut John Kasper, hasn't been able to make a go of it in that sorry role. Anyway, I guess this thing with you is just some kind of obsession for Höttl, kiddo. The mad bastard craves revenge."

"I don't understand that," Marie said.

"You don't understand revenge?" I squeezed her hand and gave her this sad smile. "I surely do."

My telegram to Jimmy was fired off. I rented a nondescript Ford, then headed back to the hotel.

I sat with a glass of wine, leafing through my address book and looking for sources who might get me some more information about Höttl. Most of my domestic OSS cronies were dead or retired and moved on to parts unknown.

Marie poured herself a cup of wine. She curled her legs up under her in a chair. Jo Stafford was crooning on the radio. Marie looked profoundly glum.

"I'm sorry for all this," I said softly to her. "I swear I'll do better for you. I'm so sorry this isn't what it seemed."

She sipped her wine; bit her lip. "Frankly, I was hoping you were very wrong about all this and you'd really cost me an opportunity. But this writer who was beaten by your car? These dead Germans? The notion this man is chasing me still, and that he really wants to *kill* me?" Marie hung her head. "I'm so damned *tired* of his shadow hanging over my life. So many years, and yet it seems so fresh in some ways. I want to hurt him back, Hector. I want to sour his life and make it last forever." She searched my eyes. "Maybe someone should write a book about Höttl. I mean, look at the grief that someone's desire to write your biography is causing you, and you're a good man."

Yeah, look at me, the good *man.*

I took her hand. "Tough for me to get my mind around it too—his still hunting you." I smiled. "Yet in some ways, it doesn't seem that long ago I pulled you out of that hole in the wall, this little wide-eyed darlin' without a word of English. Seems not long ago at all we jumped off that balcony onto that mattress before the building exploded." I kissed her forehead. "You remember any of that, kid?"

Marie shook her head. "Images, mostly. I remember Pancho from back then. I remember my time with him very clearly." She smiled sadly. "He almost saw me through college, you know."

That was a bit of a gut punch. I dearly loved that dog. So much, in fact, that I'd never permitted myself another.

Marie and Pancho. Two strays who'd gotten through that sturdy wall of my own construction back then. Chance meetings still sending out ripples fifteen years on.

Nothing is ever over. Not ever. In life there's only one ending. You die; roll the credits.

"I *really* hope you're still somehow wrong about all this," she said again.

"Sure. Me too. But I'm not wrong, Marie. Two very dead Nazi-throwback Germans in Los Angeles says it all, honey."

She sighed. "Uncle Jim is on the way, then?"

"I'll know tomorrow. He'll call me through a friend. Ex-boxer friend of mine who lives here in town. Packy will pass our messages back and forth. We'll rendezvous at a little airstrip outside Bakersfield. 'Tween now and then, it's just a matter of staying scarce."

Marie said, "Won't that 'staying scarce' cause you problems with Sam Ford?"

"He'll be livid," I said. "But then Sam's not the Webster's illustration of dependable. That cyclops is an alcoholic and his habit's getting' stronger. I don't know how much longer the suits will put up with Sam's shenanigans." I waved a hand. "Anyway, I'll say it was a woman and case of whisky keeping me scarce. Sam'll be forgiving if he thinks it was like that. He likes to kid himself we're birds of a feather."

I freshened our cups. It felt more than a little funny to be drinking with Marie. In nearly all ways, I really did still see her as that little girl cowering in her hole in the wall. But I owed her more. I said, "Duff says you brought along spec scripts you've written."

"Yes."

"We've got at least forty-eight hours, kiddo," I said. "I've written whole scripts in half that time. Let's see what you've got. Maybe see what script you and I can cook up together tonight."

Marie beamed.

43

"Jaysus, things must be fuckin' dire," Jimmy said, looking around the car's interior. "For you to be driving a fecking Ford? Must be frost forming in Hell."

Watching the mirrors, I said, "Yeah, you know me, always a Chevy man. And I guess anyone looking for me would know that, too. Hence, this sorry heap. Make any friends on your way out here?"

Jimmy frowned. "In Ohio, yes, but not German friends. Or I don't think so, at any rate. You know, Cincinnati is *lousy* with Germans, but Cleveland, not so much. They'd tend to stand out there." He paused, said, "These looked like government boys, to me."

I was incredulous. "What, like East German government?"

"No, Hector, nothing so fanciful. More like our government."

That made me wince. "Christ's sake," I said. "How'd you shake 'em?"

"Took 'em on a road trip to Chicago and lost 'em in the Loop. I flew out of the Windy City to St. Louis. Small planes and short road trips from there. Made good time. The day I can't shake a goddamn Fed's tail is the day for me to fold my hand." Jimmy jacked a thumb at his own breastbone. "I'm 'Kevin O'Day,' by the by."

"Seems to have worked, *Kevin*. I'm not seeing anyone back there."

"That's what you can expect to see when I'm shaking a tail."

"Right."

Jimmy was grayer, a bit heavier. His breath seemed to come a bit shorter. He seemed a few years older than his real age. But it was good to see him and a real relief to have him at my side. We'd come through so many crazy, odds-against-us onslaughts over the years that Jimmy's mere presence buoyed my optimism for coming safely through the other side on this escapade.

He said, "We're going to exploit this moment of safety, Hector, and no arguing on this one. We're going to send Marie to Mexico with Duff. Just the two of them. Then you and I are going to ferret out this son of a bitch and speed him to his dirt nap."

I cracked the window and primed the Ford's cigarette lighter, steering with my left hand and fishing my right pocket for my Pall Malls with the other. "You able to find anything official on Armand Vargas?"

"There is no such animal," Jimmy said. "Somebody didn't take the effort to set up even a token false identity to support that alias. Smacks of a rush job. Or hubris."

I tapped ashes out the window. "Of course I'm all for slaying this son of a bitch. But you said you thought our government might be tracking you here. If they're tangled up in this, well, it makes things… complicated. Killing him may rain down chaos on us."

Jimmy said, "Bum a cigarette?" He rarely smoked the few times I'd seen him since the last war. I passed him my pack. He said, "I've done some sleuthing these past years. I haven't learned what's really going on, not deep down, but I do know that some arm of our government is still shielding, even protecting, Höttl. Hell, all the dead ends my inquiries have run up against are enough in themselves to point up some official agency is running interference."

"You're scaring me, Jimmy."

He smiled and shook his head. "Why should I be the only one?" He looked at the cigarette smoldering in his meaty fist, made a face, then pitched it out the window. "We have to get it done this time, Hector, whatever the ramifications. We have to do that. Höttl must die."

"We'll find a way to see to that need," I said. "But you'll likely have to arm-wrestle Duff to decide who goes to Mexico. She's adamant she and I are going to hunt Höttl."

"Duff's a scrapper," Jimmy said. "She's a hellcat, and that's why I want her guarding Marie way down south. But think what that bastard was prepared to do to you in Paris when he had you to himself. Are you prepared to put Duff at the same risk?"

Checking rearview mirrors again, I said, "Of course not. Hell, I don't want to put you in that danger, either. Frankly, I'm frightened enough for myself in this. That said, I think I should maybe do this alone. Let me kill the bastard and assume the risks."

"That some more of your Gary Cooper, world-patent solo lobo bullshit?" Jimmy turned his mouth down. "No, boyo, you need a strong right arm." He gave me this look as I was looking him over again. He said, "Stop eying me that way, Hector. I may not have kept myself in your fighting trim, I may not have your tough and immortal Texas-Stryder genes, but I can fight this battle through to the end, boyo."

"So be it." I cracked my window wider. "But you have to convince Duff. I took my shot at that task and failed badly."

"You don't have my charms, Hector. Nor my dulcet tones. It'll go down like honey coming from me."

I left Jimmy, Duff and Marie with Chinese takeout and then found a payphone three miles from our hotel.

Aiming to keep the call too short for a trace—Jimmy's fears about government participation in protecting Höttl from us had me casing every angle—I propped my Timex up on the top of the payphone.

Sam said, "Rock's out of our film, I guess you'll be happy to know. Those homo rumors about him got back to the Front Office. They hear *Hush-Hush* is pokin' around. If I ever find out you had something to do with any of that, Hector—"

"I've got bigger fish to fry, frankly, and those rumors on Rock have been out there for a while," I said. "Discreet he is not. Anyway, Rock was all wrong for the part. How about going after Sterling Hayden? He really was a vet, and he's even taller than Hudson. The Viking God's about half-wrapped, but I'm friends with the crazy, magnificent son of a bitch and have this soft spot for the guy."

"*That* commie son of a bitch? Not in my fuckin' picture," Sam said. "Hec, I need you in tomorrow. Need to touch base with you on some script things. Armand has some logistical questions for you. Thought we could discuss 'em over lunch."

That got my attention. "*Did* he? Armand really going to be there, too?"

"Not clear to me. What the hell is it with you two? For two guys who've never met, you two seem to spend a lot of time thinking about one another. After this Hudson thing, well, I don't want any surprises. You haven't gone homo on me, have you, Hec?"

"Uh, no," I said. "Have you actually talked to that bastard Vargas?"

"Finally, yes."

It came out as a snarl: "Is he German?" I winced a little at the acid in my voice.

Sam sounded just a tad taken aback. "He's got some kind of accent, but I ain't a damned linguist, Lassiter. German, French, Eye-talian? It's all Greek to me."

"I'll call you tomorrow at ten," I said. "By then, I may have a better handle on my schedule. Maybe I can do a late lunch, Sam. But only if Vargas comes."

"You sure you ain't queer for him? I asked Armand if he's queer, and he nearly had a conniption."

"Just get him there," I said.

I racked the receiver and scooped up my watch. A car was idling across the street. It looked more than a little like some flavor of Fed sled.

44

Everyone was irked at me for getting them up so early. I'd roused our crew at three-in-the-morning, arguing it would be a hell of a lot harder for anyone to follow us to Bakersfield if we were the only car on the road at that crazy hour.

We made the run in record time.

But now the pilot was bitching, too.

When he finished cursing me to wander off and fetch another cup of coffee, Duff pulled me aside and said, "This sleepy-eyed air ace, he's really good? He looks *old*."

"Lee is old   and an old *friend*," I said. "We met in Mexico, during the Punitive Expedition, when I was following Black Jack hunting Pancho Villa. Lee used to fly for Villa during the revolution, here and there. He's a forgotten man and a friend I've been out of touch with long enough to make him likely incorruptible in terms of selling us out on this tight a timetable. Lee'll get you two to Mexico, safely. That said, don't tell him precisely where you're headed once you touch down, just in case. When this is over, Jimmy and I will come down there and fetch you two."

I kissed Duff and hugged her tightly to me. "Please don't take any risks, darlin'. Lay low, stay away from other Americans and keep Marie on a very short leash. To my mind, she's not nearly paranoid enough for someone so squarely in Höttl's sights."

Duff kissed me back and said, "Keep Jimmy close by you, too. You aren't going to have me to pull you out of that torturer's chair this time, you know?" She shook her head. "I still feel I should be the one staying here to keep you focused. You and Jimmy together seems a little like fuses and dynamite."

"Jim and I have always come through just fine together. He ever tell you about another little girl, Cleveland, the Ohio mob, and us back in 1950? Talk about outnumbered and outgunned. Yet here we are."

"Somehow that tale got by me," Duff said. "You stay safe so you can tell me about it next time we meet."

"Scout's promise."

Duff traced my lips with her fingertips. "I've been thinking hard about us," she said. "Maybe we could just live in sin. Marriage somehow makes us boring. I think I even miss the desert. Certainly do miss the house."

I didn't even have to think about it. I kissed her forehead, said, "It's well worth considering."

Duff smiled and kissed me again.

Jimmy and Marie were finishing their goodbyes. Marie smiled sadly at me. She hugged me and said, "Please keep Uncle Jim safe. I don't think he's as tough as he thinks he is."

I said, "Neither is Höttl, honey. Don't you worry a bit. Jimmy and I will both come for you, and with a little luck, maybe sooner than you think."

I handed her a slip of paper. "There's an address on this. I want you to memorize it on the plane, then destroy it. If anything goes wrong, if you and Duff are separated or the like, then you go there, and tell the woman's whose name is on that paper that Hector Lassiter asks you be allowed to stay until Jimmy or me comes for you. That lady owes me a big favor from a few months ago, so it won't be a problem."

Marie looked at the slip of paper. "Duff knows to go there, too?"

"*No*. Wouldn't make good strategic sense for you *both* to know about this place," I said.

Marie looked stricken. "So it's still that dangerous, you think."

I hugged her to me. "Until the moment Höttl's in a box and deep in the cold, cold ground? Yes, I do think so."

We saw the plane off, then headed back to the car. Jimmy said, "Where do we start?"

"We speed back to Los Angeles," I said. "When we get there, I'm going to ditch this crap Ford and retrieve my Chevy. With the girls out of harm's way, it's time to standout again. I want this son of a whore to show himself, pronto. Once we have my Bel Air, we're going to stake out a restaurant and see if Armand Vargas keeps a lunch date with Sam Ford and I."

"The hours of my life I've lost with my ass planted in some car, staring at some building…? *Jaysus*." Jimmy loosened his necktie and killed some time singing "The Minstrel Boy." I found myself humming along:

"Land of song," said the Warrior Bard,
Tho' all the world betray thee,
One sword, at least, thy rights shall guard,
One faithful harp shall praise thee...

After a time, Jimmy said, "Why don't we just take the chance and barge in? If Höttl *is* in there, we'll drag him off to some place private and shoot his ass dead."

There'd been no sign of Höttl going into the joint and we'd arrived at Boardner's a full hour ahead of the scheduled lunch.

Sam, disarmingly punctual, had headed in fifteen minutes back. Another fifteen minutes passed, then the director staggered out onto North Cherokee, looking drunk and angry. I shook Jimmy awake and pointed. "There goes Sam. Would you say he looks stood up?"

"Stood up, yet about to fall down," Jimmy said. "Really, he's plastered. Oh, *Christ*, look, your pal's jingling car keys. No way that lush should be driving."

No, he shouldn't. "Dammit," I said. I opened my door. "Be right back."

I slid out of the Bel Air, jogging through traffic and calling, "Sam! Sam, buddy, wait up!"

I was halfway across the street when a salmon-and-cream '56 Buick Roadmaster tore off the curb, barreling straight for me. I threw myself across the bulbous hood of a parked Belvedere to keep from being run over. The Buick veered at the last minute, just missing tearing off its sideview mirror on the fifty-four Plymouth.

My Bel Air tore off in pursuit. I gave Jimmy a thumbs-up as he rolled by. Sam said, "Christ, Hec, that some pissed-off husband or boyfriend of some dame of yours?"

"Evidently some pissed-off something," I said.

But it didn't seem like a serious attempt on my life, somehow. More like a tantrum, maybe.

I took Sam's keys from his hand, encountering token resistance. I said, "I'm getting you a cab back to your office so you can sleep this off. You get stood up, Sam?" I figured likely as not he'd course correct after I sent him on his way. Probably detour to some bordello.

Sam said, "Stood up? Yeah, cocksucker. First by you, and then by goddamn Armand."

I held up my hands. "Whoa, there, buddy. I'm right here. Tardy, but present."

Sam thought about that, then said, "A woman make you late?"

"Sure," I said, "what else?"

Sam nodded. "Okay, then."

45

I stood with my back to Boardner's façade, standing under the canopy to stay out of the steady rain, smoking a cigarette and watching the street. As I savored my Pall Mall, I thought more about the car that had tried to run me down.

The more I replayed it in my head, the more it seemed like a half-hearted effort. It was that notion that kept me out in the open now, exposed to a possible rifle shot or sidewalk snatching.

For the moment, near as I could tell, Jimmy and I were Armand/Werner's only avenue to get at Marie—to get at Duff, if Höttl was indeed after her, too.

But then I started to second-guess myself. What if this was some improvised bid at divide and conquer? If it was, it was working all too well. Here I was, alone in the heart of L.A., while Jimmy was bound for parts unknown, chasing that Buick.

Rethinking the wisdom of standing out in the open, I was about to head in when I saw my Bel Air turn the corner. Jimmy rolled curbside, leaned over and rolled down the passenger side window. "Sorry to keep you waiting, Hector. I don't know this Godless city. It took me a while to find my way back here. Getting in?"

"Nah," I said, staying under the canopy to keep dry. "I want to head in there, anyway." I pointed at the restaurant behind me. "Park her, won't you?"

Jimmy pulled in behind one of the new Edsels. He tossed me the car keys and nodded at the new Ford parked in front of my Bel Air. "What do you think of that thing, Hec?"

"I think I'll stick with Chevys," I said.

"The bastard lost me," Jimmy said, "But I did get a license plate number. I'll get on the phone inside and call back to Ohio. Get one of my buddies to get L.A. cops to run a check on the thing."

He held the door for me. "Why are we headed in here, anyway? Thought you said Höttl was an apparent no-show."

"Probably he is," I said. "But Sam doesn't know what Höttl looks like. Maybe Werner actually beat us here and is just parked in some booth, waiting to see if I would show up. Besides, we've been on the road for hours. I'm starved. Lunch is my treat."

I tossed my cigarette out the door behind me and said, "You are carrying, right, Jimmy?"

"Of course," he said. "I'm licensed to do that. Assume you're carrying, too, even though you're not licensed." He turned down his mouth. "Suppose it's that old Peacemaker."

"That's right."

"Someday, you're going to need to trade up to an automatic, Hector. The young turks, and even most of the old ones, have upgraded their hardware, Hec. More bullets and faster firing are a good thing. It *is* 1957, after all."

Boardner's was a bust so far as Höttl went. Not even a detectable minion in sight.

I grabbed a booth while Jimmy worked the phone. I ordered us each a whisky, then scooped up a discarded newspaper from an adjacent table. I pulled on my spectacles and perused the front page. The usual current stuff: racial strife of various stripes. Atomic bomb handwringing. Political wrangling that made my soul hurt. I flipped to the literary section and read a nugget on this new novel called *On the Road*, made a mental note to look it up next time I found myself in a bookstore.

Jimmy was still taking his time on the phone. I began to browse the menu. He slid in across from me and pointed at his glass. "What brand are we drinking?"

I gave my glass this look. "Islay."

"It passes." Jimmy snapped loose his napkin. "If the food is good, I have a haunt."

I passed him a leatherette menu. "Anything come of your call?"

He winked. "We did catch a break of sorts. A rookie cop I trained back in the late thirties is out here, now. He's risen in the LAPD ranks."

The waiter was suddenly loitering; we both ordered steak and baked potato. When the waiter was gone, Jimmy flipped open his notepad. "Ever hear of a boyo name of Wesley A. Swift?"

I poured a little more water in my whisky; shook my head. "Rings no bells. Should I know the fella?"

"No, I'd be surprised if you did. Seems this Swift is some kind of radical cleric. He's taking Methodism to new and fascist places. Lad seems drawn to Hitler *and* Jesus. Maybe in that order."

"And that was his car that nearly ran me over?"

"No, the car belongs to one Frederick Brown. He's some kind of acolyte of Swift's. Brown's even more the Nazi fanatic than Swift, they say. Brown splintered off and formed his own church. Local authorities believe it's really more of a militia than a house of worship. They're trying to stoke FBI interest for a federal investigation into Brown's church. There are rumors of them collecting weapons. Beating up Negros, Jews and homosexuals."

I rolled my head; felt neck muscles crack and pop. Even that last wouldn't get an anti-semite, racist like J. Edgar Hoover off the dime, I figured. "So the car belongs to this Brown?"

"That's right," Jimmy said. "LAPD is watching the church, as it can. Seems there's a new joker in that deck. Boyo with this nasty looking scar and a German accent."

I looked up sharply. "Did they follow Höttl? Maybe have an address for the son of a bitch?"

"No, Hector. But this man meeting Werner's description seems a bit of a fixture at this church. Seems maybe to be bunking there. I have the address for *that* place."

It was tempting to tear over there, but it sounded like a suicide run if just the two of us charged in.

"Joint smacks of the consummate lion's den," I said. "And they sound like they'd have us well out-armed."

"As always, the numbers are on their side, too," Jimmy said with a sigh. "No, we can't simply storm those gates. Not just the two of us, anyway."

"But *if* the LAPD is watching, and *if* they saw us taken hostage?"

"Nah, Hec, they've had to redeploy resources. Since day-before-yesterday, the LAPD has pulled back surveillance on

Brown and company. And this church site where Höttl's bunking is in county sheriff's territory."

Well, that was just about perfect. I said, "Anyway, if that happened, we'd lose a shot at a clean kill of Höttl with no fingerprints."

Halfway through our meal, a waiter appeared with a phone connected to a very long cord. He said, "You are Hector Lassiter, sir?"

I cleared some tabletop for the phone's base. "That's me."

Jimmy asked the waiter, "This caller? Did the boyo give a name?"

The waiter sat down the phone and said, "Armand Vargas."

Jimmy looked at me with raised eyebrows. "*Ho-ho!*"

I held up one hand to quiet Jimmy. With the other, I scooped up the receiver and said, "*Werner.* We miss having you at lunch. You should head right over."

This pause, then *that* voice, all sneers and menace. Hearing it again, I couldn't suppress a shiver. "Lassiter! Still glib and still ineffectual! Still a hick hack writer from Texas with delusions of literary worth. Remember when I promised you that you would sit in my chair again?"

Silence. He was waiting for an answer.

"Sure," I said, finally. "I remember you *saying* it."

"Not empty words, and that time will soon be upon us," Höttl said. "And I'll make it worse for you, this time. I've learned some new tricks. It will be much more unpleasant this time. You, and also your Irish policeman friend, will soon enough experience what I'm talking about."

"Really, Werner, why don't you come on over and eat with us? We'll talk about all this over some *meat.*"

Höttl sighed and said, "Where has *Fraulein* Sexton taken my daughter, Lassiter?"

"The girl's whereabouts are entirely at Duff's discretion," I said. "Really don't have a clue where they've run to, and Duff is one resourceful woman. And, of course, if I did know where they are presently, I wouldn't tell you anyway."

"When I break you again in my chair—"

"I didn't tell you anything back in Paris," I said, cutting him off. "I didn't do that when you had all your toys and sadism ranged against me, cocksucker. And while I'm sitting here in the City of Angels, savoring a fine steak and some single malt with my good friend the Irish policeman? Well, hell, you've got even less prospect of getting any gen from me over the phone. Dig down deep and find a pair. Come here and we'll talk plenty."

Höttl said, "I located her once, in that stupid Midwest state. I'll do it again."

"No, you won't have the opportunity," I said. "Soon enough, you'll be dead. By the way, those first little Nazis you sent after me were not impressive, Werner. The one shot the other in the head and then turned the gun on himself. What the hell kind of strategy is that? Smacks of Hitler in the bunker. Though story I hear is his woman shot him because Adolph didn't have the balls to do the deed himself."

"The two you talk about proved to be the dregs of the European stock, as you say," Höttl said. Sounded grudging. "These Americans I've recently met, they will do my bidding, zealously and without question. They're exceptionally feral. I need only unleash them against you and—"

"Brave words from a voice on a phone," I said. "All these years passed, and you still haven't succeeded in breathing life into your lost cause, Höttl. Why do you keep hunting this girl? Can't be about saving face as Germany remains divided and you Nazis have been routed."

Jimmy was watching me intently. He was chewing so hard on his bottom lip he'd drawn blood. I sensed Jim was struggling not to rip the phone from my hand and tearing into Höttl, himself.

"It's a matter of principle," Höttl said. "Principle, desire, and revenge. And I haven't yet abandoned my dream of a re-energized Nationalist Socialist Party, Lassiter. I'm destined to see that dream realized, I *know* it. Look around you—increasing numbers of your own countrymen are drawn to the cause."

I remembered what Höttl had said when he was torturing me, his bragging about being a Nietzschean. I said, "What's that cockiness based on—more 'Will to Power' bullshit?"

Jimmy blurted out, "Come here now, you Kraut cocksucker, and we'll settle your score lickety-split!"

This shadow fell across our table.

The phone was ripped from my hand and racked, the connection severed.

A youngish guy in tan suit pulled back his jacket to show us his gun.

"Easy boys," he said. "Scoot over please, Detective Hanrahan. I need to talk to you gents right now."

46

The stranger slid in next to Jimmy.

I said, "And who the hell are you?"

He smiled. "I work for your Uncle Sam. Let's leave it at that. Now, I want to have a nice, friendly chat with you gents."

"Not without sharing a name, you won't do that," Jimmy said.

"We're going to have a nice, calm discussion," the stranger said, brushing Jimmy off. "We're going to talk about why you're not going to go after this man you call Werner Höttl."

The stranger was sticking by his commitment not to reveal a name. He was six-feet, probably about two-hundred pounds. Looked like much of that weight was muscle. He wore his brown hair in a Princeton cut. He had hazel eyes and big hands. He likely fell just a shade of either side of thirty.

He wasn't FBI: suit was just a tad too edgy to meet with J. Edgar's approval. Same with the leather tassels on his spit-polished loafers. And cufflinks? Only foppish dumbasses sport cufflinks—gin drinkers, to a man.

CIA? Maybe. That, or some other goddamn Federal acronym.

The man whom I'd decided to dub "Agent X" said, "Mr. Lassiter, your military records make it clear this isn't the first time you've been officially ordered to desist in your persecution of this person. Technically, you're in danger of violating the terms of your military hearing waiver. You could be re-prosecuted in a Federal court for—"

"What? War crimes?" I smiled meanly. "Do it, kid. I'll use my time on the stand to prosecute the U.S government for climbing in bed with a mass murderer like Höttl. I'll laundry-list every one of Höttl's war crimes and shame 'Uncle Sam' in the process."

"That son of a bitch is still trying to kill my niece," Jimmy said. "He just threatened her again, not two minutes ago."

"We had the phone tapped," Agent X said. "We were listening. We know all that. We heard every word of both sides of the conversation. That's why I interrupted the call when I did. Before any more empty threats could be uttered by either party."

"Empty threats?" I couldn't help it, the words came in a snarl. "Empty threats? That bastard tied me to a chair and tortured me to try and get at that girl during the war. As Armand Vargas, he engineered things to get myself, my former wife and Jimmy's niece out here to L.A. to kill us all at a stroke. Hell, as you heard on the phone, he admits sending two hold-over Nazi goons after me the other day. He—"

"He will soon be irrelevant," Agent X cut me off. "He's an asset. One determined to be of renewed strategic intelligence value by our government. That said, we are aware of his animus toward the four of you. You'll be pleased to know we're moving this man back out of this country, permanently. He's being permanently moved back to a place he can better fulfill his strategic intelligence obligations to us. An ancillary result of his relocation will be his inability to pursue this presumed vendetta against all of you. He'll never set foot on U.S. soil again, I promise you."

"Bullshit," Jimmy said. "I—"

Agent X held up a hand. "Enough. I've already detailed the legal risks to Mr. Lassiter in continuing his pursuit of the man formerly called Höttl. Let me outline for you your own precarious legal position, Detective."

Jimmy's blue eyes narrowed. "What the hell are you talking about?"

"This man claims your 'niece' is his daughter, Detective. If that's so, she should have been sent into his care upon her mother's death."

"Höttl fucking tortured and killed her mother," Jimmy said. "Jesus Christ, you dumbasses—"

"She *should* have been assigned to him then, regardless of the circumstances of the mother's death," the stranger persisted. "But you, Lassiter and this Duff Sexton conspired to essentially kidnap Höttl's child. If we'd known about all this in 1942, it's entirely possible that child might have been returned to her natural father by agents of the U.S. government. As she's now an adult, and since it appears she might possibly be at some mild risk from our asset, we will abstain from pursuing any legal punishments for you, Lassiter and Sexton. In return for that rather generous largesse, you'll desist in your efforts to track or harm our man. You will content yourself with the knowledge he will be in no future position to harm any of you three, or to harm Miss O'Rourke."

Jimmy beat me to it. He snarled, "Look, boyo, your assurances don't mean squat to me as they come from an unnamed son of a bitch working for a no-name agency."

"Put yourself in our position," I said. "If it was you trying to protect an innocent—"

"I've explained the situation as fully as I can," Agent X said. "You're both legally vulnerable. So is Miss Sexton. She could be arrested the second she crosses the border back into the United States. Yes, we know generally where she is, but Mr. Höttl does not, I promise you. We have had him overseas for some number of years, working in an intelligence role. During a changing of the guards, his value on that front was erroneously appraised down, so to speak. He took advantage of that time to come back here, to establish a new identity, and to begin to float a career in film. He also used the time, and some contacts he made in our government, to search for Miss O'Rourke, Miss Sexton and you, Lassiter."

He smiled and said, "*We're watching, now.* You should take comfort from that. You can't conceive of the reach or depth of our intelligence-gathering potential."

Oh, I figured I could. But I said, "And what? In the meantime, this bastard runs around with these lunatics who've styled themselves as latter-day Nazis?"

Agent X shook his head. "We will be picking up Mr. Höttl in a few days and then he will be gone, as I said. The Nazis, as you call them, are a matter for local authorities Now, you three do nothing. Do that for two or three more days, and all of your problems with this man will be over. They will same as evaporate along with Armand Vargas slash Werner Höttl. Do anything else, and the price will be unthinkably high for you three. You'll die in a prison the world doesn't even know exists."

He must have thought that last was enough to cow us, because he left us then. Didn't say goodbye, or even offer to pick up our check.

Jimmy looked at me over the rim of his glass. His face was flush and his eyes were blazing. "So?"

I emptied my own glass. "So it sounds like we have less than forty-eight hours to slay that Nazi son of a bitch."

47

Alone again, Jimmy and I lingered over more drinks, mulling next moves. He said, "Let's at least move to the bar, Hec. Can't help thinking we were perhaps put at this particular booth for a reason."

"Given my recent history with listening devices earlier this year, I was thinking the same thing," I said. "Bastards are probably bugging my Chevy as we sit here. Let's find an entirely different bar."

We settled the check and then wandered outside. There was a tavern just across the street. An armless panhandler was propped up against the façade of our prospective new watering hole. I leaned down and stuck a five-dollar bill in his beggar's cup. I said, "See that Bel Air over there?"

He squinted back at me. The sun was at my back and he had no hands to shield his cataract-clouded eyes. He said, "The turquoise fifty-seven? I've been admiring it."

"You see anyone fooling with it?"

"Nope."

"Gonna be here a while, pal?"

"Till my ride comes at five," he said.

"We won't be anywhere near that long. Watch her for me, would you? Just see if anyone fiddles with her. I'll give you a Hamilton when I come back out."

"Gotcha."

Jimmy and I headed into the dank dark of the tavern. There were a couple of serious elbow-benders at the bar. We grabbed a booth near the jukebox. To thwart any handheld listening devices, I dropped coins for some new guy named Johnny Cash.

Jimmy returned with a couple of beers. He said, "Been cogitating, Hector. Despite this boy's baffling government shield, he's very thick with this Freddie Brown and his band of nouveau Nazis."

"Right…"

"So let's give the sons of bitches a taste of their own medicine," Jimmy said. "After witnessing that melee you engineered in the desert several years back—you know, in Fifty— I *know* you're not adverse to authoring real-life mayhem of some bloody scale."

Yes, 1950 in the deserts of Mexico, that had been some bloodbath.

I arched an eyebrow. "What are you thinking?"

Jimmy smiled broadly, wiping off a beer-foam moustache with the back of his hand. "Blitzkrieg, boyo! Hit 'em fast and hard and leave 'em bloody. Take no prisoners. There's not an innocent in that crew, so far as I'm concerned. They deserve our worst."

"If we're going to do that, and I think it is the only way to do it, then we're going to need more hands on deck, I said."

Now Jimmy's smile ebbed. "Yeah. Goddamn it, there isn't enough time for me to call in favors from fellas back home."

"I can maybe pull a few hombres together, but it's going to be a pretty ragtag team," I said. "I mean really motley. And most of 'em are going to be bought help."

Jimmy winced, said, "I can probably pull together a couple of thousand bucks, but more than that—"

I shook my head. "Nah, we're not talking that kind of compensation," I said. "Ragtag, remember? We're looking at doling out quantities of rotgut booze. Maybe some working girls." I waved a hand. "Don't sweat that aspect of it, it's my freight to pay."

I looked at my barely touched mug of beer. Never did care for the stuff. What inspired Jimmy to order it? Jim and I always seemed to be of the same school of thought when it came to booze. If you're going to drink, *drink*. I said, "I'm going to go get a proper whisky, then burn my pocket change giving my address book a workout. See what kind of crew I can muster."

Jimmy said, "If it comes down to the endgame, which one of us gets the privilege of killing Höttl?"

Smiling, I searched Jimmy's eyes, then decided he wasn't joking. That wiped the smile off my face. I said, "We both have good reason for killing that man, Jim. Maybe we best just make it a fast-draw competition."

48

It was dusk. Jimmy looked up at the Hollywood sign looming over us. "Picturesque place for a meeting, Hector."

"Getting out here made it harder for the Feds to follow us, if they really are watching us closely now. We can at least make 'em earn our arrests, *sí?*"

Jimmy stamped his feet and rubbed his arms. I could see his breath when he spoke. "Getting goddamn frigid now that the sun's down." He gave me this long, appraising look. "We've not had time for much other than Höttl talk since my plane touched down. These last couple of years of yours haven't been kind to you."

I squeezed his shoulder. "Please *don't*, Jim. I'm just starting to come out on the other end and okay, now. Talking about it is just going to stir it all up."

"You lost a wife and a child, Hector. Either one of those is a body blow that can crush a man, and you've sustained both." Jimmy had been present down there in Mexico when I met my late-wife Maria. He'd been friend enough to try and warn me off her in the early going. Of course, I didn't take heed.

Then, much later, troubles with Maria that Jimmy had sensed up front ended up costing us our only daughter, my poor, ailing Dolores.

I checked my watch. "Really, leave it be, Jim, I'm beggin' you. I've just reconciled myself to the fact that 1957 is not going to be a banner year—not anymore than fifty-six was. But hell, maybe 1958 will be terrific. And 1959? It might be passing wonderful."

"Okay, Hector. But if you ever change your mind... Maybe if you find yourself having some dark night of the soul down there in your desert hellhole when it's too late for the bars—"

"You're the one I'll wake up, buddy, I swear it."

There was the sound of an engine moving through the fog-bound hills. "That'll be Duncan," I said. "He's an ex-Marine. Works as a stuntman, now. He's an utter hellion and the dirtiest fighter you'll find in greater Los Angeles. A kind of living weapon."

"Charming," Jimmy said. "What's his compensation for undertaking this bloody task?"

"The body count you suggested," I said. Thinking of what Sam Ford had observed about Hollywood name changes, I said, "Duncan's current name is one he chose for himself, like Hollywood types are given to doing. Real name is David Ebner, born in Berlin. The Nazis took a hell of a lot from the man. He's still avenging all that."

Jimmy grunted. "A Jew, eh? *Good*. That makes this all *extra*-personal for him."

"Acutely so," I said.

"And in that, he sounds a solid choice for the team," Jimmy said. "Who else?"

"Guy who's supposed to be riding along with Duncan is Will Buchanan. Will is former OSS. He was part of this special unit of movie-types our side used to fox the Germans. Wild Bill assembled this crew of sound engineers who used audio equipment in theatre to make the Germans think the forest was thick with allies, for instance."

"You joking?"

"Not at all," I said. "It was all smoke and mirrors. Strategic deception, so to speak. Guys would put out cardboard or inflatable tanks and aircraft that cast convincing shadows to fool air surveillance by the Luftwaffe. I used to write scripts for radio chatter, myself. Stuff that'd play nonchalant and sound like guys shooting the breeze, but let slip little false intelligence about troop movements and the like. Get the Germans focused on place 'A', while our guys were really racing to place 'H.' Like that."

"This Buchanan guy, he's good?"

"Buck is a pro, on- and off-screen. His specialty is explosions. He got his start in Spain with the Abraham Lincoln Brigade blowing up the real items—railroad tracks and bridges and such. Here in L.A., he just blows up little models of those sorts of things. The occasional car for the odd film noir. Stuff for war pictures."

Jimmy chuckled and stretched. "He another of your Hollywood name-changers?"

"Sure," I said. "But not for racial or ethnic reasons."

"What, then?"

"Like I said, Jimmy, he was in Spain. One of those 'premature anti-Fascists.' Only way he gets work in this town is using this other name."

Jimmy said, "God, I loathe this city. Everything in it is a falsity. The notion of Marie working in this town, or worse, living in it? It sets my skin to crawling." Jimmy gave me this long, hard look. "What about you, Hec? That an adopted name? Are you really Hector Mason Lassiter?"

I said, "To the bone."

Twenty minutes later, my two remaining recruits arrived— my boxing pal, Packy Thompson whom I would quietly be paying out of pocket, and another member of the OSS strategic deception team, Barney Nettles. Barney was one of those sound wizards I'd told Jimmy about. He was short, thin and wan. Something almost ghostly about Barn. Wasn't too sure what technical boon he could bring to *this* table, but he was good with a gun, which would almost certainly be a benefit going up against a militia, as we seemingly were going to do.

We were huddled inside Will's special effect's van, trying to keep warm and talking strategy, variously quaffing coffee, or booze from various thermoses and flasks.

Duncan, aka David Ebner, said, "I've been eyeballing the place most of this afternoon. It's a converted pole barn deep in the sticks. It's in a kind of mini-hollow. It'd probably be in the flood plain anyplace with real water. Strategically, it's bad for them, because they're essentially in a basin. We have nearly 360-degrees of high ground. Place is ringed with trees on three sides and there is a road approach from the rear into the woods. I say we go in that way, slow and quiet as we can. The hillside mounding and the trees that side should cover the sound of our coming."

Will, our demolitions expert, was about five-five and barrel-chested. He turned to Jimmy and I. "Guess the main question here is, what's our primary objective?"

I sure knew what I was prepared to do, but I let Jimmy say it. He did so with gusto. "Lads, the objective is to kill a single man," Jimmy said, measuring reactions. "I mean put him down good and bloody for all time."

Jimmy weighed each man's expression. Evidently encouraged by what he saw, Jimmy said, "He's an escaped Nazi torturer and child-killer named Werner Höttl. He was chief stooge for Klaus Barbie in Lyon, France—the so-called 'Butcher of Lyon.' We confirm that Höttl is in that bunker-cum-church, and then we will make him dead. "

Will wet his lips. "That I can do easily enough, with the right stuff."

Jimmy said, "And you can obtain the right stuff?"

"Hell, I possess it," Will said. "But doing it for sure my way will vaporize that building and break big branches off a lot of those trees. If it's a stormy day, and there's enough air pressure over that basin, the shockwave could break windows for a few miles in every direction." He paused and said, "And anyone else in that building when it blows will obviously be just as dead as this goddamn German will be."

Will paused again. Now *he* searched faces. "I'm told there might be two-dozen men bunking in that place, any given day or night. We okay with racking-up that kind of death toll?"

I anted up first. "I've got a durable conscience where these types are concerned."

Duncan, dark hair, dark eyes, grim-faced, said, "They are Nazis, one way or another. So to hell with 'em. Let 'em die bloody. It's unfinished war business, that's all."

Jimmy crossed himself and said, "Amen."

Packy was the only one of the guys who was in this for the money. He was a minor local celebrity, so I could forgive him any cold feet. He said, "Christ, didn't realize we were going to total war with these Kraut-lovers." He looked at his hands. They'd administered their share of carnage, sanctioned and otherwise. He said, "Still, the last show cost me two nephews on those goddamned European beaches. The idea of these cretins trying to start that Nazi stuff up here just won't do."

I slapped his back and said to Barney, "And you, old pal? This maybe more than you want to sign on for?"

He shrugged. "If we were going to storm that place, and do this hand-to-hand, I'd tell you all to go and fuck yourselves," Barney said. "But if we're just going to H-bomb them, well, that sounds a worthy enough task. This Höttl does sound like unfinished business from the last war. Maybe even qualifies as a civic duty. How do you propose to blow those losers up, Willie?"

Will nodded, said, "What's this building's architecture?"

Duncan drew a picture in the air with his index finger. "Rectangular. Very cheap construction. Strategically, I mean from the standpoint of an assault, it's a killing jar. Only two doors and those are up front. One's a garage door; the other just a standard door, opens in."

Will nodded. "Windows?"

"None at all," Duncan said.

Will considered that. "We want them to barricade in there then, which it sounds like they'll need to do if we shoot at 'em."

"Absolutely," Duncan said. "They haven't even dug fox holes or made any kind of cover for themselves around the perimeter of that joint. For would-be storm-troopers, they haven't prepared the site at all for combat." He sniffed. "Amateurs."

"Probably because they envision taking the war to the world," I said. "Instead, it sounds like they've built for themselves an accidental Alamo. Great news for us."

"Here's what I advocate," Will said. "We go in as Duncan proposes. Then we push a truck around to the front of that joint. We start the engine on the truck at the last moment. I can rig a pretty elementary radio-control steering gizmo to work the truck's gas and steering wheel. We'll load the truck with the explosives. Then we'll roll the truck down there and up against the garage door of that place and blow it. Even if they survive the actual blast or resulting fire, the shockwave alone will kill everyone within a couple of hundred yards of that building. Turns your insides to jelly, like that." He snapped his fingers.

Barney said, "I can ring the place with some speakers. We'll use some of the tapes from old days to convince them they're surrounded and pinned down by numbers so they stay in that shack until we atomize it."

Jimmy said, "You can pull all this together before morning? We don't have much time left to get this done."

Affirmative nods all around. "Now," I said, "we just need some way of knowing that Höttl is in there before we do the deed."

"That shouldn't be hard," Duncan said to me. "A man looking like your description of Höttl was in and out of there several times while I was scouting. He came out three or four times over the course of two hours to relieve himself. Enlarged prostate, or something like that, I should think. He was constantly pissing."

"Christ, I hope he does have plumbing issues," I said. "I wish Höttl every misery, and that seems a fine one. Good then. We wait to see him take that last piss. When Werner heads back in after siphonin' the python, then we'll fix his prick for all time."

We agreed to reconvene in the morning at a roadhouse about three miles from our target's would-be compound. As our crew broke up, Jimmy put the arm on Duncan. "Hear you also lost some back there in Europe, boyo," he said softly to the stuntman.

Duncan gave him a long look, then pushed up his left shirtsleeve to show Jimmy the numbers tattooed there on his arm. "My whole family died in the camp. I was the only one got out. If the war had gone another week?" He pushed his sleeve back down. "That's why I've told Will *I* will be the one to press the button on that bomb tomorrow." This frightening smile. "I'm going to relish that." As an afterthought, Duncan said, "Hope neither of you has a problem with that."

49

We didn't get much sleep from there. After being cautioned that enough of the truck's remains might be traced to a rental agency or used car lot, Jimmy hotwired some heap and drove it to a garage for Will to equip with a remote steering rig. I went ahead and rented a tow truck so we could get the truck loaded with the explosives on site.

About four a.m., Jimmy and I decided it was best just to banish thoughts of sleep and push ahead through to the end of the thing, fueled by hi-test coffee and adrenaline.

Driving out to the site in the tow truck, Jimmy said, "Despite everything, all the precautions, the Feds are likely going to land on the two of us. They're likely to land on us *hard* for this, Hector. We'll be their prime suspects, of course."

That thought got my guts going. I said, "Of course. And that's further great reason to be on that plane to Mexico this evening. Let things cool off while we savor some south-of-the-border living. Besides, David, I mean *Duncan*, had some ideas about how to throw suspicion in another direction, well away from us."

Jimmy said, "Care to elaborate?"

"It's his idea. Better to let him explain it."

Before we pushed the bomb-laden truck into launch position, Will handed out earplugs to everyone. He said, "Even though you're wearing these, you should still put your hands to your ears and keep your mouths open until after she blows. That last will help equalize pressure in your skulls so you don't blow out your eardrums. We'll be far enough back the shockwave won't do us permanent damage, but it will maybe knock you off your feet."

Barney said, "When Hec has confirmed a Höttl sighting, and the guy goes back inside, then we'll start. I'll roll tape, peppering them with some official sounding threats. Make 'em think we're the county sheriff's boys. Hec, Packy, Jimmy and Duncan will lay down some rifle fire on the doors to keep the bastards inside. Then Will and Duncan will wrap it up with the big boom."

Jimmy and I were crouched down behind a fallen tree's big old rotting trunk, waiting for a glimpse of Werner Höttl.

I said to Jimmy, "These rifles in our hands, and with these scopes, it's going to be tempting to take a shot at Werner, to put him down first and early with a single shell. But we can't do that. If we were to miss?"

That bought me a pretty withering look from Jimmy. "I trust you're talking to yourself, Hector," he said coolly. "For *my* part, *I* wouldn't risk losing that son of a bitch again now that we've found him. That's on the one hand. On the other hand, the only satisfaction in personally pulling the trigger on him would come in Höttl's knowing *who* was killing him. But we're serving this one up cold and from far away, so I'm willing to let that camp survivor detonate the explosion. So, are you just thinking out loud because you're afraid *you* might take that reckless shot?"

"Dammit, no… I—" I slapped his back. "I'm just working my mouth, and stupidly. All this is a little unsavory and more than a little overkill. Guess it's just got me second-guessing."

"There's still time to call it off." The tone in Jimmy's voice led me to believe he might try and knock me unconscious and charge ahead if I really intended to pull the plug on this operation.

"Christ, no," I said. "We've all but done it now."

Duncan said, "Brothers! Look, the door!"

I picked up my rifle, careful to keep my finger well away from the trigger for Jimmy's benefit.

My Irish friend's soft tenor in my ear, "Is that him, Hector? Is that the German devil?"

The man who stepped outside the door was wearing a long black coat. He was also wearing a black fedora. I could only see him in three-quarter view from the back. He was fiddling with his pants zipper from the look of things. He stood there watering a plant with his poison, looking around at the countryside. I then saw the livid scar trailing down the right side of his face. I said, "It's been quite a few years, but there couldn't be two wounds like that one in the world."

Jimmy pressed, "So it *is* him?"

"Got the right scar," I said.

"Okay, then." Jimmy signaled the boys with a thumbs-up. His voice raw, he said, "Soon as the lad goes back inside, we do this."

The thin man in the black coat shook, zipped up, then turned heel, headed back inside. The clouds had grown gray and low and it was starting to rain.

Jimmy said softly, "Feds are going to be *so* pissed at us."

I got my rifle up and into firing position. Sighting in on the pole barn's garage door, I said, "They surely are."

Will turned over the truck's engine and got her in gear. He picked up his remote. "I say we start this rig down the hill," he said. "About halfway to target, Barney turns on his speakers. That way, they can't run far enough away to survive the blast. That way, if they *do* fire back, the truck will be closer to them than to us if they should accidentally trigger her explosion."

The blast was a ghastly, terrifying thing to experience at close range.

Because of the low cloud ceiling, Will explained later, the air pressure suppressed the upward force of the explosion, pressing it back to earth and intensifying the blast force.

I had no doubt that if we'd been standing when the explosives went off we'd have been knocked clean off our feet. The rush of air in our faces was blast-furnace hot and the ground shook for what seemed several seconds.

The building was *gone*, along with anything inside or immediately around it.

I was appalled by what I could see of the emerging crater. The black mushroom cloud roiling over that hole was sublime. It looked a little like a black death's head.

As Will told me later, the magnitude of the explosion wasn't entirely his work.

"I should have figured they'd have stockpiled their own explosives, and they obviously did," he said. "We're goddamn lucky we weren't killed by that blast, too." Several trees had been toppled around the back of the blast site and the grass was on fire.

Jimmy dug his earplugs from his ears and hollered, "We should move our asses, boys! This is going to draw all kinds of crowds!"

As we prepared to flee the scene, Duncan was hanging behind, drawing in the dirt with a stick. Jimmy leaned over and said, "What's that you're doodling?"

It was a crude sketch of a menorah surrounded by a circle of Hebraic text. I said, "That's our misdirection I was telling you about earlier, Jimmy. It's our fall-guy, so to speak. It's the emblem of the Mossad."

50

The plane ride to Chihuahua was a bit rough. Some storm front seemingly without end set the craft to bucking. I said, "No fretting, Jimmy—Lee could fly into hell itself and back."

Half-nauseous myself, I broke the seal on a bottle of tequila. Sour-faced, Jimmy said, "That can't possibly help."

"Can't hurt, either." I took a swig; barely kept it down.

Jimmy accepted the bottle, took a sip. He made a face and handed it back. He said, "Feels a little hollow, doesn't it? At least for me. What about you?"

"You mean this thing with Höttl? Maybe a little empty. Guess there *is* something to what you were saying about the bastard knowing who did it to him. Still, it's done now, and Marie can live her life without *that* shadow. And all the others we took out today? They're not going to be troubling my sleep."

I looked out the window. There wasn't a hell of a lot to see out there except when lightning slashed the sky. "Good news is, I think we've crossed into Mexican airspace," I said. "So we're free of Federal entanglement, for a time. If they really mean to burn us, I suppose we can just be two more gringos hedonistically living out our days here in Old *Meh-hico*. Hell, I can write anywhere."

"But I can't police just anywhere," Jimmy said. "And that's another thing. This intelligence role of Höttl's that was so important to these shadowy government types, what the hell *was* that?"

I shrugged, staring at my bottle and mulling whether to take another hit. "Guess we'll never know."

"How do you figure the story of this explosion will play in the press?"

I put the bottle aside and said, "Will was adamant the building was packed with explosives. Most elegant thing for officials to say is these Nazi-types accidentally blew themselves to hell. It'll look like they died butter-fingered dumbasses. I *like* that notion."

My ears began to pop, then. I said, "Coming in for landing, feels like."

Jimmy, looking a little greener, said, "Not a goddamn moment too soon."

Staring out the window of our cab, Jimmy looked glum again. Our driver had the radio cranked up a bit too loud and not quite squarely set on some mariachi station that was more static than music.

Over the din, Jimmy said, "I've never understood your love for this country."

"This is a good place," I said. "I like Chihuahua. They say the name comes from the Tarhumara language. Means 'between two waters.' The Sacramento and Chuviscar rivers meet here."

"I still don't care for it."

"Well, you won't be here too long," I said. "We'll get you and Marie on a plane back to Ohio soon as you want to go."

"It *will* be soon," he said. "I'm just staying here long enough to convince myself a flight back to the U.S. won't land me in irons for that bedlam back in Lotus Land earlier today." He turned to face me. "What about you and Duff?"

"I'm going to see if I can't talk her into a few weeks together down here," I said. "See if I can't persuade Duff to head down to the Yucatan, maybe. It's been good to have her back these few days. Hell, maybe with a few more years behind us now, well, maybe we could work this time, you know?"

Jimmy looked skeptical, but said, "You know I've always been most fond of that one. I haven't met 'em all of course, all of your women, I mean. But of the ones I've run into, along with Brinke, Duff's my favorite."

51

"Neighborhood is a tad better than I expected," Jimmy said, scanning the small, stucco, Spanish-style homes whipping by.

"It's a retirement district for old gringos," I said. "I got 'em a rental. And Jimmy, not all of Mexico is like a Wallace Beery film. It runs the spectrum, like all places."

I checked addresses as the cab slowed. I tapped the driver's shoulder. "Up there, the one on the left. Stop here, *por favor.*"

Jimmy braced his hands against the back seat as the cab lurched to a rubber-squealing stop. He said, "Why not pull into the driveway?"

I pointed. In a strained voice I said, "See that hanging plant?"

Jimmy squinted, then nodded. "Sure, but it's not hanging."

"Exactly. Also, those venetian blinds in the front window are slanted in, not out. They're both distress signals I set up with Duff before we left California." Anticipating his next question, I said, "And, yes, Marie knew them, too."

Distractedly, I settled up with our cab driver. I said, "Can you wait here a few minutes? We may still need you."

Rattled, I took Jimmy by the arm. "I'll go in through the front. You take the back."

Jimmy nodded. He reached under his jacket and drew his gun. "This feels bad."

"It feels very bad," I agreed.

I found Duff on the bed.

The carnage was appalling.

Jimmy found me in the bathroom, bent over the toilet. Between dry heaves, I managed, "Marie's not here. I think—" another gag, "I think she's the one who moved the plant... to warn us."

He pressed his big hand to my back. "Aw, Christ, Hector. I'm *so* goddamn sorry. But nothing can be done for her."

"I know."

Spent, I fell back against the bathtub, trying to force the image of her body on the bed from my mind. "Jesus Christ, what they did to Duff! I'll fucking tear them apart with my bare hands," I vowed. "Swear I'll kill 'em slow and bloody like nobody's *ever* been killed."

"I'm sure that's so." Jimmy fished my jacket pocket. He took out two cigarettes and my Zippo. "They didn't get to do *everything* they wanted to Duff," he said softly. He handed me a lit cigarette and dropped my lighter back in my pocket. I took my first hit of nicotine and wiped my eyes.

My voice was raw. "What do you mean, Jimmy?"

Jimmy said, "Duff was tough, make no mistake." He held up a necklace. I remembered it from France. Seeing it again sent this fresh chill through me.

"She must have held onto this from the war," he said. "At some point, Duff got a hand free. She took an old L pill, ended her own suffering and robbed them the chance to hurt her more. A lot of that bloodiness burned into your brain now, maybe even most, was post-mortem." Maybe Jimmy was lying to spare me. If so, I loved him more for it.

He hesitated, then handed me the necklace. "If we were back home, I'd make book Coroner Gilbert would say she's been dead at least twenty-four hours."

I fumbled in my pocket, got out a notebook and pen. I turned to a virgin sheet and scribbled down an address. "This is the place where I told Marie to go if there was any trouble. It's in the city, proper. Pancho Villa's widow lives there. I made her acquaintance earlier this year, and she owes me a favor. You better hurry. That cab will be going soon."

He furrowed his brow. "What will you do?"

"Call the police," I said thickly. "I'll stay here until they come. By then, I'll have a story for them. Once I've handled things here, I'll come looking for you at that address. My gut instinct is Marie is there, safe."

Jimmy squeezed my shoulder. "Okay, Hector. Better give me your gun. God knows what those Mex police would make of you carrying a six-shooter."

We tossed our cigarette butts into the toilet and I flushed. Woozy, I stood and shrugged off my jacket, then my shoulder holster. I passed the holster and Colt to Jimmy. "You need to fly, pal," I said. "You have to be on fire to get there, so please, just go."

"You're right," he said. "But before I do that, some advice. Don't look at that bed again, Hector. Remember Duff as she was. And don't force yourself to look for clues. I've already done that." He bit his lip, then said, "Soon those Mexican cops will be here. Not knowing how good they might be, I think there's a risk they might accidentally obliterate the one strange thing to be found in there."

"What's that?" I slipped back on my sports coat. My legs were shaking; my heart raced. I *so* wanted to *kill* something. I wanted to rewrite history. I wanted not to have sent Duff down here with Marie. I couldn't fathom Duff being dead.

Jimmy hid my gun and holster under his right armpit, then closed his own coat. He said it in his cop's voice. "There are three dents in the carpet, right there at the foot of the bed. To me, they look like they were left by a camera tripod."

52

We lingered for a long time in front of Donna Maria Luz Corral De Villa's old and French-style house dubbed *Quinta de Luz*. In the night, the pink stucco covering the place looked like diluted blood.

As we stood there embracing, wetting one another's shoulders, I stroked Marie's back.

She had, she said, come back from a walk and saw that the blinds had been twisted inward. Duff had evidently had enough warning to do that one thing.

As she was deciding what to do next, Marie heard the front door opening. She hid behind some shrubs. She watched two men leave. One was tallish, skinny…that was all she could make out of that one. The other was stocky, balding and bespectacled. They were speaking to one another in German. Both men's shoes and slacks were splattered with blood. The thin one was carrying a movie camera. That one had paused to relieve himself in the front yard before they drove away.

When they had gone, Marie ran inside and found the bloody crime scene that would haunt her to the grave.

"You shouldn't have gone in there," I said, rather stupidly.

"I wish that I hadn't," she said between soft sobs. "I didn't stay long. Just ran out of there, screaming and trying not to retch. I stopped long enough to move the hanging plant to the porch step."

Marie looked up at me, her dark eyes searching my face. "What will happen to Duff?"

"Police here will do what they can, their coroner, too," I said. My voice was still raw and hoarse from all the heaving I'd done earlier. "When they're done, I'm having Duff sent to New Mexico. She loved the desert. I had a burial plot there picked out for myself. Got a nice view." For the living, that was to say.

She said, "I want to be there when you, *you know.*"

"You will be. You and Jimmy. But before I can make those kinds of plans, I have to make sure the Feds aren't going to slap irons on your uncle and I when we cross the border to go home."

Marie hugged me tighter. "How will you know when it's safe to return?"

"I'm going to work the phone in just a few minutes," I said. "I'll see what Jimmy's and my status is. And I want to pursue another angle. Only one way that those men of Höttl's found you two here. There's a leak on our government's side."

"But Höttl *is* dead now?"

"Blown to dust," I said.

Marie hugged me again. "In Hollywood, I told you I couldn't fathom revenge. But now I do. Problem is, Höttl's dead, and there's no way to kill him again."

I wrapped an arm around her slim shoulders and steered Marie back toward the house. "There's the two guys who did this to Duff who still sorely need killing. If I can get a line on them, I'll give 'em even worse that they gave Duff. I'll make hell seem a holiday." Even with my imagination, dark as it runs, I couldn't conceive how I could top the suffering and carnage they'd visited upon my darling. But I'd take a bloody shot at it, afforded the opportunity.

Marie said, "What are the odds of you ever finding those men? Really?"

Too slim. But I said, "I'm wicked patient, kid. There've been times I've waited decades to get my revenge. But I do get it."

Jimmy caught me on my way out to a payphone. He grabbed me in this big awkward bear hug. The look he gave me, the pain in his eyes, rattled me. He said, "Hector, if I hadn't insisted on staying with you back there in Lotus Land...? If I hadn't insisted Duff bring Marie down here?" He pressed his fists to the sides of his head. "Christ, I truly believed this trip down here would be a milk run."

I gripped the back of his neck in my mitt and got up in his face. "You couldn't know how this would turn out, and neither could Duff or I," I said. We all agreed to this, Jimmy. Much as you might want to try, you can't take the blame for what's happened here. There's only a few sons of bitches that can do that. The ones who killed Duff, and the ones back home who told them where to find our girls. Now, to address that last bunch, I've really gotta find a phone."

I burned through four cigarettes and pocketful of change as the bastards passed me around from agency to agency. From no-name stooge to no-name federal stooge.

At last, a familiar voice:

Agent X said, "I've been apprised as to what's happened down there, Mr. Lassiter. My sincere and heartfelt condolences. Höttl's threat to you and yours was clearly greater than I thought possible. I am so sorry for your loss and very relieved Miss O'Rourke, at least, is unharmed. If it's of any consolation, I'm making it my mission to identify the leaker and to see that man prosecuted to the full extent of the law."

"Nice speech," I said. "Fact remains, this didn't need to happen. If you hadn't protected that son of a bitch Höttl for all these years things would be different now."

"Well, that's a moot point, all around," Agent X said. "You've seen to that, haven't you? You and your friends certainly ended that intelligence enterprise earlier today when you blew Höttl to hell along with all our uses for him."

"That's another thing that's eaten at me for too damned many years," I said. "What was that intelligence value that had you boys all wet?"

"Again, a moot point, Lassiter. It's over now. Guess nobody wins, eh?" Agent X paused, then added, "If I were in your position, I'd probably have done the same thing to him. Though perhaps not so destructively. My God, the carnage."

"So you're not going to come after me or mine? I mean, if we *had* done something here?"

"What would we gain, Lassiter? Your former wife is dead. Höttl is dead… along with twenty-three pieces of human debris. And, frankly, you're a public figure with far-reaching media connections. I was browsing over your file when you called. No, you're a writer—I should choose my words more carefully. I've been *wading* through your file. It's a massive goddamned dossier. But suffice it to say, I'm convinced pursuing charges against you in this matter would be a treacherous undertaking." His voice hardened. "But if you ever do something like that again? The insurance claims from the broken windows alone are shaping up to be staggering."

At least I didn't have to worry about being a fugitive. Still, I couldn't resist a dig. "How many other Nazis is Uncle Sam protecting? Whatever happened to Klaus Barbie, for instance? How about Josef Mengele? You boys maybe set that twisted cocksucker up in some backwater with a bottomless stock of twins to tinker on?"

"This conversation is over, Mr. Lassiter. *Again*, I'm sorry for your loss. *Again*, keep your damned nose clean."

I said, "This isn't over yet. Not even close."

"Hell it isn't," Agent X said. "It is over. Over and done. Put it behind you, Mr. Lassiter."

Jimmy and I sat out on the balcony of our hotel room, staring out at the lights of Chihuahua, half drunk on mezcal.

Sipping my booze and studying the moon, I said, "It's not really over you know."

Jimmy turned his head; arched his eyebrows.

"It's not over in the purest sense, I'm afraid, Jimmy. The Germans who killed Duff are still out there. They know who Marie is and they were prepared to kill her for Höttl. They probably know about you and about Ohio, because Höttl knew. If they want revenge for what happened to their chief?"

That sparked Jimmy to fury; I was the convenient target for his wrath. He snarled, "So *what?* What are you fucking saying, Hector? That Marie has to stay in hiding? That she gets some other name? That she has to move to some *other* place even though this cocksucker's already in hell? Fucking Christ!"

Figured about then, we were both flashing on memories of Duff on that bloody bed.

Seething, Jimmy stared at the moon for a long time.

I said softly, "Yeah, Jim. I guess I am saying all that."

Jimmy hung his head. "Goddamn it!" He sighed. "But you're likely too right, of course." He looked close to tears. His hands trembled with impotent frustration. "I'll break that lousy news to Marie in the morning. I can't do it now and not like this." Jimmy flung his glass over the balcony. It crashed on pavement and a dog barked.

I poured myself some more Dos Gusanos. I said carefully, "They know where you live, too."

Now I got this withering death stare from Jimmy, all cop's eyes and barely contained fury. "Are you going to hide, too, Hector?"

"Nah. I'm solo lobo again, and in the best of times, I'm a moving target. And after what they did to Duff, I'm going to be hunting these bloodsuckers."

"When do you undertake that quest, Hector?"

I fired up a Pall Mall. All gravel, I said, "First, I have to bury Duff."

I poured myself another drink; trying to get drunk enough to make me forget the nightmares I knew I'd have tonight and for many nights to come. My poor lost Duff.

But I'd been hard at the bottle that year, and could hold my liquor too well. So the booze, this time, offered no respite.

When sleep finally came, it brought some of the worst nightmares of my sorry life.

BOOK FOUR
The Garden of Suffering:
July 1971

*"A land without men
for men without land."*
— Emilio Medici

Excerpted from *Publishers Weekly*
(Starred review of *Demon's Daughter: A Survivor's Memoir*,
by Marie O'Rourke—aka Sara Tennant)

"The past is never dead," declares Sara Tennant in her startling tell-all, *Demon's Daughter: A Survivor's Memoir*.

Tennant, a novelist and screenwriter of some repute, reveals she was actually born Myriam Dreyfus, in Lyon, France.

In 1942, Myriam's parents were tortured and murdered by her biological father—a Nazi filmmaker, propagandist and sadist named Werner Höttl. Höttl was right-hand man to Klaus Barbie, the so-called "Butcher of Lyon."

Obsessed with obliterating any trace of evidence he'd fathered a Jewish child, Höttl embarked on a decades-long campaign to murder Myriam.

As detailed in Tennant's gripping account, she was rescued from her Anne Frank-like-hiding-place in Lyon by charismatic, larger-than-life novelist and screenwriter Hector Lassiter (Lassiter died under mysterious circumstances in 1967).

Lassiter, renowned as "the man who lived what he wrote and wrote what he lived," was aided by the charming, equally larger-than-life Irish-born detective whose family would adopt and raise Myriam as their own. Along for the ride was a beautiful OSS operative named Duff Sexton whom would later marry Lassiter.

From the opening, breathless description of Lassiter's characteristically violent and swashbuckling rescue of the child from a band of Nazi searchers in occupied France, to post-war Hollywood for a final showdown with a disguised and vengeful Höttl, the memoir is a white-knuckle and deeply-felt tale of courage and wily fortitude in the face of overwhelming odds…"

Headline from *Variety*:
United Artists' options *Demon's Daughter: A Survivor's Memoir*

Sidebar headline from *Variety:*
William Holden in discussions to play famous crime writer
in *Demon's Daughter*

53

It was raining hard on the coast of Oahu. Lightning forked over the chopping waves and thunder rattled the windows in their cases. Honey-voiced schmaltz on the hi-fi: Roger Whittaker's "The Last Farewell."

I stood looking out the sliding glass door, sipping coffee, watching the water and thinking about my next novel. Duff had long ago theorized I'd have to one day choose between being "the man who writes what he lives" or "the man who lives what he writes." In the late 1960s, I'd chosen to live my life very differently. I'd also chosen to write very different kinds of novels. Yet I still wasn't sure it all broke in half as evenly as Duff had seemed to think.

From deeper inside the house, I heard our phone ring. I heard my wife talking in her softly accented Spanish. But something creeped into her tone that chilled me. She put down the phone; she was coming for me.

"Héctor, it's your friend, the Irish policeman." Alicia looked very sad. "Something very bad has happened. I'm so sorry."

Jesus Christ. I hoped it wasn't another heart attack. Jimmy's ticker was all but shot now.

Since 1967, since I'd "retired" the wearisome, outsized persona of "Hector Lassiter" from the world with my own staged "murder-suicide," Jimmy and I pretty much only connected by phone. The last time was when he suffered his second heart attack, a call that Marie had made him make over his own objections, he'd said, because he didn't want "to worry or depress me" with his failing health.

I scooped up the phone, said, "Jimmy?"

His voice was cracking, "I need you to come to Ohio, Hector. I need your help, now. Marie is dead, Hector. Höttl murdered her."

"Marie? Dead? *What?*" None of this made any sense. I said, "Höttl? We killed Höttl in fifty-seven, Jimmy. Are you—"

"No, Hector. We didn't kill him. Höttl is still alive. The bloody bastard murdered our Marie yesterday! Goddamn it, Höttl had her killed!"

My son Joaquin fetched the newspaper for me.

I found a wire account buried on page 14. Marie, now "Sara," a name I'd never grown accustomed to using for her, had been signing copies of her memoir at a bookstore in Illinois.

According to reports, a stocky man wrapped in an out-of-season black overcoat approached the signing desk and passed a copy of her memoir to Marie for personalization.

As she set to that task, the man whipped off his overcoat. He was dressed in khaki pants and shirt and sporting a Nazi armband. He pointed a vintage Mauser at Marie and shouted, "Father sends his regards!"

He then shot Marie twice in the face.

As he successfully fled the scene—all those bookworms were no threat to his escape—the shooter was seen being followed by a second man who was carrying a motion picture camera. They bolted in a white Plymouth.

I sat in my chair, desolate, the newspaper crumpled in my lap.

My wife took the paper from me, knelt and hugged me to her as I sobbed into her bare shoulder.

It's a hell of a long way from Hawaii to northeastern Ohio, so I had too much time on planes to think about it all. Time to browse over articles on Marie's recent memoir and additional accounts of her murder a clipping agency hastily assembled for me.

After Duff's death, for several months I'd chased those two phantom Nazis who'd killed her. I'd hunted them with no success. In 1958, I'd gotten caught up in other matters, and early-to middle-1959 found me tangled up in *different* old business that had also clouded my life across the decades.

By July of 1959, having never found a trace of the Nazi bastards, I'd reluctantly set aside my search for Duff's killers and tried to close the door on all that. Revenge, I tried to convince myself then, was a hobby for the young and the passionately intent.

By then, Marie had adopted another name, moved out to Los Angeles, and, with a little help from myself and my screenwriter/poet/songwriter friend Eskin "Bud" Fiske, she'd established herself as head writer for a long-running CBS TV series.

In late 1967, tired of being me, I'd pulled my own disappearing act—I'd plotted and written myself right out of the public eye.

I'd not known Marie was contemplating a memoir. If I had, I'd certainly have strongly counseled her against it. That fact was probably why she kept me in the dark about her damned book. Doing that probably cost her some real money. Judging from the estimates in the trades regarding her likely advance, with my publishing connections, I could certainly have gotten Marie better than the book deal she'd signed.

But there was no advance and no movie-option money in the world that could offset what telling her true story had cost Marie.

There was not enough to make up for what it might yet cost Jimmy.

Hanrahan's house was located in a quiet neighborhood shadowed by big old trees. I parked my rental Impala in the driveway. There was a black wreath on the front door.

I buzzed and an elderly black woman in a nurse's uniform opened the door. "You must be Beau Devlin," she said. "I'm Rose. I've heard so many stories about you. I expected you to be a good bit older, Beau."

"I'm seventy-one," I said. "Just been living cleaner… Lately."

She smiled with her eyes. "Wish you'd taught your friend to do the same, Beau. I check on him mornings. See him through to lunch. Martha comes by in the evenings. His church women are filling in the gaps for the next few days." Rose shook her head. "That man surely should have married."

"His job always got in the way of that," I said. "Where is he?"

"On the back porch. He just sits there all day. Poor man."

Rose led me through the neutrally decorated house and out onto a slab patio that had been screened in. Rain pattered down on the aluminum roof. Jimmy was sitting in a chair. An oxygen tank in a rolling cart sat at the ready near his elbow. On a low table, there was a copy of my novel, *Bordertown*, and a bottle of Jameson. A single upended glass sat next to the bottle.

Even seeing him from behind, I could tell Jimmy was carrying a few more pounds. His hair was now white. He was sipping his own stingy pour of whiskey and staring off through the trees.

That familiar tenor: "Boyo, pull up a chair and pour yourself a drink."

I did that. He reached over and shook my hand. Still a killer grip despite it all. "Thank you so much for coming all this way," Jimmy said. "I can only imagine the trouble this caused you with your wife. I'm sure Alicia hates you risking coming out here. Risking exposure. And she probably already suspects why I asked you here."

"Alicia knows you are my good friend," I said cagily. "My last good friend from the early days. It's just thee and me now, Jimmy. Last men standing." I sipped my Irish whiskey, staring at the trees now, too. It was hard to see Jimmy looking so old, so frail. I said, "You should have called me earlier, buddy. I'd have been here for the funeral, you know that."

"There really *wasn't* a funeral," Jimmy said voice cracking again. "I couldn't even be there. My blood-pressure was in the danger zone. Sawbones feared any exertion or emotional stress beyond what I'm *coping with*—their mealy-mouthed words, not mine—might trigger another attack. They say the next one could be the one that at worst will kill me, and at best might make me an invalid." Jimmy shook his head. "As if there's a feckin' difference."

He sighed. The rain began to beat down harder on the aluminum roof. "So there was no funeral, per se. With Finn and Sean already gone, Marie and I were the last, anyway. I knew given how she died, the place would be thick with reporters. Those maggot journalists would turn any service for Marie into a circus."

Eyeing that idle air tank, I resisted the urge to have a smoke. I'd been cutting down for years, lately rationing myself to stingy two-a-days. But stressed like this, I felt the old craving for a smoke more strongly than I had for a long, long time. For single malt, too. Irish whiskey would have to do.

I said, "I had a clipping service send me everything they could find on—" I faltered, finished with, "—on what happened to Marie. The shooter got away, of course, but I know witnesses say he spoke with a German accent. Given what Marie's memoir centered on, it's reasonable to assume some neo-Nazi sort might snap and go after—"

"No!" Jimmy swiveled to face me, his blue eyes watery but wrathful. "Höttl did this, no mistake on that! Höttl hired that man to kill her!" He passed me an envelope. "His letter. As you'll see, like everyone else in this gullible-ass world, he fell for your so-called death in 1967. Just like you and I fell for Höttl's so-called death ten years before."

Skeptical, I turned over the envelope, raised the flap and slid out the letter inside. I slipped on my despised spectacles and read:

My dear Hanrahan,

I wish I could better savor what I've taken from you.
As I write this, your "niece" is still alive, of course.

Timing is everything and I want this letter to strike you hard, as close as possible to the news I've had that cursed girl killed.

You see, I'm sufficiently confident of my plan's success to mail this letter even before its subject has come to pass.

My daughter's murder will be attended by many members of the press, of course. That damned book of hers seems *quite* the rage. So mine won't be the only cameras running when my man puts those bullets in her. One to the heart and one to the head, as the saying goes.

All of this is rich with irony, of course.

I have only been able to strike at that girl because of her damned memoir that has made historical record of that which I've tried for so many years to keep secret—my siring of the unclean little bitch.

Given the damage she's done my reputation with her book, and, soon (more rich irony here), with the *film* based on that book, one might think I'd gain more satisfaction from finally putting her in the ground.

But her nearing assassination brings me little consolation. The fact that Sexton and Lassiter, particularly, are both already dead and so not here to witness my ultimate success makes it all a bit hollow.

By the time you read this, there will be only you and I left, Hanrahan. And I hear you are all but dead yourself. What's the line from your countryman? "An old man is but a paltry thing, a tattered coat upon a stick..."

Your time seems quite past.

Still, I have the mild satisfaction of knowing *you* know I lived on and waited for my moment and now have at last succeeded in taking her from the world.

That's some scant consolation.

Lest you think this letter some kind of hoax, I've provided the enclosed photograph of myself. I sense I've weathered the years better than you.

—Werner Höttl

P.S. I'd have preferred to send this as a *filmed* testimony, but I've no sense you have the equipment or facility to screen such a "document." So we have to make do with mere words.

I looked at the accompanying photograph. it was Höttl, no question. He was white-haired now; his face lined. He seemed very bronzed. The ugly scar showed differently in his deeply tanned face. The old man in the picture stood ramrod straight and was still quite slender. In the photo, he was glazed with a thin sheen of sweat. The foliage in the background looked lush, tropical, like some goddamn jungle.

Biting my lip, I checked the envelope again. The thing had originated from somewhere in Brazil. It wasn't much of a start for a search, but maybe if I could find some native investigator for hire there, some shamus who'd understand the way mail moved in that country?

"I've done everything possible to trace the letter to its source," Jimmy said. He was still the ace cop, ever the man who'd already anticipated, and, often as not, executed my strategies in advance of my having even stated or possibly even thought of them.

"It's likely to have come from somewhere in central Brazil, but that's all that envelope can tell us. And we can't farm out this job of finding him, Hector."

He gripped my arm; his eyes besieged me. Jimmy said, "I've never asked you for a deep favor, not once, but I'm doing that now. Look at you, Hector—you could pass for your late fifties. You can do what *I* can't. You can *go* where I can't go anymore. I know you can't do this, but I'm begging you to do this anyway, Hector. For the love of God, do what I can't do for myself. Go there and kill Höttl! Avenge our Marie. Avenge Duff. Please, Hector, I'm begging you. I can't die knowing that monster is still in this world."

54

To my shame, I'd left Jimmy with no firm commitment about chasing after Höttl. He was right—he'd never asked much of me, yet over the years he had come running to the four-corners of this sorry world for me when I'd asked favors of him.

But *this* request?

And I'd only succeeded in drawing the woman who was now my wife back into my life with an honest promise of no more bloody intrigue; no more mayhem. I'd meant to keep that promise to my own real end.

I stopped by the cemetery to pay my respects at Marie's lonely grave. The place was quiet and the sun had burned off the morning's rain. A mourning dove cooed from the branches of an old elm that shadowed Marie's plot.

The marker bore the name by which the world had come to know Marie as a writer.

I checked my watch. My first flight of three that would carry me back to Hawaii was scheduled to depart in three hours. It was a thirty-minute drive to the airport. I had the time to tarry.

But I found myself distracted.

A young man with blond hair was hanging around a grave three rows away. His hair was longish, like all the young guys seemed to wear it now. He saw me looking, nodded, then squatted down and pressed his hand to the sod, eyes closed in apparent prayer.

It was some nice theatre.

We were the only two living souls in sight in the crowded bone yard.

I moseyed over his way, fishing my old Zippo from my pocket. Stepping up behind him, I said, "Who'd you lose, son?"

Boy was a lousy liar. The headstone said old "Sebastian May" had died in 1940. No way this young guy was more than twenty-four, tops. Yet the kid said, "My father."

Lad should have picked a fresher marker or been more deft at dissembling.

Bringing my Colt from Hawaii to Ohio was more logistical trouble than I'd wanted to tackle, and getting the Peacemaker out of the house around my wife would have invited even more resistance on her part about my leaving. And, hell, I hadn't anticipated actually needing the damned thing like I did now.

But my hands were big and still steady. I jammed two fingers into the boy's kidney and flicked the lid on my Zippo to simulate a gun's cock.

"That's a lie, sonny," I said. "Check those dates on the tombstone. You should have said grandfather. Keep those hands out and pressed to that sod, son. Stay down there, boy. Now, don't get screwy or stupid. I'm pulling your wallet from your back pocket to check your I.D. Move any at all, and I will shoot you through, kid."

The boy's legs began to tremble; my gun ruse seemed to be working. That was good. As Jimmy said, I'd kept myself reasonably fit, but at seventy-one, me wrestling some young buck was not apt to have a good outcome for me.

"Sounds a real dull duty, watching that grave," I said. "How long are they paying you to stare at that plot?"

The kid blustered, "You're nuts! I'm not spying on that woman's grave."

"No? Then how'd you know it's a woman buried yonder there?"

I flipped open the kid's wallet. I squinted at his license. Putting on my spectacles would mean taking my pretend gun from his back. "So, you're one Vincent Stoats. Now, a last time, who's paying you to watch that woman's grave, Vince?"

"I don't know what—"

"What I'm talking about, yeah, yeah," I said, cutting him off. "I can supply every lame denial you're going to trot out before you finally get some sense and tell me what I want to know. Now, before we have to go through those tired motions, before you have to sacrifice teeth and maybe take a bullet to the knee, just cut to the chase, boy. I'm striving to do this civil-like."

He was still hesitating.

I tossed his wallet on the ground. "Look how quiet it is out here, Vince. How lonely. If I shoot you like this, with the gun up tight against you, it's gonna hurt my wrist, but it's also going to suppress the sound of the shot. Nobody will hear."

Keeping my fingers jabbed into his back, I began to pat him down. Kid had no weapons, but he had a pocket bulging with change. I said, "I'm assuming there's a pay phone somewhere around here so you can call in and report."

In the pocket with the change, I'd found a slip of paper with a phone number scrawled across it. I held the paper up where he could see it. "You're to call into this guy, right? Report in anyone lurking around the girl's grave?"

The kid tried to brazen it out, to stay silent on me.

I said, "Vincent, you're no hard case, so just stop this silly shit. When I call the number on this paper to tell your boss how you screwed up out here today, who's gonna pick up on the other end?"

The first crack in his veneer: "You're crazy, old man."

Kid was so green I truly was loathe to start-in beating on him. I decided to give it one more shot. "Sonny, you're just dense as a brick, aren't you? We have this place to ourselves, and it's a damn graveyard. Look over there. See that dirt pile? That pile implies an adjacent hole, Vincent. And look, someone left a shovel in that mound of dirt from that new-dug grave."

Vince said, "So what, man? It is a graveyard. So what?" There was a new quaver in Vincent's voice. They couldn't be paying the young dude too much to run surveillance on a grave on the off chance someone other than Jimmy or a journalist might happen by to gawk.

I figured this kid's courage threshold, the point at which risk exceeded paltry compensation, had been reached. He only needed a little nudge across that line, now.

"It *is* a graveyard, yes, Vincent," I said. I jabbed him hard in the back again. "If you don't affably start gushing helpful information, here's what's going to happen to you, son. I'll escort you over to that hole in the ground, then I'll put a bullet in your heart and topple you into that open grave. Then I'll ladle in just enough dirt to cover you up. See kid, nobody's going re-measure that hole now that it's been dug. They aren't going to notice it's only five-feet deep when they drop the other dearly deceased's vault in there over top your corpse.

It's the perfect place to dispose of a body, Vincent. Requires hardly any effort on my part and they will never, ever find you, sonny."

That did it. The words came in a torrent. "He's some private investigator named Jeffrey Carey. I don't know who he's working for. I was to watch the grave, like you said. Call in if anyone came by."

I could guess who was paying the private peeper's bill. I said, "Good, Vince. You just might yet walk out of this graveyard, today. Lead me to that payphone you're supposed to call from, sonny."

He did that.

I caught a break: along the way, we encountered no mourners or caretakers to mess up my quiet menacing of Vince.

When we reached the phone booth, I made the boy stand inside, facing the phone, while I checked the Yellow Pages. There really *was* a local private eye named Jeffrey Carey. His office number matched the one on the slip of paper I'd found in Vince's pocket. I tore out the yellow page with the ad. I slipped that in my pocket and then I gave Vince back the scrap of paper with the phone number. I said, "Dig yourself some of that change out or your pocket and dial that number, kid."

Vince said, "You *want* me to call him?"

"Yep. You call him and tell him just what you would if I didn't know you were spying on me, sonny. Tell him what you're paid to say. You tell this bastard you saw a man standing over the grave. Keep the description sketchy. You only saw my back. Say I'm still here, and it looks I might hang around for a while."

Vince handled it all very convincingly. When he finished, I jerked the chromed receiver cord from the box; tossed it on the ground. "Now, gimme your car keys, Vince."

Kid sounded freshly panicked. "You're not stealing my car?"

"Just taking your keys, kid." I pointed at the distant gates of the cemetery entrance. It was about three-hundred yards away. "I'll leave your keys there at the end of the driveway. But if I was you, I'd *jog* down there, fetch 'em, and keep on going out of this bone yard. I'd come back later for my car. Maybe in a week. You see, Vince, distances in this town are short, so I don't figure you have time to get your keys, get back here *and* drive out before your private-eye boss arrives. Lousy liar that you are, Carey's going to figure out you helped me finesse him away from his office and then he's going to be *very* angry at you, kiddo. Worse news? The people he's working for are even meaner."

The office door lock picked easily enough.

The private eye's place looked like something a dumbass who'd seen too many film noirs thought embodied a P.I.'s office. There was a battered desk (with office bottle in a lower drawer), a crooked coat rack, and two guest chairs. Two battleship-gray four-drawer filing cabinets held down one corner (idiot left the keys in the cabinet locks, but it turned out I didn't need 'em, anyway).

The office's window overlooked an alley and the place was scented with the rising bouquet of the garbage dumpsters below. *Très* swanky.

Jeffrey Carey seemed to have three active cases. He'd carelessly left the files atop his desk. Two dossiers were tied to tawdry divorce jobs. The other consisted of a batch of documents regarding Marie and her gravesite. That file contained some telegrams, some correspondence… Wire transfer records and preserved envelopes mailed from someplace called Mato Grosso, Brazil.

There was probably enough time to read the scant information in the file and make my own notes.

But I didn't care so much about leaving footprints, so to speak. I decided to take the file and read it on the plane.

That was the ticket, I'd decided. I'd let Jeffrey Carey carry word back to his Brazilian client something hinky had happened here in Ohio.

Höttl still considered Hector Lassiter dead, so there was no threat to me or mine in that sense.

Höttl knew Jimmy was housebound.

I was, for the moment, the *perfect* mystery man.

And, hell, as such, maybe I'd even cost Höttl some sleep.

55

I t was raining in Oahu—the daily misty downpour.

My wife said, "You're not a young hell-raiser anymore, Héctor. You're over seventy and you're seriously talking about going to a *jungle*."

She took my face in her hands. "I've been reading about this place. Héctor, there are many people who believe this Mato Grosso is the actual gate to Hades. This idea of you going there alone, to kill this man, it's loco, Héctor. They say this is a lawless, savage place. Much of it is still unexplored."

Alicia was right. It was one of the last frontiers. The rumored location of El Dorado and a place, as my wife said, that some believed was a portal to the literal Hell.

"But I have something like an address," I said. "This man, Höttl, he believes Hector Lassiter is dead. Beau Devlin is nobody to this man, nor to anybody in Brazil. Just as Jimmy, Marie and I never saw Höttl coming after his bogus death in 1957, the bastard will never see me coming his way until it's too late."

"You promised me there'd be no more of this, Héctor," she said. "You swore we were just going to have our quiet, normal life. Until now, you've largely honored that promise. If you break it now…?"

I combed my fingers through her glistening black hair. "This is the *one* thing in this world that can compel me to break that promise, and just this single time. I owe Jimmy a thousand times over. He's saved my life many times. He's my last true friend from the old days. Darling, I thought I'd saved this child. I thought I'd killed Höttl all those years ago. I never imagined this was a possibility. But he tricked us somehow. Höttl is still alive, and he had Duff tortured and killed. He had Marie murdered. Now I have a chance to kill him back for certain, up close and personal. I won't be fooled again. I can't let him cost me or Jimmy anymore."

"It sounds you've already made up your mind," Alicia said. "Isn't that so, Héctor?"

"I don't feel like I really have a choice." I awaited her verdict. My beautiful quiet life with the family I never thought I'd have now hung in the balance. I pushed a bit harder. "What if it was one of our children Höttl killed? If Jimmy was capable of doing this himself, I wouldn't contemplate this." I searched her dark eyes. "I'm the only one who can do this."

She was quiet a long time, just looking at me. Alicia said, "Perhaps. Perhaps there is no choice in this." She understood revenge better than most. She understood me better than anyone alive, God help her.

Alicia kissed me hard. "This must be the only time. This must be the last time. And you must come back to me, safe."

"I'll return just as fast as I can." I hugged her to me. "Please believe me, my love. I truly don't relish any of this that is to come. But it has to be done. Höttl has to die, and he has to know who it is who's killing him. He has to know what he's paying for."

Jimmy picked up after the third ring. He was a little breathy sounding as he said hello.

Not knowing if the line was fully secure on his end, I'd opted for a payphone to make my call. I said, "Jimmy, it's me. I'm going. I swear I'll do my best to put that devil back down in the pit forever."

A heavy sigh on his end, then Jimmy said, "*Thank you.* I wish there were more words to tell you how much I value what you're doing here."

"Hell, we don't need 'em, brother. We never have."

Jimmy said, "Then please, just make it hurt terribly for that son of a bitch."

I smiled so he'd hear it in my voice. "Rest assured, old friend, that's my goal."

56

I flew from Honolulu to São Paulo. The in-flight movie was *Double Indemnity*, prissy Ray Chandler's spin on earthy Jimmy Cain's carnal potboiler. Strange bedfellows, indeed. It was regarded as one of the great film noirs. The script and dialogue crackled, but that casting distracted me, and *how*.

Fred McMurray and the Sapphic Barbara Stanwyck?

I kept thinking, *My Three Sons* meets *The Big Valley*.

So I turned my attention to Hem's posthumous *Islands in the Stream*. I'd had a chance to participate in shaping the unfinished manuscript for publication, but demurred. I was curious to see what Hem's dotty widow had ultimately made of the book. Flashes of the brilliant Hem lurked in there, but the novel still really didn't cohere. It was going to hurt Hem's long game. That bitch.

Eventually, I turned back to the notes various investigators had gathered for me regarding the career of this Brazilian filmmaker Siron Cícero, cinematic auteur.

The critics deemed Cícero's films "dark" and "transgressive." Those were the fawners' verdicts.

The less enthralled cineastes threw around terms such as "sadistic," "misanthropic" and "diseased."

There was hand-wringing scuttlebutt in some obscure cinematic journals that an on-screen murder in his latest Portuguese-language film, *The Grand Inquisitor*, was not acting, nor a special effect. One wag had actually declared the movie a "snuff film."

Reading a synopsis of the flick, I caught myself squirming. The movie was about an interrogator and his hapless... *er*, subject. The latter was stripped naked and tied to a chair for the duration of the movie. He was "interrogated" and tortured and, finally, murdered in the final seconds of the *three-hour* film.

I didn't think anything could set my skin-crawling more than that capsule summary had, but I was wrong.

The next article I read described this Cícero's work-in-progress. It was a mysterious film he called *The Garden of Suffering*.

I splurged on the hotel. As it was apt to be one of the last chances I'd have for comfort and modern convenience for some unknown time, I decided I deserved some decadent opulence, some high-end mollycoddling.

After checking in, and after a bracing shower, I sprang for a massage from a comely, raven-haired woman who offered a bit more for some cash. It was an offer elder, happily married me found surprisingly easy to decline. Instead I headed to a Japanese quarter of the city and a purported local favorite restaurant called Rua Galvão Bueno. I ordered some *sukiyaki* and *unagui* that I washed down with butterscotch-tasting, belly-warming sake.

After my meal, I toured the city a bit more, finding that my fluent Spanish gave me enough of a leg-up to adequately communicate with the Portuguese-speaking natives.

My cabbie, on the other hand, was a French-speaker. He said there many French and Italians living in this part of Brazil. He gave me some tips on travel to the interior. "You picked a good time of year to come—winter is cooler, drier, of course," he said.

Funny to think of July as winter, but it was that part of the hemisphere where everything kind of up-ended on you.

And, hell, even for "winter," it was still nearly eighty-degrees. Call it a wet heat: I'd already sweated through my second shirt of the day.

My driver said, "Where do you go from here, *Senhor* Beau?"

"Mato Grosso," I said, dragging a sweat-slicked forearm across my damp forehead.

Although I was in the backseat, I could tell my driver was surreptitiously crossing himself to hear where I was headed.

Back in my hotel's lounge, I ordered a *Vinho tinto* and started combing back through my files on the filmmaker I suspected of being Höttl, going over again what my sources had been able to gather for me about this Mato Grosso place.

Now that I was in country and very much alone, this whole enterprise was starting to strike me as the insane under-taking it was.

Alicia had been too right. Here I was, topping seventy, and preparing to penetrate a lawless jungle populated by bands of mercenary *pistoleiros*.

The country was a kind of logging/diamond/gold mining territory—a denuded and strip-mined wasteland surrounded by the densest jungle.

The parts of the country that hadn't been raped for wood, precious stones and ore were said to be thick with malaria, capivara, soldier ants, and man-eating caimans. The rivers teemed with piranha.

I was seemingly going to be riding a train the locals called the "Devil's Railroad" to the so-called Portão de Inferno—the Gates of Hell.

The jungle areas were thick with lost tribes, mercenaries and hunted men. And sundry other Nazi war criminals if the rumors were true.

If the natives or Höttl's praetorian guards didn't kill me, yellow fever or heatstroke might easily take up the slack.

I looked up from my notes, freshly dejected.

Yes, my Alicia had been so right: at my age, and alone, this was the daftest quest of 'em all.

Some mild commotion across the room.

A tallish, thin man in a white seersucker suit was talking to the maître-d and pointing my way. The man had dark brown hair, starting to silver at the temples. He had prominent ears. A black eye-patch covered his right eye socket. He smiled and I recognized him.

Son of a bitch if it wasn't my poet-friend, Eskin "Bud" Fiske!

57

I ordered Bud a whiskey on the rocks and slapped his arm.
"Christ, it's good to see you, Bud. But how on earth?" I
winced and said, "Alicia's behind this, isn't she?"

He didn't even pretend. "That's right," Bud said. He was
in his late thirties by my reckoning. His face was a bit lined.
He was wearing glasses over that eye-patch. He'd lost the orb
on some CBS Studios back-lot, attacked by a drunken Peter
Lawford during the wrap party for Bobby Conrad's *The Wild
Wild West*.

I said, "You're the best of friends to do this, Bud, but I
want you to use my credit card and book yourself a flight
home to Tennessee, pronto. I *won't* have you take this risk,
buddy. You've got no dog in this fight. You should be back in
Nashville."

Bud got a hand up. "Drop it, Hector. And you introduced
me to Marie. She was my friend, and I worked with her for a
solid year trying to get that sit-com up and running. I spent more
time with her than you ever did. I loved her like a sister, Lass."

Oh yeah. That damned "situation comedy." Something
that was supposed to be ABC's answer to *Hogan's Heroes*. Some

whacked project called *My Chauffführer* that revolved around a decrepit Adolph Hitler, still on the lam twenty-two years after the fall of Berlin.

The way Bud had first explained it to me over the phone had made me ask him what he'd been drinking *and* smoking. The premise was Hitler faked his death in the bunker in forty-five, intent upon disappearing into South America. A booking accident, exacerbated by Adolph's notoriously shaky English, resulted in the disguised Führer's misrouting to Beverly Hills. There, the reeling ex-Reich-master would grudgingly take work as a driver for a *borscht belt* variety show host and comedian loosely modeled after Sid Caesar.

Marie seemed to have bought into the whole jaw-dropping enterprise.

As such things are wont to do in the world of television, nothing quite went to plan and the mess never got far beyond a filmed pilot.

Bud said, "Marie was a great kid and what happened to her, well, goddamn that Nazi, anyway. And besides, I gave Alicia my word, Hector." He smiled and added, "And I've got us some capable help for this thing, too."

I was still resistant. "Bud, you inject insulin. You need to have a steady diet to quell your diabetes. Where I'm going? *Hell* doesn't do it justice."

"I'll be fine, Hector," Bud said. "And I've brought really good help."

I ran my fingers back through my damp hair. "What kind of help, exactly?"

Bud smiled. "Called in a longstanding marker."

Dubious, I said, "Some friend of yours?"

"Friends of *ours*," Bud said.

"Who?" Hell, I'd been benched so long, they'd have to be nearly as old as me.

"More of a case of what," Bud said. "And that 'what' would be the State of Israel."

I nearly sprayed the poet-screenwriter with un-swallowed hooch. "Say again?"

Bud looked surprised. "Don't you remember? Nashville, December 1958? That *item* that fell into our hands and your decision to hand it over to...?"

Oh, *yeah*. "Christ, I'd forgotten that outstanding debt. It was a big one for sure." A gift that kept on giving in goddamn *spades*. Goddamned Gnashville gold, so to speak.

"Well, I didn't forget," Bud said. "I made some calls, and the upshot is we have a couple of tough operatives being sent to help us with the hunt for Höttl."

Well, well. I said, "These old boys they're sending to help, they're Mossad?"

"Frankly, I don't know what they are," Bud said, "but they pretty much specialize in hunting Nazi war criminals from the story I was told."

I sipped my red wine. "When do they get here?"

Bud signaled for a waiter and asked for a menu. "Haven't eaten in too long," he said. "With the diabetes, well, like you said..."

Yeah, *like I said*, goddamit. The prospect of Bud in the jungle with his precious, fragile vials of insulin and hypos and unsteady blood sugar side-effects tied to dieting terrified me.

Bud ordered himself a meal in faltering Spanish, but it seemed enough for the waiter to grasp Bud's request.

Watching him go, Bud said, "The two Israelis are to meet us for breakfast tomorrow. They're already based here in Brazil, hunting some other Nazis." He smiled. "They were pretty floored to hear that Werner Höttl is still alive."

"Not as surprised as I was," I said sadly. "Surely not as surprised as Marie."

"She was a great gal," Bud said softly. "And a very fine writer." Watching him, I wondered if something had happened between them, decided it did. The kid had to stay.

After Bud's meal, we wandered the city for a bit. Despite my earlier driver's assertions, I was surprised to see what a large Italian population there was in São Paulo. We found ourselves a good Italian joint for an early dinner, and I gave my Great War-era Italian a dusting-off.

Further wandering of the city took us into a tenement zone that stank of open sewers. I hailed us a cab away from there.

As we waited for our hack to make it through traffic to our side of the street, Bud eyed the dilapidated wooden *cortiços*. "We should do this quickly and go home. I'm not liking this place, Lass."

"Savor the city, Bud," I said. "This is as civilized as it's apt to get for us."

The poet opened the door of the cab and I slid in first. "So you said," Bud growled, sliding in behind me. I told the cabbie the name of our hotel. Bud said, "Alicia made it sound like you've already got a little on this guy. A general sense of where he might be."

"General at best," I said, twisting around in my seat to watch a Volkswagen microbus that had seemed to me to have been trailing us as we made our way on foot. "My files are back at the hotel. Along with some notes about where I suspect we're headed to close matters with this cocksucker. If that stuff doesn't put you on a plane back to Music City, then I guess you're crazier than many claim I am."

Bud pressed his hand to his belly. "Might be the food that chases me out. The Italian stuff was good, but that soup I had for lunch? I haven't felt right, since. What was that I ate, anyway?"

I shook his bony knee. "Sure you really want to know?"

Bud looked a little green, now. "*Oh, God*, maybe not from the sound of your voice. I kind of figured from the name it was some kind of fish."

"Some kind," I said. "That was piranha. You feelin' feisty, Bud? They say it's an aphrodisiac."

Now Bud looked extra queasy. "Those fish eat people, don't they? I could be a second-hand cannibal."

"Life's always eaten life, son." I was still focused on the VW behind us. "Pretty sure we're being followed," I said. "You carrying?"

Bud shot me this look. "Uh, *no*. Figured you'd know how to get us guns here."

This time I had taken the trouble to arrange a weapon for myself in advance. I bit my lip, then said to our driver. "Pull over for a moment, would you?"

He did that.

I leaned in close to Bud. I whispered in his ear, "I have a forty-five. Get out, keep an arm under your coat like you've got a gun, too. You take the passenger side and I'll approach on the driver's side. Just look like trouble's meaner older brother." In Bud's case, the eye patch would further the cause. He looked like a skinny badass now.

Bud nodded and wetted his lips. "Really think this is *that* kind of scene?"

I shrugged. "They're obviously not following us for no reason at all."

Bud said, "It *is* a German manufactured vehicle."

"Uh, *right*." We slid out and I reached under my coat, clicking off the safety on my automatic. The sun was on the glass on my side of the VW. I held up a left hand, trying to shield the window glass and get a look at the driver while I kept my right hand on the butt of my gun.

The window of the van was being cranked down. There was a flash of light that blinded me.

Jesus Christ! I blinked, seeing spots. Another flash.

This voice with an Asian accent: "Can we have your autograph? We're huge fans!" I was just beginning to see again. The driver was an elderly Japanese man. He thrust a notepad and pen at me. His wife, beaming, had a camera on her lap. She was twisting in a new flash bulb.

Chee-rist!

I scribbled my name on the sheet of paper. Through the VW van, I could see Bud on the other side, struggling his maintain his composure. I handed the notepad and pen back to the man. He read my name there, and, frowning, said, "A good joke, but could you sign your *real* name for us, Mr. Holden?"

His wife smiled at me and said, "We *love* your films. That movie of yours, *The Wild Bunch*?" She pretended her fingers were a gun, shooting me in the heart. "Oh, boy!"

Not for the first time, I played along, scribbling down William Holden's name. The male Holden fan said, "Can you give us a line from *The Wild Bunch*? We *really* loved that movie of yours, even *with* that bloody ending."

I managed a smile and a wink. Good thing I liked old Bill Holden well enough, since I was so often being confused for him as the years went on. And I'd recently seen *The Wild Bunch*. Hell, given how things might go in the jungle, I might be *living* that bloody film's final porch battle in a few days, I figured.

There *was* a particular line of Holden dialogue in that movie I'd found hauntingly resonant. Trying to catch old Bill's tones, I repeated, "We've got to start thinking beyond our guns. Those days are closing *fast*."

The woman clapped her hands, beaming. He husband clearly liked it fine, too.

Bud's look was harder to read.

58

Bud's Israeli friend was a tad like a saturnine body-builder. He stood right around six-feet and nearly all of that appeared to be muscle. Curly dark hair framed a beetle-brow over very dark eyes.

He grudgingly gave his first name as Eli, but wouldn't give up more of his handle than that. He wouldn't even hang a first name on his partner, and that hombre was nowhere to be found, allegedly made off to parts unknown, following up some Höttl lead.

The hotel staff set up our breakfast on the terrace of my room, cranking up the table's umbrella to cast some much needed shade over us. We were nine floors up, but the street noise at this relatively early hour was fairly intense.

"Sorry about the din," I said. "Perhaps should have taken breakfast in the restaurant downstairs."

"Not for *this* talk," Eli said, glum-faced. He tasted his orange juice. "This is good." Fella had a way with words.

I settled in across the table from him and sipped my own juice. "Bud said you boys were already here in Brazil, hunting other Nazis. Who do you suspect to be here?"

"Klaus Barbie, who we hear is perhaps some kind of agent for your government," Eli said. He sounded like he personally blamed me for that. "Also, we think, Mengele, the Angel of Death."

Bud slid into a chair. He said, "You saying Mengele is under U.S. government protection in some way, too?"

"No, not him," Eli said. "We merely think he might be here in Brazil, too. We think Barbie is on your government's payroll, and Höttl, too. How can that be?"

"That's about a thirty-year question for me," I said. "Main thing is, when we finally lay hands on this son of a bitch, *I* get to put him down."

Eli scowled. "*Put him down.* What does this mean? Be precise."

"It means I get to be the one to kill Höttl," I said.

"Kill?" A scowl. "*No.*" Eli waved a hand. "No killing him." Eli, the bastard, seemed emphatic.

Bud said, "I told you up front that was our intent."

"Your intent, not ours," Eli said. "Once we learned Höttl lives, this became a matter for us. We will apprehend this criminal and we will smuggle him out of this sordid safe haven to stand trial for his war crimes. He is an important symbol in that sense."

Couldn't help myself—it came as a snarl. "*Trial?* You're fucking crazy. You don't put monsters like this on trial. You just put 'em down, and you do it out of sight. You don't martyr the cocksuckers. Putting this kind on trial is an idiot's reasoning."

"Nonsense," Eli said. "Trial. For war crimes, as I said. Just like Eichmann."

I jabbed a finger into Eli's chest. "The only trial this bastard has in his bleak future is one of pain and then death. I'm serious, boy. I'm going kill that rotten son of a bitch, and slow, with my bare hands. I've earned that privilege, all the way up. It cost me beyond your wildest imagining."

Bud said, "Damn it, I came to get your government's help for this, Eli, not to have you try and hijack our mission."

"Your plan is no longer relevant," Eli said. "Go home before you get hurt, or before I have to be distracted from task to detain or hold you in some way until Höttl is in our hands."

Bud gave me this look of mixed contrition and rage. I held up a hand. "Calm down, Bud. I'm sure Eli here can be made to see reason."

That was lip service. Eli wasn't the kind to bend and me either.

Eli had drained his orange juice. The hotel flunky had left the sweating pitcher of juice back in the room, out of the sun. Bud had nearly polished off his juice too. I finished off my own OJ, then rose with our three empty glasses in hand.

As Bud continued to tear into Eli, I poured three new glasses of juice.

Alicia had thoughtfully packed some sleeping pills for me in case I had trouble with jetlag. I shook a few capsules out and pulled them apart. I emptied their contents into one glass of orange juice.

I had Eli spread out on the terrace floor. Sucker was snoring up a storm. As I rooted through his pockets, Bud apologized over and over for having dragged in the Israeli authorities.

"Spilt milk," I said, brushing it aside. "Pack us up, Bud. This sucker's going to be pissed off as hell when he comes to. We want to be long-gone before then."

59

Closing the cab door, Bud said, "How long do you think Eli will be out?"

"Nowhere near long enough," I said. "I sorely found myself tempted to kill that son of a bitch to keep him off our heels until we get to Höttl. But grief like the Mossad maybe hunting us because I killed one of theirs? Well, that's too much heat, even for me in my natural prime, which I surely ain't in anymore."

I looked up at the soaring apartment building. According to what useful paperwork I'd taken off Eli, he and his unnamed partner believed Höttl kept an apartment in this relatively newly built high-rise.

Bud said, "Kind of posh. At least on the outside."

"Uh-huh," I said. I was fighting the instinct to light up a cigarette. "Makes you wonder if this pad's paid for with Nazi gold or American blood money."

"Maybe film earnings," Bud said.

"Yeah, those damned movies." I slapped Bud's arm. "Let's get up there, pal. No guts, no glory, yeah?"

Bud nodded. "What if Eli's partner is up there?"

I pulled back my seersucker sport jacket and showed Bud my forty-five again. "We're well past jawin' with those humorless sons of bitches."

Eli's partner *was* there, after all. He lay dead in the hallway, just outside Höttl's bedroom. He had this terrible smile spread across his face, a kind of bemused-looking rictus.

Bud said, "My God, what killed him?" The poet was crouched down over the corpse, patting him down for papers and I.D. that might give us clues to where Höttl might be hiding *right now*.

"Whatever did this got him in the hand, I think." I pointed at the dead man's right palm. There was a little bloody hole there. I checked the knob to the bedroom. "There's a little metal prong here on the knob," I said. I sniffed at it. "Some kind of poison there on the spur. Be careful looking around, Bud. Likely to be more booby traps like that one."

Nodding, Bud, handed me what he'd taken from the corpse, then opened the bedroom door with the toe of his wingtip.

I went to toss the living room.

All-in-all, the apartment was pretty neutral; no homey touches like personal photos or mementos from Höttl's rarified travels. Rooting through drawers, I found no paperwork, bills or address books to point to other Höttl domiciles.

Then I checked the closet off the living room.

The space was packed with film canisters.

Jaw tightening as I read them, I checked labels on the metal containers.

I saw:

"Jean Moulin Interrogation/execution—negative"
"Oskar Schindler Interrogation/execution—negative"
"Amelia Earhart Execution—negative"

There were many more along those lines, a veritable who's who of "the disappeared" during the German Nazi regime.

One canister set me to shaking. I saw black spots and my pulse thrummed in my ears:

"Duff Lassiter (née Sexton) Interrogation/suicide—negative."

This gasp behind me. Bud said, "God, I am so sorry, Hector. Monster isn't enough for this one."

Nodding, I handed him another canister that claimed to contain footage of Marie's murder in the bookstore. "Welcome to my world, kid," I said.

"Now *I* want to be the one to kill him," Bud said.

"Find some boxes," I said. "Let's pack up these tins and scram before Eli comes calling."

Bud looked sick as I felt inside. "You're not thinking of actually screening these?" Another frown. "Or for some kind of *evidence?*"

"Please. We're going to burn these sorry and sick sons of bitches unscreened, Bud. History never knows about this one, not *ever.*"

60

"Beau Devlin" and "Raoul Bender" checked into a decidedly downscale but clean hotel. Sucker also had air conditioning. I kicked off my shoes, stripped off my shirt, then stretched out on the bed with my glasses and the notes Bud had taken from Eli's partner's body.

The random mail I expected, but couldn't find, had been in the dead man's pocket. Several pieces of Höttl's correspondence were business things, including a tax bill for three Brazilian properties, complete with formal addresses.

I smacked the mattress. *Gotcha, demon!*

Toweling down from a cold shower, Bud said carefully, "Those films we burned—Höttl may have prints, too, you know."

The one-eyed poet poured us both some iced tea and handed me a glass. "Yeah, I kind of figure Höttl's maybe done that," I said. "Even though he seems to be somewhere in the Brazilian interior, presently, Höttl appears to have left the air conditioning running at that apartment at some cost." I waved the German's electric bill at Bud.

"Figure he wanted climate control to protect those bloody negatives," I said. "Clearly, Höttl didn't want to risk losing them to humidity or jungle rot. Now we've just got to get to Werner's Mato Grosso hellhole ahead of Eli. Now that an Israeli operative's been felled by Höttl, I figure they're going to redouble their efforts to *capture* the bastard, wrong-headed though it is."

"I'm sorry for reaching out to them," Bud said. "I was an idiot."

"Don't beat yourself up on that front anymore, Bud. If I'd stopped to think about what we'd done in fifty-eight, and the scale of that state's indebtedness to the two of us for same, I'd probably have tried the same gambit." I smiled and held up Höttl's property tax bill. "But we have his addresses now. All *three* of 'em."

Bud looked it over. "Don't suppose we could get lucky and he's maybe in Rio."

"There last of all, I think. We've eliminated the apartment here in town, and if you're Höttl, and you're really hiding, it's got to be his place in the interior."

"Was afraid you were going to say that." Bud nodded. "We leave soon?"

"*Very* soon," I said. "First, I need to work my little black book. Looks like we're back to having to see if I can find any of my old comrades still north of the dirt."

Geezers with good trigger fingers—that's what I'd be seeking.

Three hours later I'd gathered together three men crazy enough to hire on for the river run with Bud and I.

I'd tracked Charles Delattre to a place in Cancun. He swore he was in fine shape, but the years had done little to improve his English. He said, "*Grand Capitaine,* I read you are dead! All the reporters in the newspapers said—"

"Hell, you know journalists, Charles. Damn reporters and newspapers can't get *anything* right."

"Well, thank God for that," Charles said. "I'm ecstasic to know the recorders are wrong."

"I'm ecstatic the reporters screwed up, too," I said. I told him I'd wire him some money and have a plane ticket to Brazil waiting for him at the airport.

Next I scrounged up Jésus Calderone. He'd been a cold-hearted, perhaps even sociopathic hell-raiser who'd helped Jimmy and I out of that bloody dust-up south of the border in the early 1950s. I figured he'd be about forty, now. He was running some kind of boat charter out of the Yucatan for his "*pendejo* uncle."

Jésus seemed eager for the change of scenery on my nickel. I also figured, in light of where we were headed, a spare boating expert couldn't be a bad thing.

Rounding out my recruits was a half-Pima, half-Apache Indian who had my back in a bar fight in 1960 in Scottsdale, Arizona. Boy had been a terror with a knife in his early twenties. His thirties found him bored and idling away his days as a grease monkey in a Phoenix service station.

"It'll take 'em about forty-eight hours to get here," I said to Bud. "That'll give us time to get at least our initial travel arrangements and guns and ammo stocks seen to."

Bud said, "The third guy, the Native American, what's his name?"

"Jonny Lightfoot," I said. "At least that's it in our language."

"Sounds like a fake name, to me."

"Maybe. I sense Jonny has some legal issues hanging over him. That said, I wouldn't question him about his handle, my poet. He's the touchy sort, best of times."

"Bet your ass I won't press," Bud said. "All these guys sound like lunatics and him most of all."

"Yeah, but *our* lunatics," I said.

"This must be costing you a fortune," Bud said.

"I can afford it this year, and it's money well-spent. Biggest trick will be keeping this bunch's enthusiasm tamped down enough to stop 'em from killing Höttl before *I* can."

Bud just gave me this look. Once again, it was a hard one to read.

61

B ud and I were to meet up with our recruits for a get-acquainted dinner and bar-crawl before heading out, probably badly hung-over, the following morning.

Not knowing when—or, yeah, *if*—I'd get another chance, I made a couple of phone calls, first.

I thanked my darling for sending Bud along to have my back.

"Bud will at least keep you more cautious," Alicia said. "Bud has proven a good balance for your more reckless impulses, Héctor. He has his own reasons for revenge against this man." She hesitated, then added, "Yet he's hardly enough against the German, I fear."

"We've called in some more help," I said. "We'll be five going in after Höttl, and I'll put my near-half-dozen up against three times as many of Höttl's boys, any day."

Alicia sighed across the miles. "Just remember your promises, Héctor. Do this and come home fast."

"I surely mean to. I miss you all dreadfully."

"These bloody things you sometimes do, just don't start *liking* them again, Héctor."

Across the miles, Jimmy said, "I got a copy of Marie's autopsy, finally."

That came as a gut shot. I said, "Christ, Jimmy, why the hell would you do that to yourself?"

"It was well worth it, by God," he said. His voice faltered. "She was sick, Hector. Sick with something that Marie couldn't ever have fixed. It likely would have killed her, Hector. Maybe even a worse death than the one Höttl gave her, may God forgive me saying it."

"What the hell are you saying, Jimmy? How was Marie sick?"

"She had a rare congenital disease, Hector. You can only get it one way. It comes from genes passed down by *both* of your parents. It was dormant all these years, but in the last few months, the coroner said, it became active. I think that's why she wrote the damned book." Jimmy laid it out for me. When he was finished, I was swarmed by feelings of horror, anger. But the vengeful part of me, the strongest part of me in some ways, *that* nasty slice relished the prospect of sharing the coroner's revelations with Werner Höttl.

Jimmy must have been thinking the same thing. He said, "God, how I wish I could be there when you tell Höttl. To see that bastard's face? *Delicious.*"

I said, "I'll see to it they're among the last words he hears, Jimmy. I'm going to give 'em just enough time to sink in before I kill him."

When I first met Jésus Calderone down in the desert out-side Juárez, he'd been a skinny little runt with bad skin and no meat on him. Figured then most of his weight was to be found in his clothes and the steel-toed work boots he fancied.

Jésus still wasn't much over five-feet, but his metabolism seemed to have pulled a Houdini and lit out for keeps. Now Jésus went two-hundred pounds, easy. Maybe it was all that booze he seemed to have cultivated a high-tolerance for imbib-ing. He was knocking back the Cuba Libres with awesome speed. His black hair hung almost to his ass. He kept it out of his face with a red bandana. He wore sandals, ratty bellbottom jeans with no knees and a black muscle shirt emblazoned with a picture of Emiliano Zapata on one side and Che Guevara on the other.

Jésus said, "I hate the fucking Germans. They've always meddled in my country. My *abuelo* blamed the German immigrants for all the accordions that have ruined our music. And did you know the Germans were arming one side during the Revolution, trying to get you gringos focused on Mexico instead of going to Europe in the First World War?"

"I remember hearing something about that somewhere," I said.

"And Trotsky? Killed by an ice axe in Mexico City by the Nazis." Jésus crossed himself over Che's face and signaled for another rum and Coke.

I finally allowed myself a cigarette. Firing up a Pall Mall with my old Zippo, I said, "Jésus, Trotsky was a *Russian*. He was killed by Soviet Intelligence. Some NKVD enforcer called Ramón Mercader."

Bud's brown eye skittishly roamed between us.

Jésus helped himself to one of my cigarettes and lighter. He said, "German, Russian… there's a damn difference?" He squinted at the engraving on my lighter. He read, "*One True Sentence*. What's it mean?"

"A sometimes too-elusive dream" I said. "Much like proper revenge."

Jésus smiled. His front teeth were gold-capped, now. "Revenge only truly counts if you stay alive after," he said. "And it must be the kind of revenge you can live with, hombre."

I smiled, said, "*Non timebo mala*."

Jonny Lightfoot was next to arrive. He refused hard or soft liquor and instead ordered iced tea. His first words: "Weapons?"

"I'll have plenty of guns and ammo," I said. I introduced him to Bud and Jésus. He gave 'em cursory nods and said to me, "I'll need knives. I know what I want."

I said, "After dinner we will—"

"Not hungry," Jonny said. "I should start looking for what I want *now*."

Well, God bless him for bein' a professional.

I pulled out my wallet and passed Jonny some bills. Then I handed him a slip of paper with the hotel address and room number. "That's where we put up tonight. Get what you need and find us there, Jonny."

Lightfoot had been gone perhaps twenty minutes when Charles plopped down in his vacated chair and began pumping my hand. He said, "Solicitations, *Grand Capitaine*."

"Felicitations to you," I said. "How was the flight, Charles?" He looked older, of course. Probably on the cusp of sixty, now.

Charles said, "Fine. I'm belated to work with you again."

"I'm elated, too," I said. Bud gave me this look that telegraphed, *Who is this idiot?*

Serious now, Charles leaned forward, arms crossed on the table. "I have friends in French intelligence. They tell me there are four former Nazis, low-level ones, that the so-called Nazi hunters don't waste their time with, yet. They were little ones. Hardly more than boys during the war. They are now Höttl's protestors in this country. I have their names and photos."

He handed me a dossier full of dope about Höttl's *protectors*. Bud raised his eyebrows. Charles said, "Before you worry, *Grand Capitaine*, let me just say I did not tell them it is Höttl we are hunting. I am not fool, *non?* Tell them it is Höttl we seek, and suddenly they take an *interest.* Next, they take charge."

That set Bud to squirming in his chair.

"So rest assured," Charles continued, "The French intelligence and others believe we are hunting this other, this movie man Siron Cícero."

I slapped Charles on the knee. "Get yourself a drink, Charles. Bottoms up, but do it in a jiffy, old pal. We need to get to dinner soon." I held up his files. "Come morning, we set out to make these die-hard Nazis just another piece of regrettable history."

62

For some time, I'd labored under the delusion we could take a train some distance toward the patch of rain forest where Höttl's second-of-three sanctuaries was located.

But the so-called "Devil's Railroad" had foundered, just like the Madeira-Mamoré Railway that claimed more than eight-hundred lives and resulted in about four miles of completed track—a rail line to, well, nowhere.

So we drove in by Jeep, setting off from Porto Velho to the river Madeira, where we boarded our first boat.

Strange, black-headed, white-bodied birds with beaks like axe heads stood balanced on reedy legs, watching us. Their black and white plumage was separated by red bands at each of the birds' throats. Our captain, an elderly Portuguese sailor named Getúlio, said, "Red-necked tuiuiú." He pointed at some parrots perched above them. "And those are macaws."

"Those last they sell in pet stores back home," Bud said.

That fact didn't seem to please the old salt. He said, "Between the poachers, the miners and the people who steal our birds to sell, this country is falling to pieces. Being ruined." He pointed to several other birds on shore. "Those, there—

those are roseate spoonbills. The water is unseasonably deep. Usually, they'd have migrated away this time of year. These are the *good* animals. Soon, as you go further in, you will see more of the caimans. And the piranhas."

Höttl's remotest home was in the Pantanal, a place slowly but surely being converted into a kind of environmentally protected land. But for now, it still had its share of gold and diamond hunters. Poachers, fugitives from various flavors of the law, and hired brigands.

The foliage of Pantanal, according to our captain, was nowhere near as dense or near-impenetrable as other parts of this stretch of Brazil. I was dubious. It already looked pretty wild to me, a helter-skelter tangle of under- and overgrowth. Some called Mato Grosso "The Green Death."

On shore a massive boa constrictor was killing a deer. A big cat growled from deeper in the jungle. Getúlio muttered, "Jaguar."

Bud gave me this uneasy look. I'd warned him, just as Alicia had warned me.

Three days in, we switched boats and captains, starting a seven-day journey down the Cuiabá, São Lourenço and Paraguay rivers.

On July 16, we reached Corumbá. From there, we began our land journey, aiming for Porto Cercado. It was in that region we began to see some of the "rape of the land" that had been perpetrated by the gold miners.

Construction had also begun on a highway intended to connect Cuiabá to Corumbá. When they finished that sucker in some as-yet-unknown year or perhaps century, I thought

Höttl and many other Nazis' jungle hidey-holes would be severely compromised.

I picked up a local paper from an adjacent table and read that Francisco Franco had finally named a successor. Hell, if I survived this thing, maybe I could *at last* revisit Spain before I turned tits up.

We spent the night in an un-air-conditioned hotel, then pushed on a bit further, no more than seven miles now from Höttl's jungle sanctuary by my reckoning.

Indications were it would be a hellish last trek. After all, this was country where hundreds of men died to lay those *four* miles of go-nowhere railroad tracks.

I reckoned that traversing seven miles in the Brazilian interior might be a little like crossing the Sonoran Desert back home.

The patch of ground between Höttl and us was a kind of mosquito and caiman infested bottomland with no paved roads; a boggy trail through the woods or a risky run via river.

Looking over the maps, Jonny said, "If we leave early, say, five, six in the morning, we can maybe be sure to reach there by mid-afternoon. That's *if* we go in on foot."

Jésus said, "There's another option?"

"I Iorses," Charles said. "But we would have to hire at least five. We'd have to give some sense of where we meant to take them. And in a small place like this—"

"Word would maybe get back to Höttl," Bud finished for him.

Jésus said, "For all we know, everyone in this place might be on this German's payroll. Paid to protect him or to warn him. There's that river approach we might take, but so many of us in a boat, and with all the guns we'd have to load in?"

"It'd be another eyebrow-raiser indeed," I said. "On the way in here I saw a dune buggy for sale. Figure three of us and most of the weapons can fit in that. And it looks narrow enough to pass through that jungle-cut path. Tires on the sucker shouldn't bog down in that soup, either."

Charles said to me, "Then you suggest we should split up, *Grand Capitaine?*"

"Exactly," I said. "Jésus and Bud will go in by boat. We'll set up Bud as some kind of naturalist on camera safari. Jésus, you get a boat big enough for the five of us to flee in. Once this is done, one way or another, I think we're going to be on the hard-hunted run back to civilization. Boat will be a lot faster means of de-assing these evil environs."

Bud went with me to close the deal on the dune buggy. While we waited for the papers to be drawn up, Bud said, "Sending me in that boat—you're still worried I can't cut it, aren't you, Hector? You're just trying to keep me out of harm's way."

I gripped the back of his neck, got in close and looked into Bud's one good eye. I lied and said, "You know how to steer a boat. I know you know, because I taught you. If something should happen to me, and to Jésus, you're the only one left to get those men out of there. I really don't think a land retreat's going to be even a remote possibility. When Höttl knows he's in trouble, if he learns before I put him down, he may have a radio and call in local law. Maybe even American muscle if our government's still keeping close tabs on him. Even if Höttl's dead, those cocksuckers may be vengeful."

Bud wasn't buying in, yet. I said, "And there's the fact I don't trust you to control yourself. You want that man dead as much as I do. So I can't risk you putting Höttl down before I get my shot at him. He's *mine* to kill, Bud."

"That's bullshit," Bud said. "Just like that nonsense of wanting a boat big enough to carry all five of us out. You know we *all* won't come back from this. After all these years, know one thing. I know you, Hector, and I know when you're lying."

I didn't contradict what he'd deduced. Instead I said, "At very least, we certainly need a boat big enough to stretch out our wounded." A beat. "Or our dead."

63

The morning of the raid.

Bud and Jésus were going to set off a couple of hours behind us. Barring attack from the banks by mercenaries, thieves or some stray, lost tribe of Amerindians, they were apt to make much better time. They were taking along two walkie-talkies, a couple of machine guns, spare ammo drums, two forty-fives and a flare gun in case we needed help finding the river and our get-away ride through all that tangled jungle.

Charles, Jonny and I slathered on mosquito repellant, then finished loading the dune buggy. Jonny wedged a long, oil-cloth wrapped something into the back where he was planning to sit. I said, "What'cha got in there, Jon?"

"My bow."

I smiled. "Bow as in arrows? Are you joking?"

"You want to have a chance at surprising that German in his house?" Jonny patted the wrapped-up bow. "Only way to kill quiet and from a distance."

The path to Höttl's place was hardly more than that—a weedy, boggy swath cut through jungle already threatening to grow closed.

Stray branches swatted arms and nicked cheeks scarlet. Snakes nested in overhead branches. Charles, our driver, had to brake several times as caiman lumbered across the trail.

"These alligators, they unsettle me," Charles said.

Jonny, apparently unfazed, said, "Not alligators."

Charles nodded, said, "Crocodiles, then."

"Caiman," I said.

Charles arched an eyebrow. "What's the difference?"

"Hell if I know," I said. "Croc, gator or caiman, they're all just luggage with teeth to me."

We heard the growl of another jaguar. I was beginning to lean Charles's way. Men with guns were one thing—a bloody but *familiar* prospect. Something one had experience with. Exotic animal ambush, on the other hand? That was terrifying.

Perhaps four miles in, Jonny put a hand on Charles' shoulder. "Stop," he said. I saw he'd gotten out his bow; already strung an arrow, in fact.

Jonny squinted up into the canopy, drew back and let fly with a basso *thwang*.

I heard limbs crack. Leaves rustled and low branches whipped wildly.

A body fell onto the path about fifteen feet in front of us. Jonny had put his arrow through the man's heart, coming in under the sternum.

The dead mercenary—he had knives thrust down each of his boots and a carbine was still strapped around his torso—had landed on his back.

"We should probably go in on foot from here," Jonny said, leaping off the back of the buggy. He put a foot to the dead man's neck to brace the body, then pulled out his arrow. He looked it over, said, "Good to go again. It's going to be a fine day, I can tell."

Charles and I exchanged uneasy glances as Jonny pulled an arrow from a third body Charles said, "I feel recumbent."

"Redundant," I corrected. "Ditto."

Jonny whipped the arrow once, flinging red droplets into the red dust. He pointed: "The roofline. I'll cover you two to the door. I'll keep the outside clear. You two kill everybody inside." He made it sound so simple.

I nodded. "Right. But first let me see if Bud and Jésus are in position yet." I reached for my radio.

"Be quiet about it," Jonny said. "That man, the second one I killed, he had a radio, too. If signals should cross…?"

But I couldn't get a signal, not even radio crackle to speak of. Frustrating. Troubling.

I stowed my walkie-talkie and we crept through the undergrowth until we reached a clearing and could see the house. It was a kind of bastardized, two-story colonial. The graying white paint was peeling off in strips. It looked like a haunted house, but for the noise: somewhere, a generator was working overtime to power the big central air conditioning unit at the side of the house. That sucker looked newish.

About twenty yards off the house was a separate unit, a kind of uneasy compromise between a massive garage and a smallish barn.

On the moldering front porch of the house, two men with shotguns stood talking. Not Germans—Brazilians, chatting in Portuguese. Both men were toting rifles.

Jonny whispered, "I can get one, no problem. But I'm not certain of getting both before one or the other gets a shot off."

"And there would go the element of surprise," I said.

For just a moment, I thought we'd caught a break.

The guards split—one stayed at the front door, in the shade of the porch. The other began to make his way around the house to check the back. When that one turned the corner, Jonny shot him in the back—an oblique shot that missed the spinal column but again found the man's heart.

The skewered guard fell face-first into the red dust. His falling gun didn't discharge. I sighed, said, "Very nice work, Jon."

The dead guard's buddy heard the fall of the body. With a puzzled expression, he raised his gun and moved along the wall, preparing to sneak a look around the corner. He was about to lean around when Jonny's arrow killed *him*.

"Hell, this might not be hard at all," I said.

Stupid. Of course such cockiness always invites disaster.

As we were about to step from cover, gunfire broke out from somewhere to the right of our position. A voice that sounded like Jésus' yelled, "Sons of *putas!*"

More gunfire, then what sounded like a grenade going off.

Several of the upstairs windows of the house were opened; gun barrels poked out. I grabbed Jonny and jerked him over behind a fallen tree. I rolled over the trunk behind him. Charles crashed onto the ground behind me as the first slugs slammed into the tree's trunk.

64

Charles and I returned fire. Jonny put a couple of arrows through windows. We heard high-pitched screams; saw some guns withdrawn or dropped, sliding down the roof of the porch and tumbling into the crimson dust. Blood spritzed window sashes and glass.

Several men darted from behind the house. They put down covering fire for the men running behind them—two big boys half-leading, half-carrying a white haired old man with a nasty scar down the side of his face. Old fella seemed to have trouble walking on his own. *Good.*

They were making for that garage-barn. We killed or felled at least five but the rest made it inside the big garage. I tried mightily to put a slug into Höttl or one of the men carrying him, but the big bucks up front fouled all my shots.

Sounded like several engines were turning over inside the barn. Then those engines were *gunned.* Jonny kept his attention focused on those upstairs windows while Charles and I fired into the front of the barn. Through a rear door, three motorcycles with attached sidecars tore off down the path, disappearing into the overgrowth behind the house.

One of us—either Charles or I—killed the driver of the rearmost bike. The motorcycle veered rightward and slammed into the corner of the house, nearly decapitating the sidecar rider.

But near as I could tell, Höttl was in the sidecar of the *first* motorcycle—now well out of my gun's range.

I said, "There might be another motorcycle in that garage." Jonny was out of arrows. I handed him a forty-five and some clips to handle anyone he couldn't get close enough to kill with all those knives he'd carried in. I snarled, "Cover me, because I'm going for the garage."

Charles said, "I'm with *Grand Capitaine.*"

The two of us ran for the barn, firing up at the second floor windows of the house as we went. There were two more motorcycles in the barn. One had a sidecar, the other didn't. I said, "All the things I've done in my life, I've never been on one of these things damned bikes. But how hard can it be?"

Charles pointed at the sidecar. "You sit in there, *Grand Capitaine.* "From there you can fire on the German. I can drive these. You see to the killing."

We tore out of the garage, sputtering black smoke and whipping through low-hanging foliage. To protect my eyes, I got out my Ray-Bans and put them on. I commenced to looking for a way to steady a shot at the back of the driver of the rearmost motorcycle that was quickly coming into range.

The other two bikes had a pretty good head start on us, but those fellas seemed intent upon staying alive. Seemed to me Charles had no similar ambitions. He was running flat out, sending us briefly airborne as we struck protruding tree roots and small, unknown critters dashing across our path; some kind of animals that squealed as the tires broke their backs or crushed their skulls.

"Christ's sake," I yelled over the roar of our own engine, "we can't kill this bastard if you kill us first."

The man in the sidecar of the last motorcycle was trying to twist around in that little tube to take shots back at us. But he was a husky lad and couldn't quite get himself turned around enough in the cramped sidecar to take clean shots.

And the bumpiness of the ride made any kind of competent targeting something of a pipedream. I aimed at the back of the sidecar rider's head and instead struck him in the neck. My shot maybe severed the man's spine. He slumped forward, his arm hanging out the side of the car and hand trailing the ground. He lost his grip on his gun and it bounced along in their wake, eventually striking the bottom of my car. I got lucky and the thing didn't discharge and shoot me in the ass or the like.

I screamed at Charles, "Better ease up a little, just for a minute. I'm going to shoot at the driver. If he loses control, all that metal is maybe going to come rushing back at us just like that gun did."

Charles slowed a bit, putting some more ground between us and buying himself more reaction time.

It took three shots, but I finally put one in the biker's lower back. He twisted as he took the hit and the motorcycle veered rightward off the path, crashing through brush and spindly trees. There was a splash, then some thrashing; seemed some body of water was just off to our right. Thinking that, I realized now I could smell water and figured it was probably the river.

As I was thinking that about that river, as Charles was increasing our speed to gain on the last of the bikes—the one with Höttl in the sidecar—a caiman ran across our path. He was a big enough son of a bitch, probably six-feet long and all of him one big and armored muscle.

Snarling, Charles did the best he could to steer toward the lower, backend of the giant lizard—to go over him at the hindquarters and tail where the bastard was closest to the ground.

It was *still* a hellish bump. We were pitched forward, then sideways. There was a sound of twisting metal and I nearly lost my gun. Charles managed to stay on the bike and to keep us on the trail, but now the front end of the sidecar was twisted away from the bike at a rightward angle. I looked down and saw the metal bond between me and the bike was twisted, nearly sheared through.

Though he tried to close the distance on Höttl's bike, the damage done our ride was slowing us down. I took a couple of shots at Höttl's back, frustrated by the notion of maybe killing him before he knew who'd done it to him.

The old man pitched something over his shoulder. It bounced along the path behind them, wobbling our way. I thought maybe Höttl had lost his grip on his gun, just like the other boy who was now in the river had before him.

Then I figured out what it was. Before I could yell "Grenade!" it was under us. Charles had seen it, too—given our bike all the kick he could to get us away before the detonation. The grenade slammed against the bottom of the sidecar. I figured at that point I was going to lose my legs, my plumbing and probably my life. My remains would end up in some caiman's belly.

Then the grenade was somewhere behind us. The shrapnel from a rearward explosion could still be plenty lethal to Charles and I, I figured.

But the grenade bounced off trail. A tree dampened most of the explosion's force. Yet it was still enough concussion to lift Charles's bike up off the ground. I closed my eyes against a pelting of branches and severed foliage.

Instead of rolling us over, the force of the explosion put more stress on the already damaged umbilical between the bike and the sidecar. There was again the sound of twisting, shearing metal, and then branches were slapping me in the face. I couldn't see Charles or the bike, just heard a big splash.

Realizing I was rolling out of control toward the river, I struggled to get up out of the sidecar, to make a leap before I hit the water teeming with all those caiman and ravenous, razor-tooth piranha.

I became tangled in the low-hanging brush and was ripped from the sidecar.

There was a last crash of metal through foliage and then another big splash as the sidecar slammed into the river water.

I was dangling in the branches, seeing spots and amazed to be alive. I shook my head and lowered myself to the ground. I found no sign of Charles or the bike. I had this terrible vision of him being torn apart by predators somewhere under the surface of that stinking river.

And Höttl?

That bastard was long gone, leaving me behind to try and follow that treacherous path back to his house, easy prey for the caiman I now knew were lurking in the river just a few yards from where I stood.

I'd walked—well, limped, because I'd wrenched a knee being jerked from the sidecar—perhaps two hundred edgy yards through snake and caiman infested boggy overgrowth when I heard a motorcycle engine. The sound of its approach was coming from the direction of Höttl's house. I'd lost my gun in the wreck. I had a knife and a few grenades, but that was all.

But the bike was moving slowly, just a hair above an idle. A voice called, "Hector? Charles?"

It was Bud Fiske, bumping along the path in the last of the motorcycles we'd left behind us in the barn when Charles and I had torn off after Höttl and company. The bike Bud was on had no sidecar. I stepped out into the path, waved a hand, said, "Thank God for you, Bud."

He smiled and said, "Thank God *you're* okay, Lass. You are okay, aren't you?"

"Probably bruised and will be sore as hell come morning. Need to give my knee some attention, but yeah, I'm okay."

"Charles?"

"I think we lost him," I said bitterly.

Bud hung his head. Said, "And Höttl?"

"He got away, goddamn it."

Quiet, Bud twisted and turned the motorcycle around on the path, got it pointed back toward the house. As I slid onto the seat behind him and wrapped my arms around his torso, Bud said, "Jonny's cleaning up back at the house with Jésus. Mopping up the last of them."

"We take any prisoners?"

Bud scoffed. "With Jésus and Jonny on the job? Are you joking?"

65

Jésus and Jonny had indeed "cleaned up," as Bud said. They had killed Höttl's guards to a man, then pulled their bodies into the garage and doused the bloody corpses with gasoline. "Thought we'd put the torch to this place," Jésus said.

"A fine notion," I said, "but first I want to go through Höttl's place. Might be something useful in there in terms of picking up his trail again."

But there wasn't.

Bud and I searched the house, careful to look for more booby-traps like the one Höttl had set in his apartment back in São Paulo. While Bud and I tossed Höttl's hovel, Jésus and Jonny went off again in search of Charles.

It seemed a pointless mission, to me, but I let them go and turned my attention to that other search.

If his apartment was impersonal, Höttl's house was the opposite, almost like a hellish glimpse into his interior landscape. Nazi flags and memorabilia were strewn throughout the warren of a house.

His version of wall art was decidedly macabre, too—giant framed prints of historical black-and-white photos. There was

Lee Harvey Oswald being shot. The was the image of that communist guerilla in the checked shirt, his arms secured behind his back, as he was killed by a pistol shot to the head in Cholon, Saigon.

There was Bobby Kennedy, bleeding on the floor of that L.A. hotel kitchen. There was that famous shot of a sniper hanging dead in a tree in Spain circa the Civil War. And speaking of the Civil War, several blowups of Matthew Brady's photographs of Union and Rebel dead proliferated.

One room was filled with tins filled with prints Bud had theorized Höttl might have struck from the negatives we'd destroyed back in São Paulo.

Bud fetched more gasoline tanks from the garage and we doused the interior of the house. We went outside to await Jésus and Jonny. When they returned an hour later, I could tell from their expressions they didn't bring good news.

Jésus said, "*Nada.* He might have gone in the river. On the other hand, he might still be chasing them. Either way, he's gone."

Jonny said, "We think there might be some men coming in on foot from the direction Höttl ran. Lots of men. We need to leave, fast."

"Right," I said. "Let's set fire to all this and head for the boat."

As we saw to the destruction of the house and garage, I kept looking back up the path, hoping for sight or sound of Charles returning, but nothing like that happened.

66

We reached Rio de Janeiro in the midst of an unseasonable rainstorm.

That last address of Höttl's we'd found for a small house on the outskirts of the city was the obvious next place for Höttl to run to.

But the joint looked abandoned. I got out my lock-pick tools, said, "Let's be extra careful boys. This bastard has had time if he's returned to studiously lay traps throughout this sorry bitch."

But Höttl's Rio hideout was more in the vein of the one he maintained in São Paulo, anonymous and vanilla.

There were no negatives or film prints in this place, though we did find a newish looking camera and tripod... *and* some unused film.

Those gave me this sudden, wicked inspiration. "We'll take these along," I said.

We stepped out into the warm drizzle. A black '67 Impala whipped in behind our rental car. My arms were still full of camera equipment; Bud, Jésus and Jonny drew down on the Chevy.

The driver lumbered out, hands in the air. He was grinning. I shook my head, smiling.

Charles said, "*Grand Capitaine!* You're alive!"

"You, too," I said, putting down my load and clapping his back. "But how?"

Seems when the sidecar and motorcycle parted company, Charles had stayed upright *and* continued his pursuit, "I did that competent you would survive and would want me to stay on Höttl, *Grand Capitaine.*"

Faithful to his given word not to deprive me the kill, *confident* Charles had just stayed glued to Höttl, tracking him all the way back to Rio, by-passing several chances to kill the bastard himself.

"Followed him right to this place," Charles said proudly.

'But he's *not* here," Bud said.

"Not now, no," Charles said. "The German stayed here only briefly. Now he's staying in one of those big new hotels overlooking the beach. I've been stopping back here three times a day, hoping to find some of you survived and were still hunting."

Then he hugged each of my boys in turn, all but Jonny, who flatly refused to be touched.

I said, "If Höttl should move from that hotel while you're here...?"

"No." Charles shook his head, emphatic. "Not for what he's paying. He's checked into this hotel for at least another week, and they are very expenditive commendations. He has a whole floor to himself, with privee elevator service. All that space, it's just Höttl and the man he escaped the jungle with." Charles suddenly looked glum. "But the way that place is built, he doesn't need more men, I think. With all the projections the hotel gives him, Höttl might as well have a regime guarding him."

Bud looked puzzled: "Regime?"

"I think he means regiment," I said.

"That's right," Charles said, annoyed. "Many men. "That floor is almost impossible to attack. Still, he has to leave sometime."

"Nothing's impossible," I said. "I'll ride with you, Charles. Show us the way to this place."

67

The joint overlooked the beach, as Charles had said. Overlooking the hotel was a monstrous statue of our savior—*Cristo Redentor*—looking more than a little, as Bud put it, "like a giant plastic Jesus on the dashboard of the world."

Höttl was hiding away on the hotel's second floor from the top of the hotel; reachable only via secured elevator and equally secured emergency stairs.

His joint had a private balcony that couldn't be accessed from the balconies of lower floors.

Frustrated, I took my crew into the shaded cool of the hotel's bar to introduce them to the forgotten glory of the mojito.

Motley crew we were, we drew suspicious looks from the bartender. It was just us in the bar—us and some lonely looking older woman reading a movie magazine with William Holden on the cover. According to the cover blurb, the actor's longtime marriage was on the rocks.

The woman kept looking from the cover to me and back again, deciding. So it wasn't just those Asian tourists. Being confused for Holden was something that had started in the 1940s. The older that I—*and* Holden—got, the more I found myself being mistaken for him. Sometimes I let myself wonder if anyone ever thrust copies of my novels at old Bill and asked him to sign Hector Lassiter's block-letter scrawl.

"There's a floor above Höttl's," I said. "Looks like another private space to me. It has its own private balcony, directly above Höttl's. A man *could* be lowered from one balcony to the other."

"*Oui*," Charles said. "Such a thing might be done." Then he shook his head. "But that's not to be. Even all Höttl's blood monies couldn't suture that topmost floor for him. It's the most exclusive space in the hotel. Höttl's floor can only be reached with a special key turned in a commoner elevator. That top floor has its own elevator. It's the presidential suite. They call it a 'suite' even though it's really the whole top floor. It's for presidents, as the name replies. For kings and the famous movie stars."

The woman with the movie mag was eyeing me again. I smiled at her. Then I fished out my wallet and skidded off some bills to Bud. "Buy me a couple of suitcases, Bud. If you didn't pack a good suit, buy yourself one. Something that positively screams Los Angeles, specifically Hollywood. Oh, and about that luggage, I want it monogrammed, jiffy-like."

Scowling, Bud said, "Sure. What? 'B.D.'? Maybe 'H.L' for old time's sake?"

"No," I said. "I want the bags to read 'W.H.'" I squinted at that movie mag again, checking Bill's hair color. "And get some medium-brown hair dye."

Jésus said, "What's this about?"

"We're checking into that presidential suite," I said.

68

B ud said, "Mr. Holden will be wanting *total* privacy. No calls are to be put through to him except from myself. I'm Mr. Holden's personal assistant, Raoul Bender, by the way. Also, you may put through calls by Messrs. Lightfoot, Delattre and Calderone."

As Bud said all this nonsense to the hotel's head honcho, I tried to look jaded, but affable, like Old Hollywood going through all the timeworn, tedious motions. Playing to hard-drinking character (not so much of a reach, let's agree to that up-front), I nodded at the hotel bar and said, "They know how to pour in that joint?"

"It's excellent, Mr. Holden," the hotel manager said.

"Great," I said with a grin, "and for Christ's sake, do please call me Bill."

Bud said, "One other is to be put straight through if he calls. That would be Mr. Lean."

"Mr. Lean," the manager repeated. He looked like he was trying to connect something.

"Yes, *David* Lean," Bud said in a confidential whisper, looking around like someone might care enough to eavesdrop on us. "*You* know, the director—*Zhivago*, *Lawrence of Arabia*, and *The Bridge on the River Kwai*. Mr. Holden starred in the latter, of course."

The manager wet his lips. "I see. If I may, confidentially of course, are you *filming* here?"

"More like scouting potential locations for a film," Bud said carefully. "Tell me, purely hypothetically, could your hotel accommodate a large film crew? Say, three-hundred rooms?"

"With sufficient warning, that would present little problem," the man said, barely containing his glee over the math he was doing in his head, savoring the prospect of the attendant publicity for his hotel. He was hooked, for sure. Bud reeled him in now:

"Understand," the poet said, "Mr. Lean is a notoriously *painstaking* filmmaker. We could be talking about a production schedule here of eighteen, perhaps even twenty-four months."

Riding up in our private elevator to the tippy top floor, Bud said, "God, can you imagine how worked up Höttl will get if he gets wind of William Holden and David Lean mounting a major motion picture from the floor above him?"

I laughed and slapped Bud's back. "Yeah, I surely can."

Looking down from my private balcony was a hell of a lot more vertiginous than looking up from the beach. This was going to be hell on my fear of heights.

Bud said, "When do you want to do this, Hector?"

"This afternoon. And God help you all if you drop me. I swear I'll ghost all your bones into eternity."

At four I changed into white pants, a white polo shirt and white tennis shoes—hues that would blend in against the alabaster wall of the hotel.

Bud helped me on with a canvas-colored backpack—sucker weighed at least thirty pounds. The boys followed me out on the balcony, Jésus hauling the coiled up rope; my life was dependent on the quality of his knots.

The sun was winking between the storm clouds. The not-so-nice weather had chased away the beach bunnies: the girls from Ipanema had thrown on some clothes and run for the bars or the beds from the looks of things.

Another break in my favor.

Jésus checked the knots in the rope again, then thrust the ring at one end of the rope over my left fist. I gripped the rope above it in a sweaty palm.

"Remember," Jésus said. "When you're ready, put your hand back through this loop, tug three times, then hold on with both hands, Héctor. Close your eyes and we'll have you back up here *rápidamente*."

I nodded. Apart from my damp palms, I had butterflys, overwhelmed by heights as I usually was, and this was the worst case of it I'd had, ever. Still, I swung my legs over the balcony's ledge, then cast off. I hung suspended above the concrete patio surrounding the pool twenty-two floors below.

Straining against the rope, Bud said over the balcony to me, "Really think we shouldn't have done this at night?"

"No," I said, trying not to look down. "The light is important to me."

My biggest risk was that first moment when my feet became visible to anyone who might be standing on—or looking *at*—the balcony from inside Höttl's private area. Given the size of the floor Höttl was paying for, I took it as a calculated risk there was little prospect of the two men seeing me come down.

Again, luck was with me. There was no sign of my quarry, and Höttl's single guard had his back to the balcony, watching William Shatner pitch woo at some busty, green-haired babe in an aluminum bikini on *Star Trek*.

The balcony door was open to let in a little rain-scented, cooling breeze. I slipped off my backpack, crouched, and got out the rag and bottle of chloroform packed inside.

69

I pinched Höttl's earlobes until he blinked and started to come back around.

He seemed to panic as he realized he was gagged. He became even more alarmed to find his arms tied behind the high back of the heavy hotel chair. Probably figured I was going to go for point-for-point revenge for what he did to me back in Paris.

Certainly I wanted him to think I might do that.

After what he'd done to Marie, and ordered done to Duff, it was all I could do to restrain myself from dissecting the man with my bare hands. I wanted to lay him waste.

But I watched Höttl sitting there, watched his dawning awareness of the terrible scene he'd awakened to.

The Nazi filmmaker had lost more weight. He was a kind of living skeleton now. The scar was a fat welt down the side of his face and his eyes protruded around the veined ruin of his hawkish nose. While stripping him, I'd noticed a tattoo on the underside of his left arm—a permanent mark noting his blood type. Himmler had ordered the tattoos for all SS members. Höttl had tried to burn his away with a cigarette. The tattoo wasn't very big, hardly a quarter inch, but the sadistic Nazi seemed to have lost his resolve. Must have a low threshold for pain, despite his penchant for dishing it out.

He didn't have to say it, I could see it in his eyes: "Lassiter!"

I smiled and pointed at the camera sitting on the tripod. "Sorry for the rough awakening, Höttl, but that camera only holds so much film and I don't want to lose the light." I pointed out the window at the sunset. "See, I remembered and took the trouble. It's the golden hour you described, though even its magic can't really flatter a subject like you, I'm afraid. You look like hell, Werner."

With a rubber-gloved hand, I patted his scarred cheek. He tried to turn his head. "As a cinema-type, I know you'll appreciate these touches. It's been a lot of years and we have a lot of ground to cover and little time in which to do it. I mean, little time if we want to get the best footage and effects. Now you sit tight while I fetch my cinematographer. Don't let the fella's black patch throw you. He's got the eye, so to speak."

I walked out on the balcony and gave the rope dangling there a single tug. It was pulled up, and a few seconds later, Bud was lowered down to join me. "Christ, that's terrifying," he said.

"Tell me."

Bud took up a position behind the camera. I pointed at Bud and said to Höttl, "Another friend of Marie's. Now we're rolling." The green light came on. Höttl jerked again at his bonds, raging.

I pointed at Höttl's guard, now on his back on the floor, said, "That's right, your demonic man servant is already plumping your pillows in hell."

Höttl's strangely bulging eyes got wider. He jerked at his bonds again. Looked like me might be on the verge of choking or gagging.

"*Easy* there, Werner," I said. "Too soon to check out, old pal. I'm going to take that gag out of there in a second, because if my suspicions are right, I wouldn't have you choke to death. I also suspect you don't have the pipes to scream anymore, which you shouldn't try to do anyway. Just make it harder on yourself if you do, right?"

I got around behind him and untied the gag. I said, "No blather, now. Like I said, we're on a tight shooting schedule for this one. Can't lose that magical light or run out of film before we close accounts."

He spat out the gag and I got around in front of him. I smiled. Yes, there it was, this strange involuntary movement to Höttl's bulging eyes. "Although you fancy yourself a filmmaker, you're not a storyteller, Werner," I said. "It's all about image and juxtaposition with you. Set pieces and contrived moments. But there's no build to an engaging end. No drama or character arc. No reversals and no twist at the end. Probably too late to teach you any of that now. Yet I feel a hankering to try and do just that."

Höttl was trying to speak, but seemingly struggling to swallow. He finally succeeded in that and then said in a low, reedy voice, "Did you fake your death in sixty-seven because you feared me, Lassiter?"

"Nah, that was the fault of some *other* miserable cocksucker," I said. "A countryman of mine named Hoover whose evil even you'd have a time touching in some ways. On that note, how'd you manage to escape that blast back in fifty-seven?"

"Your own government tumbled to your plan," Höttl said. His swollen, protruding eyes roamed from me to his dead guard and then to the camera. "They had little concern about you murdering those American Nazis. The agents tipped me to your plans, and I talked one of the members into posing as me in an effort to ostensibly fox the very government authorities who were secretly protecting me. I called in a studio makeup artist to put a false scar on the man. My impersonator was quite flattered to do it. Just like those fools Hitler used to use as doubles. Of course, this man didn't know he'd be dying as me."

From behind the camera, Bud said, "This fascination of our government's with you all these years, the protection you've been extended, what has all that been about?"

"Intrigue, intelligence," Höttl said in his weak voice. His words were slurred, like he was slightly drunk, maybe. Well, that too tallied with what I suspected.

Bud said, "What kind of intelligence did you have to offer them?"

"More than simple spying," Höttl said. "I had advantages and connections in certain political climes. Many of us Party members did. I was useful for passing on information and misinformation. There were some projects involving your CIA and foreign regimes tied to illicit drug trade. They used— they *continue* to use—many of us." Werner smiled. "Your own government, and a priest, made Klaus' flight to safety from France possible, you know."

"Klaus? Barbie?" I sighed. "Well, hell, that cocksucker's maybe fixin' to be a next project for me, then. Don't you go thinking he's clear just yet."

Höttl looked at his bonds, then looked back at me. "What's your aim here, Lassiter?" He nodded at the camera. "Why that? *I'd* use the footage of course, our positions being reversed. But *you*? What possible use is it to you? Even if you aim to harm my reputation, you can't possibly use that. Television would never show it and it would be evidence of a crime. Your fake death would be compromised and you'd be branded a torturer and murderer."

"My reasons for the camera are my own," I said. I shook out a cigarette and got out my lighter given me so many years ago in the Keys by Hemingway. I said, "Looks who's got the smokes now, Höttl. Look who's in the bloody chair. Maybe awaiting the attention of this baby." I held the glowing end of the cigarette up close to his eyes.

"You won't do it," Höttl said, sneering. He looked at the dead man on the floor. "Oh, you'll do *some* things, things you can convince yourself represent revenge. What you'd regard as *justice*. But you won't torture me. You're not that kind."

"But I might be," Bud said.

"You?" Höttl sneered again. "You far less than Lassiter."

I poised my cigarette's end over his bony thigh. "Prepared to bet your life on that?"

Höttl managed a wink and a lopsided smile. "Yes." He winked again. "Besides, what I did to your women aside, you should kiss my ass and thank me every day of your life for the gifts I've given you."

I took another hit of my Pall Mall, frowning through the smoke. Goddamn Höttl. So far, he was right. I couldn't make myself grind that coffin nail into him, despite everything he'd done in his too-long, sadistic life to merit it. "Thank you," I repeated. "Why the hell would I thank you?"

Höttl leaned forward with his death's head grin. "Because I *made* you."

70

"I made you," Höttl said again. He said it with fierce pride.

I blew smoke in his face, said, "How the hell do you figure?"

"What your career has been since 1945—what you've really made your name and your money on—that's all thanks to me. Don't you see it, Lassiter?"

"Nah," I said. "I really don't. Try and make me see it."

"I will," he said. "Film. *Film noir,* a style and sensibility born of German cinema. With just a handful of visionary others, I sowed the seeds of film noir, the medium with which the name 'Hector Lassiter' is most associated. All your American director friends, Huston, Welles and Ford, where would they be without the sparking brilliance, the template of Höttl?"

I laughed scornfully. "You really do yourself way too much credit as a filmmaker, Werner. John, Orson and Sam? Doubt they've even heard of you."

But he wasn't through, yet. Höttl said, "It wasn't just the money that I made you as a screenwriter for crime movies whose aesthetic I shaped and informed. No. Crime fiction, those novels of yours and others like you, they were all colored by your post-war sensibilities and film noir. Your entire creative aesthetic sensibility is owed to me, Lassiter. And your experiences in the war? In my chair? I'm not the only one to notice that your novels became richer, darker and sadder after you spent time in my chair there in Paris. Many critics have noticed the change in your post-war work, too. So, yes, Lassiter, I made you."

I was in the throes of a slow burn, now. I ground out my cigarette—in an ashtray.

"You never had anything to teach me, Höttl. You're no storyteller and you're a shitty filmmaker. The only skill you have is causing suffering and destruction. The only thing you've made me is vengeful. Fact is, as an avenger, I can only kill you once. I can only end your miserable existence once, that is to say. But as a writer, I can murder your reputation for eternity."

That brought Höttl up short.

Bud was watching me intently, too. Probably trying to figure where I was headed next. Some part of me actually relished Bud as witness, the fact he was a fellow writer made it better. I savored having an informed audience, so to speak, for this particular famous final scene.

"The only thing I've learned from you, Werner, is to confirm every kill," I said. "And you've reminded me it's true, what the man said—history is most certainly written by the winners. So, along with Marie, I've appointed myself caretaker of your memory, Höttl. I mean to place a new brand on you in print."

Höttl shook his head. "What? Another lie, Lassiter?"

"No, Werner," I said. "No lie, this. This one is real enough. Certainly tragic enough. I'm going to relish running this one through you. And Marie's going to help me do that."

"She's well past hurting me, as you too well know," Höttl said. "You, too. As you said, you can only kill me once."

"Wrong, Werner. I can only kill your body once. Your reputation I can go on murdering for as long as history endures. Marie and I can do that to you. You see, her memoir is going to be released in paperback this fall. It will be an *expanded* version, updated with material provided by noted novelist Beau Devlin. That is to say, me."

"New information?" Höttl said. "This phony murder, you mean?"

"Oh, that will move copies, sure," I said. "But that's just for starters." I looked to Bud, pointed at my watch. He checked the camera, then flashed me seven fingers. The shadows were also getting long; we'd lose the light, soon.

I needed to wrap this up. I said, "I've got a much bigger revelation regarding you to spring on the bad old world, Werner. And it has the virtue of being tragic fact. Completely provable."

Bud was all attention now. Höttl, too.

I said, "When Marie was killed, there was an autopsy performed. The coroner, medical examiner, rather, who did that was *good*. He was thorough. He found that Marie was on the verge of becoming very sick. She had a genetic disease that was just asserting itself. An inherited condition fairly peculiar to her race called Machado Joseph disease."

Höttl was giving me his death stare, now. Nothing I had to say was news to him, I was sure of that. So much of this was for Bud's benefit; for Bud and for the camera.

"This disease, it's a nasty goddamn thing," I said. "It attacks the central nervous system. Slowly destroys the body while leaving the mind cruelly untouched. You become trapped in your own body as you lose control and strength in your arms and legs. You develop trouble swallowing, have loss of eye control. The eyes themselves begin to bulge from their sockets. In the end, you're just a witness to the world, trapped in your own living corpse."

I leaned in close to Höttl. "But you know all this too well, don't you, Werner? You had to be carried out of that barn to those motorcycles because you can't walk on your own anymore, isn't that right? You have trouble swallowing and your eyes tell their own story. It causes frequent urination, too. So I figure, based on all your reported trips outside to piss, in L.A. in fifty-seven, you were in early phases then. You knew to have your double keep up those frequent trips outside when you swapped places."

Höttl said nothing. So I said, "Here's the thing about this disease, Bud. There's no question but that Höttl fathered Marie. She had Machado Joseph disease, and so does this bastard. But there's a genetic reality at work here. Both parents—both *Jewish* parents—have to carry the gene in order to pass the disease on to their offspring."

Höttl said, "*Goddamn you!*"

Bud said, "This son of a bitch Nazi is a Jew?"

"That's the reality the revised version of Marie's memoir is going to make clear to the world," I said. "Werner Höttl, this wicked Nazi and right hand to the Butcher of Lyon, was himself Jewish."

I looked at my watch. "One minute of film left," I said. I began to work on the ropes binding Höttl.

The German said, "One minute? Until what? Until you kill me? I'm sick, like you said, Lassiter. You won't beat or torture me. What are you going to do? Put a gun in my mouth and shoot me like Hans?"

"That would be far too kind," I said. I grabbed him by the back of the neck and by one wrist. I twisted that arm up behind him to control him. I hauled Höttl to his feet.

In that slurred voice he said, "What are you doing to me, Lassiter?"

"I'm writing you out of the story now, Werner. For you, this dream is over. Time to fade to black. But as you do that, I want you to think about what you did to Marie. About what you had done to Duff."

Höttl sneered. "*Had done* to her? I did it myself. I beat you down to Mexico and filmed all I did to Duff."

I nearly beat him to death then. Instead I smiled meanly, said, "*Danke*, Werner. You just made this so much easier."

I began pushing the old Nazi across the room, out toward the dying light.

Bud followed with the camera.

Höttl saw what was coming and began to scream. It was a choked, suffocated cry of fear—his lungs were already ravaged by the Machado Josephs and so he had no air projection to make any noise anyone might hear.

"That's right, scream you bloody son of a bitch," I said. "Scream all the way down, now. I would surely hate for you to land on some innocent tourist."

I pitched him over the side.

Höttl softly howled all the way down.

There were no other screams from below yet; it must still be empty around the pool, I figured. I pointed at the rope hanging from the overhead balcony. "You go up first, Bud. I'll bring the camera."

71

My boys were tying one on in celebration, really wallowing in that presidential suite pad.

Jésus called up some working girls. The gals were rough-looking local trade. Bud and I swiftly retreated to the hotel lounge.

I took my drink with me to a phone booth.

Given the difference in time zones, I woke him up of course. But I hoped the news would be worth it.

Groggy, Jimmy said, "Everything is okay, boyo?"

"Is now," I said. "It's over now."

I heard Jimmy bite back a sob; that cleaved me. He said, "Are you *sure*? You saw with your own eyes?"

"It happened by my hand," I said.

"Thank Christ." Jimmy paused, said, "God, I wish I could have seen it."

I almost hesitated, but pushed on. "Well, about that…"

72

Cleveland was in the throes of a hard summer rain; rolling thunder in the distance. The rain had seemed to follow Bud and I all the way from Brazil.

Bud was now screening the Höttl film on one of Jimmy's blank white living room walls.

I couldn't watch the goddamn thing.

Instead, I wandered out to Jimmy's back porch, staring off through the trees and watching the rain fall.

Jimmy eventually wandered out. He was looking a good bit stronger than the last time I'd seen him. His color was better. He put a big hand on my shoulder and squeezed. "I can never make it up to you, your taking care of Höttl like that."

"You don't owe me anything," I said. "Hell, I still owe you more favors than I can count, Jimmy. Besides, Marie meant the world to me. And I had to avenge Duff. And on both counts, it still wasn't enough."

Jimmy said, "I know it has to be destroyed, Hector. Hell, it's evidence of a capital crime. But I'd like to watch it another time or two. To savor Höttl's fear and hate and helplessness. His realization that, like you said, Marie is going to destroy him with her words. I don't think I could ever get tired of watching that moment."

"You roll it again, then, Jimmy. But me, I've really got to get on home."

"You do." We hugged and said our goodbyes.

Bud walked me outside. I said, "Once again, you've gone above and beyond, my friend."

The poet/screenwriter/songwriter shrugged it off. "I heard what you said to Jimmy," he said. "It's the same for me, Lass. Marie was my friend, too. There was no choosing in this."

Bud looked around, said, "Think before I head back to Nashville, I'm going to hang around here a few days. Just to make sure Jimmy really is solid."

"Bless you for doing that, son," I said.

Bud shook my hand. "All my love to Alicia."

"I'll surely pass it along."

Before I hit the airport, I made a last stop at the cemetery to pay respects to Marie.

I stopped by the graveyard's chapel and lit two candles.

AUGUST 1971

The in-flight movie was *Patton*. I tore off my earphones and read a book instead.

I picked up my Chevy from the airport's long-term lot and flipped on the wipers. More goddamn rain. Seemed to be raining, like some writer said, everywhere in the known universe.

Close to home, the setting sun finally dipped beneath all that cloud cover. It was a red sun that made the sky look like a Technicolor matte painting in a Selznick picture.

A skinny dog was flirting with a suicidal road crossing. He was a black Lab that looked about half-starved. I pulled curbside and popped the passenger side door and whistled.

Skittish, the Lab approached my car. He had no tags; not even a collar. He looked like he had been days on the run.

It had sure been a long time since I'd had a dog. I patted the seat. He hesitated, then climbed in, collapsing next to me.

I reached across, closed the door. I scratched his head and rolled back into traffic.

A country song on the radio: Buck Owens warbling "Act Naturally." Buck sang, "They're gonna put me in the movies."

I turned that off, dialed around and found Ray Price singing "For the Good Times."

I drove into that big bloody sunset, one hand on the stray and the other on the wheel.

Roll the credits.

READER DISCUSSION QUESTIONS

1. Hector Lassiter's WWII activities have been loosely hinted at in previous novels. What most surprised you about his now-revealed World War II adventures?
2. Werner Höttl was first glimpsed in *One True Sentence* as another artistic intellectual haunting 1920s Paris and another member of the Lost Generation shaped or damaged by WWI. Did the Paris flashback in this novel give you any fresh insights into prior novels' themes?
3. Hector Lassiter is an author and Werner Höttl a filmmaker. How do their respective careers inform their lives and define their very private war?
4. In this novel, we at last come face-to-face with Duff Sexton, one of Hector's eventual wives (and one namechecked in an earlier book). What about Duff do you think so strongly appeals to Hector sufficiently to result in matrimony?
5. A number of characters from prior Lassiter novels make cameos or return appearances in this book. Was there a particular character you were pleased to see back? Who were you most pleasantly surprised to see make a return?

6. Film and *film noir* drive and inform *Roll the Credits*. How did you feel about Hector's use of film at the novel's climax to punish Höttl?
7. This is the first novel since *Head Games* to be narrated by Hector. Did the shift in voice in any way affect your attitude towards Hector?
8. Do you prefer your Lassiters in first- or third-person point of view? If you have a preference, what drives it?
9. Bud Fiske, Hector's *Head Games* sidekick, returns in this novel. Did anything about the direction of Bud's intervening life surprise or disarm you?
10. Apart from Duff, another Lassiter wife is revealed in this novel. Were you surprised to see who the much older Hector was married to? Did that union please you, or...?

ABOUT THE AUTHOR

Craig McDonald is an award-winning author and journalist. The Hector Lassiter series has been published to international acclaim in numerous languages. McDonald's debut novel was nominated for Edgar, Anthony and Gumshoe awards in the U.S. and the 2011 Sélection du prix polar Saint-Maur en Poche in France.

The Lassiter series has been enthusiastically endorsed by a who's who of crime fiction authors including: Michael Connelly, Laura Lippmann, Daniel Woodrell, James Crumley, James Sallis, Diana Gabaldon, and Ken Bruen, among many others.

Hector Lassiter also centers short stories that appear in three crime fiction anthologies, *Dublin Noir* (Akashic Books), *The Deadly Bride & 19 of the Year's Finest Crime and Mystery Stories*, (Carroll & Graf) and *Danger City II* (Contemporary Press).

Craig McDonald is also the author of two highly praised non-fiction volumes on the subject of mystery and crime fiction writing, *Art in the Blood* and *Rogue Males*, nominated for the Macavity Award.

To learn more about Craig, visit *www.craigmcdonaldbooks.com* and *www.betimesbooks.com*

Follow Craig McDonald on Twitter @HECTORLASSITER

https://www.facebook.com/craigmcdonaldnovelist